Also by Sharon Sala

Don't Back Down
Last Rites
Heartbeat
Left Behind
Bad Seed
The Next Best Day

Blessings, Georgia
Count Your Blessings (novella)
You and Only You
I'll Stand by You
Saving Jake
A Piece of My Heart
The Color of Love
Come Back to Me
Forever My Hero
A Rainbow Above Us
The Way Back to You
Once in a Blue Moon
Somebody to Love
The Christmas Wish
The Best of Me

Crossroads
Sunset
Midnight

DAYBREAK

SHARON SALA

Cover design by Ervin Serrano
Cover images © rahnuma/Shutterstock, Creative Travel Projects/Shutterstock, Hank Shiffman/Shutterstock

Published by Sourcebooks Casablanca, an imprint of Sourcebooks
1935 Brookdale RD, Naperville, IL 60563-2773
(630) 961-3900
sourcebooks.com

Cataloging-in-Publication Data is on file with the Library of Congress.

Printed and bound in the United States of America.
VP 10 9 8 7 6 5 4 3 2

Chapter 1

Dallas Homicide—Central Division
6:12 p.m.

It was the time of Mother Nature's uncertainty, also known as the lull between the last gasp of spring—right before the hellfire of a Texas summer.

Homicide detective Gunner Kingston hit Save on the report he'd just finished, printed out a hard copy for his files and another for his boss, Lieutenant Andy Samuels, then signed off the computer.

"I'm outta here," Gunner said and headed for the door.

Gunner's partner, Cliff Beale, glanced up from his phone conversation, nodding an acknowledgment while still on his call, wishing he had Kingston's leg length and swagger.

Unaware of being on anyone's radar, Gunner took the stairs down to the ground floor and out the back to the parking lot, shifted into a lope, and ran all the way across the lot to the black Mustang GT, wincing at the stifling heat as he got in, fired up the engine, and turned the AC to morgue.

He noticed as he was leaving that he was low on gas, so he stopped at a Gas and Dash to refuel. Afterward, he went inside to get a cold drink and a candy bar and, on impulse, used the change to buy a lottery ticket and drove away, downing the Hershey bar he'd purchased, three squares at a time. The cold drink lasted longer, but once he segued into traffic on the Loop, he settled in for the drive. Another twenty minutes or so and he'd be home.

The fact that he lived alone was his saving grace. It was the bolt hole he needed to let go of the stress of working homicide, without having to explain to a wife why he didn't want to talk about his day.

In his world, every case began with identifying a dead body, getting a time of death, and then working backward from the last twenty-four hours of their victim's life to figure out who did it and why. The most frustrating cases were the victims who died from acts of random violence, because there were no obvious starting points to look for perps.

The past few days had been even more hectic. All levels of Dallas law enforcement were on alert. The only witness in an upcoming federal murder trial was missing, and the four special agents who had been with him in the safe house were dead.

Freddie Welsh, a key witness in the Burgess Dixon trial, had disappeared two days ago, and every callout that Homicide attended, they half expected it to be him. The fact that it was the FBI who'd lost him, despite him having been secreted in a safe house, was all over the media, while Burgess Dixon, the defendant in the case who was out on bail, was claiming innocence of any knowledge.

The Feds and the Dallas PD knew Dixon was behind it, but they couldn't prove it. The special agents who'd been guarding the witness had just enough time to alert their superiors that they'd been made when the call suddenly ended in a hail of gunshots. By the time the Feds showed up at the scene, Freddie Welsh was gone, and the special agents who'd been guarding him were dead.

Gunner had known one of the agents personally and sent his condolences to the widow and her son, but it was yet another reminder of why being single in his job was a plus. He had only himself to worry about.

As soon as he got home, he locked up his weapon, changed into sweats and a T-shirt, ordered DoorDash, then spent the evening with Chinese takeout and a King Kong movie before going to bed.

Sometime before midnight, he heard thunder, and then rain blowing against the window and hoped it would quit raining before morning. Driving on the Dallas freeways added a whole other level of risk when it was wet.

He rolled over and went back to sleep, only to have it disrupted again with a phone call a couple of hours before daybreak. Groaning, he reached for the phone.

"This is Kingston." Then he listened intently. "Text me the address. I'm on the way."

All Yankee Dan wanted was to get out of the rain. The city had already cleared out their squat at the warehouse months earlier, but he had an infected blister on the heel of his left foot and walking was hell. He'd been scrounging in the dumpsters for food when the storm rolled through, and the warehouse was his nearest refuge.

The warehouse was locked and boarded up, but he knew another way and got himself inside. The downside to his entrance was the water dripping rapidly from the ceiling and onto the floor, so he made his way up to the second floor, which consisted of a loft on the opposite side of the building where the old offices used to be. The roof on that side didn't seem to be leaking, and the floors were dry. He knew from experience that it was warmer on the wooden floors above than the cold concrete below.

He found a corner and curled up. Still shivering and trying to ignore the misery long enough to fall asleep, he was startled to hear the screech of hanger doors rolling back downstairs and panicked. This place was off limits, and the last thing he wanted was to get picked up by the cops.

He slipped out of the cubicle and moved to the railing just as he saw the silhouettes of two men in the open doorway, dragging a third man between them.

What the hell? Those aren't cops!

Yankee Dan went belly down. The shivers he was feeling now were not from the cold—they were from fear. He was witnessing a body dump. It took a few seconds for his panic to subside, and he began to assess his situation.

It was pitch black, and the dripping water echoed eerily throughout the building. He knew they couldn't see him, but he was also blind to who they were or what they looked like.

The men, unaware that they were silhouetted by the streetlights coming in through the giant doorway below, dumped the body in the middle of the open floor, then walked out, talking between themselves.

Yankee Dan could hear their voices, but he couldn't discern the words, and they'd been nothing but silhouettes, both coming and going. He waited until they pushed the doors shut, and waited even longer until he heard them drive away.

Acclimated to the absence of light enough to maneuver, Yankee Dan made his way downstairs to see if the victim was still alive. He felt for a pulse and found nothing, then quickly removed both shoes. He was going for the socks when he found the phone stuffed into the upper part of the sock on the dead man's right foot.

He didn't need the phone, but he didn't have it in him to rob a dead man and leave him lying, so he decided that an anonymous call to the cops would save the body from the rats, and maybe a little of Yankee Dan's soul for the theft.

But the good idea fell flat when he couldn't open the

phone. It took him a few seconds to realize it had to be opened with a fingerprint. Taking a chance, he pressed the dead man's thumb against the icon. The phone screen opened with a multitude of other icons.

"Bingo," he muttered and immediately called 911, told the dispatcher that he found a body, gave them the address, then hung up without giving his name.

Satisfied he'd done his moral duty, he wiped the phone free of his prints, slipped it into the man's pocket, then headed for the stairs. Desperate to get the new shoes on and get the heck out of the building, he sat down on the bottom steps to change his shoes. He winced as the scab on his heel pulled off with the leather, but for the first time in months, he had socks to pad the sore and shoes that didn't rub. He was about to make a run for it when he began to hear sirens.

He hadn't expected the police to respond so quickly, and now he was trapped. If he ran out onto the streets at this time of night, in this part of town, he would be looked at as a possible suspect in this man's death. In a panic, he ran back up the stairs, hoping to hide among the discards of the company, forgetting that he'd left his old shoes behind.

Yankee Dan was running for his life in a dead man's shoes. It did not bode well for him.

The first wave of police arrived, spilling into the warehouse in twos and threes. Fearing they would begin a search, Dan slipped into an office, crawled beneath drop cloths covering old filing cabinets that had been piled in the corner, and held his breath, praying that they didn't search too hard.

There was a door at the far end of the second floor that would take him down two flights of stairs to the street below, but it would be locked. He could hear voices downstairs, but they stayed distant and muffled.

Just when he thought he might get out of this without

being discovered, he heard more voices—louder voices, and then footsteps on the stairs, and in that moment, remembered the old shoes he'd left behind, and the body without any.

Reality hit. They would find him and blame him for the death. His only option was to run and hope for the best, and so he did, unaware that the man who was chasing him had once chased down a runaway longhorn on foot. He was already caught and just didn't know it.

One wild ride through the rain-drenched city later, Gunner rolled up on the scene at an abandoned warehouse. Crime scene tape was up, streets were already blocked off, and cop cars were everywhere. His partner, Cliff Beale, was just pulling up behind Gunner as he reached for his tac light and got out of his car. He paused, waiting for Cliff to catch up.

"Hell of a wake-up call, isn't it?" Cliff muttered as he approached.

"Aren't they all?" Gunner said and ducked under the crime scene tape and headed into the warehouse with Cliff beside him.

They knew the area as a homeless squat, but when they entered the warehouse, the entire lower floor was empty. No boxes. No obvious signs of recent occupancy. Just the body lying on the concrete, surrounded by growing puddles of water. There was no power in the building, but the high-lumen work lanterns set up near the body spotlighted the tragedy, and the water puddles at their feet reflected that light back. Clearly, the roof was leaking.

The officers standing just inside the warehouse ended their conversation as the detectives approached.

Usually, it was forensics that set up lights on a crime

scene, but they had yet to arrive. Gunner pointed at the lanterns.

"Where did all the light come from?"

A patrol officer named Davis spoke up. "We brought them in. Couldn't see shit in here, sir, and after we found the body, we didn't want to walk on evidence."

"Right, so what do you know?" Gunner asked.

"An anonymous tip was phoned in to PD. We were dispatched to the scene, found the body, and called it in. We don't know who called, and we haven't checked the body for ID," Davis said.

Gunner took a couple of steps closer and swept his flashlight over the body, noted the missing shoes and socks and the bruised and battered face, then saw a small shamrock tattoo on his neck and sighed.

"Cliff. Look." He aimed his light at the tattoo. "It's Freddie Welsh. This is our crime scene and the Feds' missing victim. Better let Lieutenant Samuels know. He can be the bearer of bad news."

"Right," Cliff said and walked a short distance away to make the call. Gunner was still sweeping the area with his tac light when he saw the old shoes beneath the stairs. Suddenly, the reason the body was barefoot made sense. A homeless person found the body and took the shoes. He glanced back at Cliff, who was still on the phone, then headed up the stairs to the second level.

He began sweeping his light across the empty expanse and was headed toward the ramshackle cubicles when he caught a brief glimpse of a bearded man in rags running west.

"Runner!" he yelled and took off after him.

Downstairs, they all heard Kingston's shout, and Cliff turned around in dismay. He didn't know Gunner had gone up alone.

Cliff pointed at one of the officers. "You! Stay with the

body. The rest of you take the west stairs up to block him off. I'm with Kingston."

There wasn't a man on the force who could outrun Gunner Kingston, but Cliff was his partner, which meant Cliff was also his backup. He took off up the stairs, two steps at a time.

The second Gunner saw a fleeing suspect, he shouted.

"Stop! Police!"

When the man kept running, Gunner kicked into gear, vaulting over an empty crate, side-stepping piles of ragged bedding left behind by the homeless who'd once sheltered here, and easily caught his runner at the door.

"Don't shoot! Don't shoot! I didn't kill him!" the runner cried.

Gunner flashed his badge. "Detective Kingston. Dallas Homicide. What's your name?" he asked.

The old man spun, his eyes wide with fright. "I didn't kill him! I didn't kill him!" he kept saying.

Gunner saw the shoes on the homeless man's feet and knew he'd guessed right about the shoes. "Sir, your name, please."

"Dan Helford. I go by Yankee Dan. I didn't kill him. I was looking for a place to get out of the rain and came in the back way. It was so dark I couldn't see shit, but I knew the layout because I used to squat here."

Gunner's eyes narrowed. "And that's when you found the body?"

"I didn't find it. I was up here in the old offices bedded down for the night when I heard the big doors opening downstairs. I sneaked out to the landing to see what was going on because I didn't want to get caught by the cops doing another sweep. There was a faint light coming in through the open doors from the outside streetlights, but all I saw were silhouettes. Two men were dragging one between them. They dumped him and left," Yankee Dan said.

"Could you identify them?" Gunner asked.

"No way. Look around you. It's black as the pits of hell in here, except for the lights you brought with you. If they hadn't opened those big doors, I would never have seen a thing. I thought the man they left behind might just be hurt and came down to check for a pulse, but he didn't have one. I took the shoes and socks. I needed 'em, man. I got a big sore on my heel from what I been wearin.'"

"We got a call from 911 about a body. Was that you?" Gunner asked.

Yankee Dan nodded. "I found the phone only because it was hidden in the top of his sock. I opened it by pressing his thumb on the ID screen. Called 911, then put the phone in his pocket. I didn't search his body. I'm not a thief. But I did touch the body by taking off his shoes."

Gunner nodded. "Okay, Dan. I need you to come with me."

Dan stepped back in fear. "Are you arresting me?"

"No, sir. But I need to get your statement for the record, and we're going to have to confiscate the shoes and socks you took. They're evidence."

Yankee Dan groaned. "Ah, man. Then I'm going barefoot because I can't put those old shoes I was wearing back on. I already have an infected sore from wearing shoes too small."

"I'll get you fixed up with replacements," Gunner said. "And we might round up some meds for your foot and some food in your belly while we're at it. How's that sound?"

Dan rubbed his face as he slumped against the wall. "Like a better end to this day than I could have imagined."

At that point, Cliff and three cops arrived on the scene.

Cliff was out of breath as he approached, his flashlight aimed straight at the duo near the door. The patrol officers who'd taken the west staircase were coming toward them from the other direction.

"Good, you caught him," Cliff said. "Who is he? What's he doing here?"

"This is Dan Helford. He is the one who found the body and called it in. We need an evidence bag for these shoes. His DNA will be on them because he took them off the body, but he's not being arrested. We just need to get his statement for the record," Gunner said, then saw the patrol officers approaching.

Cliff pulled an evidence bag from his pocket, and Gunner dropped the shoes and socks in it.

Gunner pointed at Officer Davis. "You and your partner take him to Central Homicide and put him in an interrogation room. I'll be there shortly. And tell somebody in the office to get him a pair of shoes and socks. He also needs some first aid on one of his feet and something to eat. Tell them I said so, okay?"

"Yes, sir," they said and cuffed him.

Dan panicked. "You said I wasn't under arrest!" he cried.

Gunner gave him a pat on the shoulder. "It's just protocol. I promise," he said and gave the patrolmen a look. "He's old and he's hurting. Take it easy, right?"

They all knew Kingston well enough to know not to push his boundaries. "Right, sir," they said and slowly escorted Dan down, then walked him barefoot through the continuing drizzle, seated him in their patrol car, and drove away.

Cliff flashed his light around the area, making sure there weren't any more surprises up here. Satisfied he wasn't about to get jumped, he threw out the obvious question. "Hey, Gunner, do you think the old man was telling the truth?"

Gunner glanced at him and frowned. "About what? That he found a body and stole the shoes and socks? Yes. Do I believe he used the phone on the corpse to call it in? Yes. And you and I both know that Freddie Welsh was beaten, tortured, and dead at least a day before he wound up here. I don't see an old homeless man with nothing but dirt on his hands doing any of that, do you?" Gunner said.

Cliff nodded. "Yeah, right… I wasn't thinking."

"Your call to Samuels lasted a while. What else is on your mind besides the job? Who else did you call? Your bookie? We pay attention to the evidence, not the obvious."

Cliff felt seen. He had called his bookie, and he was looking for the obvious to get this over with.

"So, he didn't see anyone?" he asked.

Gunner frowned. *What the hell is wrong with him?* They were standing in the farthest, darkest corner of the upper level. Was he really going to have to explain this like his partner was five?

"Turn off your flashlight," Gunner said.

Cliff flipped it off, and within seconds, Gunner turned his off, too, putting them both in immediate darkness.

"Can you see me?" Gunner asked.

"Well, hell no," Cliff said.

Gunner turned his light back on. "Right, and Dan Helford didn't have a flashlight, and there were no lights on anywhere in this building. He only heard the doors opening… and all he saw were the silhouettes of three men coming in and two men going out. He was a good fifty yards away on the second level, in a warehouse without power. I couldn't even see your silhouette when I turned off my flashlight, and you were standing less than five feet from me. We're going down now. You wait for the Feds until they're on-site and then head back to the station. They'll bring their own forensics team, and they can call the shots. I'm going to the station to get his statement on record. Did you tell Samuels who the victim was?"

"Yes. He said he'd deal with it," Cliff said, but he was frowning all the way down.

He and Kingston had been partners for seven years, and the man still scared him a little. He'd just made a fool of himself and lost the last thousand dollars in his savings account, all in one night. If Gunner didn't kill him for stupidity, his wife would do it for his betrayal.

An ambulance arrived as Gunner was leaving the premises. He glanced over the Dallas skyline to the east, then down at his watch. Daybreak wasn't far away, and he knew where coffee and sausage biscuits could be found at this hour of the day.

Less than an hour later, he was walking into the precinct carrying a sack of sausage biscuits and two large coffees.

Frankie Adams, the only female detective in Homicide, was in the hall as he came off the elevator. She saw the food he was carrying and grinned. "Hey, Kingston! You shouldn't have!"

He glanced at the circus of colors in her spikey hairstyle. "Nice look. Where did they put my witness?"

"I don't know. Ask Rowdy. The patrol officers handed your guy over to him."

Gunner called out to the detective coming out of the break room with a coffee cup in his hand.

"Hey, Rowdy! Where did you put my guy?"

"Interrogation room A," Rowdy said. "He stinks."

It was the tone of his voice that stopped Gunner. He turned, frowning at the smirk on his face.

"He's homeless. That means no change of clothes, nowhere

to bathe, and no hot coffee. No freaking food to eat," Gunner said and walked out.

Rowdy glanced down at the coffee he was holding and tried to shrug off the disapproval in Kingston's voice, but it was unmistakable.

Frankie Adams was not surprised by Kingston's defense of a homeless guy. For a hardened homicide detective, Gunner Kingston had an unexpected soft side. A shiver of wishful thinking rolled through her as she watched him walking away—admiring his broad shoulders and the way he moved. It was more like stalking…but sexy stalking. Hard case or not, no man should be that hot, that sexy, and unattached. And he was a lookalike for her favorite actor of the moment. Brandon… Brandon something.

"Oh, fudge. I never can remember that man's name," she mumbled, grabbed her phone, pulled up Google and typed in, "actor who plays Spencer Dutton on the TV series *1923*." The name Brandon Sklenar popped up. "That's it. Brandon Sklenar. No wonder I can't remember his last name. I can't even pronounce it." She walked away, still mumbling. "Yeah, he looks like that dude…only better."

Unaware he was the object of a Frankie Adams fantasy, Gunner stepped into the interrogation room with the coffees and the sack of sausage biscuits, then stopped. Shock followed by pure anger rolled through him. The old man was still barefoot, and still in handcuffs.

"Did they look at your foot yet?" he asked.

Dan shrugged and shook his head.

Gunner frowned. "Did they bring you any food?"

"No, sir."

Gunner put down the food and took a deep breath. "I'll be right back," he said, then stormed out of interrogation and up the hall and into Homicide, shouting. "Rowdy! Why the hell is my witness sitting in interrogation wet and cold, still handcuffed, no shoes or socks, his bad foot still untreated? Is there not a single cup of hot coffee in this place to be shared? He's not under arrest. He's just here to give a statement. Son of a…"

Then Gunner stopped mid-sentence, took a deep breath, and glared at the people sitting at their desks. He pivoted with more grace than a man his size should have been able to manage and was making calls as he slammed the door on his way out.

The silence he left behind was telling, and everybody was suddenly busy thinking about something else besides their sins of omission.

Gunner stormed back into interrogation, removed the handcuffs, took a packet of wet wipes out of his jacket pocket and laid them on the table for Dan, and then began unpacking the food.

"I apologize for how you've been treated. Detective Rowdy should have removed your cuffs."

Yankee Dan shrugged. "He was okay. He wasn't mean or anything. Just curious about the situation. Real talky… You know."

Gunner was through talking about Rowdy. "Do you want sugar in your coffee, or do you take it black?"

"I wouldn't mind a little sugar, since you're asking," Dan said, as he reached for the wet wipes and began wiping his hands.

Gunner emptied two packets into the large coffee and stirred it, then took two sausage biscuits out of the sack and put them down with his coffee.

"These are for me?" Dan said.

"Yes, sir, they are," Gunner said. "I'm hungry and need the coffee. I thought we could kill two birds with one stone and talk while we eat. You okay with that?"

Dan took a deep breath, and then nodded.

Gunner caught a glimpse of tears and looked away. Yankee Dan was about his dad's age. *But for circumstance and the grace of God it could have been*—Then he reached for his coffee without finishing the thought.

As soon as Dan had some food in his belly, Gunner called in Lieutenant Samuels and asked him to witness the statement. After Samuels arrived, they began.

It was the same story Dan had given Gunner at the warehouse, but now they had it on record, and as they were finishing up, there was a knock at the door.

The EMT Gunner called was here to treat Dan's foot, and another officer came in with a pair of prison-issue slippers and socks.

Lieutenant Samuels liked Kingston. The man was brutally honest and never backed down from a situation. Kingston drove his car like a bat coming out of hell on fire and waded into whatever was going down without hesitation. It was Samuels's personal opinion that if Kingston didn't get himself killed, he could go as high up in law enforcement as he wanted to go, and the EMT's arrival was Samuels's signal to leave. He eyed the horrific wound on the old man's foot and then put a hand on Gunner's shoulder.

"See that he gets a ride to wherever he wants to go, okay?"

Gunner nodded. "Yes, sir. I'll take him, myself."

Samuels nodded and left the room.

A short while later, Gunner and Yankee Dan were walking out of the precinct when they met Cliff, who was just returning from the scene.

"Where are you going?" Cliff asked.

"Just giving Dan a ride home. Did the Feds show?"

"Yes. I left when they took over the scene, but I don't think they're gonna get much," Cliff said.

Gunner shrugged. "That's because it was the dump site.

No telling where the scene of the crime took place, and it's the Feds' case anyway."

Cliff eyed the old man, nodded at him, then walked away.

As soon as Gunner got Dan out of the building and into his car, he headed toward a shelter.

"Where are you taking me?" Dan asked.

"Where do you want to go?" Gunner asked.

Dan shrugged. "Home. I want to go home. But it doesn't exist anymore. Just take me back to where there are places for people like me to hole up at."

"I know some people. They run a decent homeless shelter. You need somewhere to be so that your foot can heal. Are you up for it?"

Dan nodded, and for a few minutes said nothing as Gunner sped through the streets. When they came to a stoplight, he glanced at the cop.

"Why do you care what happens to me?" Dan asked.

Gunner didn't hesitate. "The way I see it, you were minding your own business when you became a witness to a crime. We're the ones who dragged you further into it. And now I'm taking you out of it."

The relief on the old man's face was evident. "Much appreciated, officer."

Gunner almost smiled. "No problem, dude. I'd share a sausage biscuit with you anytime."

Dan laughed, and the moment passed.

By the time they reached the shelter, Gunner had already been on the phone with Wilson Trainer, the director, and as they neared the shelter, saw Wilson waiting for them outside the door.

Gunner pulled up to the curb and pointed. "That's Wilson Trainer. He'll get you settled in." Then he gave Dan his card and a hundred dollars. "Get a shave and a haircut, dude. They'll give you clean clothes and a place to sleep.

And if you're willing, they'll help you find work. You never know when the opportunity for something better will come knocking. Be ready to meet it head on."

"I don't know how to thank you," Dan said.

"No thanks needed," Gunner said, then waited until the men were inside before returning to the precinct to write up the report.

Cliff was gone when he returned but showed up an hour later, and just in time to answer the phone ringing at his desk.

"Detective Beale, Homicide."

Gunner hit Save, then glanced up as Cliff pointed at him, and then the door, indicating they were getting a new call.

Gunner nodded, grabbed the jacket hanging over the back of his chair, and waited for Cliff to finish the call.

"What's up?" Gunner asked.

"Somebody's dead," Cliff said.

Gunner grinned. "No shit, Sherlock," and threw a wad of paper at him.

Cliff caught it in midair and laughed as he dropped it in his wastebasket. "Let's go, and I'm driving. You drive like you're running from the devil," Cliff said as they headed for the parking lot.

"Maybe I am," Gunner said and kept walking.

Burgess Dixon was having breakfast at his estate outside of Dallas, enjoying waffles and the morning news, when he caught his name being mentioned. He turned up the volume just in time to hear the commentator speaking…

"Federal authorities have identified the body found in the warehouse as Freddie Welsh, the missing witness from the FBI safe house."

Dixon frowned. *What the hell? I told Garza and Letourneau to bury the body, not leave it lying around out in the open.* He picked up the phone and called Beau Whistler. Whistler was his chauffeur, bodyguard, and the man who disappeared Dixon's enemies when the need arose.

Whistler was outside in the six-car garage, getting the limo ready for Dixon's morning ride to the office in downtown Dallas, when his cell rang. "Morning, Boss. What's up?" he asked.

"Tell Garza and Letourneau to get their asses over here ASAP. They screwed up, and I want to know why. I'll be in the library."

"Yes, sir. Calling them now," Whistler said, wondering what screw-up they'd done now. But when he pulled up Garza's number and called, Letourneau answered the phone.

"Do you know what time it is?" Letourneau mumbled.

Whistler frowned. The jerk was either hungover or still drunk. "Is Garza there with you?"

"As, with me in bed? Hell, no. He's in his own room," Letourneau muttered.

"Then why do you have Garza's phone?" Whistler asked.

Letourneau sat up, stared at the phone, and then frowned. "Shit. He must have mine. We partied hard after the dump."

"Clearly," Whistler snapped. "Go wake up your cohort, and both of you get your asses over to the estate, ASAP. The boss wants to talk to you."

Letourneau groaned. "Yeah, yeah. It'll take at least forty-five minutes to get across town."

"I suggest you hustle. He sounded mad," Whistler said and hung up.

Letourneau swung his legs over the side of the bed to sit up, then called his own phone number.

Garza answered. "What the hell? It's not even 8:00 a.m."

"You have my phone. I have yours. Whistler just called. Dixon wants to talk to us ASAP. He said Dixon was mad. Get dressed," Letourneau said.

"Shit," Garza said and rolled out of bed.

Neither of them knew that the body they'd dumped last night had already been found. They'd been partying when the boss called and were already high when they got the nod to get rid of a body.

The only problem for them had been the storm. Digging a grave with lightning cracking all around them seemed foolhardy, and dead was dead, so they'd opted to dump him in a long-abandoned warehouse, assuming decomposition and rats would take care of the rest.

Dixon was still in the dining room when he got a phone call. He recognized the number as a burner phone from one of his informants inside the Dallas PD and frowned. This was never good news.

"What?"

"There was a witness to the dump. A homeless man—an old dude who goes by Yankee Dan. He claims it was too dark to see or hear anything, but he was there on the upper floor of an abandoned warehouse where the dump was made. The cop who caught the witness took his statement and then dropped him off at Wilson Trainer's homeless shelter."

"Just a minute," Dixon said and got up, cursing beneath his breath as he went straight to the library and shut the doors for privacy. "Damn it! A witness and a cop? Could this get any worse?" Dixon shouted. "Who's the cop?"

"A homicide detective named Gunner Kingston."

There was a long moment of silence, and then Dixon asked, “Is he any relation to Asher Kingston, the special investigator for the State Attorney General?”

“Brother.”

Dixon took a deep breath. “Shit. Do you think the witness told the cop something that didn’t go in the report?”

“I told you what I know.”

The line went dead in Dixon’s ear. The news just added to his aggravation. He’d dealt with the federal witness. Now all this was happening because Letourneau and Garza didn’t do what he said. All they had to do was bury the body, and they couldn’t even do that right.

Despite the fact that it wasn’t even 9:00 a.m., Dixon went straight to the wet bar. He poured himself a double shot of bourbon and downed it like medicine, then sat down to wait.

Chapter 2

WHISTLER WAS IN THE FOYER OF THE DIXON ESTATE, watching for the two screw-ups to arrive, and when they did, he escorted them to the library, knocked, then opened the door and stepped inside.

"Garza and Letourneau are here."

Dixon was standing with his back to the windows when they walked in. Whistler started to leave when Dixon stopped him. "Whistler. You wait in here with me."

"Yes, sir," Whistler said and shut the door, then leaned against it.

Garza and Letourneau suddenly realized they were in trouble, but weren't sure why.

Dixon took a deep breath and then unloaded. "What did I tell you to do last night?"

"Pick up a body and dump it," Garza said.

"No. That's not what I said. My instructions were specific. I said, pick up a body and bury it where it'll never be found."

Letourneau shifted nervously. "It was storming when you called. Raining like hell and lightning zapping all around us. The road to the gravel pit was underwater. We did a dump in an abandoned warehouse instead. Hell, by the time the body is found, decomp and rats will have obliterated it."

Dixon crossed the room, stopping directly in front of them, and slapped Letourneau across the face so hard it knocked him off his feet.

Garza gasped and started whining. "We were high when you called, Boss. We weren't cognizant enough to make good decisions. We'll go back today, pick the body up, and do the job right. Give us a second chance."

Dixon shook his head. "There are no second chances in this business. Someone saw you make the dump and called the police. The Feds already have the body, and it's been identified. Your only saving grace is that it was too dark for the witness to identify anyone. Now, here's what I need you to do. The witness was a homeless man who goes by the name Yankee Dan. He's staying at a shelter run by a man named Wilson Trainer. Find Yankee Dan and make sure he becomes the victim of a hit and run. And then both of you head for the border, and don't come back. If I see either of you again, I'll kill you myself. Understood?"

"Yes, Boss. Understood," Garza said and dragged Letourneau to his feet and out of the mansion as fast as they could move. He shoved his partner into their car and left rubber on the pavement behind them as they drove away, with Burgess Dixon watching their exit from the same library windows.

"What do you want me to do, Boss?" Whistler asked.

"The only reason they're still breathing now is because I didn't want their blood and brains on my floor. Make them disappear, and you do the witness. I don't know what he looks like. Homeless people are victims of something every day. A hit and run won't be looked at as an actual hit. And I'm going to have to think about that cop. I don't need the Feds *and* the State Attorney General's office on my heels. Heist a car to do the job. Make sure whatever you use is untraceable."

Whistler nodded and walked out of the library, quietly closing the door behind him.

Cliff and Gunner arrived on the scene of their next call to see a man's body hanging by his neck out of the fourth-floor window of an apartment building. The officers first on the scene had assumed it was a suicide until forensics showed up and found scratch marks in the paint on the windowsill, and the same paint beneath the victim's fingernails.

It was obvious the young man had not committed suicide, but someone had wanted it to look that way, which is why Homicide caught the case. Within moments of their arrival, Gunner and Cliff began interviewing witnesses, and when other detectives arrived, they sent them door to door to interview residents in the apartment building and gather footage from security cameras in the surrounding area.

Across town, Whistler had followed Garza and Letourneau straight back to their apartment building, which showed him they weren't in any big rush to carry out Dixon's orders. He pulled around back and parked, gloved up, and pulled a burner gun out of a bag, attached a silencer to the weapon, and went inside. He already knew the place didn't have security cameras, but he had a medical mask over his face anyway. Ever since that Covid outbreak a couple of years ago, it was no longer unusual to still see people walking around in public wearing masks, so no one was going to pay attention to him.

He went to Garza's apartment first, saw a few drops of blood in front of the door, and guessed he'd taken his partner inside to clean him up before they went out looking for Yankee Dan. He had part of a plan, but it all depended upon how they reacted to his arrival as he knocked.

Letourneau was sitting on the sofa with an unopened bottle of cold beer in his hands, holding it onto the bruised side of his face when they heard the knock. "Are you expecting anyone?"

"I owe the landlord," Garza said. He pulled a handful of hundred-dollar bills out of his wallet and went to the door.

The moment the door swung open, Whistler kicked Garza in the balls. The money in his hand went everywhere as he fell backward, clutching his crotch in utter agony. Money was still floating down as the door swung shut.

Whistler was inside. Garza was doubled over, holding his balls with both hands, groaning and cursing, and Letourneau was on his feet and coming at Whistler with his fists doubled.

Whistler waited until Letourneau was only a few feet away and then shot him between the eyes. The sound was little more than a pop, and Garza was on his feet and coming at him from behind. Whistler pulled a knife and, as he spun, stabbed the knife into Garza's throat.

Garza's eyes widened in disbelief. The last thing he saw was Whistler's eyes above the mask he was wearing, and then cognizance for Garza no longer existed. He fell forward on top of Letourneau. The deed was done; now to set the stage.

Whistler picked up Letourneau's lifeless hand, cupped it around the knife hasp, and squeezed it to imprint DNA and fingerprints in the right position, making it appear as if he'd been the one to stab Garza in the neck.

Then he shoved the gun with the silencer into Garza's left hand. A dying reflex was the squeeze he needed as he watched Garza's fingers curl around the grip. At that point, Whistler added to the pressure and squeezed off one more shot that went into the sofa, making sure gunshot residue would be on Garza's clothes and skin, and making sure his fingerprints and DNA were all over it, then stepped back, watching the blood beginning to pool beneath the bodies.

He glanced at his watch and grunted in satisfaction. *Seventy seconds.*

He was eyeing the scene as he backed toward the door—bodies entangled, the rent money scattered beneath and around them, the gun, the knife—knowing the cops would assume they'd had a fight over the money. As he was leaving, he picked up the car keys on the table by the door and left the door unlocked.

When he got to the parking lot, he unlocked the door to Garza's car, left the keys in the ignition and the door ajar, and drove away. It wouldn't take long for someone to heist the car. The more confusion to a crime scene, the better.

His next stop was to steal a vehicle to do the hit and run. He knew Wilson Trainer by name, and knew where the shelter was. As he was driving, his phone dinged. When he stopped for a red light, he opened the message. It was two words. Yankee Dan. And a photo. The boss was nothing if not thorough. Now he had a face to go with the name, but he had his own crime scene to scrub first.

He went home, stripped and bagged up the clothes he'd been wearing, stowed them in his closet, and went to shower. Afterward, he removed the tags from new clothes he kept on hand for days like this, then dressed and left his apartment.

Next stop was to heist a car, and he drove straight to a convention center and began cruising the massive parking lot filled with vehicles belonging to the current attendees. He found a big newer model black Dodge truck with tinted windows parked at the far end of one lot and grabbed his Slim Jim and a paintball gun as he got out. He shot black paint balls at the nearest security cameras, then tossed the paint gun in the back of the truck and popped the lock.

A set of car keys fell into his lap as he pulled down the visor. Score. He wouldn't even have to hot-wire this one, he thought, and drove out of the lot. With the tinted windows for cover, he didn't have to worry about being seen. And if they did, they would assume it was the owner, which was even better. If they ever tied the truck to a hit and run, the owner would take the fall. It was time to head to the other side of the city, to Wilson Trainer's homeless shelter.

For the first time in years, Yankee Dan had taken a hot shower, shampooed his hair and beard, and been given clean clothes. He had food in his belly, his foot had been treated and dressed again, and the day wasn't over. The money Detective Kingston gave him was burning a hole in his pocket. Get a shave and a haircut, the detective said, and by God, he was going to go do it while he was still full of resolve. This was a new chance. Not his second chance, or even his third, but it was a new chance.

He stopped by the front desk to ask where the nearest barber shop was located, then signed out and left the building.

It was nearing dusk. The people who lived on the streets were already sheltering in place. Most of the storefronts in the area were vacant, so once it began to get dark, the streets cleared of heavy traffic.

According to the information Dan had been given, the shop wouldn't close for another two hours. He had plenty of time to get it done and get back before the shelter locked up for the night.

He patted his pocket as he walked out the door to reassure himself that he had the money with him and headed down the street. According to the guy at the desk, it was four blocks north, then two blocks east. All he had to do was watch for the old-fashioned barber pole at the door.

After the intermittent rain they'd had the past few days, and the midday heat they'd had earlier, the night air was still thick and muggy. The back of his neck was sweaty by the time he got to the intersection to walk east.

Dan was curious as to what he looked like now. He hadn't been clean-shaven in at least ten years, and the gray interspersed within his hair and beard had to be hiding age-related wrinkles as well. Except for the occasional car full of gang members driving by, car traffic was almost nonexistent in this part of the city, and he was still at the corner, waiting for the light to change.

Finally, the lights turned red, and the signal for foot traffic lit up. He stepped off the curb, barely wincing at the sore on his heel, and was halfway through the crosswalk when he heard the roar of an engine coming out of an alley behind him.

In the few seconds it took for Dan to realize what was happening, he'd missed his chance to run. The oversize truck hit him from behind, breaking every bone, every rib, turning the shattered shards inside his body into shrapnel and deploying a force that caused instant internal decapitation.

The impact threw Dan's body a good twenty feet across the pavement, but he never felt the pain. His last chance to start over had been a short one.

A few moments later, a woman came out of a nearby bodega with her shopping bag full of purchases, saw the body lying in the street beneath a spreading pool of blood, and started screaming.

Cop cars soon descended upon the scene, and people were coming out of surrounding buildings to see the aftermath. Officers began taking control of the gathering crowd and stringing crime scene tape around the area.

And in the distance, the high-pitched shriek of an ambulance's approach somehow seemed less urgent to the onlookers, considering the old man's body didn't have enough unbroken bones left to hold it together.

Whistler was back across town in the convention center parking lot. The space where he'd stolen the car had been taken, but there was another one close by. He put the keys back behind the visor, got his Slim Jim from the seat, and locked the door from inside before getting out. He couldn't do anything about the dent in the truck grille, or the blood splatters on the hood, but he left the paintball gun in the back of the truck. A little added evidence against the actual owner. Explaining it away was not his problem.

After a quick glance around, he got back into his truck, drove out of the lot, and returned home without incident.

He removed the clothes he'd been wearing, bagged them up with the other clothes he'd left in the closet, then dumped all of his kitchen and bathroom garbage in the bag on top of the clothes and carried it outside to the dumpster. The timing was good. Trash pickup was tomorrow.

He went back inside and sent Dixon a text.

Boss. I'm feeling better. Do you want me back tonight, or come tomorrow as usual?

It was code for "the job is done."

Within a couple of minutes, Dixon replied.

Tomorrow is fine. Get some rest.

"Damn straight," Whistler muttered, then ordered a pizza via DoorDash, grabbed a beer, turned on the TV, and settled down to wait for the food to arrive.

Gunner and Cliff were back in the department, writing up their reports on the hanging-man case, when Gunner got a phone call from another division of the Dallas PD.

"Homicide, this is Kingston," he said.

"Detective, this is Officer Waters in Traffic division. We're working a hit and run, and have a victim here who had your card in his pocket, along with a hundred dollars. Does that ring a bell?"

Gunner's heart sank. "Does he have long gray hair and a beard?"

"Yes. Do you know who it is?" the officer asked.

"If it's who I think it is, his name is Dan Helford. Where are you taking him?"

"The morgue. If you'd be willing to make a positive ID, it would be helpful. I know it's late, but they're loading up the body now. I'll tell the medical examiner you're coming to make an ID."

Gunner hung up, looked across the desk at his partner without speaking, then got up and walked into Lieutenant Samuels's office.

"I have to go down to the morgue to ID a body," he said.

Samuels looked up, saw the expression on Gunner's face, and frowned. "I hope it's none of your family."

"No, sir. I think it's the old homeless man who found Freddie Welsh's body. The one we brought in this morning to get his statement."

Samuels frowned. "Well damn, what happened, and why did they call you for the ID?"

"Hit and run. I gave him my card when I dropped him off at the shelter. They found it on his body."

"Take Cliff with you," Samuels said.

"I'd rather not. I'll be back," Gunner said and walked out.

Samuels frowned, got up from his desk, and walked out of his office, eyeing Gunner as he grabbed his jacket from the back of his chair.

Cliff started to get up. "What's up. Where are we going?"

"I've got this," Gunner said and kept walking.

Cliff glanced at the boss. "Is everything okay?"

Samuels frowned. "You tell me."

Cliff shrugged.

Samuels turned around, walked back into his office, and shut the door.

Gunner hated the morgue. Hated going into it. Hated seeing the bodies in varying stages of being autopsied. Hated the smells and the fact that it always made him want to cry. Grown men aren't supposed to cry. Gunner had taken that to heart at an early age.

Dr. Delores Paige, the medical examiner, was at her desk when the detective arrived. She'd met him before, but she couldn't really claim that she knew him. She just knew the stories and the reputation, and she could tell by the look on Kingston's face that he was bothered by this call.

"Hey, Doc, I'm here to ID a body," Gunner said.

Doctor Paige got up from her desk. "Yes, and thank you for coming, detective. Follow me."

Gunner followed her into the autopsy room and stood aside while the coroner pulled out a drawer and lifted the sheet from the deceased man's face.

"Damn it," Gunner muttered, unaware he'd said it aloud, and then nodded. "Yes, that's Dan Helford. His street name was Yankee Dan. Once you do the autopsy, I want a copy of the findings. If there's any way of knowing if this was intentional or an accident, I'd appreciate the heads-up."

Dr. Paige replaced the sheet and pushed the body back into the drawer. "You suspect foul play?"

Gunner sighed. "Less than twenty-four hours ago that man had the misfortune to witness the body dump of a material witness in a federal case. It was at night, in an empty warehouse with no power. All he saw were a few shadows, and then they were gone. But he went down the stairs and found the body, then called it in. I took his statement and dropped him off at a homeless shelter. He didn't see anything, or hear anything except doors opening and doors closing, but certain people may not see it that way. They could have viewed him as more trouble."

She frowned. "I don't know what I'll find, but I will keep that in mind. Best guess is that it's going to be next to impossible to tell if it was an accident or purposeful, but I'll make sure you get a copy of the findings."

"I appreciate that," Gunner said and walked out, but his heart was pounding. Every instinct he had told him this was because Yankee Dan had been in the wrong place at the wrong time, and Burgess Dixon was still tying up loose ends.

But there was another issue attached to this tragedy that was bugging Gunner. The media knew nothing about a witness to the body dump. Twenty-four hours had yet to elapse from the time the police had arrived on the scene, and yet that witness was now lying in the morgue, which led

Gunner to believe that Burgess Dixon had a dirty cop on his payroll, and it was someone in this department.

He drove back to the precinct and went straight to Samuels's office. The door was open. He knocked and then entered.

"The witness we brought in from the body dump is dead. Victim of a hit and run. No witnesses. No working security cameras. No leads. My Spidey senses tell me Burgess Dixon has a dirty cop on the payroll."

Samuels frowned. "That's a dangerous insinuation, detective."

"I'm not insinuating. I'm saying it outright. Somebody is keeping Burgess Dixon abreast of anything ongoing related to him. I took Yankee Dan's statement, and you witnessed it. I assume you sent a copy to the Feds. The officers on scene at the warehouse heard him identify himself as Yankee Dan. I told Cliff his given name, and everyone in this division knew who he was and why we brought him in. And now he's dead, and I can't help thinking that we're the ones who put him in danger by bringing attention to his presence there. I'm pissed, and I'm sick to my stomach. I hate dirty cops, and I'm saying we have one…somewhere."

"Where are you and Beale on the dude found hanging out a window?"

"No leads. Waiting on forensics," Gunner said.

"Then go home. Get some food and rest, come back tomorrow ready to focus on that, and leave the rest of this to me. I'll notify the FBI about a possible connection to Dixon, but the rest is up to them. This is not our case. Right now, in the eyes of the law, it's an unfortunate hit and run. Not a murder."

Gunner didn't like it, but he didn't argue. He just turned and walked out, stopping at his desk long enough to log off his computer.

"What's going on?" Cliff asked.

"The old man we brought in from the warehouse is dead. Killed by a hit-and-run driver. They asked me to ID him."

"Why you?" Cliff asked.

"Because they found my card on him. I gave it to him when I dropped him off at the shelter. I'm going home. See you tomorrow."

Cliff frowned. "Damn, that's tough."

Gunner turned, looking Cliff straight in the face. "No, it's suspicious as hell. That's what it is," and walked out.

Cliff nodded but didn't respond. Ever since they'd worked the body dump case, he and Gunner had lost traction. He felt the distance between them but didn't know how to get it back.

Gunner was in a mood, and going home to an empty house with no groceries wasn't going to make it better. He'd been putting off a shopping trip for almost a week and decided that walking down aisles among strangers to the piped-in music from the eighties was better than thinking about stuff he couldn't change, so he stopped at the nearest Whole Foods, grabbed a shopping cart, and headed down the first aisle.

This was Texas. It was common to see cowboys. But it wasn't every day you saw one like Gunner Kingston. His badge and the shoulder holster with his weapon were obvious. It branded him as a cop. But there were perks. His hair was black as night, and he was tall enough to reach the top shelves without the need to stretch. Even the brim on his black, gambler-style Stetson couldn't hide the handsome cut of his face, or the grim expression he was wearing. Women looked, then looked away, unwilling to be caught in the icy glare he was giving to a box of cereal.

Unaware of being watched, Gunner was focusing on finding a box of cereal that didn't have marshmallows in it, and unaware of the shopper behind him until the sudden stop of motion in his peripheral vision made him turn and look.

The first thing he saw was a woman with a wild mane of auburn curls, and then he saw her face and realized she was calling his name.

"Gunner… Is it really you? It's me, Holly. Holly Dillon."

He blinked, then a slow smile spread across his face. "Damn, kid. You grew up, and did a fine job of it, at that."

Holly beamed, then threw herself into his arms without a shred of hesitation. "I haven't seen you since you graduated high school. Are you as badass as you look, or is this all just fashion and flash?"

He grinned. She'd never been one to hesitate about speaking her mind, and clearly, she had not changed.

"I haven't seen you since you were what…ten years old?"

"Twelve, and the only bat girl Crossroads baseball team ever had," she said, then realized she was still hugging him and let go. "Sorry. I got a little carried away."

He touched the tiny little scar on her forehead. "I seem to remember you getting on the wrong side of a fly ball and dropping like a dead fly out near the dugout."

"Yes, and you picked me up and started running toward my mom and dad who were watching the game from our truck, dumped me in Mom's lap, and told them to get me to a doctor. I believe you also told them they better not let me die, because I was the best bat girl they'd ever had."

Gunner grinned. "You were. It's great to see you again. Do you live in Dallas?"

"Yes, and the real estate office I work at is in Dallas, too, but I work all over the metroplex," she said.

"You sell houses?"

"I take a listing occasionally, but my main job is keeping up with all the paperwork regarding buying and selling, and verifying deeds for the other Realtors. What about you?"

He pulled back the front of his jacket, revealing the weapon in his shoulder holster and the detective badge clipped to his belt. "I've been with the Dallas PD from the start of my career, but the last eight of those years in Homicide."

Her eyes widened. "Awesome. Can you still run like the devil is chasing you?"

Without thinking, he lifted a wayward curl from the corner of her eye.

"Yeah, only now I'm the one chasing the devil and his cohorts. Are you married, dating, attached in any way, etcetera, etcetera?"

She grinned. "No to all, even the etcetera. What about you?"

His eyes narrowed as he watched the expressions coming and going on her face, and he made a knee-jerk decision that was very unlike him.

"My only attachment is my job. Want to trade phone numbers?" he asked.

She yanked her phone out of her pocket without bothering to answer. They traded numbers and one last hug, and then she pointed down the aisle behind him. "I still have shopping to do. Don't forget me."

"That's never gonna happen. Have dinner with me... If you're not busy," he said and then nearly choked on his audacity. He wasn't a spur-of-the-moment kind of man.

Holly beamed. "You mean now?"

"I guess I do. Like as soon as we finish shopping...before either of us go home. Somewhere nearby. I have a rare need for some company, and I would love to catch up with you."

Holly was trying not to giggle. "I would love to. There's a

little Mexican taqueria just a block from here… If you're in the mood for that."

"I'm in the mood," Gunner said. "Thirty minutes?"

She threw back her head and laughed. "Thirty minutes it is. I'll shop fast."

"I drive a black Mustang GT," Gunner said.

"White Chevy SUV. Meet you there," Holly said.

Gunner watched until she was out of sight before he made himself refocus and finish what he'd come to do. Today had been rough, but this unexpected meeting and asking her for a date before they'd barely said hello could be excused because of their past relationship.

Granted, she'd been the pesky little kid who trailed his every step, but she was no longer a pesky kid. She was drop-dead gorgeous. At that point, all of his walls went up and his warning system kicked in. It was no big deal. Just a meal with someone from home.

Gunner was at the taqueria when Holly entered the parking lot. She made one sweep through the cars before finding a place to park, and then tried not to run when she went to meet him.

"This is the best thing that's happened to me in ages, and I can smell that grilling meat from here," she said.

"Smells like a Texas barbeque," Gunner said as he took her by the hand and walked her across the parking lot and into the little café. They were seated quickly, handed menus, and turned in their drink orders, then took the time to look—really look—at each other.

"Sorry for staring," Gunner said. "You're just…so beautiful. I'm trying to find the kid I knew in that amazing face, and the only thing left that's really familiar is your hair."

"It's not red," she said.

He laughed. "Oh, I remember the rule. It's auburn, right?"

She laughed. "You did remember."

"I remember you shouting at the catcher every day because he called you 'red on the head' and it made you mad."

She was still smiling. "The whole team gave me grief, but I loved being the bat girl. I got to hang out with all the cute guys at practice and at games. Made my girlfriends so jealous."

Gunner couldn't stop smiling. Their coach used to call her the little rattle-bucket, because she also never stopped talking, but she'd been a good sport about getting teased.

"The waitress is heading our way. Do you know what you want to eat?"

She nodded. "Shrimp tacos on flour tortillas. Chips and queso."

"Sounds good to me, too," he said.

The waitress took their orders and soon came back with their drinks and a tray with chips, salsa, and queso for the table.

"To old friends," Gunner said as he toasted her with his drink.

"And new friendships," she countered as she toasted him back.

They ate a couple of chips before curiosity got the best of her, and Holly asked the question she'd been dying to ask. "How is it that you have managed to stay single for all these years?"

Gunner glanced up, still chewing, which gave him the moment he needed to figure out how to answer that. "Uh… Picky, I guess."

She nodded. "Still the loner, aren't you?"

He frowned. "What do you mean?"

She fired back. "How many girls did you date in high school?"

"Well, I took Linda Carver to a school dance."

"That wasn't a date. It was that girl-asking-the-boy dance. I remember."

He threw a wadded-up paper napkin at her. "Don't blow my image. I'm the hard-nosed, take-no-prisoners cop who has the best record on the gun range, and an unbroken record on the track when we work out."

She giggled. "Don't worry. I always had your back. I always will. I also don't throw away old shoes or worn-out T-shirts, so I don't know what that says for me, either."

Now he was laughing. A thing so rare that it almost felt like he was coming out of the dark. "I think you are good for what ails me. Do you want sopapillas?"

"Too full, but thank you," she said.

"Maybe next time." He glanced at the time. "We better get a move on. We've both got groceries in our cars, and it's at least a forty-five-minute drive home for me."

"About the same for me, but toward Fort Worth," she said and began gathering up her phone and purse.

Gunner left money on the table with a sizeable tip, then walked her out the door and across the lot to her car.

"This was the best day I've had in forever," Gunner said. "We have to do this again, and soon."

"You have my number. And I'll save room for dessert next time. Thank you for dinner. Don't forget me, okay?"

It was the poignant tone in her voice and the blue sparkle in her eyes that got him. Before he could change his mind, he cupped his hands on her cheeks, brushed a quick kiss across her lips, and then gave a wayward curl a quick tug.

"You're impossible to forget. Drive safe, Hollyberry. Talk to you soon," he said.

Holly was still coming down from the shock of his mouth on her lips and allowed the use of her old childhood nickname to pass. "Yes, soon," she said.

He opened her door, waited until she was seated and buckled in, then gave the top of her car a quick tap as she closed the door and drove away.

He knew he'd just come to a personal crossroad. Now all he had to do was figure out where to go from here, and if she was willing to go with him.

Chapter 3

Holly was so elated that she felt like bouncing. She glanced at the time as soon as she got into the car, noting that it was just shy of 9:00 p.m. She couldn't wait to tell her mom that she'd just had dinner with Gunner Kingston. But when she didn't get an answer, she guessed they were probably busy outside somewhere and decided she'd try later. Instead of leaving a voicemail, she disconnected and took her exit off the Loop and headed home.

She was still smiling about her chance meeting as she began bringing her groceries into her town house and putting them up. She was on her way to the bedroom to change clothes when her phone rang.

She looked down, saw her dad's name on Caller ID instead of her mom's, and frowned. "Hey, Dad, what's up?"

She heard the panic in her dad's voice, but he was so choked up and rambling that she couldn't understand him.

"Dad! Dad! What's wrong? I can't understand what you're saying!"

Then suddenly her younger brother, Travis, was on the phone. His voice was shaking. She could hear her dad sobbing in the background and felt the ground falling out from under her.

"Sis, it's me. Mom is dead. She was a quarter of a mile from home when a truck came over the hill in the middle of the road and hit her head on. Please come home. Dad's coming undone, and I don't know what to do." And then he broke down in sobs.

"Oh my God, oh my God," Holly mumbled. She wanted to scream, but she could tell from the sounds in the background how bad it was.

"Travis! Listen to me! I just got home. It'll take me about thirty minutes to pack some clothes and notify my boss. Just know that I'm on the way. Who hit her? What happened to that driver?"

Travis's voice was still shaking. "It was Lee Peters, my best friend. We'd gone to Amarillo this morning, and he'd just dropped me back off at the ranch. He was on his way home. He's dead, too."

Holly's legs went out from under her. She dropped into the nearest chair to keep from falling.

"Oh, dear Lord. Travis! I can hear it in your voice, but none of this is your fault. Call Granny Dillon. She's just across the border in New Mexico. She'll get there before I will, but I'm coming, honey. I'm coming home. Tell Dad I'm on the way. We'll get through this together. I love you."

"Love you, too, Sis," Travis said and hung up.

Holly was shaking so hard it was all she could do to make the call to her boss, Gene Morris. Even as they were talking, she knew she was sounding like her father, rambling, shattered, not making a lot of sense as she began to explain to him what had happened, and that she had to go home.

After extending his sympathies, Gene reassured her that her job would be waiting, and to take as long as she needed.

The moment they disconnected, she began dragging out suitcases, then dragging them up the stairs to her bedroom, tossing clothes at random, sobbing between every breath as she dragged them back down and loaded up her car. She set the security alarm at her home and headed northwest out of Dallas. It was a long drive to the panhandle of West Texas. A long, sad way to go, knowing her mother would not be there to welcome her home.

Gunner was still thinking about Holly Dillon long after he got home, and was stretched out on his bed, scanning through texts and updates from Cliff. The TV was on in the background when he heard the word "lottery" and remembered tonight was the night for the Mega Millions draw. The amount was over seven hundred and eighty million dollars, so he turned up the volume just in time to hear the announcer.

"....winning lottery ticket was sold at a Gas and Dash just off the bypass. Somewhere within this city, there is a man or woman carrying around a seven-hundred-and-eighty-million-dollar lottery ticket. Check your pockets, folks. Someone's life is about to change. The winning numbers are posted at the bottom of the screen, and also on the Texas Lottery website."

A shiver ran up Gunner's spine as he rolled out of bed and reached for his wallet. He pulled out the ticket he'd bought at a Gas and Dash, read the numbers posted on the screen, then looked at the numbers on his ticket.

"No way," he muttered, then took a picture of the numbers on the screen and reread the numbers on his ticket again, and felt the blood draining from his face. "Sweet lord," he whispered and put his head down to keep from passing out from the shock.

His head was still spinning when reality hit. Until he got this ticket to the Texas Lottery Commission, it meant nothing, but for his future, it meant everything. He put the ticket back in his wallet. He put the wallet under his pillow, got his gun from the lockbox and put it beside his pillow, too, and then got up and walked through the house to recheck the windows and doors, making sure his security system was armed. It was a knee-jerk reaction to the amount of money, because in reality, there wasn't a soul on earth who could know who was holding the winning ticket. Still, his heart was hammering as he went back to bed, but he couldn't sleep.

Everything about his life was in sudden free fall. He sat back up and sent a text to Lieutenant Samuels, telling him he was taking a personal day tomorrow, then called his lawyer.

The phone rang four times, and then Gunner heard the call pick up.

"Hello?"

"Bradley, it's me, Gunner. I need legal help in the morning. Are you free?"

"I can be. Are you in trouble?" Wes Bradley asked.

"It's not bad, but it's way out of my wheelhouse, and I have to do it ASAP."

"Where do I meet you?" Wes asked.

"I'll pick you up at your office at 9:00 a.m."

"Works for me. Just give me a call when you arrive, and I'll come out to meet you. Save you the trouble of trying to find a place to park."

"I really appreciate this," Gunner said and disconnected, then sat up in bed with the gun in his lap, waiting for daybreak.

It was just shy of 4:00 a.m. when Holly Dillon drove through Crossroads, Texas. A couple of miles farther, she took a right off the highway, and the moment her tires hit the blacktop, she was already home. Everything from as far as the eye could see, in any direction—west, north, and east—was Dillon property. The house was still a quarter of a mile north.

She was coming up over the rise when the bits of scattered debris across the road suddenly caught light in the moonlight. She slowed down, hesitant to drive through it for fear of damaging her tires, then she saw more of the same debris glittering from both sides of the ditch, and that's when it hit her!

This is the wreck site!

This is where her mother and Lee died.

"Oh my God, oh my God," Holly moaned and sped through it like she was driving through fire, then pulled over and stopped, sobbing uncontrollably. The whole time she was trying to unbuckle her seat belt, she knew she was going to be sick. When it finally came loose, she all but fell out of the car, staggered into the headlights, and threw up until there was nothing left inside her to reject but the grief, and it was going nowhere.

She stumbled back to her car, grabbed a half-filled bottle of water from the console, and rinsed her mouth, then sloshed the rest of it in her hands and scrubbed her face. The last thing her family needed was for her to arrive in a state of hysterics. She got back in the car, took a deep breath, and buckled up.

Within minutes, the security lights on either side of the entrance gate to the homestead came into view. The lights of the long, rambling ranch house were visible now as she drove over the cattle guard. As she neared the house, she saw her granny Dillon's car parked beside Garrett and Travis's trucks. The only vehicle missing was her mom's blue Toyota.

She parked beside her grandmother's car, popped the trunk, and killed the engine. Her legs were shaking as she circled the car to get her bags, but then the front door opened and Garrett and Travis were coming toward her in long, hurried strides.

"Baby girl," Garrett said and wrapped his arms around her.

"Oh, Daddy, wake me up now. This is a nightmare," she said and broke into sobs.

Garrett's voice was thick with tears. "I know, honey, but I keep reminding myself that we're not the only family grieving. Lee was Travis's age, and he's gone, too. It was a freaking tragedy, but we're gonna get through it together."

Travis gave Holly's shoulder a quick squeeze. "I'll get your bags."

Holly was exhausted and so sad it was hard to breathe, but she was home.

Garrett was at a loss for words as he walked Holly into the house. Every time he took a breath it was like a knife to the heart.

Travis came in behind them with Holly's suitcases. "I'll take these to your old room," he said.

"Dad... Travis... You both must be exhausted, waiting up for me, but I'm here now. I assume Granny is asleep, and I can get myself to bed. Both of you are officially relieved of duty. We'll talk tomorrow."

Whispered words and one group hug later, Holly was alone. She knew no one was going to be able to sleep, but rest was needed. She slipped out of the room and went up the hall to the kitchen, looked for a can of anything cold to take away the bad taste in her mouth, and took it back to her room, sipping it now and then as she began to unpack. Finally, she stretched out on the bed just before daybreak and closed her eyes, drifting in and out of sleep for a couple of hours before she was awakened by the sound of a calf bawling and, before she opened her eyes, wondered where the hell she was at.

Then her eyes flew open, and she remembered. Fresh tears rolled as she threw back the covers and got out of bed, tied up her hair, and took a quick shower. A short while later, she was in the kitchen frying bacon and listening to the burp and bubble at the coffee station as fresh coffee dripped into an oversize carafe.

Garrett appeared a few minutes later, with Travis on his heels. "Holly, you didn't have to cook."

"We all need food. Where's Granny?" she asked.

"Mom's up," Garrett said. "She'll be along later."

Holly pointed. "Coffee is done. Toast and bacon are on the counter. Scrambled eggs are in the skillet. Help yourselves. We can talk while we eat."

Moments later, Garrett's mother, Trudy, came into the kitchen in yoga pants and a loose sweater. Despite the silver in her hair, she could have passed for a woman twenty years younger than her actual seventy-one. She wrapped her arms around her only granddaughter to hug her, then didn't want to let go.

"Holly, darling, I'm so glad you arrived safely. Sorry I didn't wake up in time to help you. I'm not as perky as I used to be."

"I'm just glad you're here, Granny. Breakfast is ready. Have a seat."

But when they were all seated, sitting down to a meal without Helen seemed like a betrayal of their grief. They had food on their plates but were either picking at it or staring off into space, until Trudy intervened.

"My dear loves. Listen to me. Food in mouth. Chew and swallow. Even if it tastes like sawdust and sits in your stomach like a rock, the day ahead of us is going to be long. The crew will tend to the chores. We have other stuff to decide between us."

"I don't think I can eat, Granny," Travis said and laid down his fork. "I should call his parents, but I don't know what to say when I can't believe we've lost Mom, too." Tears were streaming down his face, and he was swallowing sobs between words.

Garrett took his son's hand and gave it a quick squeeze. "Mom's right, Trav. Eat something, even if it's just toast. I don't know the propriety of sending our condolences to the Peters family when we're in our own state of shock and grief. This is a waking nightmare."

"We'll send flowers and let them respond or not," Trudy said. "We'll figure it out as we go."

They all managed to get a decent meal down and then helped Holly clean up afterward. By then, the first delivery of flowers arrived, and Garrett and Travis's phones began to ring.

"I'll deal with deliveries," Holly said. It was tradition for friends to bring food to a family in need, and she knew it would be coming.

"I'll go make up the beds and start some laundry. I saw the hamper was full when I arrived last night," Trudy said and left the room.

Garrett shoved a hand through his hair. "I need to talk to Sheriff Reddick. I need to know how long the autopsy is going to take. We are at a standstill as to making any arrangements until they release her body," he said and walked out of the kitchen.

Travis was still standing at the sink, looking out at the corral and horse stables beyond.

Holly reached for his hand. "Talk to me," she said.

"I need to talk to Mr. and Mrs. Peters, but I don't know how to feel. On one hand, I am crushed that Lee is the one who hit Mom head on. But who's to blame? The police said they were both in the middle of the road. So does that mean Mom killed Lee, or Lee killed Mom?"

Holly took a deep breath. "It was a terrible accident, but there's no blame to claim. Understand?"

"What if the Peterses don't feel that way?" Travis said.

Garrett walked up behind his children. "Lee's parents were at the scene of the wreck just like I was. They heard the police just like I did. Neither driver swerved, nor hit the brakes. They hit head on, and unless the autopsy gives us specific answers, we'll never know why. We hugged and cried together when they finally removed their bodies. They already understand and expect you to be as devastated as they are."

Travis ducked his head, his voice barely above a whisper. "Lee and I were going be roommates at A&M. Mom and Mrs. Peters were already planning to help us fix up our room."

"Plans are made. Plans change," Holly said. "I am your big-sister backup. We'll figure it out. You can call Mr. and Mrs. Peters, or you can go visit them. Your choice. Your decision. This sucks, but life has just handed you big shoes to stand in, whether you were ready or not."

Travis picked up his phone and walked outside to the back porch.

Holly's eyes welled. "What do you want me to do, Dad?"

"I'm leaving my phone with you because this is the number everyone will be calling. I have to go talk to the men. We're separating cattle today, and I need to be on-site. The calls will likely be condolences, but if they have to speak to me, then take their names and numbers and I'll call them back tonight. Is that okay?" Garrett asked.

"Absolutely," Holly said, watching as her dad left the house. She knew he needed to stay busy, and this would help. If he got enough of it, he'd come back to the house.

Life as they'd known it was over, and her urge to go to ground like a wounded animal was real, but sticking together through this was how they were also going to survive it.

Holly checked her phone for messages, then laid it beside her dad's phone and went back to the sink. As she looked out the kitchen window, she saw Travis out by the barn, leaning against the corral fence and talking on the phone. She looked away. The next time she glanced out, he was standing with his arms braced against the corral and his head down.

She pocketed both phones and walked out of the house. She could hear him crying as she neared the corral and slipped her arm around his waist as she walked up beside him.

He turned and wrapped his arms around her, sobbing. "Damn it, Sis, that phone call about did me in. What do I do next? Do I stay here with Dad and give up my scholarship, or go to A&M on my own and leave him here alone?"

Holly was shocked. "First, you do not give up that scholarship! Mom and Dad were so proud of you. The last thing you do now is throw it away. There are over twenty hired hands here every day, beside Dewey, the foreman. Dad is only in his fifties. He's not old. Don't insult him by even suggesting this, okay? Besides, I'm here, and I'm not running back to Dallas the first chance I get. I took a leave of absence with my boss's approval. I'm here as long as I want to be."

"Really?" Travis said and wiped his eyes with the sleeve of his shirt.

"Yes, really. Our business now is getting Mom put to rest, crying when we need to, and reminding ourselves how blessed we were to have had her for a mother. Dad will figure out his own things, and they're far different from ours. He's just lost the love of his life. He needs to do what he does in his own time, okay?"

Travis nodded. "Yes, okay. I'm really glad you're here," he said.

"I wouldn't be anywhere else," Holly said. "If none of this had happened, what would you be doing about now?"

"Online classes, but I graduated in December. I've just been biding my time here helping Dad until Lee graduated at Crossroads."

"Then get your hat and gloves. He left his phone with me, so go ask Dewey. Get dirty. Cuss a stubborn steer or two. I know they're separating cattle somewhere. That's where he said he'd be."

"Oh, then I know where he is," Travis said. "I'll have my phone if you need us."

"That'll work," Holly said. She gave him a quick pat on the shoulder as he headed for the stables while she walked back to the house, her feet dragging with every step.

Unaware of the Dillon tragedy, Gunner was showered, shaved, and dressed before daybreak, making breakfast with an eye to the time. Even as he was putting a second slice of bread in the toaster, he kept thinking this lottery win couldn't possibly be real, and that he'd wake up any minute and realize it was just a dream. But he'd also checked his wallet at least four times since he started the coffee to make sure the ticket was still there, and it was.

He took another sip of coffee and finally smiled. *I don't know how this is going to impact my life, but I'm about to find out.*

His last piece of toast popped up; he grabbed it, smeared it with grape jelly, and wolfed it down. It was time to go pick up Mr. Wes Bradley, Esquire.

Wes Bradley went to the office early to finish up some paperwork ready to file and was waiting when he got Gunner's text. He left the air-conditioned comfort of his office and walked out into the bright light and building heat of a sunny Texas morning, then slid into the front seat of the detective's car.

"Is this thing as fast as it looks?" Wes asked as he buckled up.

"Yes," Gunner said and drove out of the parking area and back onto the bypass, heading to Stemmons Street.

"What's the big secret, and where are we going?" Wes asked.

"I won the seven-hundred-and-eighty-million-dollar Mega Millions jackpot, and we're going to the Dallas Claims Center to claim it."

Wes laughed. "No, seriously dude. What's up?"

Gunner's focus was on the bypass traffic, and he never broke his gaze as he repeated himself.

"I won the Mega Millions jackpot. The ticket is in my wallet. I'm a cop. I want a lawyer with me for legal backup when the money gets to the bank. I'm not telling anyone else but my boss, so this is privileged information, got it?"

Wes's shock was real. He took a deep breath and then forgot to exhale as he watched Gunner's calm demeanor.

"Holy shit, man. This is amazing! What are you going to do?" he asked.

"Still be a cop," Gunner said. "Just one with a whole lot of money now."

Wes grinned. "This is amazing! Absolutely amazing! Congratulations, Gunner."

"Pure luck of the draw. I did nothing to deserve it. I also read up on the lottery rules, and I'm taking a lump sum payment, which should come to about half the jackpot, or less. Also, it's likely to take four to six weeks before the payout happens. I also need to update my will and get a financial advisor. That's where you come in."

Wes realized how serious Gunner was about the responsibility of having that kind of money and was somewhat surprised that a single, good-looking man like him wasn't thinking about a little bit of a wild spending spree and seeing the world.

"Are you going to eventually tell the people you work with?" Wes asked.

Gunner shrugged. "Not on purpose, although I suspect they'll figure it out later. I don't intend to become their bank and money lender. I'm not looking forward to the big reveal. I don't like turmoil in my personal life."

"Understood," Wes said as Gunner moved into the lane on the right and took the exit ramp off the bypass and onto Stemmons, straight to the Dallas Claims Center.

A few minutes later, they were in the claims office. After a brief explanation of their visit and a quiet round of congratulations, Gunner and Wes were escorted into the boss's office. The winning ticket was presented, verified, and the paperwork began.

It took a bit less than two hours to complete the change to Gunner Kingston's life. He and Wes left the claims office as calmly as they'd entered, and then Gunner returned Wes to his office.

"I'll message you with specific details regarding the change in my will," Gunner said.

"And I'll send you the details to the best financial planner in Dallas, although you won't really need him until the payout shows up in your account," Wes said. "In the meantime, what's next?"

"Back to the case my partner and I are working on," Gunner said.

"Are you going to tell your partner?" Wes asked.

Gunner didn't hesitate. "No."

"Really? Why not?" Wes asked.

"Long story. He gambles. He already owes me more money than he will ever repay. I've already cut him off, but he'll see me now as his personal piggy bank, and…I don't entirely trust him anymore."

After that, the conversation ended until Gunner pulled up in front of Wes's office building again.

"I really appreciate that you rearranged your schedule for me this morning. Don't forget to bill me for the time," Gunner said.

Wes grinned. "I'll add it to the charges for reworking your will. Take care of yourself. I'm wishing you a long and happy life, and that you loosen up and spend a little of your fortune along the way."

Gunner reached out and shook his lawyer's hand. "Thanks. I'll be in touch."

Wes was headed for the entrance when Gunner took off like he'd been shot out of a cannon, tires squealing as he left a little bit of rubber behind. Wes shook his head and watched until the sports car slipped into the traffic flow and disappeared, and thought how aptly that man had been named.

Gunner went straight home, got out the copy of his will, and read it through before deciding how he wanted it reworded, then emailed his notes to Wes. Only after he'd done his due diligence did he grab a cold pop from his fridge and go outside on his patio. He sat down in the shade and kicked back in one of the Adirondack chairs before he popped the top on his drink. It was still fizzing when he lifted it in a toast to himself.

"Gunner Kingston, you are one lucky son of a bitch," he muttered and took a big drink.

He knew his dad and both brothers would be at work, so he sent a group text to all three of them with a single cryptic message.

We need a family meeting. Make yourselves available for a 10:00 p.m. call tonight. Highly confidential.

Asher Kingston was in Austin on a stakeout when he got his youngest brother's text. He frowned when he read it and wondered what fresh hell he'd gotten himself into now, but he made a mental note to be available when the time came.

Dylan Kingston was at a job site, waiting for a city inspector to pass judgement on the electrical and plumbing work so they could begin putting up sheetrock. When he saw Gunner's text, like Asher, his first instinct was to wonder what kind of trouble his little brother was in now.

Jacob Kingston was behind his bar, hooking up a fresh keg of beer to the tap when he heard his phone signal a text. He finished what he was doing, then wiped his hand and picked up his phone.

He read the text with interest, wondering what Gunner had to say. Maybe he'd finally met a girl. Maybe he was getting a promotion. And there was always the possibility that he was up to his eyeballs in a mess not of his own creation, but not once did Jacob ever doubt his sons' honor or honesty.

Now he was curious, and more than a little anxious about the call. Tonight, he was closing the Tumbleweed Bar a little early and hoping for good news.

With the business of becoming shockingly rich out of the way, Gunner drove to his dealership to get his car serviced. He was sitting in the waiting area of the showroom while the maintenance crew was rotating his tires and changing the oil. Waiting with nothing to do was pure torture for him, so he'd brought his laptop with him to continue gathering background on the case of the hanging man.

After learning there was a hefty payout from a life insurance policy belonging to the deceased, Barry Caldwell, and that his twin brother, Perry, was the recipient, he began digging into the living twin's background.

Perry was gay and living with his partner of seven years, Ron Ames, but witnesses they'd spoken to were clear about how close the two brothers were, and that they were in business together. What he did find interesting was the amount of debt that Ron Ames held. He made a note to tell Cliff they needed to find out if Perry Caldwell knew his partner Ron was in financial trouble and see if that went anywhere, so he made notes to that effect to share with Cliff.

As he kept working, a bright light flashed through the plate-glass windows and into his eyes, causing him to look up, and he was surprised to see Cliff's car pulling up to the curb across the street. Curious, he closed his laptop and leaned forward, watching as Cliff got out and took a nervous glance around before slipping into the passenger seat of the car beside him.

Gunner was already suspicious of Cliff since that night in the warehouse, so he wrote down the tag number of the other car, curious about who Cliff was meeting. The car door opened. As Cliff got out, he slipped an envelope inside the inner pocket of his jacket, then got in his car and drove away.

At that moment, the skin crawled on Gunner's neck. If he'd been on a stakeout, he would have sworn he'd just witnessed some kind of payoff. But he also knew Cliff was a notorious gambler, and that might have just been a payoff from a bookie. The hard part for Gunner was the feeling that there was a dirty cop somewhere in Homicide, but he wasn't at the point of placing blame.

He leaned back in the chair, stretching his long legs out before him as he began thinking of tonight's phone call with the family. He could only imagine what they must be thinking. His brothers would think he was in trouble, and his dad would probably be hoping it would be news related to him finally settling down. Being the only unmarried brother in his family meant he was the stooge for all of the single jokes and blind date suggestions.

At that point, his thoughts went straight to Holly Dillon. Of all the people to run into. Having lunch with her had been an impulse, but it left him wanting to know more about her. The skinny little redhead with the oversize baseball cap constantly blowing off her head had grown up to be a knockout. He knew she'd be at work now. Maybe tonight after office hours he would give her a call and see if she was free to go out this coming weekend.

About an hour later, his car was ready to go. The toast he'd eaten this morning was long gone, and he'd already missed lunch, but he hated eating in public alone, so he made his usual choice. It was either food to go or food ordered in. And today, it was barbeque to go from the Texas Smokehouse, which he picked up on his way home.

Today, the quiet of his house and the food going in his stomach was the solace he needed. In a couple of hours, Holly should be off work, so he occupied his time with doing laundry. The house cleaners would be here tomorrow, but he'd be at work, and they wouldn't have to clean around him.

Despite his best intentions, it was after 8:00 p.m. before he sat down to call her. The phone rang enough times that he thought it was going to voicemail when he heard her answer.

"Gunner? Is this you?"

The quaver in her voice let him know something was amiss. "Yes, it's me. If you are ill, or this is a bad time, I can call at a later date."

"I'm at home, on the ranch. Mom was killed in a wreck yesterday. It's absolute chaos here. We're all between lost and losing our minds."

Shocked, Gunner's empathy was instantaneous. "My God, Holly! Honey, I'm so sorry. You have my deepest sympathy. Losing your mother at any age is devastating. Please give your dad and Travis my condolences. I won't bother you further and…"

"No, wait. Don't hang up. It's good to hear your voice. Talk to me about something you've been doing. Oh, wait… You can't talk about cases. So, tell me what's going on in Big D that I might need to know about. I heard on the news that somebody in Dallas finally won that huge Mega Millions jackpot last night."

Gunner took a deep breath. He didn't want to lie, but he wasn't ready to reveal it to the world.

"I know it happened, but no identification has been issued. I've just been chasing bad guys and keeping myself out of trouble," he said. "I don't know how long you plan to stay, but I'm going to be heading to Crossroads soon for a quick visit with Dad and Pearl. If you're still at the ranch, maybe we could grab a meal at the Rose. Pearl and Dad are together at his place now, but she's still running the café. It wouldn't be the Yellow Rose without Pearl in the kitchen, right?"

Holly sighed. "I would love that. I know this madness will fade and we will find our own levels of peace, but right now it's all just so awful."

"It couldn't be anything else," he said. "Of course, I'll let you know my arrival date, and if you're still in the area, we'll make that happen. Again, honey, I'm so sorry."

Tears thickened the words, making them hard to get said. "So am I, Gunner. God, so am I. Thank you for calling, and for not forgetting about me."

"I already told you that's not likely to happen. Feel free to call me any time you need to vent. I'm a good listener and a safe place to fall."

The call disconnected in Holly's ear. She was grateful that he actually called her, and for the honest empathy she'd heard in his voice. And then she thought of the Kingston family history, and how young those three boys had been when their mother took her own life. That was a whole other kind of tragedy. But all she kept thinking was that Gunner Kingston had kept his word and called her back.

Her eyes welled again. "Oh, Mom, how did this happen? I wish you were here to talk to. There's no one left to share my dreams with now."

Chapter 4

Gunner was in shock as he hung up the phone. He'd known Garrett and Helen Dillon all his life, and Holly had been the little kid in the background of his high school years, following him around like a shadow. Seeing her in the supermarket all grown up had been great, interesting, even mind-blowing.

But this tragedy just put a whole new light on Holly Dillon. She was hurting, and in a way he understood. He glanced at the time and then went to shower. As soon as he made the call to his family, he was going to bed. He was way past needing sleep and had to get the call over with before he fell asleep standing up.

By the time he had shaved and showered, it was time to make the group call. He called Asher first, then connected Dylan, then last but not least, their dad, Jacob.

"Okay, we're all here," Asher said. "What the hell have you done?"

"Are the ladies on the call?" Gunner asked.

All three of the men said yes, then Jacob added, "We can ask them to leave if you need to—"

Gunner interrupted. "No. We're all family, but I am asking every one of you to please keep this to yourselves. It's all going to come out eventually, but I need the time to get some stuff in place before it happens."

"Gunner, we're here for you, bud," Dylan said. "Just spit it out. Whatever is wrong, we've got your back."

"A couple of days ago, I bought a Mega Millions lottery ticket, and it turned out to be the winning ticket. I won. All of it."

There was a brief moment of shocked silence, and then Asher said, "Is this a joke?"

"Nope."

"The seven-hundred-and-eighty-million-dollar jackpot?" Dylan said.

Gunner sighed. "Yes."

There was a communal response of "good lord" from all three men, plus the background chatter from the women in their lives, and then silence again as Gunner kept talking.

"My lawyer and I have already been to the Dallas Claims Center and done the paperwork. I opted to take a cash settlement, which will amount to something around four hundred million plus. I'm also telling you this now, and you don't have the option to refuse. Asher and Nora, Dylan and Angie, Dad and Pearl, you're each going to get a million dollars apiece outright, so just know that's going to happen. I'm still going to be a cop. Just a rich one. I was told it will take several weeks for the payout to show up in my account at the bank. My lawyer is recommending a financial advisor, and no, I'm not going to buy anything stupid or do anything stupid."

Dylan cleared his throat and then took a deep breath. "Oh man… Gunner… I don't know what to say other than thank you, brother. This is college money for CJ and any other children we might have when they grow up."

"Same for Nora and me for little Jake. We won't waste such a gift," Asher said.

Jacob chuckled. "This is a blessing, son, and I might waste a little and remodel the kitchen in this old house for my sweet Pearl."

The laughter made Gunner smile. It was going to feel good to be able to make life easier for all of them.

"Okay, guys, I love you, but I need to get to bed. I haven't had enough sleep in the last two days to make sense right now. I'm almost at the point of walking into walls."

"Sleep well, son, and take care of yourself. We love you, too," Jacob said.

Gunner hung up, leaving the others on the line talking excitedly among themselves.

Melvin Ashworth, the owner of the black truck that Whistler used for the hit and run, had just checked out of the convention center after a five-day conference and was way past ready to get home to Denton. He made the long walk across the parking lot to get his truck, but when he arrived at the numbered space where he'd left it, it wasn't there. He knew he was at the right place because he'd parked beneath a security light on purpose, and he was at the point of panic when he saw it just a few spaces down. He cursed, guessing it had been someone's joy ride, but at least they'd brought it back.

And then he saw the damage to the front end and dropped to his knees to look beneath, checking to see if there had been damage to the frame. To his horror, he saw a man's shoe wedged between the frame and the chassis. He fell backward in shock, and while sitting at that angle, also saw a scrap of cloth caught in the grill. His first thought was a hit and run. Somebody used his truck and committed a crime!

Within seconds, he was calling 911. He gave the dispatcher explicit instructions as to the location of the parking space and sat down on one of his suitcases to wait, eyeing his truck as if it had become a monster.

It didn't take long for a half-dozen police cars to arrive,

including an officer from the traffic unit, who caught the call. They could tell from the start that the owner was beyond horrified as he showed them what he'd discovered and then pointed to a paint gun in the truck bed that did not belong to him.

A couple of officers headed into the convention center to check out his alibi, and it didn't take long for them to find out where Melvin had been for the last five days, with video evidence of him all over the conference.

The truck was taken into evidence, and the shoe and cloth scrap sent for testing for DNA. When the results came back, they matched the DNA of a man named Dan Helford, aka Yankee Dan.

They had a time of death for Dan, and security footage of Melvin Ashworth on stage giving a speech at his convention.

Melvin was released, but without a truck. He took an Uber to rent a car and drove himself home, with a message from the Dallas PD that they'd be in touch as to when he could pick up his truck when it was no longer evidence in a crime.

Unknown to Beau Whistler, the scene he'd left behind had a flaw. The man he'd marked to be the fall guy had an unbreakable alibi.

The hit-and-run case against Dan Helford was no longer considered "just an accident." They were looking for a killer, and that's when it fell to the homicide division on that side of the city.

Mason Walters, the super in charge of Letourneau and Garza's apartment building, was making his second round of door knocks for the week, collecting from residents who had yet to pay up their month's rent.

As he approached 12, he frowned at the odor in the hall but couldn't quite place it. It wasn't unusual to smell weed, but this was more like garbage that needed to be taken out.

It was Thomas Garza's apartment, so none of those odors were surprising, given the man who lived there. He knocked. When he didn't get an answer, he knocked again. As he was about to slide a notice under the door, he saw what appeared to be dried blood drops on the floor in front of him and frowned.

He knocked again, called out, then reached for the master key, but when he grabbed the knob to insert the key, the door swung open. He took one look at the fly-covered bodies of two men and the money plastered to the floor in the dried blood and gagged. If that was the rent money, it had just become evidence. Although it was too late to hide the scent, he backed out and shut the door, called 911, and went downstairs to wait.

Cops, detectives, and a crime scene crew were all over the apartment before the medical examiner arrived. The detectives had already bought into the story Beau Whistler left for them to read. They weren't looking for anyone else to blame it on, and from the rap sheets of both victims, they made their own assumptions based on the scattered money. In their minds, if anyone had come in to rob them, they wouldn't have left the money behind. This was going down as a fight between two men gone wrong, and unless the medical examiner found evidence to refute that, the case would be closed.

Burgess Dixon was at the breakfast table when he got a call that Garza and Letourneau's bodies were in the morgue, and the detectives were ruling it a fight gone wrong. The gunshot residue on Garza's arm and hand, and Letourneau's fingerprints on the hasp of the knife, plus the money all over their bodies and the floor, was all the proof the cops needed to prove they'd killed each other. Case closed.

As soon as the call ended, Dixon reached for his fork to finish his waffle and bacon. The federal witness against him was gone and the men guarding him—collateral damage. The homeless man who found him was gone. And the two losers who'd screwed up the body dump had been dealt with without a single finger pointing at him. That's why he kept Whistler on the payroll. It wasn't the first time Beau Whistler had gotten away with murder.

He finished eating, gathered up his briefcase, and buzzed Whistler to bring the car around. It was business as usual at the office downtown, and while he made good money running a commercial cleaning business called Dixon Down and Dirty, it was basically a front for his side businesses, the ones that had made him rich. But that much money coming into a cleaning service was also what had alerted the Feds.

Whistler was outside in the limo, waiting when Dixon emerged. He nodded a good morning as Whistler opened the door to the back seat. He was inside and buckling up as Whistler drove away from the estate on their way downtown.

It was going to be a busy day today with the grand opening of his eleventh Dixon Down and Dirty cleaning services in a new location. He had his iPad in his lap, going through the checklist for the opening, when his phone rang. He set the iPad aside to answer, glanced at the number, and then answered in quiet disapproval. "Why are you calling me on this phone?"

"Because you still have a loose end."

Dixon's gut knotted. "Text me the info on the other phone, and don't ever use this number again."

As soon as he got to the office, he got his burner phone out of the safe and frowned when he read the name. It was the same damn detective who'd brought Yankee Dan in for questioning. He cursed beneath his breath and made one more call, then worked until it was time to go to the grand opening.

By night, ten hired hit men were vying for the fifty-thousand-dollar bounty on the head of a homicide detective named Gunner Kingston.

The morning after the hit went live, Gunner was merging into the traffic on the Loop, carefully working his way into the fifth lane of a six-lane highway as he headed to work. His entire focus was on telling Lieutenant Samuels about his lottery win, and he had left home earlier than usual, hoping to talk to him before the workday began.

As always, he had an eye on the traffic around him—from the guy in the Mercedes riding his bumper, to the woman in the Ford Focus in the fourth lane beside him who was putting on her makeup as she drove, to the guy in front of him pulling a metal trailer with landscape equipment who kept hitting his brakes. While the traffic in lanes one, two, and three kept moving and exiting from the Loop onto feeder roads to get to their destinations, the sixth lane was left for switching highways. It was nothing short of a miracle that any of these people lived long enough to grow old.

A couple of minutes later, he saw a flash of something purple in his side-view mirror. It was a rider on a Yamaha motorcycle coming up fast behind him on the outside lane nearest the concrete barrier. He expected the rider to go flying past, except he didn't. Instead, the rider braked slightly and began matching his speed to Gunner's car.

It was a bright flash of light coming through the driver's side window of his car that caught Gunner's eye. The light was bouncing on his arm and then on his shirt, and he chanced a glance away from the traffic in front of him to see what it was. The rider on the Yamaha was aiming a handgun straight at his face.

Gunner stomped the brakes instinctively, knowing the biker would sail straight past him as he fired, and it worked. The first shot went over the hood of Gunner's car and into the back window of the little Ford Focus belonging to the woman putting on makeup.

With only seconds to react, Gunner made a hard swerve to the left and ran the bike straight into the concrete barrier, knocking the biker into the air like he'd been ejected from the cockpit of a fighter jet. He came down hard on the hood of Gunner's car as Gunner was already stomping the brakes to keep from running over him.

Gunner spun the car sideways, which slung the shooter off onto the pavement to his right, then jammed his car in Park to block the lane from the traffic behind them. Cars were already swerving into other lanes to get out of the way. The woman in the Ford Focus had swerved and spun out, and was now stopped sideways across lanes four and five, screaming bloody murder inside the car without being heard.

Gunner's mind was spinning in a hundred different directions as he hit the lights and sirens on his car, then he jumped out and began waving off traffic into the three open lanes to the right.

Traffic was slowing down to a crawl as he made an urgent call for backup and an ambulance, then he ran to the biker to see if he was alive. To his surprise, the biker was not only alive, but beginning to regain consciousness.

At the same time, the driver of a concrete truck and the driver of a semi both stopped, purposefully parking in a way that completely blocked off all traffic around the wreck to protect Gunner and the victim and to protect the little blue Ford Focus from being T-boned by oncoming traffic.

Gunner was looking around for the gun when he saw it lying against the barrier, beneath the wrecked Yamaha. He grabbed an evidence bag to recover the gun, then went back to the shooter.

The man had a serious case of road rash along with some obvious areas of missing skin. His helmet was in two pieces and lying on either side of his head like a hamburger bun, open and waiting for mustard. Two of the fingers on his shooting hand were broken and dangling like wet noodles, and he was moaning something about his leg and reaching for his head and chest.

"What's your name?" Gunner asked.

"Kevin Warren. Sorry… Sorry," he kept saying.

"Why did you pull a gun on me?"

"Needed the money," he muttered.

Gunner frowned. "What does that even mean? You expected money if you shot someone?"

Warren moaned. "Hurts… Bounty on your head."

"Bounty? On me? Do you even know who I am?"

"Kingston. Cop. Black Mustang GT." Then he quoted Gunner's tag number.

The skin crawled on the back of Gunner's neck. "Who the hell put out the bounty?"

"Don't know.… Tying up loose ends… Am I gonna die?"

Rage followed shock. In that moment, Gunner knew.

Damn Burgess Dixon and his loose ends.

Four dead FBI agents.

Freddie Welsh—dead.

Yankee Dan—dead.

Gunner Kingston.

All of them dead…but him.

Gunner rocked back on his heels as the biker took a slow, rattling breath and closed his eyes. He checked for a pulse. The biker was still alive, and now he could hear sirens.

Gunner stood, looked at the wrecked Yamaha the biker had been riding and then at his own car, not as pretty as it had been ten minutes ago but still in one piece. And so was he.

But not for long if this was only the beginning. He had to take some drastic action fast, but right now, it was all about getting the wreck off the highway and traffic moving back at normal speed.

He stood aside as the ambulance rolled in, followed by two units from the Highway Patrol who began redirecting traffic. He gave the gun he'd recovered to two cops in a patrol car while the EMTs made short work of stabilizing Kevin enough to transport, then loaded him up and headed to a hospital with the police car behind them. Warren was already under arrest for attempted murder, and Gunner was anxious to get back in his car and off this freeway. Where there was one fool, there could be a hundred others.

As soon as the tow truck loaded up what was left of the Yamaha and the officers cleared the highway, Gunner turned his battered car around and headed to work.

By the time he got to Homicide, he was in a most shitty frame of mind. He entered the department disheveled and bloody, moving like a soldier going to war.

Cliff stood abruptly. "Gunner, what the hell happened?"

"Hell just froze over," he muttered and kept walking—straight into Lieutenant Samuels's office without knocking, closing the door behind him.

Samuels was on the phone when Gunner entered, but when he saw his detective, he ended his call and stood.

"What happened?"

"There's a fucking fifty-thousand-dollar-bounty on my head. I know that because a biker on a purple Yamaha tried to take me out on the Loop this morning. His first shot missed me and hit the car in the lane beside me. I ran his ass into the concrete wall. The impact threw his body a good ten feet in the air before it landed on the hood of my car and slid off. He's on the way to the hospital. He's already under arrest for attempted murder...if he lives."

Samuels paled. "What's going on that I don't know about?"

"I believe I asked him the same question. All the biker said was that there was a bounty on my head, and someone was tying up loose ends. Federal agents dead. A federal witness dead. Yankee Dan dead after finding the body, and because I brought Dan in, clearly, I am the last. I don't know what Dixon thinks I know, but he's not taking any chances. And I'm going to say this again. This is happening because some dirty cop in this division is feeding Dixon privileged information."

"I want you to go home and stay there until we can get this figured out," Samuels said.

"Like hell...sir. I'm about to have a Come to Jesus meeting with the bastard at his office, and if I don't come back, then you'll know it's on him. And there's one other thing I was going to tell you this morning for legal purposes. I am the unidentified man who won the Mega Millions lottery. My lawyer and I have already been to the Dallas Claim Department, signed the paperwork, and set up the payout. It won't show up for a few weeks, but I'm telling you now so that no one thinks it's dirty money when that shows up in my bank account."

Samuels's eyes widened. "Are you serious?"

"Yes, sir, and I don't intend spreading the news around. It will eventually leak after the money shows up, but I don't want to face all that until I have to, so I'd appreciate you keeping that info to yourself."

Samuels shook his head in disbelief. "You win the lottery, and someone puts a hit out on you. That's the craziest dichotomy of personal issues I've ever heard, but my lips are sealed, and you have my support. I'll order escorts to get you home and get a patrol at your house."

"No, sir. Keep everyone else out of this, or they'll just become another name on Dixon's hit list. Just know that I'm about to yank a knot in Dixon's ass and tie up some loose ends of my own. And for God's sake, don't say anything to the detectives out front. I don't need someone giving Dixon a heads-up that I'm coming for lunch."

Samuels was still arguing, shouting, "Wait, Gunner, wait!" as Gunner left his office.

Cliff knew something serious had happened and grabbed Gunner by the shoulders, stopping his exit. "Bro, what's going on?"

Gunner paused. "I had a wreck on the Loop. I'm going home to change clothes, drop my car off at a body shop, and rent a car until it's fixed. Are you still going through security footage from the area of our hanging victim?"

"Uh… Yeah, I am," Cliff said.

"I have some notes I'll forward to you regarding the victim's personal life. Barry Caldwell has no ex and no children. He and his twin brother, Perry, are co-owners in his business. Perry has a significant other named Ron Ames. Ames has a staggering amount of debt. Check both of them out. Barry Caldwell had a two-million-dollar life insurance policy with his twin as the beneficiary."

"When did you figure all of this out?" Cliff said.

"When I took my laptop to the dealership yesterday to get my tires rotated and the oil changed," Gunner said.

"Oh, right. Good work," Cliff said.

Gunner nodded and let the door slam shut as he exited the department.

Chapter 5

DIXON WAS STANDING AT THE WINDOWS IN HIS OFFICE overlooking downtown Dallas, going over his notes for the little speech for the new opening and memorizing the name of the manager so he could include him in the kudos, when he heard shouting in the hall outside his office and then his secretary screaming. He heard Whistler curse, but before Dixon could react, there was a hard thud against his door, and then it opened inward.

Whistler was unconscious and handcuffed on the floor, and his secretary was making a run for the ladies' room. And an exceedingly tall man was walking over Whistler's body with care, as if he was dodging dog shit.

"I'm calling the cops!" Dixon shouted and leaped toward his desk.

"Already here, you son of a bitch!" Gunner said and flashed his badge.

"Who the hell are you?" Dixon shouted.

"You know damn well who I am, and I'm here to tell you this crap stops now! You just put a fifty-thousand-dollar bounty on my head for nothing. You also killed an old man for nothing."

Dixon bolted toward his desk, and Gunner pulled his weapon. "That's not happening. You're going to hear me out or I'll shoot you where you stand. Sit down in that chair. Not behind your desk, and keep your hands where I can see them."

Dixon was in shock. Kingston had laid Whistler out like it was nothing. He sat.

Gunner started talking. "The old man from the warehouse heard nothing. Knew nothing. He was fifty yards away on the second floor of a warehouse with no power. It was pitch black in there and pouring rain in the dark outside. He saw nothing but shadows. His only offense was taking shoes and socks off a dead man because he had a sore on his foot and needed new shoes. But you had him killed. I can't prove it, but I know it. And you put a hit out on me because you think the old man told me something, and you're all about tying up loose ends."

Dixon blustered. "I don't know what you're talking about!"

"Bullshit. I just sideswiped a hit man on a purple Yamaha about an hour ago and watched him skid sideways on the concrete for taking a pot shot at me on the Loop. He's not dead, but he's broken in enough places he's not going anywhere, and according to him, the bounty on me has to do with tying up loose ends. I don't have loose ends, you sorry shit, so that leaves you, and you screwed with the wrong man. My boss knows where I am. Anything happens to me, he'll tell the FBI the last place I was headed. And I suspect by now, your dirty cop knows where I am, too. The whole Dallas Homicide Division knows where I am. Anything happens to me from this day forward...the cops are coming after you. Even if someone else is responsible, they're coming after you. It is in your best interests to stop this now. The FBI knows about the hit and run, and I will be making a call to the Texas Attorney General's Office about a bounty on my head. So, if someone takes me out now, your ass is grass. Call your dogs off now, or there won't be enough left of you to bury. Do we understand each other?"

Dixon's gut knotted. He *had* misjudged this man, and when the detective pointed a finger in his face and then turned his back and walked out, stopping long enough to remove Whistler's cuffs, Dixon knew he'd met his match and then some. That son of a bitch wasn't afraid to die, and he had to stop the landslide he'd started before it buried him under it.

Gunner was shaking inside when he got to his car. That bald bodyguard was the size of a bull, with a funky scar on his eyebrow that cut the eyebrow in half. He also knew that man was the kind who was going to hold a grudge for being decked, but that was for another time. Right now, he had to get somewhere fast until word got out that the bounty was off, and he needed to let Samuels know.

Lieutenant Samuels was gathering up some files for a meeting with the deputy chief when his phone rang. "This is Samuels."

"This is Gunner." Then he proceeded to tell him what took place and what he said to Dixon. "Bottom line, Boss, I'm still a target until the word gets out that the bounty has been voided."

"What makes you think he'll pull it?" Samuels said.

"Because he doesn't want the Dallas PD, or the Feds, or the State Attorney General's office in his business again, and I made it clear that there was now a target on him, as well. Anything happens to me, they're coming for him."

Samuels shook his head. "I hope it works, but I still want you off the streets and in your house for the next week."

"I'm going one better, Boss. I'm going home. To Crossroads. You know how to contact me if you need to. Tell the team what happened and why I'm gone, but don't tell them where I'm going. And it wouldn't hurt to drop a hint about somebody leaking info."

"Are you and Cliff on the outs?" Samuels asked.

"I don't know what we are, but from the second we took Yankee Dan in for his statement, Cliff has challenged everything I've said and done. Acting like the old man gave us information during his interrogation that we didn't share, and all that makes me wonder how Dixon ever found out the identity of the old man, or that I was the one who took his statement, when the only people who knew worked in our department."

"Understood," Samuels said. "I'll let all of them know about the bounty and why you're gone. I'll also do some checking on my own. Be safe, and let me know when you get there."

"Yes sir, will do," Gunner said. Then he drove straight to the body shop, stripped his car of his personal effects and left it to be repaired, and called an Uber to take him home. It was only after he was sitting in the back seat with the sun in his eyes that he realized he'd left his sunglasses in the Mustang.

Samuels picked up his files and walked out into the Homicide department. He could tell that they were all curious about what was going on with Kingston.

"Detective Kingston will not be with us for a while. Someone has put out a hit on his life with a fifty-thousand-dollar bounty to go with it. He found out the hard way this morning when a biker rode up beside him on the Loop and took a shot at him. He missed Gunner and hit the car in the other lane. Kingston reacted with precision and ran the biker into the concrete wall and sent him flying. That was why he came into the precinct pissed and bloody."

There was a communal gasp, and then everyone started talking at once.

"Damn it! Who did that? Who ordered the hit?" Cliff asked.

"Kingston suspects it's the same person who ordered the hit and run on the homeless man who found the body of the Feds' missing witness. When Gunner left here, he was on his way to Burgess Dixon's office to confront him. I was not privy to the confrontation, but Dixon kept claiming his innocence until Kingston told him it didn't matter, and that if anything happened to him now, the cops were coming after Dixon. Even if someone else is responsible, Dixon is going to be their first suspect, and the Feds are just itching to have another reason to arrest him. He'll either call off the hunt or go down for it."

The silence that ensued was telling.

Finally, it was Cliff who spoke up, and his voice was noticeably shaking. "I knew Gunner didn't pull punches, but even I didn't know he'd have the balls to do that. Damn. So, what happens next?"

"He is officially off duty until we are confident that the contract on him has been pulled. You'll be working with Detective Rowdy until he comes back. And nobody goes to see him. Nobody calls him. Everybody minds their own damn business. I don't want to think that I have a dirty cop in our midst, but Kingston is convinced that Dixon had far more information about our business than he should have. I have a meeting with the deputy chief. I will be filling him in on all of this and updating it with the Feds as well. He'll be back when we see him walking through the door and not before. Understood?"

"Understood," they echoed, and as soon as the lieutenant left the department, the guesses started flying, until Detective Frankie Adams bolted up from her desk. Her sunglasses were on top of her head, half-buried in a nest of magenta-colored curls, and there was a visible coffee stain on the leg of her pants.

"Shut it! Shut it now! Unless you have an actual fact that you wish to share, we do not tear into our own!"

The room went silent and then returned to a barely audible murmur.

Cliff Beale and Tom Rowdy looked at each other and shrugged, then Cliff began filling him in on the case they'd been working and gave him Gunner's notes he'd just received to refer to.

Dixon was in a rage, but there was no one to blame but himself. He'd gone overboard on his desire to tie up loose ends, and it had backfired in a very big way. Not only were the loose ends still hanging, but things were beginning to unravel.

He sent his secretary home, threw a glass of water in Whistler's face, kicked the bottom of his boot, told him to get up, and then left him on the floor in the outer office, gasping for air and wiping water out of his eyes.

Dixon went back into his office and closed the door, then got on the phone and called off the hit.

"End this today. The hit is off. No money will be forthcoming. Make the calls now, and don't go to bed tonight until every last one of them has been notified."

Two words from the voice on the other end of the call: "Message received."

Dixon ended the call, laid down his phone, and then went to the wet bar and poured himself a double shot of scotch, downing it in one gulp. It had been a long time since he'd been bested, and it was a bitter pill to swallow, but he wanted nothing more to do with Gunner Kingston.

The Uber driver let Gunner out at his house. He locked the door behind him as he went inside, then sat down and called his dad.

It was loud and raucous inside the Tumbleweed Bar when Jacob's phone rang. He glanced down, saw it was Gunner calling, and walked through the hall and into their home to answer.

"Hey, son! What's going on?"

"I want to come home. If that's okay."

Something was wrong. Jacob could hear it in Gunner's voice, but he didn't let on.

"Of course it's okay. Your room is always ready. Are you heading this way today or—"

"I'm packing now. I should be there before sundown."

"Drive safe," Jacob said.

"Always," Gunner said and disconnected, then pulled out two suitcases and started packing. With his sports car in the body shop, that should slow down the men hunting for him. Now he was glad he still had the 2018 Jeep Rubicon Wrangler, and a back exit from his two-car garage. It led to a blacktop driveway across the backyard and into the alley behind his house, and he never drove that vehicle on the job, so no one would be looking for him in it. All he needed was to get packed and set the lights in his house on timers so if anyone was looking, they'd think that he was home.

Within an hour, Gunner was driving through neighborhoods, taking back roads and old highways to get out of Dallas alive. Once he hit US 287, he relaxed. It was a good five-hour drive on a four-lane highway all the way to Amarillo, but he wasn't going that far north. Once he got to Esterline, it was westbound on Highway 86 all the way home.

He stopped once for fuel and to get some snacks and took the time to call Asher. He needed him to know the shit he was in and who to blame if this all went wrong. As soon as he put his drink in the console and opened a bag of chips in the seat beside him, he made the call via Bluetooth, leaving his hands free to drive.

The call rang four times, and just as he thought it was going to voicemail, Asher's voice was in his ear.

"Hey, little brother. Are you on the job?"

"No, I'm pretty much on the run from the job. I found out this morning that there's a contract out on my life and a fifty-thousand-dollar bounty to go with it. A biker on a Yamaha took a shot at me on the Loop. I ran his ass into the concrete barrier and sent him flying before we had a discussion about why he tried to kill me."

Asher was in shock and trying not to let on how suddenly scared he was for his youngest brother.

"Do you know who ordered the hit?" Asher asked.

"Yes. Burgess Dixon, but while I can't prove it, I still paid him a visit after the fact. I went to his office downtown, left his bodyguard unconscious and belly down on the floor with his hands cuffed long enough to have a polite conversation with the man himself, so if anything happens to me, it's on him."

At that point, Gunner began relating the whole story, from the Feds' missing witness to Yankee Dan being killed in a hit and run. "Because I took the old man's statement after he found the body, I'm guessing I became the last loose end in Dixon's quest to clean up everyone related to that pending trial."

"Damn it, Gunner. What a nightmare," Asher said.

"Yes, and I'm telling you now, I'm positive there's a dirty cop in our department. I don't know who, but they were the only people who knew I was the one who brought the old man into the precinct to get his statement. My lieutenant sat in on the statement with me, but I think he's hesitant about admitting the dirty cop theory. However, the hit and run on the homeless guy less than twenty-four hours after he found the body was suspicious, then the contract put out on me right afterward is an obvious sign that someone in the department is feeding Dixon info. I can't do background checks on any of them without the whole department knowing what I'm doing, so that's where I am."

"You can't dig, but I can," Asher said. "As soon as you get to Crossroads, send me some names."

"I will, and thanks."

"Safe travels home. Call if you need me. Meanwhile, if I uncover anything suspicious, I'll let you know," Asher said.

"Thank you for hearing me out," Gunner said and disconnected.

The Dillon and Peters families were on hold. They could not lay their loved ones to rest until the medical examiner released the bodies. It had only been a few days since the accident, but it felt like an eternity to all involved.

This morning, Garrett and Travis were at the stables with the farrier who was making his monthly round at the ranch.

For the time being, Trudy was dealing with the condolence visits while Holly stepped into her mother's role, keeping books, paying bills online, and cooking for the family. The house cleaning crew from Amarillo had just left the property, and Holly was transferring a load of laundry from the washer to the dryer when her cell phone rang. When she saw Briscoe County Sheriff's office pop up on Caller ID, her heart skipped.

"Hello?"

"Holly, this is Sheriff Reddick. We have just received the medical examiner's findings, as well as finished up our investigation into the wreck. Is Garrett available to speak to?"

"Not at the moment. The farrier is here. But I could have him call you, or you could tell me what you need to say."

"Why don't you just let him know that I'm coming your way in about an hour. That will give all of you time to gather at the house for the results. I'm not trying to be mysterious, but the accident wasn't as straightforward as we believed."

"We'll all be at the house when you arrive," Holly said. "I'll make sure of it."

"Thanks. See you soon," Reddick said.

Holly disconnected, turned on the dryer, then went out to the stables to get her dad. Knowing there was something more to the wreck than they'd first believed made her anxious. It didn't change the reality of their world, but accepting a new reason for how it happened felt threatening. She didn't want to think about the new revelation as she entered the stables.

She heard her dad's voice and a loud bang, followed by the sound of Travis laughing. Whatever had just happened, at least no one got hurt. Then she saw Travis leading one of the geldings back into a stall and started walking toward him.

"Where's Dad?" she asked as Travis came out of the stall carrying a halter.

"In the corral with the farrier," he said.

"Is he close to being done?" she asked.

"We're on the last horse. He's nailing on a new shoe. Why?"

"Sheriff Reddick is coming to the ranch to talk to us. He's bringing the autopsy results. He'll be here within the hour.

Would you please tell Dad? The sheriff wanted to talk to him personally," Holly said.

Travis frowned. "What does that mean?"

"I don't know, honey. But we'll find out shortly. I'm going back to the house to wait for him. Now, go tell Dad."

Travis went to get his dad as Holly returned to the house to tell Trudy.

This trip back to Crossroads was one Sheriff Reddick could have done without. The cause of death was unexpected on both counts, and both families were going to have to readjust to the actual truth. He would stop by the Peterses' home on his way back to the office in Silverton, but the Dillon Ranch was the farthest one away, so he was going there first.

He glanced at the Tumbleweed Bar as he drove through Crossroads, wondering how Jacob Kingston was faring, and had a sudden yen for some of Pearl Fallon's coconut cream pie as he passed the Yellow Rose Café, but that would have to wait for another day. Instead, he kept going west until he reached the turnoff on Highway 86 that led to the Dillon Ranch. It was the only road in and out to the ranch, and he knew that tragedy would forever mark it as the place where Helen died.

He pulled up to the house and picked up the envelope containing Helen Dillon's personal property they'd recovered from the wreck. As he got out, he settled his Stetson a little firmer onto his head against the wind, went up the steps, and rang the doorbell.

A few moments later, the door swung inward. Garrett Dillon was standing in the doorway.

"Matt, good to see you. Come in."

Holly, Trudy, and Travis were already in the living room when Garrett led him in to join them.

"Holly said you have new information for us," Garrett said.

Reddick sat. "I do, and I'll get right to it. The autopsy on Helen revealed that she died from a massive heart attack. She was already gone before the wreck happened."

There was a mutual gasp from the Dillons.

Trudy put her arm around her son as he dropped his head, and Holly reached for her brother's hand.

"Oh, my God. It's like she died twice," Garrett muttered.

Trudy gave his shoulder a quick squeeze. "Only to you. For Helen, she was already with the angels before any of that happened. She wouldn't have known it or felt it. You have to hold on to that."

Holly shuddered. "I have been struggling with the image of her being hit head on, and imagining her shock and fear, knowing she was going to die. I am going to hold on to this and tell myself that the heart attack happened so fast she didn't suffer. Her body was still in the car when she and Lee collided, but knowing she was already gone helps take away that horror for me."

Matt cleared his throat and handed them the last piece of information. "One other thing. We had a phone call from Lee Peters's girlfriend, telling us that she and Lee were texting back and forth when the wreck happened. We had recovered Lee's phone from the wreck and checked it. He *was* texting her, and likely not looking up when Helen's car came over the hill. Helen was no longer in control, but her foot was still on the accelerator. If Lee hadn't been texting, he would have seen her and swerved. I don't know if this helps or makes it worse to hear, but these are the facts, and you all deserve to know the whole story. I will be giving the Peters family the same information."

Travis swiped a hand across his face, as if to wipe away the horror of what he'd just heard.

"Trisha is…was Lee's girl. The last thing he said to me when he dropped me off at the house was that he was going to see Trish. I don't know how many times I told him not to text and drive. If only he had looked up, he could have swerved and missed her. Damn it," he muttered, and he got up and walked out of the room.

"The bodies are being released to the respective funeral homes. You can contact them to make the arrangements. I'll see myself out, and I'm so sorry for your loss," Reddick said.

Garrett got up, turned in a random circle, then sat down again and put his head in his hands. Trudy stood. "I'm going to make some coffee."

Holly moved to where her dad was sitting and put her arm around his shoulders. "Love you, Daddy."

Garrett reached for her hand. "Love you, my sweet girl. Thank you for being here with us."

Burgess Dixon was more tied up in knots than he had been when the Feds put the witness against him into protective custody. He'd dealt with that problem without a shred of evidence pointing back to him, knowing that they could suspect all they wanted, but unless or until they had proof, he was, once again, a free man.

But he'd made one small mistake in going after a cop who'd called his bluff, turned the tables on him, and put a target on Dixon's back. Anything happens to Kingston, Dixon would be the assumed guilty party.

Even though there was no evidence to show that he had ordered the hit, Kingston had publicly pointed the finger at him. And that put Dixon back in the crosshairs of the Dallas PD, the Feds, and the State Attorney's office. Although he'd called the contractor and ordered a stop on the hit, he wouldn't rest easy until he knew that everyone gunning for Kingston had been notified that there was no more bounty.

Whistler no longer knew where he stood with the boss, and Dixon wasn't showing his face anywhere until the bounty-hunting fiasco had blown over.

Dixon would have breathed a lot easier had he known Kingston had put himself on ice, but his only choice was to ride it out and hope the hunters were all pulled in. He only had himself to blame for the mess he was in, but what worried him more was that his contact in the Dallas PD had gone quiet. *What was happening? What the hell was going on?*

The black ribbon of highway Gunner was traveling on was visible only within the extent of his headlights, unrolling before his eyes as the miles he'd already traveled disappeared into the darkness behind him. Other than the occasional coyote intersecting the light from his headlights as it loped across the highway and meeting a couple of bull haulers going in the opposite direction, they were his only visible signs of night traffic on 86.

Then seeing the faint glow of light from the little town of Crossroads on the horizon made his heart skip.

Finally.

It was the beacon he'd been watching for—the light that would guide him home. Nearly six steady hours of driving and he was almost there. Lord, it would be good to sleep in his old room tonight and wake up to the sound of his dad's voice, and the scent of coffee and toast wafting down the hall.

There was a level of comfort in knowing the room he'd grown up in was still considered his. He belonged to Crossroads. The people there helped raise him and his brothers, him more so. He was the baby…the seven-year-old without a mother. Part of him knew she had once loved them, but not enough to be faithful to their dad, and not enough to face the consequences of her actions. She'd taken the easy way out and left them drowning from her sins.

That was his identity then, and he'd been running from it ever since. Going to Dallas had been his solution to putting it behind him, but it hadn't taken long for him to realize there wasn't enough distance in the world to outrun his past.

This threat to his life was a wake-up call. He wasn't happy. Hadn't been happy one day in Dallas since he arrived. He was good at his job, but he'd isolated himself because he didn't want people to dig into his past, and it hadn't helped a damn bit. A bad man was trying to kill him, and somebody in his workplace was aiding and abetting.

In all the years since Gunner had moved to Dallas, he'd never put down roots or had any desire to do so. And all the years in between, when he came back to Crossroads for holidays and family time, the hardest part had been leaving it, time and again.

But the lottery win, the attempt on his life, and the distrust he now felt within the workplace had changed his focus. During this long, silent drive, he'd come to a life-changing decision. This trip to Crossroads was different. This time it was a homecoming, and if he could make it work, maybe for good. It was time to pay back the people in Crossroads for all they'd done for him and his family, and to be there for Jacob as he continued to age.

The glow on the horizon was getting brighter, and then

in the distance he saw the usual assortment of cars and trucks packed in the Tumbleweed parking lot, and the lights blazing from every window like the beacon on a lighthouse, and every tense muscle in his body let go.

He took the turn off the highway and drove through the narrow lane on the west side of the bar that took him to their house behind it and parked, breathing a huge sigh of relief as he killed the engine and got out to get his bags.

He was in no danger here.

Nobody was hiding in the shadow to try and kill him.

He was home.

As he started up the back steps, the door opened inward, and Pearl was standing in the doorway.

"Welcome home, honey! Come in! Come in! You must be exhausted."

Ever since Pearl had moved in with his dad, the whole atmosphere of the house had shifted. Something good was always baking or on the counter, and his dad was lighthearted and happy.

"It was a long drive, for sure," Gunner said, then dropped his bags and gave her a big hug. "It's so good to be home."

Pearl was beaming. "Park your bags. Have you eaten? I brought fried chicken and potato salad from the Yellow Rose, and there's coconut cream pie here from yesterday."

"I have not eaten, and that sounds amazing," he said.

"Then go do your thing and say hi to Jacob. I'll have your food heated up by the time you get back."

"Yes, ma'am," Gunner said and pulled his bags through the kitchen and down the hall to his room, then went to wash up. He could hear Pearl humming and banging lids and cabinet doors as he went back up the hall, then through a door that led to another hall and into the bar.

Jacob was behind the bar, popping the cap off of a bottle of Lone Star beer and sliding a little bowl of salty pretzels in front of the man sitting at the counter. He wiped his hands as he was turning and saw his son standing at the other end of the bar. He also saw exhaustion and stress on his face, and something else—something that was probably the reason he'd come home. But that was for later.

He started smiling and headed toward his youngest son with arms wide open.

"You made it!" he said and gave Gunner a big hug and a pat on the back.

"Yes, I did. I can see how busy you are, and Pearl is about to feed me. We'll talk later, okay?"

"Absolutely okay," Jacob said and beamed with pride as his customers began shouting out greetings of their own to his son.

Gunner waved. "Don't be giving my dad any grief now. I'm too tired to have to whip someone's ass."

A roar of laughter followed him as he left the bar. He was smiling when he sat down at the kitchen table to the food awaiting him. "Sit with me," Gunner said as Pearl poured herself a cup of coffee. "I want to hear all about what's going on, and what's already happening. Is Davey your fry cook still living in the apartment above the Rose?"

It was all the invitation Pearl needed to unload, and the first thing she started with was the tragedy of Helen Dillon and Lee Peters's wreck.

Gunner let her talk without mentioning he already knew that, because he didn't want anyone to know that he and Holly had been communicating. He cleaned his plate and downed a big piece of pie before Pearl finally ran down and began asking him about work and any plans he had for his big windfall.

"Work's been a headache, but that's mostly a cop's life," he said as he got up and carried his dirty dishes to the sink. "Can I put these in the dishwasher?"

"Yes, but I—"

"No, ma'am. You're not at the Rose. You're at home, and you already fed me. I can at least clean up after myself. I do it at my house all the time." He rinsed the dishes and loaded them in the dishwasher, then dried off the counter. "Is there anything I can help you with?"

Pearl hugged him. "No, baby. Just kick your boots off and watch some TV or stretch out on the bed. If you fall asleep, Jacob will wake you up to say good night."

Pearl's head barely reached the middle of his chest, but he hugged her anyway. "I'm happy you and Dad are together," he said.

Pearl sighed. "So am I. You look like you haven't slept for days. Go lie down."

"Yes, ma'am. On the way," Gunner said and walked out of the kitchen.

Pearl watched him leaving and could tell by the way he was moving that, for whatever reason, he was carrying the weight of the world on his back.

Gunner heard the TV come on in the living room and guessed Pearl was settling in to watch some shows. All he wanted was to get off his feet. Even if his feet did hang off the end of the mattress now, it was still where he felt the most relaxed. He sat down on the bed, took off his belt and shirt, leaned down to take off his boots, and then rolled over on his belly and closed his eyes.

Muffled voices from the bar on the other side of his bedroom wall were as familiar as the faint sound of the country music—the lullaby of his childhood. He knew the song he could hear playing—an old Lee Brice song that was an anthem of what he'd become.

"I'm hard to love, hard to love... Oh, I don't make it easy..."

There was an ache in his heart as he fell asleep.

Chapter 6

Jacob locked up the bar, left all the nightlights on, and went into the family quarters. He knew Pearl would be asleep because she had to be up and gone by 5:00 a.m. But tonight, his youngest son was back under his roof, too.

He opened the door just enough to see him sprawled belly down on top of the bed, still wearing his jeans and socks. He shook his head and smiled at the sight of Gunner's broad back and his long legs, with his feet hanging off the end of the bed. All of his sons had his height and thick black hair, only now, Jacob's hair was a thatch of silver gray, and he didn't stand as tall as he used to. He picked up a blanket and spread it over him, like he'd done when he was a boy.

He'd known the moment he'd seen his son's face that there was something off. But he'd find out tomorrow. Tonight, Gunner needed to sleep.

Holly woke up with a gasp, her heart pounding. The sound of her mother's scream was already fading from memory, but there was no way she could go back to sleep. From the moment she'd learned of her mother's accident, her greatest horror had been believing Helen had seen death coming too late to escape. Learning that she had passed before impact was an odd relief. Now she just had to reset her emotions to a new reality and hope for no more nightmares.

Her bedroom window was up enough to hear coyotes howling nearby, and to hear a horse nicker disapproval. They had new foals in the area. She didn't know if her dad was awake or not, but it wouldn't be the first time she had shot at coyotes to run them off.

She traded her pajamas for jeans and a T-shirt, stepped into a pair of sneakers, and headed down the hall when a door opened behind her. Travis had come out of his bedroom in a pair of ratty green gym shorts—the same shorts he'd been wearing to bed for the last four years.

"What are you doing up?"

"Bad dream, then I heard coyotes. I just wanted to make sure the foals were all okay," she said.

"Dad's already out there," Travis said.

Holly sighed as she thrust her fingers in her hair to comb the wayward curls away from her face. "I should have known, but I can't go back to bed yet. Feel like raiding the fridge?"

Travis grinned. "I could eat. Give me a sec to get a shirt," he said and ducked back into his room. He came out moments later wearing a T-shirt wrong-side out, with his hair sticking up like a rooster comb.

Holly grinned. Except for his height, he looked like he did when he was twelve.

"How about ice cream?" Holly asked.

"I'll get the spoons," he said and slid his arm across her shoulder as they headed for the kitchen.

The moment she opened the freezer, she didn't hesitate at the choice. There were three cartons in the freezer, but rocky road ice cream had solved a world of troubles when they were growing up. Maybe a little cold and sweet treat would take away the bad memory of her dream.

For a few moments, they ate without talking, using their spoons like swords, taking swipes at each other's eating territory trying to get the clump of marshmallow, or the nut poking up from the surface before the other one could get it, just like they'd done when she still lived at home.

Then Travis surprised her and leaned back, letting her have the good bite.

"I'm really glad you're here, Sis. Sorry for the reason why, but I've missed you," he said.

The bite of ice cream was melting on her tongue when she looked up and swallowed. "I should have come home more often. I wish I had now, for sure."

"No way," Travis said. "It's a hell of a long drive from here to Dallas, and you're on the far side of the city, to boot. You have a job with a lot of responsibilities, and we're all proud of you. Mom especially. We won't hear or see her anymore, but she gave us the best life, and more love than a lot of people ever get in a lifetime. Right?"

"When did you become the grown-up in this family?" she asked.

He grinned. "I just finally caught up with the rest of you."

"You're going to love college," Holly said. "I'll help you get settled, and Dad and I will always be your best backup."

"Can I ask you something?" Travis said.

"Sure, anything. My life is an open book," she said.

"When you're not at work, what do you do for fun?"

"Oh… I… Uh…" She frowned. "Well, I meet friends for lunch sometimes, but I'm around people all day long, and most of them are complaining about what's missing in the houses I'm showing them, or my boss is throwing a fit because a house someone just sold doesn't have a clear title. That's also part of my job, researching that stuff and filing all the paperwork to clear it. So, I do like my quiet evenings at home."

He nodded and pointed at the pint of ice cream between them. "You gonna eat that last bite?"

She pushed it toward him. Travis scooped out the last big bite and stuffed it in his mouth. “So, I’m hearing no boyfriend, no significant other,” he said.

She frowned. “Don’t talk with your mouth full.”

He laughed and was still smiling when Garrett walked in.

“What’s going on?” he asked.

“Bad dreams, good brothers, and ice cream,” Holly said. “Is everything okay out there? I heard coyotes.”

“All clear,” Garrett said. “Is there any ice cream left for me?”

“In the freezer,” Holly said and wondered when Gunner was coming to Crossroads. Hopefully, before she left. Life was so much simpler here. Sitting at a table with him in the Yellow Rose would have been almost like a date. Not just lunch with an old friend.

She’d been so elated to run into him again, and then all of this happened. She felt a bit like she had when she was a kid, watching him getting on the bus and leaving for Dallas. She’d been too young for him to see her in that way, but their chance meeting at the supermarket felt like a gift, and then their early dinner at the taqueria—the fancy bow. She hadn’t felt that happy and carefree in forever.

He made that promise not to forget her, but the wreck happened and she left Dallas. Now they were a world apart and in limbo. The timing was all wrong again. There wasn’t one fair thing about any of this.

Her dad came to the table with a spoon and another pint of ice cream. His voice was a little shaky, but he was smiling. “Strawberry, in honor of my sweet lady,” he said, then took the lid off the little carton and dug out his first bite and popped it in his mouth. “So, what were you two talking about?” he asked.

“Holly’s lack of a social life,” Travis said.

Garrett watched Holly’s cheeks turning pink. “I suspect there’s more than she’s willing to talk about.”

Holly shrugged. "Actually, I ran into Gunner Kingston in Whole Foods the same day I left Dallas. He took me to a local taqueria for an early dinner… Sort of a catch-up reunion. He promised to stay in touch, but then I left. He called me the day after I got home. I told him what had happened. He was shocked and very sympathetic. Sent his condolences to all of us, and said he'd see me when he came to Crossroads."

Travis's eyes widened, and then he held up his hands in a gesture of surrender. "Okay, officially minding my own business now. And I got a text from Lee's girlfriend, Trish. The Peters family is moving away. They're taking Lee's body to Tulsa to bury. I think that's where both families still live."

Garrett nodded. "I heard that, and Helen's services are this coming Saturday at the Baptist Church in Crossroads. The pastor said the Ladies Aide has graciously offered to provide the food for family and friends afterward."

Holly was silent, contemplating what was ahead of her—like a thousand handshakes and hugs, and "so sorry for your loss." Her mother and father had grown up here. People loved them. It was friends wanting to show their respect. But it was going to be a hard day, for sure.

She waited until her dad put the ice cream back in the freezer, then got up and gave him a quick hug.

"I'm going back to bed. I don't get up before daybreak unless I have to."

Gunner woke with a start, thinking he'd overslept and was going to be late for work, then rolled over in bed, saw the Coors Beer nightlight and remembered he was home, and Dixon was supposed to be calling off his dogs. He glanced at the clock. Fifteen minutes to 5:00 a.m.

He could hear water running across the hall and guessed Pearl was getting ready to go to the Yellow Rose to start her day, which meant Dad was probably still asleep.

Their working hours made it difficult for both of them to spend quality time together, but he also knew that after all the years of them being apart, they were grateful for whatever time they had now.

Gunner wanted that kind of forever love, but he'd never let his guard down enough to let a woman into his world. He thought of Holly again and wondered what was happening at the ranch, and where they were in the process of autopsies and funerals.

He would call her later to let her know he was here. Then he remembered the list of names from Homicide that he was supposed to send to Asher to check out. Back in Dallas, he would have rolled over and gone back to sleep, but not here. Daybreak in Crossroads was nothing short of holy.

Without hesitating, he put on his boots, put the shirt back on he'd worn yesterday, and left it unbuttoned as he walked out the kitchen door and into the backyard. He took a few steps more and then turned to face the east.

Standing within the silence of the sleepy little town, he watched as the sky began to turn from dark to light, slowly coloring the vast horizon to introduce a new day.

Just as the first flash of sun topped the horizon, Pearl emerged and saw him, a tall, unmoving silhouette against the sky. But instead of getting in her car and hustling up the highway to her café, she walked up beside him.

"It never gets old, does it, baby?"

Gunner slid his hand across her shoulder. "No, ma'am. It does not."

"I'm so glad you're home. I've got to get to work. Davey doesn't have a light hand with the biscuit dough. You know where to come if you're wanting a meal. Your daddy is still asleep." Then she gave his hand a quick squeeze and hustled back to her car and drove away.

Gunner watched her leave, but instead of going back inside, he turned to the south, eyeing the land behind the house and trying to remember how far back their property actually went. A thought was forming in his head, but he needed to talk to his dad before it went any further.

He was still gazing across the scrub brush and spiny shards of Yucca plants when he heard the sound of a big rig and a driver shifting gears, then saw the headlights of the semi coming in from the east. The driver was hauling ass, taking advantage of the long stretch of highway and the lack of traffic, and bringing an end to Gunner's brief moments of meditation.

He went back into the house, claimed the shower, and came out later minus the dark shadow of whiskers he'd gone to bed with, then began unpacking. Once he was dressed for the day, he headed to the kitchen with his laptop. He wanted coffee and needed to send Asher that list.

The Tumbleweed Bar always opened at 10:00 a.m., but Jacob was up by eight. And this morning he dressed quickly, anxious to talk to Gunner before the day got too busy.

When he entered the kitchen and saw his son at the kitchen table with his laptop, his fingers flying across the keyboard, for a moment it was like every morning of Gunner's life in high school, knowing he'd waited until the last minute to finish an assignment.

Then Gunner looked up, and the face looking back at Jacob was the face of a man with a problem.

"Morning, Dad."

Jacob smiled. "Morning, son. Did you rest well?"

"Better than I have in ages," Gunner said. "I can make you breakfast if you want."

"A bowl of cereal and this brew will be enough," he said as he filled his cup and then a bowl of cereal and carried them to the table. "I'm going to eat while you tell me what's wrong, and don't tell me nothing. I raised you. I can see it in your eyes."

Gunner took a deep breath. "I took a leave of absence because here I'm safe, and in Dallas, there is contract out on my life, and a fifty-thousand-dollar bonus for the delivery."

Jacob felt the blood draining from his face. "My God." His hands were shaking as he leaned back and took a breath. "Talk to me."

So, while Jacob ate, Gunner went through the entire scenario again, just as he had with Asher during the drive home.

"Good lord. Are you worried they'll come for you here?" Jacob asked.

"No, and I wouldn't be here if I thought for a second that I was putting anyone in danger. I just needed to lay low until the word gets out to all concerned parties that the bounty was called off as promised."

Jacob frowned. "Can you trust this Dixon to keep his word?"

"Hell no, but he knows without doubt that after the target I put on his back, he's the one who's going to be blamed if anything happens to me. He doesn't want to get sideways with the Feds again, and he also knows the State Attorney General's office is aware of the hit that was put out on me, too."

A slight smile slid sideways on Jacob's face. "You were my wild child, and you grew up to be an indomitable, take-no-prisoners man of honor. I'm proud of you, Gunner, but it's good you left Dallas until this all blows over."

Gunner leaned back in his chair. "I have a question."

"Ask it," Jacob said.

"How far south does your property line go?"

"I own twenty acres. There's about an acre's width to the east of the Weed, then the rest of it runs straight south. Why do you ask?"

"Because I'm thinking, since I won all that money, I might want to build a house and move back to Crossroads. Being in law enforcement has lost its shine for me. I think it hit me when the old man was killed in that hit and run, and then the bounty on my head, and a dirty cop in my division, and I no longer have a desire to go out on a call with people I do not trust. It's too easy to get shot in the back and blame some mythical crook that's how it happened."

Jacob picked up his cereal bowl, put it in the sink, and refilled his coffee before he sat back down.

"I'll gladly deed you land to build a house, Gunner, but will you be happy in this little town, after all those years in Dallas?"

"I have a job in Dallas, but I don't have roots there. I'll figure something out to keep me busy, but in the meantime, I'll be your bouncer for free."

Jacob grinned. "In the evenings after Pearl is home, if it gets too loud in the bar, she comes stomping up from the house with an air horn, blasts it once, and she returns to the house without saying a word."

Gunner grinned. "Are you serious?"

"As a heart attack," Jacob said.

"What do they say? Does it make them mad?" Gunner asked.

"Nobody gets mad at Miss Pearl. She's the reigning queen of Crossroads—her and the Yellow Rose. They just laugh and throw her kisses, but they do tone it down."

Gunner shook his head. "That's priceless. Lord, I am

missing out on all the good stuff. This just makes me want to come home even more."

Jacob stood. "Well, you're already here, so that's the first step. The next one will be going back to officially part company with your job. In the meantime, I need to get to work. Want to help me carry up some kegs to store under the bar? I have two that are going to need changing out before the day is over. I wouldn't mind having them at the ready."

"Absolutely. Just show me which ones you need," Gunner said and followed his dad into the bar.

Asher received the list of names Gunner sent him and went straight to his boss, Robert Ivory, to tell him what happened. To say the attorney general was upset that an actual hit on a law officer was circulating was putting it mildly. And to be told that Burgess Dixon was the number one suspect of who'd done it and why made it worse.

"This is appalling," Ivory said. "You have my permission to do background checks on all of the names on that list. If there's a dirty cop in that division, I want to know about it. Also, share everything you learn with the FBI, because they will be the ones who prosecute. Don't share your information with the Dallas PD or your brother. Understand?"

"Understood, and thank you," Asher said and walked out.

The moment he was gone, Robert Ivory was on the phone with the FBI. The Feds were still reeling from losing four of their special agents and a material witness to their case. They knew Dixon was responsible, but they had yet to find a shred of evidence to prove it.

Unaware that Asher had set new wheels in motion, as soon as Jacob opened the bar and customers began trickling in, Gunner went through the house and out the back door and started walking the land, looking for a site to build a home. He walked and walked, pausing often to look around as the sun moved higher in the sky and the day kept getting hotter.

Finally, he stopped and turned around to check the view. From the rise where he was standing and looking back at the bar and Crossroads in general, it was West Texas in all her beauty, and the little town that he called home.

This is it, he thought, and he began picking up rocks and stacking them up like a pylon to mark the spot. He had to wait for the lottery money to hit the bank before he did anything drastic, but he needed to get a hydrogeologist out to see if there was water anywhere beneath his feet and get an architect to draw up the blueprints.

He knew what he wanted.

A place to call home.

A woman to love and grow old with, and children to fill the rooms beneath his roof.

Money could buy the house. It would be up to him to let down his distrust of all people. He wasn't sure he knew how to be in love, or if he'd know it was happening. But Holly had opened him up to the prospect.

He glanced at the time. It was nearly noon, and he was getting hungry. Time to go back and check on his dad, then go to the Rose to get them some food. Orders from Pearl were not to be ignored.

But instead of walking back, Gunner took off at a jog, and then finally an all-out run. For the first time in years, he wasn't chasing after a suspect. He was running for the pure joy of it—just because he could.

The parking lot at the Yellow Rose was like a revolving door. Drivers pulling in to pick up to-go orders. Other diners leaving as new ones were arriving. Truckers traditionally pulled off onto the shoulder of the highway across from the Rose and walked over. Today there were six big rigs lined up on the other side of the highway when Gunner pulled into the parking lot and went inside. People began calling his name and waving him over to sit with them. It was the best feeling he'd had since the last time he'd been here with his brothers.

He wound up sitting at a table with two guys from his high school football team. Billy Barrett, who'd been their kicker, was now a cowboy on his granddaddy's ranch, and Will Devlin, who'd been the star quarterback, was now a trucker. His truck was one of the six parked on the other side of the highway.

As soon as Gunner turned in his order to Cheryl, and a to-go order for his dad, they started talking, and the first thing they asked was about his marital state.

"Are you still on the most-eligible-bachelor list?" Will asked.

Gunner nodded. "Hard to have a personal relationship when your every waking hour is devoted to trying to solve murders and find killers. What about you two?"

"Lindsey and I got married the year after we graduated high school," Billy said. "We have two kids. A boy and a girl."

"I got married, but the wife didn't care much for my trucker life. She took off for Vegas, and my mom and my sister are helping me take care of my two boys," Will said. "I never saw you becoming a cop."

"Likely comes from overcompensating for having a criminal for a mother. It wears on you, for sure, and it's good to be home. Did either of you go to college?" Gunner asked.

"Nope. All I ever wanted was ranching. Granddad was there. I fell into working in the world I love," Billy said.

Will shrugged. "I didn't go, but I also won't ever regret the mistakes I made, because my boys are all I live for."

Gunner was listening without comment, and they were still talking about Gunner's speed on the football field, and old times and football games won and lost, when Cheryl brought his food. After that, the conversation shifted to the most recent tragedy of Crossroads—the deaths of Helen Dillon and Lee Peters.

That's how Gunner learned of the upcoming funeral services, and he reminded himself again to call Holly as soon as he delivered his dad's food.

A few minutes later, Pearl came out of the kitchen with Jacob's food.

"For your daddy, and keep your money in your wallet," she said and gave his shoulder a quick pat. A loud bang from the kitchen put a frown on her face. "Oh, for pity's sake," she muttered and went stomping back to the kitchen.

Billy grinned. "Reckon we might need to say a prayer for Davey's ass?"

Gunner laughed. "Why not?"

Will took off his cap and bowed his head. "Lord, protect Davey from Miss Pearl's wrath."

"Amen," Billy said, which elicited a round of chuckles from surrounding tables. Then he glanced at the time, picked up his ticket, and left Cheryl a tip. "Gotta go. Good seeing you, Gunner," he said and headed to the front counter to pay.

Will also got up. "I need to hustle. Got a load to get to Amarillo, and back to Silverton before dark."

"Is that where you live?" Gunner asked.

Will shrugged. "It's where my mom and sister live, and I'm there so they can take care of my boys when I'm on the road."

"Safe trip," Gunner said and got up and left the Rose while Will was at the front counter, paying for his meal.

Gunner got home, left the bag on the kitchen table, and went into the bar.

"Dad, your food is on the table. Go eat. I've got the bar until you get back."

Jacob looked surprised. "You don't have to—"

"I know, but we both know I know how. Go. Eat. I can put a good head on a glass of beer with the best of them, and I can pop the top off a longneck, too."

Jacob nodded. "Don't forget the pretzels."

"I won't," Gunner said.

Jacob came out from behind the bar with a big grin on his face and went into their house. Having the time to sit and eat was a treat. He turned on the little TV in the kitchen to catch the noon news, then washed up and started pulling food from the sack.

Customers were thinning out, which was business as usual at a bar around noon. Gunner spent the time sweeping up crumbs and wiping down tables until a truck pulled up and two men walked into the Tumbleweed and headed for the bar.

"What'll it be, boys?" Gunner asked.

They both looked startled. "What happened to Jacob?"

"Nothing," Gunner said. "He's eating lunch, and I'm his son. On tap, can, or longneck?"

They grinned. "Two Lone Star longnecks," they said and sat down at the bar.

Gunner grabbed two longnecks from the cooler, popped the tops, then filled a bowl of pretzels and set it down between them.

The short one slid a twenty-dollar bill on the counter.

Gunner put the twenty-dollar bill in the till, gave them back four dollars in change, and left them to their beer and pretzels, yet well aware that they were giving him the eye when they thought he wasn't watching.

Finally, the short one spoke up. "You look like your old man," he said.

Gunner shrugged. "All of us boys look like him, but I'm not nearly as kind or patient."

They laughed. "Duly noted." They toasted him with their beers. "To attitude," they said and took a big swig.

At that point, Jacob returned. He gave Gunner a pat on the back. "You are officially relieved, and thank you, son."

"You're welcome, Dad. I've got some calls to make. Give me a shout if you need me."

Jacob nodded, then saw the two men sitting at the bar and went to greet them as Gunner left.

"Your son's a pistol, ain't he?" the short one asked.

Jacob grinned. "Let's just say he does not suffer fools gladly."

Gunner got as far as the living room before he sat down to call Holly. His stomach was in a knot the whole time the phone was ringing, and he was wondering what message he would leave on voicemail when she finally picked up, obviously out of breath.

"Hello, Gunner."

"Hey, lady… You sound out of breath. If I've called at a bad time, I can call you later," he said.

Holly walked out to the back patio and took a seat on the porch swing to talk. "No, it's fine. I'm glad to hear your voice again. It's been pretty hectic here."

"I just wanted you to know I am in Crossroads. I got here last night, and I'll be here for a while."

Holly closed her eyes, letting the deep, husky rasp of his voice wash through her.

"Mom's services are at 10:00 a.m. this Saturday, at the church in town."

"I heard them talking about it in the Rose when I went to pick up Dad's lunch."

"I didn't know, but I'm not surprised. Word does get around in small towns, doesn't it?"

Gunner had heard enough witnesses giving statements to hear that she was bordering on panic. There was a moment of silence, and then Gunner asked, "Is there anything I can do for you today?"

Holly didn't hesitate. "I wouldn't mind the sight of your face and a hug if you're free, of course. The thought of Saturday looms."

Gunner didn't hesitate. "I'm about as free as a man can be. Is now okay?"

"Now is very okay," Holly said.

"Then I'll see you soon," he said and disconnected. He went to get his hat—a black gambler-style Stetson with a thin leather hatband studded in small pieces of turquoise. It was his only bow to fashion.

There were only a few customers in the Weed when he walked into the bar. "Hey, Dad, I'm going out to the Dillon Ranch to see Holly."

Jacob nodded. "Give them my best," he said, but Gunner was already walking out. Jacob smiled to himself.

First time I've known Gunner to be in a hurry to get to a woman he wasn't about to arrest.

The moment her call with Gunner ended, Holly made a run for her bedroom, changed out of the T-shirt she'd been working in to a pretty summer blouse, took the clip out of her hair and finger-combed it into place, and started to put on lipstick, then changed her mind. She didn't want to look like she was trying too hard.

Her grandmother was coming up the hall when she noticed Holly's door was open and she had changed her clothes and her hair.

"What's going on?" Trudy asked as she walked in.

There was no way to lie to Granny and get away with it, so Holly just spit it out.

"Gunner Kingston is in town. He called to let me know and asked if he could do anything for me. I said he could come talk to me about anything except the funeral. He's on his way."

Trudy gave her a hug. "Good for you, and say hello to him for me. I remember him as a child, and then when he was in high school, but he was always such a loner. However, Jacob did raise some fine men."

"Yes, ma'am, that he did," Holly said.

"I'm going to lie down for a while. One of the neighbors brought chicken and dumplings for our supper, and we still have pie from previous days, so no worries about cooking tonight," Trudy said.

Holly paused. "Granny, is Dad going to be okay?"

Trudy sighed. "As okay as anyone can be who loses the love of their life. I lost my Jamie twenty years ago, and when I'm here, it still feels like he should walk into the house at any moment. It's why I moved to Santa Fe. It was too hard to be here without him. But I'm okay, right?"

Holly wrapped her arms around her Granny's neck and kissed her cheek. "I never thought of it that way. I'm sorry we mistook your strength of purpose. Thinking you were getting over it… Moving on, you know? We didn't realize it was how you were dealing with your grief."

"It's all good," Trudy said and gave Holly a light swat on

her backside. “Go on with you. If you need me, you’ll know where I am.”

“Yes, ma’am,” Holly said and went to watch for Gunner’s arrival.

Chapter 7

Gunner was just leaving Crossroads when he got a phone call from Dylan. He guessed he was going to get chewed out for not telling him what was going on and braced himself as he answered via Bluetooth.

"Hey, Dylan, what's up?" he said.

Dylan snorted in his ear. "You tell me."

"Who ratted me out?" Gunner said.

"Dad, and then he was upset thinking he'd said something out of turn."

Gunner sighed. "I'll make it right with him, and I'm sorry, brother. I didn't say anything because I did not want you in the middle of it."

"I assume Asher knows," Dylan said.

"Only because it's sort of a big deal for someone to put out a hit and a bounty to go with it on an officer of the law. His boss is on it. I've already been shot at once and missed. The hit is being called off because I put the fear of God in the man who did it, but I didn't want to hang around Dallas and get shot because the hunters hadn't been called off."

Dylan groaned. "Oh my God. Gunner. You don't have to work another day in your life now. Get out of that business before it swallows you whole."

"Already in the process," Gunner said. "I have plans… and I'm moving back to Crossroads. Dad's giving me a place to build on his property back up in the hills behind the house and bar."

"Thank God," Dylan said. "Does your boss know this?"

"Not yet, but he will when I go back to get my car out of the body shop."

"What happened to your car?" Dylan asked.

Gunner related the purple Yamaha story again.

Dylan took a breath. "Okay then. Who's building your house?"

"Hell if I know. We're in the middle of nowhere out there. Probably some construction company out of Amarillo."

"I wish I could," Dylan said.

Gunner smiled. "I wish you could, too, but you can't drag a whole crew of men and equipment that far from Austin for the months it will take to make that happen, so let go of that."

Dylan laughed. "You're right. But just for the record, no more secrets, okay?"

"Deal. Also, hello to Angie and my nephew," he said, then refocused on the big sign notating the way to the Dillon Ranch and took the turn. The moment he turned north, the thought of seeing Holly again made his heart skip. He recognized the crash site almost instantly when he drove up on it. It was the sparkling bits of glass shining in the grass and on the blacktop that gave it away, and he wondered how long it would take for the Dillon family to travel this road without thinking, *This is where she died.*

For Gunner, his last memory of his mother was when he was seven and she dropped them off at school. He never saw her again, and for years, he thought she'd left because she didn't want them anymore. Now, his memory of her was vague. Shadowy images of incidents and moments of joy with her and his brothers that became faded by time. There were no pictures of her anywhere. And he didn't care. He couldn't even remember what she looked like. Only that her selfish choices had blown up the family they'd had.

He kept driving with an eye on the road and soon saw the ranch house and all of the outbuildings in the distance. His eyes narrowed against the glare of the sun, and he wished he'd brought his sunglasses, then remembered they were still in his other vehicle. The one in the body shop back in Dallas.

A couple of minutes later, he pulled up to the house and got out. The front door opened before he reached the steps, and Holly walked out.

The last time he'd seen her, she'd been wearing a pantsuit and makeup. Today, there was no makeup, just pure beauty—a picture in motion, and he was thinking how perfectly she fit the image of a rancher's daughter. Bootcut jeans, the Ropers on her feet, and the loose summer blouse the wind had plastered to her curves. But it was that fiery crown of misbehaving curls framing that beautiful face that made his heart skip a beat.

"You came," she said.

"I could never tell you no. Seeing you sitting in the dugout at baseball practice, sneaking the last two Fritos in my snack, or drinking the last of my pop I left sitting there." He walked up the steps, opened his arms, and she walked into his waiting hug.

Curls beneath his chin. Her cheek against his chest. He could feel her shaking as he finally let her go.

"Thank you for coming, Gunner. Shall we go inside out of the heat? I'll pay you back with a whole cold pop of your own."

The side of his mouth tilted upward. The only sign of the smile bursting inside him. "Lead the way, lady."

A few minutes later, they were sitting on one of the sofas and facing each other. Condensation was forming on the outside of the cold drinks, and a plate of cookies was on the table beside them. Gunner could see she needed to talk, but he'd conducted enough interrogations to guess she didn't know where to start.

"Talk to me. I'm really good at keeping a confidence," he said.

Holly picked at a piece of lint on her jeans, and then her shoulders slumped. "This isn't a secret, but it's also not public knowledge…yet. Sheriff Reddick was here with autopsy results we weren't expecting. Mom had a massive heart attack. Her foot was still on the gas, but she was already dead when Lee Peters came over the hill and hit her. And he didn't see her because he was texting his girlfriend. If he'd just looked up in time, he could have swerved. But he didn't."

Gunner was stunned. "My God! I have seen all kinds of freak accidents, but nothing like that. It must have been a shock to all of you…and to the Peters family. But the question is… How does it make you feel?"

"Relieved. All this time I kept imagining in that split second before they collided, knowing she was going to die… Imagining her fear and despair, you know? If that was her day to die, somehow, the sudden death she didn't see coming seems like the blessing. I still feel so bad for the Peters boy, but at the same time, it wasn't Mom's fault that he hit her. It's all such a horrible mess, and I'm dreading the funeral."

Gunner reached for her hand. "Honey, every funeral is its own level of hell. What you're feeling is what everybody feels when they've lost someone they love, no matter why or how."

Holly sighed. "I forgot you work in Homicide. I guess you've seen your share of death."

He nodded. "The worst part is always notifying the next of kin, and then trying to find out who killed them. All of my cases are murders."

"How do you do it?" she asked.

He shrugged. "Focus. Mind over matter." He sighed. "That's a lie. But finding the killer always helps. And then before you can dwell, there's another call out or two, and you don't have time for someone else's grief because you're trying to find out what happened to the next victim."

"Everybody says you're really good at it," Holly said.

Gunner's only comment was noncommittal. "I was raised to do a job right the first time."

Holly kept looking at him—at the steady gaze in his dark eyes and the stubborn cut to his jaw—and knew in her heart he was a keeper, but would he ever see her that way?

Impulsively, she took a cookie from the plate beside them and handed it to him. "Granny made them, and I owe you. They have chocolate and toffee bits in them."

Gunner grinned. "First time I ever got paid in cookies." He took a bite, chewed, and then his eyes widened. "These are good!"

"Yes, they are," Holly said. "Mom was a great baker, too. Granny was a good teacher."

"What about you? What do you like to do for fun?" Gunner asked.

"I don't know what I do for fun. I work. I get takeout. I go home to TV and bed. I like to bake, but I don't have anyone to bake for, and I'd just sit there and get fat eating it all myself."

He grinned. "I nominate myself as your official taster if the urge happens again."

Holly smiled. "Maybe when we get back to Dallas."

He stuffed the rest of the cookie in his mouth, chewed and swallowed, and then took a drink.

She frowned. His lack of response wasn't promising. "I wasn't hinting for anything," she said.

"It's not that. I made a recent decision to get out of the

cop business. For a number of reasons. Bottom line, I'm not going back. I'm moving home to Crossroads and building a house up on the rise above our house."

She gasped. "Oh wow!"

"Don't say anything yet. I need to notify my boss first before it becomes public knowledge."

"Right! Oh Gunner, how awesome. I have wanted to do that, too. I even talked about it with Mom once, but we finally agreed that jobs in real estate are scarce here, even in Amarillo."

"You know Garrett would love it if you came home."

"Yes, but then I'd be that girl again, asking Daddy for money, and I think I've outgrown that era of my life," she said.

He wanted to unload his plans and dreams, and tell her about the lottery win, but it was too soon, and there was the funeral to get through. First things, first. Instead, he threaded his fingers through hers.

"You never know what your future will bring, but I'd love it if you'd keep me in it."

Holly's heart skipped. "Count on it."

All of a sudden, there was a lot of shouting outside. They both glanced out the window overlooking the barns and stables and saw a horse running hell-bent for leather toward the cattle guard, which they all knew he could clear without breaking a sweat, and men running after it spinning loops to try and rope it before it got away.

Gunner bolted out the front door, outpacing the horse's angle of escape, and blocked the path, waving his arms high above his head to distract it.

The stallion reared up on his hind legs, then pawed the ground, but Gunner didn't budge and kept waving him back.

It slowed the horse down long enough for two of the

cowboys to get lassos over his head. The stallion snorted and tossed his head in disgust, but he was well and truly caught, and he knew it.

Garrett was out of breath when he got to the horse, but he was grinning at Gunner.

"You sure can run, boy. Thanks for the help. If he'd cleared the cattle guard, he'd be gone."

"Beautiful stallion," Gunner said, eyeing the big gray.

"I bought him from Sonny Bluejacket a couple of years back. He's a beauty, but he has an attitude, for sure."

"I guess he needed to kick up his heels a little," Gunner said.

Garrett shook his head. "No, there's a mare in heat in a nearby pasture, and he had love on his mind."

Gunner laughed. "Ah, something we can all understand. I came to pay my respects to you and your family and was visiting with Holly when we saw the runaway. I am so sorry, Garrett…for everything."

Garrett's shoulders slumped. "Thanks, Gunner. It has been a shock for all of us. Will we see you at the services?"

"Yes, sir. Dad, Pearl, and I will be there. I have very fond memories of Mrs. Dillon when I was in school. The women of Crossroads all helped raise me and my brothers after everything fell apart, me especially because I was so young. I owe all of them a huge debt of gratitude."

Garrett waved at Holly, who was standing on the porch. "I won't keep you any longer, and I'm glad you came. Holly is struggling. She and Helen were very close." Then he waved at his men. "Get that big fool back in the stables, and this time, don't turn your back for a second," he said, then followed behind them as they led the big gray away.

Gunner started walking back to the house, but his gaze was fixed on the woman waiting. The walls he'd lived behind were cracking from within.

Holly smiled as he came up the steps. "Way to go, Roadrunner. You've still got it."

Gunner hadn't heard his old high school nickname in years. "When the need arises," he said, then reached out and cupped the side of her cheek. "You need to rest. Thank you for the invitation. I'll see you at the funeral, okay?"

The urge to lay her head in the palm of his hand was so strong it made her ache. "Yes."

"I'll just get my hat," he said and followed her back into the house, then settled it on his head. Holly's hand was on his shoulder, but he still saw tears in her eyes.

"Thank you so much for coming," she said. "Talking to you was a good reset. And getting to see that famous Kingston sprint wasn't bad, either. I'll walk you out."

The last look Gunner had of her was in the rearview mirror. She was still on the porch, watching him driving away.

Gunner's partner, Cliff Beale, was on his way home from work when he got a phone call. The name that came up on Caller ID made him sweat, but he wasn't answering. Last night he and his wife had the worst fight of their fifteen years of marriage. She found out he'd been gambling again, and worse yet, discovered how much money he'd lost doing it. It was only after he got down on his knees, begging, and sobbing, and swearing on the lives of his children that he would never gamble again, that she finally gave in.

"One more time, and we're gone. Do you understand me, Clifford Beale?"

It was still an echo in his ears. His family was his world. Gunner had warned him time and time again it was going to get him in trouble, with either his job or his wife. Gunner was right, but now he was gone. Cliff didn't have anyone to talk to, and if he started going to some program for gambling addicts, Internal Affairs would find out. If they didn't fire him, he would at least be put on suspension. He was as desperate as a man could be, and not answering that phone call from the bookie he owed was about to make everything worse.

It was a casual conversation between a cop and his uncle in the FBI that led to the special agents in charge of the Dixon case finding out about the deaths of Garza and Letourneau. They already had dossiers on both men from the evidence they had on Burgess Dixon and knew those men were part of his syndicate. After viewing records of the case, they couldn't fault the conclusion of the crime scene, but from what they knew of Dixon, they also doubted the men had killed each other.

It was more likely they'd done something that displeased Dixon, like dumping the body of the witness in that old warehouse instead of hiding it, and this was the end result. It wasn't anything they could prove, but it was info to add to the case against Dixon they still had on the back burner.

To Burgess Dixon's knowledge, there was only one hit man who had yet to confirm he knew the bounty had been pulled, and Dixon was furious with the contractor who'd sent them out. The warning he unloaded on the contractor was quiet and deadly.

"I don't care if you don't know where he lived. You had contact numbers, damn it! So, leave messages, and you will keep calling until he verifies the message that it's off, or I will make sure you never see the light of day again! Do you hear me?"

"Yes, sir, I—"

Dixon ended the call in the middle of the man's response, then threw the burner phone across the room and pounded his desk with both fists in frustration.

In that moment, Whistler was wishing he was anywhere but in Dallas with this man. He was going to get both of them killed or sent to prison. And yet he stayed—a silent witness to the threat. He didn't have to comment. He'd seen and heard it all before.

Asher Kingston was steadily working through the list of names Gunner gave him, running background checks and accessing phone records and financial information. A dirty cop was probably using burner phones, but he had to check off all the boxes. Unless there was an offshore account somewhere, it would be financial records that gave it away.

So far, he knew Cliff Beale, Gunner's partner, was a gambler and up to his eyeballs in debt. A man desperate for money could become suspect for selling information.

The female detective in the division was clean as a whistle with finances, but she was barely making it from month to month. She had a brother with priors, but he lived in Mississippi, so that pretty much ruled her out.

He kept going down the list while waiting for various background checks to show up, hoping the notifications about the hit being canceled had reached all the killers they'd set on Gunner's trail.

The sites where Asher was not allowed to breach, like digging for offshore accounts, he'd given to his wife. Due to Nora's line of work—finding online hackers and fraud within worldwide corporations—her security clearance was about as high as it got.

The moment Asher told her what Gunner was dealing with, she dropped everything she was doing and began devoting her attention to searching for secrets within the list.

Finally, it was the day of Helen Dillon's funeral.

Business in Crossroads was about to come to a screeching halt. It was just after 9:00 a.m. when the black wreaths and black ribbons went up on the door fronts of businesses. Some stores were leaving skeleton crews to stay open, but the Tumbleweed Bar, among others, was temporarily closed.

The Yellow Rose Café was open with Davey the fry cook and Cheryl the waitress staying behind to keep it open.

Their menu was, for the time Pearl was gone, a small buffet with two meats and three sides and salad. All Cheryl and Davey had to do was keep the trays full. Pearl had already cooked what was meant to be served until she got back.

Belker's Grocery was at half staff.

The bank had a black wreath on the door, but it was open for business.

Even though Lee Peters's funeral service would not be held in Crossroads, school was still out for the day. He would have graduated high school in May.

The whole student body was in shock. People their age didn't die. Or weren't supposed to. It was their first experience of losing one of their own. Even if people weren't planning to attend the services, they cared enough about the grieving families to honor their passing.

Sheriff Reddick had sent a uniformed officer to Crossroads for traffic control.

Gunner was ready and waiting in their living room when his dad and Pearl finally appeared.

“Mama Pearl, you sure look pretty,” Gunner said.

Pearl patted his arm. “Thank you, baby. It’s a shame someone had to die for me to bother about what to wear or how to look.”

Jacob kissed her cheek. “You are always beautiful in my eyes. Let’s get going. I expect parking will be a mess.”

“Don’t worry. I’m going to let you both out at the front of the church. I’ll find a place to park and meet up with you inside,” Gunner said, and he did.

As soon as he parked on a side street a block away, he hurried back to the church, then took a seat beside Pearl, leaving her sandwiched between them.

People were still arriving. There were pockets of people quietly visiting with each other, but the unusual silence was as noticeable as the single casket covered in a blanket of pink roses at the altar, and the two cowboys in starched Wranglers and pearl-snap white western shirts, standing like soldiers on guard at either end of the casket.

Finally, the music sounded, and with it came the family being ushered into the church and the long walk they had to make down the aisle to the pews reserved for them.

As he was watching it all happen, Gunner realized this had not happened for his mother and supposed she’d lost her right to be honored. He had no memory of ever seeing her grave and no idea where she was buried, or if her ashes had been cast in the wind.

He didn’t know Jacob was watching him, or that Pearl had slipped her hand in the crook of his elbow. His focus was on Holly and Travis’s arm around her shoulders. Like everyone here, his regret for their loss was real and deep.

He had given notifications of death to many families over the past ten years, but that had always been where his connection to the family ended. And once the murder was solved, the case became a number in their system, and they moved on to the next tragedy.

Only nobody killed Helen Dillon, or the boy who hit her drifting car. His lack of attention to driving ended his life, and an unknown heart problem ended hers.

Garrett's eyes were blurred with tears. He and Helen got married in this church. What was happening felt surreal. This was wrong—so wrong. It was beginning to dawn on him that the time was coming when he would sleep alone in that big house. Travis would be in college. His mom would go home to Santa Fe, and Holly would go back to Dallas. The light in his world had gone out. His heart was broken.

Holly felt sick. If she'd had to speak right now, it would have been nothing but a scream. Travis hadn't stopped crying since they walked into the church, and she was determined to keep it together for him. Entering the church with all eyes on them was the worst.

She knew Gunner was here. She'd seen him with his family as they were going down the aisle, but she wouldn't look at him. Couldn't look at the sympathy on his face without coming undone.

She held it together all the way through the prayer and the first song, but when Garrett's old friend, Wes Duggan, a cowboy preacher from Amarillo, began reading the eulogy, the sob she kept swallowing finally came up, and the sorrow in it was so palatable it was felt throughout the congregation.

It was an emotional slap Gunner didn't see coming. Her sadness was heartbreaking, and the thought of her in so much pain without being able to help triggered every protective instinct in him. Just like the day she'd been knocked out by that baseball and he thought they'd killed her. He'd never been that scared for someone else before.

Meeting up with her again now felt like she'd been a gift from the universe, but before they could further the idea of a relationship, life had knocked her out again, and it was going to take time for her to find her way back. He wanted that for her. But it wasn't going to be easy, and it might not work out. Him in Crossroads and her back in Dallas. Gunner was a pro at maneuvering through hard times and hard choices, but sometimes life just sucked.

For Holly, the rest of the service was a blur.

After the eulogy, the pastor took the podium and began to speak. She tried to focus, but every time she lifted her head, all she saw was the rose-covered casket and the two cowboys with their heads bowed—honor guards standing with their hats in their hands.

So, she bowed her head instead and let the words roll over her until the last song was sung and the service was ending.

God give me strength. I have to look at their faces now.

Feet were shuffling in the aisle. The congregation would move past the closed casket on the way out of the church, and they would stop to acknowledge her and her family on the way out.

There was the church dinner yet to endure. All she could

think about was going home, crawling into bed, and pulling the covers over her head like she'd done as a child when she had bad dreams.

And then out of the blue, her grandmother leaned over, kissed the side of her cheek, and whispered in her ear. "Chin up, my darling girl. This, too, shall pass."

Holly heard the shuffling of many feet as the ushers began moving the congregation down the aisle one by one. She took a deep breath and whispered in her brother's ear. "We can do this."

And they did, maintaining a measure of composure through every touch—every kind word—every offer of regret. Until Gunner. He said nothing, but the touch on her shoulder as he passed was enough to trigger the tears rolling down her face.

Gunner took Jacob and Pearl home so they could get back to business, then caught up with the procession going to the cemetery. He just needed to let Holly know he was there.

The sun was high in the sky when he found a place to park. As he started toward the little tent where the family was seated, he saw movement in the distance. It was a lone coyote watching, likely bothered by the number of humans who'd suddenly appeared on his route to somewhere else.

He glanced down to sidestep a broken tombstone, and when he looked up, the coyote was gone and the pastor was saying a prayer. A passage was read from the Bible, and then it was over. He stayed long enough for Holly to see him, and when she did, she quickly motioned him over.

"You are welcome to come to the dinner," she said.

He cupped the side of her face. "Thank you, honey, but I wouldn't want to intrude on family time."

She leaned into his hand and whispered. "Intrude, please."

He blinked. "Is something wrong?"

Her eyes welled. "Distant cousin. He has been hitting on me ever since they arrived last night. He has bugged me off and on our whole lives and can't even see how inappropriate it is to do that when we're in the midst of all this."

"Ah… Just point him out and leave the rest to me," Gunner said.

Holly sighed. "His name is Carl Warwick. A second cousin once removed from my mother's family. Black Wranglers. Blue shirt. Bolo tie. Belt buckle the size of his ego. Thank you, a thousand times."

"For you…anything, anytime," he said. "See you back at the church."

The tension she'd been feeling was gone. She knew from childhood that when Gunner Kingston made a promise, he kept it, and she suspected he was going to make an impression on Carl Warwick he wasn't going to forget.

Chapter 8

Gunner called his dad to tell him where he was going, then got to the church ahead of the family and waited in the car until after they'd all gone inside.

The dining hall was filled with people milling about and keeping the trail hot between the bathrooms before sitting down to eat. He paused in the doorway, searching the crowd, and spotted her almost immediately. It was already obvious that Carl was in her personal space and using every excuse he could to touch her.

It was Gunner's first introduction to a "get your hands off my woman" feeling. Even if she wasn't, he realized how much he wanted her to be.

"To hell with that," he muttered and headed toward them with single intent, then walked up to her as if Carl wasn't even there, slid his hand beneath the hair on her neck, and kissed the side of her cheek. "Sorry I'm late, darlin'. I had to make sure Dad and Pearl got home. Come sit and cool off. I'll get you something cold to drink and some food."

"I'm just glad you're here. The cold drink sounds wonderful. Not so sure about the food," she said.

Carl had yet to close his mouth. The man was huge and disgustingly handsome, and even worse, seemed to have an in with Holly he knew nothing about.

"Holly, aren't you going to introduce us?" Carl asked.

Gunner turned as if seeing him for the first time and introduced himself. "Gunner Kingston, and you are?"

"Uh… Carl Warwick. Holly and I are cousins."

Gunner nodded. "Cousins. Nice to meet you," he said and ushered Holly to a table where Garrett and his mother, Trudy, were already seated. "Sit here, honey. I'll get your plate; save me a seat."

As soon as he walked away, Trudy reached for Holly's hand. "Are you okay? You're too pale."

"Just exhausted, Granny. I invited Gunner to eat with us. When are Alicia and Carl leaving?"

"After the dinner. They packed and loaded up their car this morning."

"Thank God," Holly whispered. "Carl is a bit much."

Trudy's eyes widened. "Was he bothering you?"

"Not anymore," Holly said and grinned. "Gunner made sure of that."

"Oh, good grief. I'm sorry, baby. You should have said something," Trudy hissed.

Holly shrugged. "Daddy doesn't need the grief."

Trudy sighed. "I understand. Carl was spoiled rotten. He's nearly thirty and still lives at home with his mother, for God's sake."

Carl was still in shock from the big man's sudden presence and followed him to the buffet.

"So where are you from?" Carl asked.

"Here… Crossroads, same as Holly," Gunner said and picked up a plate.

Carl frowned. "So, you live here."

"No, I live in Dallas. I'm a homicide detective with the Dallas PD. What do you do for a living?" he asked.

"Uh… I…" And at that moment, Carl's mother waved him down. "Oh, excuse me. I'm being paged," he said, pointing toward his mother, who had her arm in the air, waving at him, and then he scurried off without answering.

"And that's the end of that," Gunner muttered.

He gave the buffet a quick glance—eyeing the cheesy toppings on most of the casseroles, the buttery juices in bowls of vegetables, six versions of macaroni and cheese, and equal amounts of church potatoes—and knew none of that would appeal to someone with a queasy tummy.

He headed straight for a platter of biscuits, picked up two, forked up a thin slice of baked ham, and made her two little ham biscuits. Then he added a spoonful of dilled potato salad, slid a piece of coconut pie on the plate, swooped up a cup of sweet tea, and headed back to where she was sitting and set it in front of her. Travis was behind him with a plate for his granny and pie for his dad.

Holly looked at the plate, and then up at Gunner. "You are scary good at reading the room. Thank you."

He felt her praise from the inside out. "I'll be right back."

Gunner and Travis walked back to the buffet together and then picked up their plates. Gunner could only guess what Travis was feeling, but he also knew that sympathy was not what he needed.

"Somebody raised you right, taking care of your grandmother's needs first. You're going to be okay, Travis. We make plans, and life drop-kicks us onto a new path, whether we like it or not, right?"

Travis paused, eyeing the man's demeanor. Everybody in Crossroads knew their story. And everybody knew how Jacob Kingston's three sons came to his rescue a couple of years ago, when he was nearly killed in a robbery at his bar. "Do you like my sister?" he asked.

"Yes. Not sure where she is with it, but is that okay with you?" Gunner asked.

Travis nodded.

Gunner put a spoonful of church potatoes on his plate and then ham and two kinds of salads, and he skipped dessert.

"What's in those potatoes?" Travis asked.

Gunner shrugged. "Not real sure, but the jalapenos I saw decorating the top gives me hope that they have some spice to them. Mostly they're scalloped potatoes with a buttload of cheese."

Travis grinned, scooped some onto his plate, and by the time they got back to the table to sit down, he was walking with his head up and his shoulders back. Holly already told him whether he was ready for it or not, he'd been given big shoes to stand in. Lee was dead. His mother was dead. And he was still here, so that meant he needed to live his best life for the friend he'd lost and for the mother who'd wanted all of his dreams to come true.

By the time the meal was over, Carl Warwick had seen enough from where he and his mother were sitting to know his chances of snagging a distant cousin for a wife were slim to none.

And Holly had seen enough of Gunner to know that if he ever let someone love him, he would give it back a thousandfold. She wanted him. And she wanted to be that woman, but time would tell.

It was difficult to get a bite of food chewed and swallowed before someone from the community would stop by their table with the same words of sympathy and/or asking pointed questions too personal to answer.

Finally, it was Holly who initiated their exit. "Dad, can we please go home now?"

"Yes. I just need to thank the ladies for providing the food for us," Garrett said and got up from the table.

At that point, the rest of them stood as well.

Gunner caught Carl Warwick eyeing Holly again and slid his arm around her shoulder.

"I'll walk you out," he said.

She leaned against him. "My white knight."

Travis was right behind them with Trudy on his arm.

The limo from the funeral home was parked at the front door, and the driver was standing outside, waiting. When he saw them coming, he began opening doors.

The wind was whipping the skirt of Holly's dress and putting more tangles in her curls that she would have to brush out later, but right now she didn't care. She was so tired her legs were shaking.

Gunner could see she was moving on autopilot.

"Darlin', I know you feel like the world's been cut out from under you, and that's part of the grief. But what you need to focus on now is that you are no longer on any schedule. Your time is your own, to sleep and rest when you want. To still cry when you want. Tomorrow will be the first day of a new reality for all of you. The business of death is behind you. It doesn't alleviate any level of sadness or grief. But your responsibilities to your mom are over. Right?"

A wave of understanding moved through her. She nodded, stumbled, and he caught her. They stopped, giving her time to regain her composure.

"I know we made a promise to each other back in Dallas not to lose touch. If you're on the same page, when you're ready to be out in the world again or you just want company, call me. I owe you a meal at the Yellow Rose before you go back to Dallas," Gunner said.

"Count on it. If it's not too personal to ask, are you for sure moving home?"

"I am so sure that you could bet a million dollars on it. We can talk about the whys and what-ifs another day," he said. They resumed the walk, but he was holding on to her now and didn't turn loose until she was seated in the limo.

He stepped back as the driver closed the door, then stayed, watching until the limousine was out of sight.

The Tumbleweed parking lot was full when Gunner got home. He made a quick change out of dress clothes, then he sat down at the kitchen table with his laptop and began checking his phone and email for messages.

There were text messages from at least eight of the detectives from his department, including his partner, Cliff, expressing their outrage at the bounty and hoping he was okay, and there was one message from Lieutenant Samuels regarding the man on the motorcycle.

> An update on your would-be assassin. He was patched up enough to be arraigned and has been moved to a prison hospital. Also, word on the street is that the hit has been officially called off. Hope you are okay.

Gunner paused, frowned, and reread the message three more times, trying to figure out what there was about it that seemed off. Then the skin crawled on the back of his neck when it hit him.

There had never been any "word on the street." It was never public knowledge that a hit had been issued. Not even Gunner knew it until the man on the Yamaha. Dixon never admitted being the one who'd set it in motion, so how did Samuels come to know this? Where did he get his information?

His heart was racing as he picked up the phone and called Asher. It rang twice, and then his brother's voice was in his ear.

"Hey, kid… You okay?"

"I just got a message from my boss, asking me if I was okay and telling me that word on the street was that the hit had officially been called off."

"Okay… Isn't that good news?" Asher asked.

Gunner pinched the bridge of his nose in frustration. "Explain this to me like I'm in kindergarten. Since Dixon never admitted to ordering the hit and it was never public knowledge that it was happening, then how did Samuels get his info? Who told him that? How would he come by that information when the hit men were unknowns?"

Asher stilled. The pause between their conversation grew longer and longer, and then he sighed. "Well, shit. I can't say as I can answer that right now. Are you okay at Dad's?"

"Yes. All is well."

"And no one knows where you are, right?"

"Samuels knows. I told him," Gunner said.

"Well shit, again," Asher muttered. "Just stay vigilant. I don't know why you would still be on anyone's radar now. Not after you presented Dixon with your ultimatum."

"Consider this," Gunner said. "If there was a dirty cop who was desperate to hide his tracks, and I'd already unknowingly admitted to that dirty cop that I thought there might be one in our department, and that cop knew I'd already publicly fingered Burgess Dixon if anything happened to me, then that dirty cop would have no trouble getting away with my murder."

"Damn it, Gunner. I don't like how this is playing out one bit."

"Neither do I, but right now, if it is my boss, he has no idea he said too much, or that I caught it. Just dig into his background. See if you can find a reason why he would even do this. He's been my lieutenant for seven of my eight years in Homicide. I would have trusted him with my life. Now I'm not so sure. I would hate to think he'd been dirty all this time."

"On it," Asher said. "Have you responded to the texts you've been getting?"

"No, not to any of them," Gunner said.

"Then don't, and tell Dad that if anyone calls asking to speak to you, tell him to say that you went back to Dallas," Asher said.

"That won't be a lie. I am going back. I have to. Staying here won't stop this situation. I'm not going to put my family in danger. I can hole up in my house as easily as I can here. I've given Dixon enough time to call off his dogs, which makes him think he's in the clear. But if there's any truth to this, Samuels won't see this coming, and if he hadn't given himself away, neither would I."

Asher sighed. "I hate to admit you're right. You're a really smart cop, Gunner. Just stay aware. I'll be in touch soon."

Gunner was now regretting he'd come home. Even the notion that his presence could endanger people he cared about was terrifying. All of his plans had just come to a screeching halt. Until the dirty cop was caught, he would be a constant target. He needed to get back to Dallas before anyone knew he was on the move, let Samuels know he was back, then set up a trap at his house and wait. If he was wrong, then thank God. But if he was right, they'd come for him there. His plans to quit law enforcement hadn't changed. But they were going to be delayed.

He glanced at the clock. It was just after 3:00 p.m. He hated that this was happening, but the sooner he was gone, the quicker any danger to Jacob and Pearl would be removed. And then there was Holly. He didn't want anyone to know he was in the beginning of a relationship with her. If someone wanted him dead and couldn't find him, they'd use someone he cared about to draw him out.

If he left within the hour, he would be back in Dallas around 10:00 p.m. His dad was busy in the bar, and Pearl was at the Rose, so he went to pack, loaded up his Jeep, and then sent his dad a text.

> Can you pop into the kitchen a minute? I need to tell you something.

Less than a minute later, he heard his dad coming into the living room and heading to the kitchen.

Jacob walked in smiling. "What's up?"

"I'm packed and heading back to Dallas. Stuff has come up that can't be ignored. If anybody calls here asking for me, just tell them I'm in Dallas and nothing more."

"What's wrong?" Jacob asked.

"I'll just say… The dirty cop may have just revealed himself without knowing it, and it could have put me in his crosshairs. But forewarned is forearmed. Asher knows and is working on confirmation, and I'll be holed up in my home, waiting. Just know that I am in no more danger now than I would be just doing my job every day, okay? It's just coming from another direction."

"Does your boss know you're going back?"

"He will soon enough, but I don't want that happening until I'm already there."

"What the hell, son? Don't you trust him anymore?"

Gunner shrugged. "Right now, Dad, I trust no one from that department, and that's all I'm going to say. Tell Pearl I'm sorry I won't get to say goodbye, but the sooner I leave, the sooner I get to Dallas and end this."

"What about Holly? I thought you two were hitting it off."

"We are. But she's in healing mode, and we'll reconnect later. I'll let her know I'm leaving, but nothing more needs to be said about her to anyone outside of our circle, okay?"

Jacob wrapped his arms around his son and hugged him long and hard. "Godspeed, son. Stay safe. Call when you can."

"I will. Sorry about all this," Gunner said.

"Hell no, you have nothing to apologize for, understand?"

"Understood. Love you, Dad, and I'm still moving back here. It's just been delayed a bit," Gunner said.

Jacob nodded. "Love you, too, boy. Love you, too." His shoulders slumped as Gunner walked out.

After all these years, Jacob had learned that the hardest thing about parenting was after the children are grown and gone. Whatever was going on in their lives from one day to the next was now off-limits and beyond his control.

Then he remembered where he was supposed to be and went back inside the bar, pretending everything was fine. He'd have to tell Pearl when she got home, but that was a secret to share for later.

Gunner pulled out onto Highway 86 eastbound with the sun behind him and didn't look back. He didn't want to think about things that could go wrong or the last memory of home he might have would be the Tumbleweed, disappearing behind him in the distance. He'd rather remember the feel of his dad's arms around him and the look of expectation on Holly Dillon's face.

The urge to call her was huge, but she'd just gone home to rest, and the last thing he wanted to do was give her something else to worry about. He'd call after he was back in Dallas, when there was more time to explain.

Once Dixon was convinced all parties had been notified that the bounty had been nullified, instead of being relieved, his embarrassment at being outsmarted by a cop began to overflow into his legal business.

Whistler became witness to Dixon's random acts of rage at other people, including his secretary at the office, the staff at the estate, and even the managers at his Dixon Down and Dirty cleaning services.

Whistler had never seen the boss so uncertain or afraid, and he knew it did not bode well for his place in the system.

Dixon's solution to a problem was just to kill all persons involved, and Whistler was now in that mix—because he'd let a cop catch him off guard, and in Dixon's eyes, that meant he was no longer trustworthy. Which also meant Whistler's days were numbered. Now he had to decide if he should just disappear or first get rid of the man who knew all of *his* secrets, and where they were buried.

Unaware of Gunner's hasty exit from Crossroads, Holly had showered, changed into pajamas, and then crawled up on her bed with her laptop to go through her email. Her boss at the realty office was sympathetic to her situation but was now asking when she planned to return, and she didn't know that answer for herself. The thought of her dad all alone in this big ranch house made her sad. And knowing Gunner was planning to move back to Crossroads made going back to Dallas even less appealing.

She was still going through the messages when Trudy saw her and knocked.

"Mind if I come in?" Trudy said.

Holly put the laptop aside and patted the side of her bed. "Of course not. Are you okay?"

"I'm as fine as any of us can be right now. Is everything okay at your work?" Trudy asked.

Holly sighed. "Funny you should ask. I just got an email from the boss, wanting to know when I plan to return."

"I wondered as much. Are you worried about your dad?" Trudy asked.

"Yes. When we leave, and Travis packs himself off to college, Dad will be alone. The thought of that breaks my heart," Holly said.

"I've been thinking the same thing," Trudy said. "If it helps for you to know this, I intend to move back to the ranch to be with him. Santa Fe is just where I went after I was widowed. It was hard to be here without my cowboy. I have friends in Santa Fe, but no one I can't bear to leave. What I can't bear to think about now is leaving my son alone."

Holly gasped. "Oh, Granny! That's wonderful. Have you talked to Dad about it?"

"We've talked. I think I've convinced him that the older I got, the less I looked forward to being alone, and it would break my heart to leave here again, knowing he would have no one to come home to when the day's work was done."

Holly went weak with relief. "I've felt the same way, and I've been thinking it was going to fall on me to stay."

"Absolutely no need," Trudy said. "Garrett and I will get Travis settled at college. You leave when you're ready. Don't jeopardize your livelihood for us. We'll be fine. Just take as long as you need to rest up before you begin that long drive back to Dallas, okay?"

Holly's shoulders slumped with relief. "Thank God for you, Granny. When Travis called me about the wreck, the first thing I told him was to call you, because I knew you could get here quicker. You are our rock. You always have been. You always will be."

Trudy gave Holly's hand a quick squeeze. "Family matters. Never forget that. Now you get some rest. If you want food later, there are countless leftovers in the fridge. Help yourself."

"I will, Granny. Love you."

Trudy smiled and patted her knee. "Love you, too, sugar," she said, then left Holly on her own.

Holly's relief was huge. She logged out of her laptop, turned off the lamp beside her bed, then crawled beneath the covers and closed her eyes, unaware that Gunner was already gone.

When Gunner stopped to refuel, he checked his phone again and found an innocuous message from Cliff, thanking him for the notes on the hanging-man case, that they'd arrested the brother's partner, and that Gunner had been right all along.

It was a good message to receive, knowing they'd brought another killer to justice, and then he thought about how he was going to feel, no longer being a part of that world. *Am I going to miss it? No. These last few weeks have destroyed all the faith and trust I had in it.*

The gas pump kicked off. He grabbed the receipt, got back in the Jeep, buckled up, and resumed the trip.

It was nearly 10:00 p.m. when Gunner drove into his neighborhood. But instead of driving straight to his house, he turned into the alley behind it, shut off his headlights, and used the security lights to guide him into the garage from the back way.

Grateful that the long drive was finally over, he retrieved his bags and deactivated the security alarm long enough to get inside, then reset it. The timer he'd set for the lights was obviously still working. The two lamps in the living room were on, and a light was on down the hall toward the bathroom, just as he'd set it. But if anybody had been watching his house, they should have figured out by now that the lights were on a timer, so he turned off the timer and went through the house, turning on lights as he went. If someone had been watching the house, they needed to know he was home.

He carried his bags to the bedroom, then went straight to his closet, unlocked the gun safe where he kept his service weapon, made sure it was loaded, and then put it by his bed and began unpacking.

The whole time he was putting up clothes and tossing others in the laundry basket, he was counting on something from Asher that would identify the guilty party and get the target off his back.

Cliff Beale had just finished typing up the details of the arrest they'd made on the hanging-man case. It was the notes Gunner left for them that set them in the right direction. Perry Caldwell, the surviving twin, was enraged and in despair, finding out it was Ron Ames, his own partner, who'd killed his brother, and when the police confronted

Ron Ames in front of Perry, he fell apart, admitting it all. Thanks to Gunner, this case was closed.

Cliff leaned back and looked across his desk to the empty chair where Gunner used to sit. That man had saved his life twice in the years they'd been working together, and he considered him a friend and a confidant, as well as his partner.

He missed him. Something had gone wrong between them, and he didn't know what. He was hoping when Gunner came back that they would be able to work it all out. Lieutenant Samuels told all of them not to call him. But Cliff had sent him a text and wasn't going to apologize for it. All he wanted was to see him walking back into the department in his long, hurried stride, with his usual blank-face stare barely visible under that black cowboy hat, and a zero sense of humor.

He sighed, logged out of his computer, locked up his desk, and walked out. Supper would be waiting, and he was on a tight leash with his wife.

Burgess Dixon was going home. He was fed up and ready for the dinner his chef would have prepared. He'd already sent Whistler to bring the limo around, so he locked up the office and headed for the elevator.

The trip down was swift. As he was moving through the lobby, he saw Whistler through the entrance, standing by the limo, waiting. He had depended on this man for everything for a very long time, but the man knew too many of his secrets. And after being taken down by that damn cop, Dixon was beginning to think Whistler was losing his edge. It was something to think about, but he couldn't replace the man until he had a surefire replacement waiting in the wings, and one he could rely on to do what needed to be done.

The evening sun was low in the west, but clouds were gathering on the horizon. It looked like rain, which would likely come in the form of thunderstorms, but he'd be home long before that.

Whistler opened the back door of the limo as soon as Dixon exited the building and closed the door after Dixon was seated, then took his place in the driver's seat.

"Home, Boss?" Whistler asked.

"Yes," Dixon said, then opened the door to the little bar and poured himself a stiff shot of whiskey for the ride.

Asher Kingston walked into his house with two bags of food from their favorite Asian restaurant, set them on the kitchen counter, then went down the hall to Nora's office.

Their son Jake was asleep on a pallet in the corner of the room with a stuffie tucked under his chin and a half-eaten vanilla wafer still clutched in his hand.

Asher smiled at the scene. Their son, blissfully sleeping while his mother's fingers were flying across the keyboard. She had an eagle-eye fix on her computer screen when he walked up behind her and kissed her on the cheek.

It was like turning off one switch and turning on another when she stopped, stood, and wrapped her arms around his neck.

"Ummm, I'm not in the habit of kissing the DoorDash driver, but I can make an exception this time."

Asher laughed. "DoorDash my ass. It's your hardworking husband just bringing home the bacon."

"Smells more like Pad Thai, fried rice, and egg rolls, to me."

"With fortune cookies," Asher said. "I'll get little Jake. I got the noodles he likes. Come eat while it's hot and tell me you've found something I can work with to keep my little brother alive."

Jake was already waking to the sound of his daddy's voice when Asher leaned down and gently scooped his son up in his arms.

"Daddy came home," the little boy said and patted Asher's cheek.

Asher kissed his little cheek, tasted cookie crumbs, and smiled. "Yep, Daddy's home. I brought noodles."

"Noodles!" Jake said and handed Asher the cookie he was holding.

They went into the kitchen where Nora was removing the containers of food onto the table and had Jake's highchair ready and waiting.

"There's my sleepy boy," she said and kissed the top of his head as Asher seated him in the highchair and snapped on a bib.

They began filling their plates, then chopping up some of the noodles in a bowl to make it easier for Jake to manage, and handed him a spoon. It was only after they'd eaten enough to satisfy the hunger rush, and Jake had abandoned his spoon and was intently focused on chasing down slippery noodles with his fingers, that Asher and Nora began to talk.

She began counting off the people she'd marked for deeper research.

"There are three people in that list who have serious financial issues. One gambles. One is paying alimony to two ex-wives, and one has a child with serious health issues… However, I feel like eliminating the one with the health issues, because their child is at Saint Jude's Hospital, and those children are treated for free."

Asher nodded, listening as he snitched the last shrimp from a bed of noodles and popped it in his mouth.

Nora was still itemizing her suspects. "I was just moving on to seeing if any of their names showed up in offshore databases when you came home. We can't overlook the possibility that it's all about padding a retirement fund. You don't have to be needy to turn bad. But you do have to be greedy and seriously heartless. Unfortunately, those traits don't show up in databases, so it's going to take more time."

"You're doing a great job, honey, and Gunner and I really appreciate it," Asher said.

Jake finally caught a noodle and offered it to Asher to eat.

Asher grinned. "You eat it."

Jake nodded and proceeded to lick it off the palm of his hand.

Nora rolled her eyes. "There's a piece of noodle in his ear," she said and dug it out with a napkin. "You never have to thank me for helping family. And you know how I feel about your youngest brother. He's such a loner. I wish he'd find someone he trusted enough to give his heart to. As soon as we finish here, I want to go back to what I was doing before I lose my train of thought, okay?"

Asher nodded. "Sure thing. I'll clean Jake and the kitchen, then bathe him so he's ready for bed. We'll watch some TV until he passes out. I'm home now, and you can be on your own time clock here."

"We have to do fortune cookies first!" Nora said. "You can have my cookie. I just want to read the fortune."

She cracked it open, pulled out the little slip of paper, read it, and then slapped it on the table in front of him.

"There you are! Wisdom straight from some dude who works at the fortune cookie factory." Then she got up, blew him a kiss, and headed back to her office.

Asher picked up the fortune and read it. *Perseverance will pay off.*

He shook his head and began cleaning up the table and his son. That fortune teller, whoever it was, scored with that one. Nora always persevered.

Chapter 9

By the time Gunner was ready to go to bed, he had everything set up for unwanted guests and the security system armed. He made a big deal of turning out the lights in the house except for nightlights and making sure the last light to go out in the house was in his bedroom.

Then he turned around and walked down the hall in the dark and into the spare bedroom at the end of the hall, locked the door behind him, put his gun under his pillow, and slipped into bed in the dark.

Even if somebody got past the security system, or broke into the house to get to him, they would go straight to the room where the last lights went out. It would be all the edge he needed to take them out.

He wanted to call Holly, but it was too late. And at this point, he couldn't tell her much about what was going on. He wanted Asher to know where he was, but it was too late to call him, too. Right now, the only people who knew where he was at were his dad and Pearl.

The last thing he thought as he was drifting off to sleep was, *Whatever will be, will be.*

As predicted, a thunderstorm came through in the night.

Burgess Dixon was awakened by the wind and thunder and turned on the TV long enough to make sure there were no tornado warnings, then turned it off and went back to sleep.

Gunner heard the wind and something rattling outside the window, then remembered he was in the spare room, and that had to be limbs of the lilac bushes slapping against the house.

He got up in the dark and went to the living room to turn on the TV for a weather check. Even if it was that time of year in Texas, this storm was all about rain. No tornadoes on the horizon tonight.

He went back through the kitchen, stopped to get a couple of cookies and a can of Pepsi, turned off the security, and went onto the patio. The weather was as unfettered as he felt, standing in the dark eating cookies and drinking pop—with the wind blowing rain against his feet and legs, and watching lightning flashes slicing through the storm.

It didn't rain in West Texas as often as it rained here in Dallas, but when it did, the storms that rolled across the High Plains were wild and fierce—kind of like the people who lived there.

He glanced at the clock as he was finishing his snack. It was close to 4:00 a.m., but since he wasn't going to work, it was far too early to stay up. He went back inside, reset the security alarm, then walked the perimeter within the house, looking out windows as he went, just to make sure all was well before going back to bed.

The next time he woke up, it was just after eight. He rolled out of bed and went to shower and shave. The blinds were open. The curtains pulled back. He was ready for the day.

He'd just finished cleaning up the kitchen when his cell

phone rang. He saw Caller ID and thought how fortuitous it was that he'd come home, because it was the body shop.

"Hello."

"Mr. Kingston, this is Bill from the body shop."

"Great… Is my car ready?"

"It sure is. Do you want us to deliver it, or…"

"No need. I'll get an Uber and head that way," Gunner said.

"See you then," Bill said.

Gunner immediately called for an Uber, then put on his shoulder holster and gun, added a lightweight jacket over it, and clipped his badge onto an upper pocket. His ride arrived a short while later. He set the security alarm as he exited the house, and after a quick glance around, hurried out to the car and got in.

"Where to?" the driver asked.

Gunner gave him the address and sat back for the ride.

Traffic was heavy. Runoff from the early morning thunderstorm was still flowing from gutters and into sewer grates as they took an on-ramp onto the Loop. He had a moment of déjà vu as they passed where the shooting had taken place, and then it was gone.

When they finally arrived at the destination, Gunner exited with a quick thanks and went inside to the man at the front desk.

"Gunner Kingston. I'm here to pick up my car. It's a black Mustang GT."

The man pulled up the invoice and printed it out. "This is the total amount owed. Will that be check or card?"

"Card," Gunner said, then waited while they ran it through the system, signed for the charge, and slipped it back in his wallet.

"I'll have one of the boys drive it around front for you," he said, then grabbed the keys and headed into the service area.

While Gunner was waiting, he received a text to rate the Uber driver, and when he did, he added a generous tip.

A couple of minutes later, a clerk drove his car up from the back parking area to the front of the shop and went inside. "Mr. Kingston?" he asked.

Gunner nodded.

He dropped the keys into Gunner's hand. "Have a good day."

Gunner slid into the driver's seat and retrieved his sunglasses from the console where he'd left them. Moments later, he was gone.

Now the real test had begun.

Had Dixon really called off the bounty?

Did Lieutenant Samuels actually know what he was talking about?

He was about to find out.

The city traffic was one thing, but getting back on that six-lane loop and trying to watch his back at the same time was impossible. All he could do was hope the hit was really off and no one knew he was back in Dallas.

Every car that rode his bumper. Every vehicle that roared past him on both sides. Every time the traffic slowed to a crawl because of some incident up ahead—the skin crawled on the back of his neck.

By the time he was home and pulling into the garage, his knuckles were white from the grip he'd had on the steering wheel. He sat in the car without moving until the garage door was all the way down, then got out, disarmed the alarm and went inside, then reset it.

He needed a stiff drink, but he decided to call Holly instead.

Holly woke up with a jolt with the sun coming through her bedroom windows and flew out of bed before she remembered that everything was over. There was nothing to rush around about, no random visitors to deal with. It was business as usual again, except for the absence of her mom. A quick sheen of tears blurred her vision before she blinked them away as she went to shower and dress.

She could hear people talking on the back porch as she entered the kitchen to get some coffee, noticed Travis's truck wasn't parked in its usual place, and guessed he was already somewhere out on the ranch. Then her focus shifted to the muffled conversation her dad and grandmother were having outside on the back steps.

Garrett's hand was on his mother's shoulder.

Her hand was cupping the side of his face.

The moment seemed poignant and private, but it dawned on her that her dad could more easily reveal his sadness and grief to his mother rather than to his children. A parent is always supposed to be strong for the family, but a man who's lost his way and his wife can still be a child in need of comfort with his mother. Seeing this moment between them was going to make going back to Dallas so much easier.

She poured herself a cup of coffee and put a piece of bread in the toaster, then buttered it hot after it popped up, and ate standing up at the island. She kept wondering what Gunner was doing as she went to gather up her laundry. The least she could do was take her clothes back clean.

A couple of hours later, her dad came into the house calling her name. She stepped out into the hall.

"I'm here," she said. "What's up?"

Garrett came striding toward her with purpose, almost like his old self. "Mom said your boss is on your ass."

Holly grinned. "I wouldn't exactly put it that way, but he did ask me when I planned to return to work."

He shook his head. "Baby girl. I love you with all my heart, but Mom wants to move home, and I'm all for it. At her age, she doesn't need to be living alone so far away from family. She thinks she's gonna be taking care of me, but I suspect we'll be taking care of each other, and right now, that's good for both of us. I'm not running you off, but if you need to go back to Dallas, then start packing."

"I kind of already am," she said. "I've been doing laundry this morning and thought about heading back tomorrow morning. I just want to spend one more night with everyone."

"You have my blessing," Garrett said and hugged her. "We'll all talk tonight when Travis is at the table. We keep forgetting that he lost two people in that wreck. Going away without Lee is going to be hard for him, and I need to reassure him that Mom and I will be the ones to get him settled at college."

"Thank you, Daddy. I guess finding a new level is what's next on our agenda."

"Yes, and for what it's worth, if you and Gunner get together, that will make all of us happy. Tell him thanks for standing up for you at the funeral. Mom told me what a pain in the ass Carl has been."

Holly smiled. "Gunner took care of all that. He's been a good friend during a bad time for all of us."

"The look on his face when he thinks you're not watching tells me he would like to be more than a friend. Now go do what you need to do, and I'll see you at supper."

"Where's Granny?" Holly asked.

Garrett rolled his eyes. "Oh, she's out at the office in the sale barn, rearranging everything back to how it was when she ran it."

Holly laughed. "I love it." And in that brief moment of joy, she knew they were going to be okay.

Garrett left the house, and Holly went back to her laundry. She was still sorting clothes when her phone rang. Seeing Caller ID made her heart skip.

It was Gunner.

"Hey, you," she said, as she sat down on the side of the bed to take the call. "What's going on in your world today?"

"Hi, pretty girl… That's why I'm calling. I had to make a flying trip back to Dallas last night. It's something to do with loose ends on an old case. I had to come back anyway, but I didn't plan on it happening this soon."

"Oh wow! You're already there, and I'm leaving tomorrow. My boss is requesting my presence. Will you have time we can spend together before you go back to Crossroads?"

There was a long moment of silence, and just when Holly feared she was about to get a telephone version of a Dear John letter, he started talking.

"There's something I need you to know, but you absolutely cannot breathe a word of this to anyone…and I mean, anyone."

Holly's heart began to pound. "You have my word, but you're scaring me. What's wrong?"

"I left Dallas because some Texas crime boss ordered a hit on my life and added a fifty-thousand-dollar bounty to go with it. I had no idea until the first hired gun took a potshot at me on the Loop."

Holly gasped. "Sweet lord, Gunner. Is it even safe for you to be there now?"

"It's hard to say. The bounty was called off after I confronted him in a way he did not expect. I came home to Crossroads because of that, but there are underlying issues regarding the whole thing that I can't ignore. I'm in Dallas to finish what he started, and right now, I don't want anyone to know about you or that you matter to me. I don't want them to know we're even friends. Do you understand?"

"I matter to you?"

Gunner sighed. "You know you do. We have had tacos together once, and funeral food together once, and I don't even know what your favorite color is. I haven't kissed you. We haven't made love, although God knows it's all on my mind."

Holly's heart was still pounding, but for a totally different reason. "Gunner Kingston, I am never going to tell you no. We barely know each other as adults, but I've always known your heart. I just never dreamed you would give it to me. I want it. I want you. And I will wait for as long as it takes. That's a promise."

He breathed a sigh of relief. After all of that, it hadn't scared her off.

"Thank you. Just give me time to fix this. There's so much more I have to share with you, okay?"

"Just stay alive. That's all I ask, and after I get back, feel free to sneak over to my place if you get too lonely."

"Giving it my best shot," Gunner said. "Text me when you get back to Dallas; just let me know you made the drive okay. I'll see if I can figure out a way to visit."

"I will," she said, and then the call ended.

She dropped the phone on the bed and sat staring out the window, shocked by what he'd told her.

After talking to Holly, Gunner was more determined than ever to end this, and using himself as bait seemed to be his only option. As much as he was dreading it, it was time to resurrect himself. He was hoping for some information from Asher before he walked back into the hornets' nest, but time was not on his side.

Dixon had opted to work from home today and was in his office. As usual, Whistler was nearby, but when he noticed the boss opening the safe and taking out the big black ledger, he frowned. The only thing in that book were names. Names of people Dixon used for different tasks. But it wasn't until Dixon walked over to the door and shut it in Whistler's face that he knew this job needed to end before Dixon ended it for him.

Unaware that he'd completely pissed Whistler off, Dixon was at his desk making calls, checking availabilities of the men he had in mind. He expected some of the numbers to have changed, but he was surprised by how many of them were deceased or imprisoned. His sources were dwindling with every phone call, and he finally decided this had been a stupid move. He tore page after page out of the book to remove the names that were no longer of value, then locked what was left of the ledger back in the safe and carried the pages to the fireplace and burned them.

Whistler smelled smoke, hoped the bastard had just set himself on fire, and walked out of the hall and downstairs.

Moments later, Dixon was standing on the second-floor landing, roaring out Whistler's name. "Damn it, Whistler! Where the hell are you?"

Whistler appeared in the foyer below the staircase.

"Where have you been?" Dixon shouted.

"When you shut the door in my face, I assumed you wanted me gone. Is there something you need?"

Dixon blinked. That man had never talked back to him before, and he didn't quite know what to make of it. "No! But you're my damn bodyguard, so guard me," Dixon shouted.

"I am, sir. Unless you're afraid of the staff, I always stand between you and the entrance to this house. Do you want me upstairs in the hall, or down here where I can see who's coming?"

The two men stared at each other in deadly silence, neither moving, neither speaking, until Dixon finally walked away.

Whistler's eyes narrowed at the sound of the office door slamming shut, then walked away, muttering. "Some days it just sucks to be you, doesn't it, Boss?"

This was the last night at the ranch for Holly, and she was watching and listening to the chatter at the table, storing up new memories for the nights when she was back in Dallas eating her meals alone, and no visits or dates with Gunner until he got the all clear.

Trudy noticed the pensive expression on Holly's face but said nothing. Parting was never easy, and this visit had not been one of joy.

"Holly, you said you were leaving early?" Garrett said.

"Yes. Tomorrow is Monday. Back-to-work traffic will suck. I'm shooting for an arrival between one and three. The noon traffic will be over, and the end-of-day traffic doesn't get bad until five. I'll plan on leaving before you guys get up for the ranch work. Granny can see that we're all out and go back to bed for a while."

They laughed and then called out "Good night, sleep tight," as she walked away.

She set her alarm for 6:00 a.m. and fell asleep.

The next thing she knew, the alarm was going off. She groaned, thinking of that long drive, then got up, dressed, and carried her luggage down the hall so as not to wake the house, then loaded it in her car.

She made herself coffee to go and a peanut butter and jelly sandwich, wrote I LOVE YOU ALL on the pad they kept for making grocery lists, and left it on the counter.

It was easier to leave without more hugs and tears. Maybe even a little cowardly, but it was all she could manage.

She sent Gunner a brief message.

I just left the ranch. I'll let you know when I get home.
Take care of you.
I need my Roadrunner to be safe.

She added her home address so he'd know where she lived, then buckled up and drove away.

Gunner's sleep was restless.

He was already up when he got the text from Holly and smiled. Good thing none of the guys in the department had ever heard him called that, or it would have stuck years ago. To them, he was just Kingston.

He was debating with himself about calling in to let his lieutenant know he was back in town when he got a call from Asher. He answered quickly, hoping it was good news. "Hey, Asher. Please tell me you have info."

"I know the Feds have info I'm not privy to. I know the Attorney General's office is working with them, but it's not shareable. We think Burgess Dixon is losing hold of his organization. Two more of his men were found dead. Supposedly they got into a fight and killed each other. That's how the police who caught the case read it. But the Feds also know both men worked for Dixon. They aren't sure if he's cleaning house for a reason or just running scared."

Gunner frowned. This was news, but none of it helped him. "So, nothing so far on fingering any dirty cops?"

"Nora is researching names in offshore accounts. That takes more time, and some of them are inaccessible. I'm sorry, buddy," Asher said.

"It's okay. I appreciate the effort. This kind of solidifies something I've been considering," Gunner said.

"Like what?" Asher asked.

"I think I'm going to go fishing?"

Asher frowned. "What are you saying?"

"If you want to catch a fish, you need the right kind of bait. I need to know if there's still someone out there who wants me dead, and I'm going to set myself up as bait and find out."

Asher groaned. "What do you mean? What the hell are you planning to do?"

"I'm going to let everybody know I'm home, then wait and see if someone comes knocking."

"That doesn't make sense. How will you tell if it's friend or foe?" Asher said.

"Nobody has been in this house but me and the cleaning company since I moved here, because I never invited anyone to come. Nobody will come knocking on my door to welcome me back. They will say it to my face when I walk into the department or not at all. Whoever comes to my house uninvited or unannounced will be here to destroy."

"I don't like it," Asher said.

"Neither do I, but I also refuse to hide. I finally found someone to love, and I can't even acknowledge her presence in my life for fear she'll be used as bait to draw me out. Understand?"

Asher was surprised. "You have a girlfriend? When did all this happen?"

"Not so long ago. I ran into someone from home when I was in Whole Foods, and she's all grown up."

"Well, don't keep me guessing. Who?" Asher said.

"Holly Dillon."

Asher didn't quite know what to say. "The little kid who was the bat girl for the baseball team?"

"Like I said… All grown up…and going through some serious grief right now since her mother's death."

"Dad told me about that. About Helen and some teenage boy hitting head on."

"The medical examiner's autopsy report told another story. Helen was already dead when the wreck happened. Massive heart attack. Likely slumped over on the steering wheel with her foot still on the gas when the boy came over the hill. He never saw her until it was too late because he was texting with his girlfriend," Gunner said.

"My God… What a horrible, freak incident," Asher said.

"Yes, the heart attack couldn't have been prevented, but if the kid had been paying attention to driving, he'd still be alive. It's been hard on the whole Crossroads community."

"Is Holly still at the ranch?" Asher asked.

"No. She's on her way back to Dallas as we speak. And I need this shit over with so we can get on with our lives," Gunner said.

Asher felt like he was failing him. "Since this has all gone to the Feds, I don't have access to much of anything now. If we discover anything else, it will be because of Nora. I'll be in touch. Please don't get yourself killed, kid."

"Don't plan on it. I have a woman to love, and a buttload of money to cushion the blow of early retirement," Gunner said, and he could hear Asher chuckling as he disconnected.

He sat gathering his thoughts for a few moments, glanced at the time, and as he did, noticed the date. Birthdays were synonymous with his mother's suicide, and he'd never been able to work up an interest in that celebration since.

"Well, hell. It's my birthday. Maybe I'll just pick up a cake to use as an excuse for a visit. Might even be inclined to strike a few matches and see what sparks," he muttered, then made a quick call to the bakery at his local deli, told them what he wanted, and was soon on his way to pick it up. He was armed up with everything but the bulletproof vest as he settled his hat on his head and headed for the garage. It was time to take a ride down to the precinct.

Lieutenant Andy Samuels was having lunch at his desk, as were the detectives still in the office. They were all kicked back, eating and chiding each other back and forth across the room when the door opened.

Gunner Kingston came striding in carrying a sack and a large, rectangular box that looked suspiciously like something from a bakery. The room went to an immediate uproar, with everyone asking questions and welcoming him back, all at the same time.

He put the box down on his desk, removed the lid, took paper plates and plastic cutlery out of the sack, and stepped aside.

"Yes, I'm here. No, I'm not coming back on duty yet. Today is my birthday; help yourself."

Samuels came out of his office in the middle of the noise, saw who'd caused it, and came toward him with a big grin on his face. "Good to have you back, Gunner."

"I'm not back. I'm just here celebrating my birthday."

Samuels looked down at the cake and burst into laughter. "Are you kidding me?"

Everybody crowded around to see the cake, expecting

to see a Happy Birthday greeting on it. But all it said was BULLETPROOF in big red letters.

"Enjoy," Gunner said, then gave Frankie Adams, their lone female detective, the side-eye as she sauntered up beside him.

"You should have the first piece!" she said.

"So, today your hair is green?" he said.

"Little sister's latest lesson at beauty school. The better to notice me," she fired back, and then saw the writing on the cake.

She frowned. "What? Is this like a money-back guarantee that comes with a product you're buying?"

"More like a statement of fact that *I'm* not for sale," he said.

His emphasis on the word did not go unnoticed.

Frankie wasn't fazed. "Then let them eat cake!" she cried. "I want the piece with a B on it. B for *bitch has to be mine*," she said, then she laughed at her own joke, took her cake and a little plastic fork, and winked at Gunner as she walked away.

"Do you want to talk?" Samuels asked.

Gunner shrugged. "I don't think so. Enjoy the cake." He turned to walk out.

"Cliff will be sorry he missed you," Samuels said.

"Then save him a piece of cake," Gunner said.

"So, you don't know when you're coming back?" Samuels asked.

"Did you talk to Internal Affairs about my concerns?" Gunner asked.

Samuels's face flushed in sudden anger. "I can't go to IA with just a suspicion or gut feeling."

Gunner nodded. "Then I guess it's up to me to do the dirty work, because I'm not coming back to work until I know whoever sold me out to Dixon is gone. A cop has to know who's got his back, and for me right now... That's an unknown."

He walked out, letting the door slam behind him.

One detective eyed Gunner's exit and then looked down at the cake. "He's really pissed. I suppose this cake is still safe to eat?"

A nervous laugh ran through the room, but a cop never turned down free cake. They cut themselves a piece and took it to their desks.

Samuels frowned. He'd just been called out in front of his detectives. He didn't like it, but he couldn't fault the man for being leery.

"Somebody save Beale and Rowdy a piece of cake," he said, picked up a piece for himself, and went back to the office.

The hair was standing up on the back of Gunner's neck when he turned his back on everyone in the room and walked out. This game of taunt and test was a little like playing Russian roulette, and it didn't feel good.

He got back in his car, ordered a catfish dinner from an area restaurant, then picked it up on the way home. He'd poked the bear with no way of knowing what would happen. Likely, he'd soon find out.

When Holly saw the Dallas skyline in the distance, she breathed a sigh of relief. Another forty minutes or so, and she'd be home. She was tired and hungry, and she knew whatever leftovers had been in her refrigerator would have to be discarded, but she just kept driving.

As soon as she got into her neighborhood, she took a side street to a fast-food place and picked up some food to go. Finally turning the corner in her residential area and seeing her residence was her finish line.

She went up the drive as the garage door opened and she drove straight in, then lowered the door before getting out—something she always did for safety's sake. After disarming her security system, she went in through the utility room and into the kitchen, set her food on the island, then began turning on lights as she went. She had lived in this two-bedroom, two-bath townhouse ever since she moved to Dallas, and even though the primary was upstairs, she loved it. Once she was satisfied her house was as she'd left it, she went back to get her bags, dragged them up the stairs to her room, then washed up and sat down to eat.

The burger was good. The onion rings were better. While she was eating, she sent a text to Gunner.

> I'm home, having a burger and onion rings. I'll go back to work tomorrow. I hope you haven't stirred up a wasp's nest for yourself. I've been holding on to all the precious things you told me like my life depended on it, because it does. Hope to see you soon.

She hit Send, then picked up an onion ring and dunked it in ketchup before taking a bite, wondering what fresh hell was waiting for her at work. Whatever it was, it was obviously stressing the boss that it wasn't done, and if it wasn't done, that meant there was a deed that hadn't been cleared from one owner to the next. She ate what she wanted of the food and trashed the rest, then went to unpack.

A short while later, she had everything hung up and was getting ready to store her luggage in the closet of the downstairs bedroom when her cell phone rang.

When she saw Gunner's name pop up on Caller ID, she dropped the bags in the hall and answered.

"Hey, you."

"Hey, darlin'. Did you have any trouble on the road?" Gunner asked.

"Not a bit, but I'm tired from the drive. What about your situation?" she asked.

"Well, it's a situation, for sure. I will say, this is probably the best and the worst birthday I've ever had."

She groaned. "Today is your birthday?"

"Yep. I took cake to my workplace and left them with egg on their faces. Now I have to see how it all plays out."

"I don't like the sound of that, but I know you are confident in what you're doing, or it wouldn't be happening. I promise I will not bug you or give you grief about any of this, but any time you feel like reassuring me that you're okay will be just fine with me," she said.

Gunner leaned back in his chair with a big grin on his face. "Why do I feel like I just got a pep talk from that kid who fielded our bats and foul balls?"

"So, was that too much go get 'em?" she said, then shivered when the soft laugh in her ear made her ache.

"You are never too much. I just need to make sure I am enough for you. I want this over. I want you in my arms. The end."

Holly sighed. "No, that will be the beginning. You have my address. Just let me know you're coming. And you can call me whenever you want. Personal calls are allowed on the job."

"I will, but for the time being, when you contact me, text. I might have my phone on mute from time to time," he said.

She frowned at the implication of caution he had to take. "Heard and understood. Happy birthday, Roadrunner. Goodbye for now."

"Bye, honey. Get some rest."

Gunner pocketed his phone and then went to his laptop and ordered enough groceries to get him through an undetermined stretch of isolation.

And Holly went back to stow her luggage, then sent a text to her boss, letting him know she would be at work tomorrow. Then she made a grocery list and ordered groceries online to be delivered today. She was too tired to shop for herself, and she didn't even have milk for cereal.

Ready or not, it was back to her usual routine.

There was one homicide cop who went home that night uncertain what the next move should be. Gunner Kingston had thrown down a warning that couldn't be ignored. The man was relentless. They all knew it.

But being made as a dirty cop was as good as being dead.

Chapter 10

DIXON WAS SITTING IN HIS DINING ROOM ALONE, EATING his ribeye because it was there, not because he craved it. He was still pissed off at Whistler for daring to talk back and had sent him to the kitchen to eat with the hired help.

He was bothered that the cop who'd been feeding him info had gone silent and tried to convince himself that it was because there was nothing to share, but it felt like he'd left something undone.

Whistler was eating steak in the kitchen and listening to the chatter from the rest of the staff. As soon as the meal was finished and the kitchen cleaned and set up for tomorrow, they would go to their suite, and he'd be going home. He had his own set of issues and future to think about and knew he'd soon be moving on, and if there was one thing he'd learned from his boss, it was leaving no loose ends behind.

Detectives Beale and Rowdy returned to the division to file reports on the case they were working on and walked in on a very subdued crew eating their way through what looked like the remnants of someone's birthday cake.

"Who died?" Rowdy said and laughed, then frowned

when no one laughed with him. "What? Did someone really die?"

Frankie Adams's spiked hairstyle was grass-green today, and she'd already been teased about it. But being outrageous was what kept the men from hitting on her. She thought it was funny they considered her too weird to fuck.

"Gunner was here," she said. "He brought cake. Said it was his birthday."

Cliff groaned. "Damn it! Is he okay? Why didn't he call?"

Frankie shrugged. "I don't think it was a celebration. I think it was a warning. His cake didn't have Happy Birthday written on it. Just the word *Bulletproof.* I'd say it was a message to whom it may concern, that he wasn't afraid of shit. He thinks there's a dirty cop in the division, and he's still pissed about the bounty that was put on his head, so I don't see him coming back until this is resolved. And since he no longer knows who he can trust, I don't blame him."

Cliff paled. Now he knew why Gunner had been acting so weird, but to think Gunner didn't trust him was a shock. *What the hell did I do to make him think I would hurt him?* He felt sick.

Lieutenant Samuels walked up behind them. "Gunner told us to save you and Rowdy some cake. It's on my desk. I've been staring at it for over two hours, so come get it or donate it to the cause."

Rowdy was eyeing the crumbs in the box. "What cause?"

"Cause I'm going to eat it if you don't," Samuels said and walked off smiling.

Rowdy let out a big belly laugh and followed the lieutenant into his office, picked up the two plates, and carried them back to their desks.

"Here you go, Cliff," he said and set it down on his desk.

Cliff stared at the cake, then pushed it aside. "I'm going

home," he said and walked out with his head down and his shoulders slumped.

Rowdy shrugged and ate both. By the time he was finished, the only people in the room were janitors. He tossed the paper plates in the trash and left the building.

Gunner was on edge all evening. He scrambled eggs and made toast, then ate them in the living room in front of the TV. When the local six o'clock news came on, one of the lead-in stories had to do with the mysterious, and as yet unnamed, winner of the Mega Millions lottery.

One of the co-hosts was teasing the other one, reminding him that whenever the payout happened, his identity would become known. Once that amount of money landed in a bank somewhere, someone was bound to tell all.

Gunner frowned. That was also on his horizon and would likely complicate his life even more. All the more reason to get the first monkey off his back before the handout horde descended.

He was still sitting in the dark, with only the light of the TV flickering in the room, when his phone rang. He looked down, then immediately answered.

"Hey, brother. Hammered any thumbs lately?"

Dylan laughed. "Nail guns, buddy. The hammers on our tool belts are just there to look sexy."

Gunner grinned. "Right… How is Angie? How is CJ? Still digging up worms in his mama's flower beds?"

Dylan laughed. "He's a busy little three-year-old, and he never stops moving. We recently had to fence in the whole backyard with an eight-foot privacy fence because he learned to climb over the other one. Angie nearly had a heart attack. We're considering razor wire around the top. We also built the new fence with the smooth side of the fence facing inward, so he doesn't have anything to grab or get a toe hold in. All of the braces and supports for the fence now face the street. It ain't pretty, but so far, it's climb proof."

Gunner laughed out loud, picturing it happening. Colter John—CJ, for short—was Dylan's mini-me in looks, but he had his mama's fire-and-brimstone temperament.

"I know you are not calling me to complain about CJ. And I'm assuming Asher told you I came back to Dallas, and I'm also assuming you know why. Rest assured that I have boarded myself up behind all kinds of security systems and Ring doorbells, and I am waiting for the other shoe to drop."

"I know you are good at your job," Dylan said. "But you don't have eyes in the back of your head."

"I know," Gunner said. "That's why I'm making them come to me. Because here, I have eyes everywhere. Understand?"

Dylan exhaled softly. "Understood. I just want you to be careful. You matter so much to all of us. We don't want to lose you."

"Thanks for calling. Love to Angie, and tell CJ that Uncle Gunner loves him, okay?"

"Will do."

The call ended, but Gunner's mood had lifted. He went to bed later, still thinking about the little monkey his nephew was turning into.

He was sound asleep in the back bedroom when the same vehicle circled his block four times, driving slowly past his house each time before finally driving out of sight.

Gunner saw the replay the next morning, and when he tried to get a close-up of the tag number and realized it had been completely covered, the hair stood up on the back of his neck.

And so it begins.

Dixon was in his office going over the bookkeeper's monthly updates on Dixon Down and Dirty services. All of the locations were making a profit, but his best locations were in the higher-income residential areas. So, the wealthy women of Dallas kept their manicures pretty, and Dixon's cleaning services kept their great mansions clean. It was a win-win situation.

It was the side job to his business that had raised red flags with the Feds and got him in trouble. They frowned upon using his cleaning vans to move drugs, and his special cleaning crews who changed the bedclothes only after they'd had sex in the sheets with the resident dilettante. Some people had pool boys. Dixon provided gigolos who did dishes.

His narrow escape from prison had come at a high cost. It was one thing to be in the drug and sex trade, but killing had not been on his bingo card. Still, Burgess Dixon was pragmatic. One did what one must to survive.

He had just pulled up the spreadsheet on the financials at one of his locations when the burner phone in his desk began to ring. He quickly unlocked the drawer and answered.

"You better have a good explanation for not answering my calls," he said.

The male voice in his ear was gruff but shaky. "Since you called off your hunting dogs, there's nothing to report, and I'm out. Don't call me again. I'm about to set this phone on fire, so don't bother trying to call."

"You don't quit me!" Dixon shouted. "I own you."

"You own mop buckets. If you out me...you out yourself. You went too far."

Before Dixon could respond, the line went dead. He stared at the phone in his hand in disbelief, and when he tried to call the number, he got a recording saying, "This number is no longer in service." He rolled his eyes as he dropped his phone back in the desk and locked the drawer.

"Son of a bitch."

Holly came to work early to put a thank-you note on her boss's desk for the flowers that were sent to her mom's funeral and then began sorting through her own messages.

The most urgent ones were follow-ups on deeds that had not gone through probate and needed to be updated so the sales of the houses could go through. After that, it was all about running down other deeds that had been misfiled at court clerks' offices in the surrounding counties. She had her work cut out for her today and would work through the oldest requests first and go from there.

The thought of Gunner using himself for bait to catch a dirty cop was horrifying, but she had to trust that he knew what he was doing. She knew he would initiate phone calls when it was safe for him to do so, but she needed to let him know she was thinking of him.

She reached for her phone and sent him an emoji greeting.

Gunner heard his phone ding a text. He opened the message from Holly, saw the good morning GIF with a sun rising above the horizon, and a good morning message to go with it, and smiled.

He returned the message with a kiss emoji and wished he could deliver that in person, then called a florist near her place of work and ordered her flowers and had them sign the card *Roadrunner*. He paid through PayPal rather than giving them a credit card number more easily traced.

Soon, darlin', soon, he thought, then kept going through that piece of video from the security camera over and over until he finally spotted something he hadn't noticed before.

On the driver's third trip past Gunner's house, he met a car coming from the other direction, and in the moment just before they were passing, the car's headlights briefly flashed on the windshield, revealing a blurry image of the driver.

He tried to enlarge it, but it only blurred the pixels more. He didn't have an editing program on his laptop, but he knew who did. He sent a clip of that video to Nora, explaining what it was, and asking if she could clean it up enough to identify the driver.

Within a couple of minutes, Nora replied, verifying she'd received it and that she'd begin working on it ASAP, and when she was finished, she'd send it back as clean as she could make it.

Satisfied that he was finally making headway, he sent his dad a message that all was well. It wasn't exactly the truth, but close enough for Jacob to rest easy.

It was midafternoon when a floral delivery man with a bouquet of yellow roses entered the realty office where Holly worked.

"Delivery for Holly Dillon?"

"That's me," she said and quickly cleared off a place on her desk for him to set it down. "Thank you. They're lovely!"

He nodded. "Have a good day," he said and hustled out the door.

At that point, her boss, Gene, and her colleagues, Leigh, Josie, and Lisa, stopped what they were doing and turned to look.

"Wow, Holly! Have you been keeping secrets from us?" Leigh asked.

Even before Holly took the card from the bouquet, she knew in her heart who sent them, but seeing the brief affirmation for herself was everything.

Roadrunner.

She flushed a delightful shade of pink as she clutched it to her heart. Twelve perfect yellow roses from the perfect man for her. Her eyes welled. *If only I could call Mama. She waited years for me to tell her I was in love.*

"Who sent them? Do we know him? Was it a client?" Josie asked.

The questions were coming from right and left. "None of your business. No, you don't know him. No, he's not a client." When her desk phone rang, she slipped the card in her pocket. "That better be from the Tarrant County Court Clerk," she muttered as she went back to her chair to answer, which ended her coworkers' moment of curiosity, but it didn't end Holly's delight. The roses on her desk were a beautiful reminder of the man who'd sent them.

Lieutenant Samuels hadn't been able to get past the look on Kingston's face after admitting he hadn't talked to the higher-ups about the possibility of an informant in their midst.

But Samuels had an obligation to also protect his detectives against false accusations, and he could not, in good conscience, do it without proof and a name to go with it. The thin blue line in law enforcement was real. They had to have each other's back at all times, and it was bothering him greatly that Gunner Kingston was so certain he'd been betrayed by one of their own.

He was standing at the window behind his desk when he felt a tightening across his chest. Within seconds, the tight feeling turned into a sharp, stabbing pain.

"Oh God," he muttered and stumbled out of his office. "Call 911. I think I'm having a heart attack." And then he dropped.

Six detectives came out from behind their desks so fast they knocked over their chairs getting up.

Cliff Beale grabbed his phone and made the call while Rowdy and Frankie Adams began doing CPR.

A silence came over the room, Frankie and Rowdy doing chest compressions and breathing for him—all praying for the arrival of the EMTs. Then finally came the thunder of running footsteps out in the hall, and they ran to open the door.

Another kind of orderly chaos began, getting Samuels stabilized to transport, and then silence again as they carried him out.

The detectives were motionless. The boss was gone.

Cliff walked back to his desk and picked up the phone again, but this time to call the captain to alert him of what had just happened. He spoke briefly, answered half a dozen questions, and then hung up.

"What did he say?" Frankie asked.

"Carry on and that he's sending a stand-in," Cliff said.

"Oh great," Rowdy muttered. "Hope they don't send some hard-ass."

Frankie snorted. "Anyone with a pay grade higher than ours *is* already a hard-ass or a badass. How about we just focus on our boss surviving this, instead?"

"She's right," Cliff said. "We know what to do. Like the captain said. Carry on."

It didn't take long for the news to spread about Andy Samuels's heart attack. Samuels had been divorced for years, and his only son was in the military and stationed somewhere overseas. His daughter lived in a nearby state. The detectives from his department who weren't actively on cases were gathered in the hallway of the ER, waiting for an update. The longer they waited, the quieter they became.

Finally, a doctor came out, asking for the family.

"We're it," Frankie said. "He's our lieutenant. What's the word?"

"He's stable. We're still running tests. He's going to CCU for continued monitoring. I assume his family has been notified?"

"One son, in the military, stationed somewhere overseas. A daughter notified and flying in." Frankie said. "Can he have visitors?"

"Maybe tomorrow, and follow the usual orders and visiting times," he said and went back inside.

A visible sigh of relief spread through the gathering.

"He is one tough dude, and we have to believe he's going to be okay," Cliff said. "This has been one hell of a day, and I think I'm done. See you tomorrow. Come on, Rowdy. I'll give you a ride back to the precinct to get your car."

At that point they scattered. Some took the stairs down. Others chose the elevator, until the hall was empty of cops.

Cliff let Rowdy out in the parking lot of the precinct, then called Gunner as he was driving home.

Gunner had just put a couple of pork chops on the grill when his phone rang. When he saw who was calling, he answered.

"Cliff... What's up?"

"Hey, Gunner... We had an incident in the department this afternoon. Samuels had a heart attack and collapsed. He's in CCU at Baylor Scott and White Uptown. I knew you'd want to know."

Gunner grimaced. "Damn it. Thanks for letting me know."

Cliff sighed. "You don't trust me anymore, do you? I'm not sure what I did to make you feel that way, but I'm sure sorry. I'm a fuck-up as a husband, and I'm going to Gambler's Anonymous, but I would never betray you. You've saved my life twice since we've been partners. I would take a bullet for you without thinking. I just wanted you to know," he said, and then he disconnected without giving Gunner a chance to respond.

Gunner laid his phone aside and turned down the grill on the chops. He didn't know what to believe and hoped to God Samuels didn't die. He had one question to ask that only Samuels could answer. *Who told you it was safe for me to come back?*

Smoke was rising from the grill up into the hood vent. Gunner shifted his focus back to the meat he was cooking, then dumped a handful of salad mix into a bowl and added some cherry tomatoes. He was sorry as hell about Samuels, and sorry Cliff was upset, but this was his life on the line, and if feelings were getting hurt in the process, then so be it. The longer this shit continued without a resolution, the easier it was going to be for him to walk away.

Later, as he ate, it dawned on him that with Samuels in the hospital and Cliff already acknowledging the distrust, it was likely safe for him to move around. At least for the time being. The truck that had driven past his house might not have had anything to do with him. It could have been someone just looking for an address, or a thief scoping out a place to hit. And with his security cameras in plain sight on both the front and back of the house, as well as on the gates leading into his drive, his house would never be a thief's first choice.

He wanted—needed—to see Holly. If ever there was a time to take that chance, it was tonight. As soon as he cleaned up the kitchen, he sent her a text.

> I miss you. If I happened to show up in the same Jeep I was driving around Crossroads, would you mind letting me in?

Holly wasn't expecting that text, but her hands were shaking when she answered.

> I miss you, too, Roadrunner. If you come a'running, I will absolutely let you in.

It was all he needed to know. He grabbed the keys to the Rubicon, left his hat and gun behind, and left the TV playing. Then he went through the house, turning on lights in various rooms, and set the security alarm before leaving via his back gate.

Getting on the Loop felt like running away from chaos. He was on the way to the answer to his prayers—chasing taillights of the cars ahead of him, aiming for the exit ramp that would take him to Holly.

Holly was standing in the dark in her bedroom, looking out the upper window of her townhouse, watching for his arrival. She knew what was going to happen between them. It was a heart-stopping moment, waiting to make love for the first time with someone you'd known all your life.

When she saw the headlights of a vehicle turn down the block and come toward her house at the speed of "trying to outrun the cops," she started laughing.

He was the cop, and he drove like he ran. She bolted from the bedroom, heading for the stairs as Gunner pulled up in the drive, exiting the Rubicon in long, hurried strides.

The door opened as he was coming up the steps, and there she was, silhouetted in the doorway from the backlit room behind her. Then she was in his arms.

The door swung shut behind them.

The first kiss lit the fuse.

The second kiss sparked the fire.

Gunner took a breath. "Where are my boundaries?"

"You have none. Like the land from which we come, the wide-open spaces of my heart are yours. All we have to do is climb some stairs."

He glanced at the staircase and then reached for her hand. "Stairway to heaven? I can do that," he said, and up they went.

She led the way to her bedroom, then turned to face him, but he was already out of his boots and shirt and reaching for the hem of her T-shirt.

Over her head it went, and then she stepped out of her shorts as he was reaching for his jeans.

He popped the buttons in one smooth move, and then the rest of their clothes went flying and they were standing face to face in total silence, as naked as the day they'd been born.

He shook his head, his voice gruff with emotion. "Beautiful from head to toe."

She held out her hand. "Come lie with me now."

So, he did.

Foreplay was not on their agenda.

Not now.

Not their first time.

This was for soothing the ache of desperation and answering all of the questions they'd been asking themselves.

In a tangle of bedclothes, with his hands fisted in her hair, he moved between her legs, into her body, and lost his mind.

Holly wrapped her legs around his waist and pulled him deeper, meeting him thrust for thrust until every nerve ending in her body felt like it had coiled itself into a knot—growing bigger and tighter to the point of pain.

At the moment of climax, conscious thought disappeared.

Gunner was moving on instinct until she moaned, arching her body beneath him and ending the last of his control.

He buried his face against the curve of her neck and took her over the edge with him, then held her close, riding the aftershocks rippling through them.

Their hearts were pounding. Steady breath returned in the form of soft, shaky gasps.

Gunner had collapsed on top of her, but he couldn't bring himself to withdraw.

Holly was still holding on to his neck and shoulders as if she'd never let him go.

Finally, he managed to raise up on one elbow and looked down at her face. "Where have you been all my life?"

Tears were on her cheeks, but she was smiling. "Growing up so that you would finally see me?"

He brushed a soft kiss across her mouth.

"I see you, Holly Dillion, but I don't play," Gunner said. "I don't second guess my feelings. I don't want to pressure you into saying anything you don't feel. But I am offering everything I am to you. You are in charge of how fast you want this relationship to go, and I will honor everything you need. But you might as well know now how much I want you, how much I care for you. I knew you first as a young girl on the verge. Now here you are again in my life, a woman who's torn down all the walls I've kept around me. You have to know, I am so falling in love."

Holly cupped his face with both hands. "I adored you from afar when I was growing up. Even after you left Crossroads, I would see you around when you came home for visits. And then I grew up and moved away and I lost that opportunity to let you know the woman I'd come to be. No more waiting for either of us, Gunner Kingston. Tonight was my pledge to you. It's you and me, from daybreak to sunset for the rest of our lives. We can fill in the blanks as we go."

He kissed her again, this time slower, reluctant to initiate the parting that was inevitable. "Fill in the blanks as we go is just about perfect. Right now, there are all kinds of blanks and holes in the job I used to love. My timing is all wrong, and yet this is the best night of my life. I don't want to leave you, but I can't stay."

"I didn't expect you to stay. Tonight was the beginning of us; now go do what you must. Just don't go and get yourself killed. I can't lose anyone else and survive it," she said.

He kissed her hard and fast, then before he could change his mind, got out of bed and began getting dressed. Holly got up and put on a robe, then walked him down the stairs. Just before he opened the door, he turned and held her.

"I love you, girl. Remember that," he said and then slipped out the door, pulling it shut behind him.

She double-locked the door again, then moved a curtain panel aside to watch as he headed for his ride. Broad shoulders. Long stride. She knew him now, and he knew her. An unbreakable bond would grow between them, but for now, it was love. Sweet love.

Gunner left with regrets for not being able to stay, but more at ease within himself than he'd ever been. Still, there were things yet to be done, and the lottery money was now a shadow in the background of his reality. Was Burgess Dixon still determined to take him out? Was there really a dirty cop in Homicide? Or was all the danger to his life over? He needed answers before he could acknowledge her existence in his life.

Chapter 11

Burgess Dixon was getting ready to go to a business dinner. He was treating the managers of his Dixon Down and Dirty sites to a night of fine dining. He could have just given them a raise, which is what they would have preferred, but these public get-togethers had been his habit for years, and no one was brave enough to approach him with the other option.

He'd lost points with all of them when the FBI began to dig into his business practices, although the managers and certain employees had been well aware of what was going on. The fact that they were no longer going to be called to testify at his trial was a huge relief for all of them, and this night was his thank-you to the managers for not betraying him as Freddie Welsh had done.

Freddie had been the manager of his first launch location. They'd known each other for years, and Dixon was shocked when Freddie agreed to testify against him. In Dixon's mind, it was Freddie's fault he was dead.

He gave himself a last look in the mirror, accepting that at the age of sixty-four, he looked like some boxer's old sparring partner. Nose slightly sideways on his face. Dirty-blond hair swiftly thinning. The broad chest of his younger years was down around his waist, and not for the first time, he was wondering where his green, frog-like eyes and cleft chin came from. He looked nothing like his mother or the man who'd been his father. So, his mother maybe slept around, but he never held it against her. He had sins of his own to worry about.

He picked up the phone and called Whistler.

"Yes, Boss?"

"Bring the car around. We need to leave for the restaurant."

"The car awaits, as do I."

Frickin' asshole. Whistler was still pissed. He could tell it. Dixon ended the call and put his phone in his pocket as he left his suite and headed down the stairs.

Whistler was in his chauffeur uniform, as requested. It was Whistler's public role in Dixon's life, and as far as the rest of the world knew, his only role.

Dixon walked across the foyer, then out onto the verandah, moving past the pillars to the white stretch limo. Once he was seated inside, he poured himself a drink and began sipping it as they went. By the time he got to the restaurant, he was relaxed and curious as to how much pushback he was going to get from the men who would be present. Freddie Welsh had been well-liked among the managers, but they all knew the score.

Whistler stopped in front of the restaurant, then jumped out to get the door for his boss. Dixon liked the attention of having his own limo and chauffeur for public affairs. As soon as Dixon was inside the restaurant, Whistler drove the limo to a parking spot and settled down to wait.

Wine was flowing. The food was four-star rated, and the ambiance of the location was everything it should be, but there was an undercurrent of reserve among them that made Dixon nervous. Then one of them made an announcement during dinner that sadly, this would be his last time to celebrate with them, and that he and his family were moving back to Canton, Ohio, to take over his father-in-law's business, due to his ill health.

Dixon frowned. "I would have thought you might have had the courtesy to let me know in person beforehand."

"Oh, but I did, sir. I personally took the letter to your office myself. I thought that you would be there, but your secretary said you were gone for the day. I saw her take it straight to your desk before I left. As I stated in my letter of resignation, I will work out the end of this month while my family goes on ahead. We're all worried about my father-in-law's health."

"Ah... Sorry about that. I took a couple of days off to work from home," he said and made himself smile. It all sounded innocent, but he and Freddie had been really good friends, and he had a feeling the man wanted out from under Dixon Down and Dirty before something similar happened to him.

By the time the dinner was over and the last manager was leaving the restaurant, Dixon was in a mood. He messaged Whistler to pick him up, paid the bill with a hefty tip, and headed for the exit, half hoping Whistler would be delayed and give him something to complain about. But Whistler was there, standing by the limo, waiting to open the door.

He glared as he got in. "Have you been eating in my car?"

"No, sir. I stood outside in the dark and ate standing between the two cars I'd parked behind, threw my trash in a garbage can, and sprayed my uniform with the lemon scent you prefer so no food odors would be evident." Then he closed the door and got into the driver's seat.

Dixon's eyes narrowed. Whistler was making no attempt to disguise what was obviously a very passive-aggressive attitude.

"Are we going home, sir?" Whistler asked.

"Yes," Dixon said and sat back as they left the parking lot.

As soon as they were home, Dixon got out and went inside, leaving Whistler to park and go home. He knew Reggie and Linda, the husband and wife who lived on-site, had already retired to their quarters.

Whistler parked the limo, got into his truck, and drove away. But he went less than a block before parking in an alley out of sight and running back to the property. He slipped in a back gate, then into the house, guessing Dixon would go straight to his office to check what was happening on the stock exchange before he retired for the night.

He stood at the foot of the stairs, still wearing his uniform and driving gloves while eyeing the closed doors on the landing above, then doubled his fists and started up. As suspected, there was a light beneath the door of Dixon's office. It was time to get down to business. He pulled a gun from the waistband beneath his jacket and walked into the office without knocking.

The look on Burgess Dixon's face was a mixture of shock and anger, but when he saw the gun aimed at him, he panicked. That was his gun! The gun he kept hidden beneath his desktop.

"What the hell?" he cried.

"You are planning to get rid of me," Whistler said.

"That's not true! I never—"

"Shut it, Dixon. I'm not stupid. The day you shut the door in my face was all the warning I needed. And since I know where all the bodies are buried, I don't see you giving me a gold watch as a send-off."

Dixon's gut rolled. All that rich food and wine from his dinner suddenly felt like an anchor. He couldn't think. He couldn't move.

"I wasn't trying to replace you, I swear. I'm down two men, and you know who and why."

Garza and Letourneau? Whistler shook his head. "Bullshit. You don't need privacy in this house to hire replacements for them. You have contacts far beyond the borders of this state. I've seen the way you look at me and the derision in your voice when you shout out orders, and it all began after that cop caught me by surprise. So, here's what's going to happen. I'm going to do you a favor and quit on my own. I always wanted to see Mexico. I think it's time to check it out. But because I don't trust you not to hunt me down later, I'm going to be needing a little insurance."

"Like what?" Dixon asked.

"How about the names of your cop informants. That way I'll know who to look for should you decide to use one to take me out. They'd easily get away with it under the auspices of a justified shooting. I want a list titled INFORMANTS, and then the names and contact numbers of every cop who has been feeding you information."

"That's absurd," Dixon said. "That won't—"

Whistler moved to the front of Dixon's desk and shoved the barrel of the gun between his eyes. "I get the names now, and I'm gone, or I shoot you now and leave anyway," he said.

"Yes, yes, fine. The names and then you're gone, right?" Dixon said.

"Right," Whistler said.

Dixon pulled some paper from an open ream on the shelf behind him and started writing, beginning with INFORMANTS as the heading, then one name after another, from different precincts and adjoining suburbs in the entire Dallas/Fort Worth area, until he listed them all and the contact numbers.

"That's it," he said and pushed the list toward Whistler.

"Fair enough," Whistler said. "And here's your gun. No hard feelings?"

Dixon breathed a sigh of relief as he reached for it, and the moment Dixon took it, Whistler grabbed his hand and shoved the gun to Dixon's temple.

"No… Don't… You said—"

Whistler squeezed Dixon's hand and trigger finger, just like he'd done with Garza and Letourneau. The little handgun went off, splattering blood and brains from the exit wound all over the left side of the desk and onto the floor.

Dixon slumped forward—his forehead hitting the desk with a thump—still holding the weapon.

Whistler carefully inched the informant list away from the spreading blood and stepped back to eye the scene, then nodded. *Damn, I am good. How sad. Dixon just committed suicide.*

But instead of a suicide note, it now appeared that Dixon had left an incriminating list behind instead, maybe as a last dig at the cops who tried to put him away. He was gone, but his intention was to take them down with him.

Satisfied by the look of the crime scene, he quickly exited the office, closing the door as he went, and ducked down the hall to the room housing the estate security system. He quickly pulled up the video feed and deleted everything that had been recorded right after Dixon walked into the house and Whistler was seen driving away. Then he turned off the entire camera system and hustled down the stairs. As he was going out the back door, he reset the house security alarm, then ran through the alley to get to where he'd parked, and drove himself home.

Gunpowder residue would be on the sleeve of his chauffeur's uniform, and blood could likely be on his glove and shoes. So as soon as he got home, he tossed the shoes and driving gloves into his kitchen trash, dumped some leftover

Thai food on top of it, and carried it to the dumpster. Then he gathered up his uniform, dropped it off at an all-night cleaners, and went home.

Chapter 12

Gunner was dreaming of Holly when he woke, rolled over to see what time it was, and sent her a text.

> Best night of my life. Love you. See you as soon as I can.

Then he rolled out of bed and went to shower and shave. A short while later, he was in the kitchen waiting for the Keurig to deliver his morning coffee when his phone dinged. It was a text from Nora.

> Check your email.

Nora had returned the video. His heart skipped when he realized he could see a man's face behind the glare on the windshield, but it didn't help. He didn't know who he was. Either it was somebody cruising to find a house to rob or a straggler who didn't get the word on the voided bounty hunting. He needed to talk to Andy Samuels, but the man was in CCU, and Gunner didn't know if he was even conscious, let alone able to talk.

He sent Nora a thank-you for the trouble and made a note to follow up on getting an ID from existing mug shots. He got up to get his coffee, poured a bowl of cereal, and was eating it standing up at the island when Holly sent him a text.

I couldn't sleep. You make me crazy. I won't be worth a nickel at work today. Love you, Gunner. So much. Stay safe for me.

He was grinning from ear to ear as he sent a heart-shaped emoji. *She loves me. Hot damn, she loves me.* He wolfed down the rest of his cereal and coffee and was getting ready to get back to his laptop when he heard sirens, and then a lot of voices, and looked out the front window. The moment he saw the patrol cars, he grabbed his badge, clipped it to his belt, and was out the door.

Patrol cars were already parked in front of the house three doors down. He knew the elderly couple—a retired postman and his wife, and he could hear an ambulance siren approaching in the distance. He jogged down to the scene and flashed his badge to the officers outside the house.

"Detective Kingston, Homicide. I live three houses down. What's going on?" he asked.

"Robbery. Old couple tied up. Cleaning lady found them and called it in."

Gunner immediately thought of the video Nora just sent back. "Who's in charge?"

"Detective Harmon. He's inside with the family."

At that point, the ambulance arrived. The EMTs rushed in, and a few minutes thereafter, brought the elderly couple out on gurneys, loaded them up, and drove away with sirens blaring.

Gunner moved past the officers and into the house where Detective Harmon and his partner were moving through the crime scene. Harmon looked up as Gunner walked into the room.

"Hey, Kingston. Long time, no see. There's nobody dead here."

"I live three houses down," Gunner said. "I don't know

where you are in the investigation, or what intel you've gained from the victims, but I have some video from one of my security cameras that you might want to see. When you finish here, I'll show you what I have. The house number is 440. Third house down on the west side of the street."

Harmon's eyes widened. "Thanks, man. We'll be there shortly."

Gunner jogged back to his house, pulled up the first video he'd captured on his camera, then went back to the living room to wait. A few minutes later he saw them coming up the steps and got up to let them in.

Harmon was all eyes as he walked into the place. Gunner Kingston was something of an enigma within the department. Not much was known about his personal life other than he was originally from West Texas, and then the big story about his mother and the armored car robbery she had been involved in before committing suicide.

"Nice place," Harmon said. "Oh… This is my partner, Jerry Rimmer. So what do you have?"

"I assume you've got people checking the area for security footage, but I have some from a few days ago that might interest you. My laptop is set up on the kitchen island. Follow me."

As soon as they were gathered around him, he opened the laptop. "The time stamp on this was just after 2:00 a.m. I didn't see any of this until the next morning," he said and clicked on the video, then stepped aside to give them the better view. "You will see this same blue truck with the headlights off circle this block four times in less than five minutes. The license tag is covered up. That was the first flag. They didn't want to be identified. Nothing changes about the video on the second trip, or the third trip, but as the truck is coming past my house again, you can see headlights coming at the truck from the other direction. Look!

There! That moment when the headlights flash on the windshield just before they pass!"

Harmon leaned down. "Back it up a sec. I want to see it again."

"I can do better than that," Gunner said, then clicked a few keys and pulled up the still shot Nora just sent him. "There's the driver."

"Damn… How did you—"

"I have a friend with a really good editing app. I asked if it could be made clearer. I got this back just this morning. Good timing, right?"

"Damn, Gunner. Your friend is good. But what made you want to dig deeper in the first place? I mean…besides the hidden tag?"

Gunner shrugged. "Everyone in my department knows this, but I guess they've kept it somewhat under wraps. A little less than two weeks ago, someone put a fifty-thousand-dollar bounty on my head. I didn't know it until the first hit man took a shot at me on the Loop when I was going to work."

Harmon's eyes narrowed. "That was you? The dude on the Yamaha?"

"It was me. And my lieutenant immediately put me on leave until they could find out who ordered it. I had an idea. Confronted the bastard. He denied it, but we came to a mutual understanding as to why it would be in his best interests if he called the whole thing off. Then I sort of crawled into a hole and waited for the all-clear signal. That's why I was so over-cautious about the truck."

"Good lord," Harmon said. "No… We didn't know anything about it. Glad you're okay."

"So far," Gunner said.

"The truck fits the description of one a neighbor caught on their security camera," Rimmer said.

"Good. If you'll give me a few minutes, I'll upload a copy of the video and the still shot to a thumb drive. You can take it with you. Help yourself to coffee if you want. Cups are in the cabinet above the Keurig. Cookies in the cookie jar. I'll be right back."

Gunner made a run for his office, grabbed a new stick from the blister pack, and headed back to the kitchen. Both detectives were sipping coffee when he returned. He popped the thumb drive in a port and began the upload, and then the still shot from Nora's email. As soon as the upload ended, he removed the drive and handed it to Harmon.

Harmon was all smiles. "Man, this is a big break for us. Thank you! We'll give you cred for the find and upload that still shot into facial recognition. If the dude has a record, we should get a hit."

"I don't need cred. Happy hunting," Gunner said.

"Stay safe, buddy," Harmon said, and then they were gone.

Gunner sent a quick text to Nora.

> It wasn't who I was looking for, but we just IDed a neighborhood thief. Robbery is on his ass. Thank you for the trouble, sister.

It wasn't any help for Gunner's situation, other than knowing the man was not connected to Dixon's list of hit men.

The next thing on his agenda was to check on Samuels. He called the hospital and got the news that Andy Samuels was in CCU but had been cleared for visitors.

Gunner's badge was still clipped to his belt; he wouldn't be carrying a weapon into the hospital, but he wasn't traveling without it. He put it in the console as he got into the car and drove away.

It was a morning for chaos in Dallas, as was often the case. Reggie and Linda Townsend lived in a small suite on the lower level of the Dixon mansion. Reggie was the resident caretaker, and Linda was Burgess Dixon's personal chef. They had been waiting for almost an hour for the boss to come down to breakfast and were beginning to be concerned.

"He's never late," Linda said.

Reggie shrugged. "Maybe he just overslept."

"He could be ill. Or had a fall. You go up and check on him right now!" Linda said.

"He'll give me hell if we're wrong," he muttered, but did as she asked and went up the stairs and down the hall to Dixon's bedroom and knocked.

When he didn't get an answer, his first thought was that he was already up and in the office, but to be sure, he opened the door enough to peek in and then swung the door all the way inward after what he saw.

The bed had not been slept in!

Reggie pivoted and made a beeline for the office, opened the door and then gasped, then turned and ran down the stairs, stumbling and shouting.

"Linda! Linda! God Almighty, call 911."

His wife came running. "What happened? What's wrong?"

"The boss is dead. Looks like he killed himself! Call the cops!"

"Oh, my lord!" she cried and ran back to the kitchen to get her phone.

She made the call, her voice shaking with every breath, and was still holding the phone when the police began to arrive.

In the middle of the uproar, Whistler arrived for work to drive the boss to his office. He parked behind the cops and got out running.

"What's happening? What's going on?" he said.

One of the officers stopped him at the door. "You can't go in there."

"I work here," he shouted.

"Who are you and what do you do?" the officer asked.

"I'm Beau Whistler, Mr. Dixon's chauffeur and sometime bodyguard. I drive him to work every morning. Why the hell can't I go in? What's happened?"

Donny Sheets, the detective who'd caught the case, appeared in the doorway. "Let him pass." Then he pointed at the room across the foyer. "You'll wait in there with the rest of the staff. We're going to need statements from all of you."

"For what?" Whistler roared. "What the actual fuck is going on?"

Reggie heard Whistler's voice and came out of the library and grabbed him by the arm. "We're in here, Beau. The boss is dead."

Whistler froze. "What? What happened?"

"I found him, dude," Reggie said. "He shot himself."

Whistler's eyes widened, and the stricken look on his face would have won him an Oscar.

"Well damn," he muttered. His shoulders slumped as he lowered his head and followed Reggie into the room.

Detective Sheets was well aware of Burgess Dixon's background and near miss at winding up in prison. He also knew there was gossip about Dixon being behind ordering a hit on another cop. And if that big dude who called himself a chauffeur worked for Dixon, he'd bet his retirement that he did more than drive a limo for the man. He gave them all a hard look and went back upstairs.

A few minutes later, Sheets came back to the library. "There are security cameras inside and outside this place. Where is the main system housed?"

"It's the door down the hall past the boss's bedroom. Everything is in there," Whistler said.

"Thanks," he said and went back up the stairs.

A few moments later, another detective walked into the library and sat down with the trio.

"I'm Detective Blake. I need to get some info. Names and contact information, and are you three the only staff that live on-site?"

"I'm Beau Whistler, but I don't live here. I just spend my workday here, or wherever the boss wants…wanted to go," Whistler said, then gave him his phone number.

"I'm Reggie Townsend. This is my wife, Linda. We live here," Reggie said. "We have a small suite of our own down the hall from the kitchen." He gave them his phone number.

"And what is your job here?" Blake asked.

"Groundskeeper, basic repairs on the property," Reggie said.

Blake nodded. "And you, ma'am? What is your position here?"

Linda was still teary and shaken. "Personal chef and minor household stuff. We have a weekly cleaning crew who cleans the whole house. I do the little stuff in between."

"So, you made dinner for him last night? How was he behaving? Did he seem different in any way?" Blake asked.

"Oh, he wasn't here for dinner last night. He had a big to-do at the Cattlemen's Restaurant for his Dixon Down and Dirty managers."

Blake shifted focus to Whistler. "And where were you last night?"

"As his chauffeur, I took Mr. Dixon to the restaurant, then parked in the lot to wait for it to be over."

"How long were you there?" Blake asked.

"Right at three hours, sir."

"Do you know who he was dining with?"

Whistler shrugged. "Like Linda said…the managers. Not sure how many of them were there because I didn't go inside. The list is probably on his laptop, but that was not in my job description."

Blake made a couple of notes. "Okay… So, when the dinner was over, what was his mood. How was he behaving?"

Whistler shrugged again. "He has a temper. I got the impression that something at the dinner set him off. He was kind of wound up, but the boss and I did not have a chatty relationship, so he would not have shared anything with me. I am an employee, not a friend." Then he wiped a hand across his face. "Was an employee. I still can't believe he's dead."

Blake frowned. "So, you expected to take him to work today?"

"He didn't tell me not to, but he also didn't tell me goodbye last night, either. He just told me to park the limo and go home, so I did."

"What do we do now? We live here," Reggie said. "If this is a crime scene, do we have to leave?"

Blake frowned. "Do you have someplace else to go for a few days?"

"No. It's here or a hotel. We could stay in a hotel, I guess," Linda said.

"Nobody is going anywhere until we've viewed security footage. Sit tight. I'll be back," he said, then spoke to an officer in the foyer and headed up the stairs.

Whistler knew the drill. The officer was standing guard on them until they were cleared, and he already knew what they would see—him letting Dixon out, parking the limo, and driving away. Then sadly, nothing more.

Upstairs was a whole other scene. It was the list of informants lying beneath Dixon's elbow that had caused the biggest stir. The congealed blood all over the desk, wall, and floor, and the gun still in his hand took second place.

The forensic team had already bagged the list as evidence, along with the gun and everything on the desk. They'd bagged his laptop and were in the act of gathering DNA from every surface, knowing full well that they would also have to take samples from the staff as a process of elimination, because their DNA was all over the house and in every room.

Sheets and another officer located the security system, but to their dismay, realized the system had been turned off. They booted it back up and then began watching within the time they left to go to the business dinner, to right after they came home. At that point, there was nothing more. They'd been hopeful answers would be in that video, but it was blank after that. Either Dixon had done it before he did himself in to keep from having his suicide revisited on video forever, or someone came into the house and did it to him and erased the evidence. But there was no evidence of forced entry, and the Townsends had already told the first officers on the scene that the house was still locked up when they awoke, and the security alarm for the doors was still set. The missing time frame seemed to suggest that Dixon turned it all off upon entering, then did what he did.

"But why the informant list?" Detective Blake asked.

"Maybe he knew something we don't. Maybe he knew the Feds were coming after him again. We need to find out. Maybe this list was his suicide note. 'Yes, I'm dirty, but so are you.'…meaning cops. If he killed himself without outing them, then they would be free and clear. Maybe he's just mean enough and resentful enough to want to take them down with him. We need to talk to the managers before any more suppositions are made," Sheets said.

"What about the staff?" Blake asked. "The Townsends live on-site."

"And they heard nothing. Seems fishy," Sheets said.

"Their suite is on the lower level, and down a long hall behind the kitchen area. They may have had the television on or were already asleep. The door to the office was shut when Reggie found him. It was a small revolver. Easy to believe they heard nothing," Blake said.

Sheets nodded. "Okay… If you have the staff's contact info, let them go for now. Warn them not to leave town and that we'll be in touch if we have more questions."

"On it," Blake said and went down to give them the word. "You two are free to go pack a bag before heading out. Stay with friends or family or at a hotel. But don't leave town. And you, Whistler, are also free to go, but same rules. Don't leave town."

The trio stood up. Reggie and Linda went to their suite to pack while Whistler walked out the front door and drove away, remembering the cop who had downed him like a felled ox. It still rankled, and he wasn't sure what he was going to do about that.

Detective Blake frowned as he watched Whistler driving away. There was no way he was "just" Burgess Dixon's chauffeur, but there didn't seem to be an obvious reason for him to want his boss dead, and his alibi checked out. This left the managers who'd been at dinner with Dixon last night. Before he left the scene, he made a call to the precinct and had another detective begin contacting the managers and get them into the precinct ASAP, with orders not to tell them Dixon was dead. They were only to say there were some questions about their boss.

The phone calls to each manager had them in a panic. They were all afraid of getting charged with some crime related to their boss again, but none of them wanted to end up like Freddie Welsh. Being the good guy got him killed.

Blake was ready and waiting when the first of the managers began to arrive. None of them knew the others had been contacted until they began to gather.

Finally, a man named Wilson Case was the first to speak up. "What the hell's going on? We get called here with no explanation, and I have a job to do. Unless I'm under arrest for some unknown reason, I'm leaving."

At that point, Detective Blake entered the room. "My apologies to all for the delay. We were given to understand that you were all present at a dinner last night with your boss, Burgess Dixon. Were you all there? Just hold up your hand if you were not."

"We were there," they echoed.

"During the dinner, did you see Mr. Dixon exhibit any unusual behavior or mention that he wasn't well?" Blake asked.

They all looked at each other, shrugged, then shook their heads. "Nothing," Wilson Case said. "He was fine, conversing with all of us. We had steaks with all the sides, and the wine and champagne kept coming. It wasn't a business dinner. It's just something he does for his managers a couple of times a year. Now, that's enough. We have a right to know what this is all about."

Blake decided to blurt it out and see their reactions.

"Burgess Dixon was found dead in his office this morning. First look is that he committed suicide. We're still waiting for test results."

The communal gasp was encompassed by cries of dismay, and then Wilson said what everyone else was thinking.

"I don't believe it! That man would never kill himself."

Blake was surprised. The vehemence of their denials was a little hard to ignore. Maybe they needed to take another look at the scene.

"Why are you so certain?" Blake asked.

"If you had known him as well as we did, you wouldn't have to ask. He was actually proud of his cleaning services. We just had a grand opening for a new location. Dixon Down and Dirty was his baby. Did you check his finances? His bank accounts? The man was loaded."

"What about the manager who was going to testify against him?" Blake asked. "You know the FBI fingered him for all of that."

"Well, of course we knew it. We were all grilled mercilessly for months by them. But asking if we knew anything again changes nothing. So, what do we do? Are we all out of jobs? There's no one left to run the businesses," Wilson asked.

The other managers were waiting, obviously satisfied that Wilson seemed to have constituted himself their spokesperson.

"I couldn't say. This will all be adjudicated through the courts," he said.

Wilson frowned. "If we aren't going to be paid, then we aren't going to work. Before we shut down, we will do payroll for money already owed to our employees and to ourselves, and then we're out of there. This is your official notification that we are shutting down today. The fleet of vans will be in the parking lot. The buildings will be locked with the keys locked inside, but you need to go back to the drawing board. No way did that man kill himself. Are we done here?"

"I got the answers I wanted," Blake said. "You're free to go, but be aware that an audit will be done of property and debts if he died without a will or an heir."

They walked out in silence, afraid to look back. That cop was actually looking for a killer among them, but they didn't have a motive. They'd just lost their jobs because of this.

Blake watched them leave, then shoved his hands in his pockets. He was about to return to the crime scene when he got a message from their captain.

In my office. Now.

Blake frowned. *Now what?* He headed down the hall to the captain's office and walked into a wall of federal agents.

"Captain?"

"The informant list found at the scene throws this back to the federal case they were working on with Dixon to begin with. One of the names on this list is quite likely the man responsible for giving away the location of their safe house, and for the death of four special agents and their material witness. We are stepping back and giving them access to all the evidence we gathered. They will run their own tests, but we're not investigating a murder, so—"

Blake interrupted. "According to the managers of all his Dixon Down and Dirty sites, they are certain he would never kill himself." Then he shifted focus to the agents. "You might want to review all of the evidence. You may be looking at a murder, after all, and there are three full-time staff members. Two who live on the premises, and the chauffeur who drives to the estate every morning. The husband and wife are presently at a hotel. Their info is in the file, as is the chauffeur's address."

The agent frowned. "What's the chauffeur's name?"

"Beau Whistler," Blake said.

The agents gave each other a look. "He's not Dixon's chauffeur. He's the clean-up man we couldn't nail, and thank you for the info. We'll be reviewing everything," the agent said, and then they were gone.

Blake looked at his captain and shrugged. "Oof... I did not see that coming. But I'm not going to lie; I'm glad to be rid of this case."

"As you were," his captain said.

Blake went back to his desk while the agents from the FBI were gathering up boxes of evidence to take with them.

Chapter 13

GUNNER WAS IN THE HOSPITAL ELEVATOR ON HIS WAY TO the Critical Care Unit to visit his lieutenant. It was just shy of eleven o'clock, so unless there were others waiting to visit, he wouldn't have to wait long.

When he got to the CCU waiting room, he scanned the faces but didn't see anyone from their precinct or anyone else he recognized. And when the clock ticked over, he got in line with other visitors, flashed his badge and ID at the door, and stated his name and who he was visiting.

"He's my lieutenant," Gunner added.

"He's in Bay 4. Ten minutes," the nurse said.

"Yes, ma'am. Thank you," he said and entered critical care, then went straight to Andy Samuels's room.

Samuels appeared to be sleeping, but his eyes opened as Gunner neared his bed.

"How's it going, Boss?" Gunner said and pulled up a chair by the bed.

"I've been better. But I'm stable and will be out of here soon. What's going on out there? What about you?" Samuels asked.

"Mostly staying holed up. Without proof, I don't really know if all the hit men are gone."

Samuels frowned. "I was told they were."

Gunner's heart skipped. "Right… I remember the text. So, someone told you that?"

"Yeah, Rowdy stuck his head in the office that day and

said the hit had been called off and everybody on the street knew it."

Gunner nodded. "Ah… Yeah… Rowdy always has his ear to the ground, right? Is there anything you need, sir?"

"I don't need anything but to get well, but thanks for asking," Samuels said. "And my daughter is on the way. I think her plane lands sometime late this afternoon."

Gunner stood. "I don't want to outstay my welcome. Get well. Talk to you soon."

"Thanks for coming," Samuels said. "You're the first, by the way."

Gunner frowned. "You mean, you've been in here by yourself since they brought you in?"

"I don't remember being brought in. They may all have been there then, but I don't need a babysitter. I've got pretty nurses for that. The team needs to be out there doing their jobs."

Gunner shook his head and gave Samuels's leg a quick pat. "Get some sleep," he said and left.

He got all the way to the elevator before he let himself be indignant on his boss's behalf. *A whole freaking department full of cops and not one showed up? Even if they were there when he was brought in, no one has followed up? Do you have to get shot to be worthy of a visit? Unless a crime wave has suddenly hit, they have a lot to answer for.*

But there was one positive thing about his visit. Finding out that Samuels was just repeating what Rowdy told him. For Gunner, that eliminated his boss from suspicion. But while he was driving home, he remembered something from the day Yankee Dan had been brought in to give a statement and how pissed off Gunner had been to find the old man still handcuffed with no food and nobody to see to his foot. That day, Yankee Dan mentioned something about talking to Rowdy, and the detective had not mistreated him, but seemed curious about him. Now Gunner wondered if Rowdy had actually questioned Dan about everything he'd seen and done before Gunner's arrival and read between the lines and told Dixon.

That was two black marks against Rowdy now. Something to dig into when he got home. But thinking of home brought him back to the robbery in his neighborhood and the two elderly people who'd been beaten and tied up while they were being robbed. If the Robbery division was able to identify the bastard from the still shot Nora sent, then they had the opportunity to find him and get him off the streets.

He wanted to call Holly. He wanted to hear her voice. God, he was sick of this cat and mouse shit. He wanted it to be over and wanted her in his arms, but not yet… Not quite yet. He had some digging to do on Tom Rowdy.

He exited the Loop and was driving into his neighborhood when he noticed a For Sale sign in a yard down the street.

It was the house that had just been robbed. The one belonging to the retired postman and his wife. That was fast! Bless their hearts. He didn't blame them for not wanting to come back.

Hours later, Gunner was still on the computer when his phone rang. It was Asher, and his first words were, "Are you okay?"

Gunner frowned. "Yes, why? What do you know that I don't?"

"Wondered if you'd heard Burgess Dixon is dead. It appears to be a suicide, but the only note on his desk was a list of informants. I know the Feds demanded a copy of the list, on the grounds that whoever gave away the location of their safe house abetted in the ensuing murder of their agents and the loss of a witness. They couldn't nail Dixon, but they're all fired up about the informant."

"My God...and no, I didn't know. We had a neighborhood robbery down the street this morning, and I went to the hospital to see my lieutenant after that. He had a heart attack at work."

"Do you still have reason to suspect him?" Asher asked.

"No, but a homicide detective named Tom Rowdy is the one who told him the hit was off and it was safe for me to come home. And Rowdy also talked to our homeless guy who was later killed by a hit and run. If Rowdy's name is on that list..." His voice trailed off, but Asher wasn't through delivering news.

"Then I may have one more nail to put in Rowdy's coffin. Nora has been researching all the names, remember?"

"Yeah, so what did she find?" Gunner asked.

"She mentioned it in passing this morning and wasn't sure it would mean anything to the big picture, but it was a rather shocking connection. One of the special agents murdered at the safe house was Tom Rowdy's brother-in-law. That could have given Rowdy inside knowledge of the location of the safe house, too, but that only matters if his name is on the list."

Gunner stilled. "You're right. I'll just have to wait and see how this all plays out, but it's now out of my hands. I suppose the Feds are all over it."

"I would assume," Asher said.

"Right... Anyway... Thank you for the info," Gunner said.

"Any time, brother," Asher said and hung up.

Gunner leaned back, absorbing the new information. With Dixon dead, and Samuels and Cliff no longer under his suspicion, and the Feds all over the list, it felt like the skies were clearing faster than he'd hoped.

He glanced at the clock. Nearly 5:00 p.m. If Holly wasn't working late, she'd be getting ready to head home. The usual suspects were either dead or cleared of his suspicions. And with Dixon dead, there would be no automatic guilty party for someone else to blame if they wanted to take a potshot at him.

The storm in his life was passing. He was ready for blue skies.

The phone was still in his hands, and the thought of Holly in his arms was too strong to deny.

She answered on the second ring.

"Hello?"

"Hey, darlin'. How's your day been?"

Hearing his voice became the best part of her day. "Crazy busy, but winding down. How about you?"

"I could say productive and not tell you a lie. Do you have plans for tonight?"

Her heart skipped. "No."

He shifted from one foot to the other. "I would love to have dinner with you and stuff." Her laugh sent shivers up his spine.

"Fabulous idea. What's your plan?"

"If you're too tired to go out, I can bring dinner to you," he said.

"I'd love that," she said. "I had peanut butter crackers and a Pepsi at my desk. I'm starving, and I don't care what we eat."

Now he was beaming. "Great. Is seven o'clock a good time?"

"The best. Do you have plans tomorrow?" she asked.

"I'm not on any schedule, if that's what you mean," he said.

"Then feel free to bring your toothbrush and a change of clothes. We live too far apart for all this driving," she said.

"That's the best invitation I've ever had. I won't have to sleep with my teddy bear tonight."

She laughed out loud. "You do not sleep with a teddy bear."

"Well, maybe not anymore… But only because it finally fell apart. I can't wait to see you again. I have a small confession to make. It's not bad, but it's something you sure need to know, okay?"

"You're always okay, with me. See you soon. Love you, Gunner."

"Love you more," he said, and the call ended. He was smiling the whole time he was packing. Choosing food to order was a whole other thing, but he knew he could do better than peanut butter crackers.

A few minutes later, he was calling in an order to pick up and driving the Mustang. No more hide-and-seek.

Holly shut down her computer, gave her roses a quick sniff, and then headed out the door.

"See you guys tomorrow," she said.

"What's the rush?" her boss asked.

"I worked through my lunch hour, remember? My tummy has been complaining about not being fed. Going home to eat and relax. See you all tomorrow."

Then when she left work, she decided to take the old way home and skip the Loop. Five o'clock traffic on it was the fifth circle of hell, and she had yet to get home without seeing at least one wreck.

She'd never slept all night with a man before. But she'd also never been so certain of a forever love. She didn't want to take a chance on being delayed due to traffic, and as she drove through the city streets, she was remembering the quiet on the ranch and lack of traffic jams on the highway.

Coming to terms with her mother's death now had nothing to do with a traffic or a collision. She'd grown up hearing her mother say over and over, "When it's your time to go, it's your time to go, and any other decision is not ours to make."

The last time Holly called home, Travis answered. When she asked him how things were going, his only comment was that they were burying Lee Peters in Tulsa today, and the family was already gone.

All she'd said was, "I love you."

There was nothing to be said in defense of that death. It was a tragedy, and life was full of them.

When she finally arrived at her townhouse and parked in the garage, the first thing she did was go shower. Her home was cool, but it was the hot time of year in Texas, and dressing for the heat was a must. She chose slip-on sandals, a pale-green T-shirt, and a pair of white pull-up shorts. They weren't going out, and she seriously doubted if they'd be dressed all that long, either, so shorts it was.

As she settled in to wait, she was curious as to the confession Gunner said he was going to make and wondering what deliciousness he was bringing for them to eat.

Gunner was on a mission and had just picked up their food. He hoped she liked Thai and sushi, because that's what he was bringing. He'd come a long way from his hamburger patties and french fries he preferred as a kid. Living in a big city could do that to a man. But he'd never found anyone here who made better pies than Pearl Fallon. In Crossroads, she was the queen of cuisine, and he loved that she and his dad had reconnected. It was going to be great living close to them again.

It was still daylight when he arrived at her house. He got out, grabbed his overnight bag and their food, and headed for the door.

He didn't have to knock.

"You're here!" Holly said and gave him a quick kiss. "Let me have your bag. I'll leave it at the foot of the stairs. The little dining area is that way. I'm right behind you."

Her energy was like stepping into a whirlwind. Before he had time to think, she'd parked his bag and was in the kitchen behind him. He put down the bag with the food.

"I'm gonna need to do this greeting thing all over again," he said, then slid his arms around her and kissed her like he needed it to breathe.

When they finally came up for air, Holly was weak in the knees and uncertain whether it had to do with him or her lack of food.

Reluctant to let her go, he tunneled his fingers through her curls, marveling at their tendencies to curl around his fingers like vines. *I'm already caught and don't give a damn. God, she's worth it.* Then he kissed the middle of her forehead and let her go.

"I hope you like Thai and sushi. I didn't get anything raw, though. Okay?"

She laughed. "I love it all, if it's cooked."

He breathed a sigh of relief. "Good. You get plates. I'll get the boxes out of the bag."

She brought the plates and flatware and then went to make their drinks. "Sweet tea, pop, or beer?" she asked.

"Sweet tea, please, and yes, I'm gonna need one of those forks. Me and chopsticks have never made friends."

"This is so fun. Thank you for bringing it here," she said and went to fix their drinks.

As soon as she sat, it felt just like the day she met him at the taqueria for an early supper. Like they were just picking up from where they'd left off all those years ago.

"They have little labels on the sides of the boxes with the names of the dishes, and the same with the sushi. One is a veggie roll, and one has smoked salmon. And the sauces are there, too."

"Did you get wasabi?" she asked.

"Wow… Didn't see that coming," he said. "I sure did. It's a must for me, too, when I want sushi. I think there's some inside each tray of sushi."

"Oh! Yes, I see it," Holly said and scooped a little bit onto her plate along with a couple pieces from each roll.

They talked as they ate, adding a serving of something new when they'd made room on their plates.

Holly was eyeing the chicken-veggie stir-fry he was eating. "Is that good?"

He pushed his plate toward her. "Take a bite and see what you think. It's spicy, but since you handle wasabi like a boss, I don't think this will bother you."

She tasted, then rolled her eyes in delight. "That's delicious, and the sweet chili sauce with the chicken and veggies is the best." She put some onto her plate, and the meal continued.

"What's your day been like?" she asked.

So, he told her about the robbery, and the video, and then going to visit his boss.

"Also, Asher called with some news. I'm sure it's all over the local news tonight, but I wasn't watching. Remember I told you about how I suspected Burgess Dixon of being the one who put the hit out on me?"

Still chewing, she nodded, then swallowed and reached for her glass.

"So, they found him dead in his office this morning. I

don't know any details, but it appears to have been suicide. So whatever mayhem he might have still been planning, it's not happening now."

Holly gasped. "Oh, my lord! Is it wrong to call that good news?"

"Not from where I'm sitting," Gunner said. "And there's something else. About that confession I need to make."

She reached across the table and gave his hand a quick squeeze. "Just spit it out and then it's done. Nothing is ever going to change my opinion of you or how much I love you."

"You would love me no matter what?" he asked.

"No matter what."

"How can you know it's not something bad?"

She shrugged. "Because I know you. You never could lie. You punched a kid for making me cry once. And you always gave me the biggest piece of your cookie. You're one of the good guys."

He smiled. "Best bat girl, ever. Okay... So here goes. You remember asking me about someone finally winning the Mega Millions lottery?"

She nodded.

"So... That was me. My lawyer and I went to the Dallas Claims Center. I told my family, my boss, and now I'm telling you."

He was watching the disbelief in her face moving to shock, and then unmitigated joy.

"Are you serious?"

"As a heart attack, darlin'. I chose the lump sum. The payout is a little over four hundred and fifty-eight million dollars. It takes a few weeks for it to show up in my account, but I set up a separate account for it."

Holly bolted from her chair. He knew she was going to land hard unless he stood up, and he was right. She launched herself into his arms, laughing and crying, and then laughing all over again.

"Oh my God, oh my God. How wonderful for you, sweetheart!"

He frowned. "Well hell, Holly. Not just for me. For us. We can go back to Crossroads without worrying about where we're going to work. We'll be close to family again. I've already picked out a location to build on. But I'm waiting for the money to get in the bank before I start spending some of it."

"You were given such a blessing!" she said.

He nodded. "And then the universe decided to make me earn it. Having a bounty put on my head left me wondering if I'd live long enough to claim it."

"What a nightmare, and all this time you were carrying that concern alone. I'm so sorry."

"But I'm not alone anymore, thanks to you. And now that Dixon offed himself, the danger to my life is over. I know that, too. So, that's my confession, but I still need to keep it quiet."

She nodded. "Done."

"Thank you," he said.

She frowned. "For what?"

"For loving me even when I was still a sitting duck," he said.

Holly shrugged. "Couldn't help it. I've loved you during all the years when half the population of Crossroads was still whispering your mother's name behind your back. I loved you more after you carried me across the baseball field to my mom and dad after I got hit on the head. I have huge regrets for not being able to remember it. And I loved you all over again when you put Carl Warwick in his place at Mama's funeral. Money or not, when you finally saw me as a woman and not a child, I could not see my life without you, either."

"I do not deserve you. But you have sealed your fate with me. I'm a hard man to love, and I know it. I've shunned women for years because of nothing more than a lack of trust, and that all goes back to my abandonment issues as a kid. I've gone to therapy about it, but it didn't take. . .until you. You didn't just break down the wall I've lived behind. You climbed over and made me look at you. I love you, girl, but you're the one in charge of how fast this all goes. Deal?"

"Deal," she said.

He laid his cheek against the top of her head and hugged her.

His confession had become their dessert. After that kind of news, the meal was over. They stored leftovers together, cleaned up the kitchen together, and finally returned to the living room to watch some TV.

"What do you usually do in the evenings?" he asked as they settled down on the sofa.

"Watch TV. Sometimes, I read the paper online. Just normal stuff," she said.

"Are you going to be okay with giving up your job and the big-city living?"

"Lord, yes. When I left work today, I took the old-fashioned way home, driving through city streets to get to my neighborhood because I wanted nothing to do with the Loop. All the way here, I kept thinking of where I grew up, and how we'd never had to deal with real traffic anywhere, unless we were in Amarillo, or on the road to some rodeo or horse show. Crossroads doesn't have traffic problems. Even Mom's death had nothing to do with traffic. Are you sure you want to give up law enforcement?"

He shrugged. "When someone wants you dead, and you don't know who to trust anymore, or who's safe to turn your back on, then the job loses all of its shine. I know someone in my family needs to be closer to my dad and Pearl. They are fine right now, but with age comes hardships in mobility and health. I don't want them to be dealing with all that on their own."

She slipped her hand through the crook of his arm and laid her head on his shoulder. "That's how I felt about leaving Dad. Travis is going to college this fall, and I couldn't bear thinking of him in that big house on his own. When I found out Granny was going to come back to the ranch and live with him, it was the best news ever. They're both happy about it, which alleviates whatever guilt I had coming back here."

"And now here I come barging into your life, requiring you to readjust again. I promise you will not be sorry, okay?"

"My darling, Gunner, you are the best thing that's happened to me. I promise not to be a royal pain in the ass, okay?"

He laughed. "Back in the day, I kinda liked watching you pitch a fit. You were damn good at it."

She gave him a look. "Daddy always said it comes with the hair. But my hair is not red, it's auburn," she added.

Gunner burst out laughing, and in that moment, the sound of his own laughter shattered the last brick in his wall.

Two hours later, the movie they'd chosen to watch was over, and Holly was asleep with her head in Gunner's lap, safely secure beneath the gentle touch of his hand on her shoulder.

She woke up when he turned off the TV, and she sat up with a groan.

"Some hostess I am. I fell asleep on you," she muttered.

"Girl, I did not come here just to be waited on. I came here because I love you. And if you're in the right frame of mind, to also make love with you, and know what it's like to sleep with you curled up behind my back."

"I'm in that frame of mind, but I need to set the security alarm," she said, then got up and quickly keyed in the code.

"Lights on or off downstairs?" he asked.

"There's a nightlight at the foot of the stairs and one on the landing. They'll come on when the lights above go out."

"Perfect, just like you," he said, then picked up his bag and followed her up.

"I'm going to wash up while you unpack," she said. "You can hang your stuff in my closet or on that hook on the back of the door."

"Thanks, darlin'," he said and put his bag on the bed, then pulled out a pair of jeans and a shirt and was putting them on hangers when she came out of the bathroom.

Gunner had already kicked off his boots and was holding the bag with his shaving stuff in it when she walked out. His heart skipped, then pounded once so hard against his chest that he felt the thud. The only thing she was wearing was a smile.

"Uh..."

She waved her hand at him in an offhand manner. "I sleep in the nude. Take your time, sweetheart," she said and began to turn back the bed.

Holy shit. Take my time? That might not be happening.

He headed for the bathroom with his toiletry bag and washed up and stripped in ten seconds flat. When he came out of the bathroom, the lights were off and she was lying on the sheets with the covers at her feet, waiting. He flipped off the bathroom light, leaving them bathed in the blue aura of her nightlight.

She turned to face him as he lay down beside her. Her skin was like silk, and the graceful curve of her neck fit perfectly into the palm of his hand.

"Your eyes are the color of bluebonnets."

She brushed her thumb across his lower lip. "When I was younger, I thought your eyes were dark because you were sad. Now when I see you, those dark eyes melt me where I stand. You are one big, beautiful man, Gunner Kingston." And then she put the flat of her hand on his chest. "Your heartbeat is as sure and steady as you are."

"The better to love you with," he said and lowered his head.

Then his mouth was on her lips, then down to the hollow at the base of her throat, following the trail through the valley between her breasts.

Holly lost focus after his hand slipped between her legs, and then the room began to spin. When he moved over her, then inside her, she closed her eyes and went along for the ride.

Nerve endings were flashing and flaring, winding up the ache within her, dancing to the rhythm of the act of making love. One slow steady stroke after another, over and over without stopping, until finally the climax washed over them, and when it did the music stopped.

Gunner's arms were tight around her, holding her until the drumbeat of their hearts began to fall back into normal rhythm, then he pulled the covers up over both of them and kissed her softly as he watched her eyes beginning to close.

"Love you," she said.

"Love you more. Sweet dreams," he said.

And the room went quiet.

Traffic was intermittent outside the townhouse apartment complex. The later it became, the less traffic passed by.

Gunner was sound asleep when he felt Holly stir, then mutter.

"Did I just dream it when you said you won the lottery?"

He grinned. "No. It's real."

She sighed. “Okay,” she mumbled and rolled over.

He rolled with her, tucking her into the curve of his body and closed his eyes, and didn’t know anything more until the alarm on her cell phone went off.

Holly mumbled beneath her breath and reached for the phone to shut it off.

“I wasn’t ready for that,” he heard her mumble, then opened his eyes just in time to see her and her naked backside as she walked into the bathroom.

He rolled over, waited for the sound of the shower to come on, and then got up, slipped into the shower with her, and changed her attitude altogether.

By the time they dressed, they had just enough time for toast and coffee before Holly had to leave for work.

Gunner kissed her cheek to keep from messing up her makeup.

“Light of my life, you look beautiful. Raise all the hell you need at work and have the best day. I’ll call you tonight.”

She was on the doorstep waving as he backed out and drove away, and then she grabbed her things, set the security alarm, and left on the run.

That morning shower had completely messed with her body clock and routine, but it was the best damn shower she’d ever had.

Chapter 14

GUNNER DROVE STRAIGHT HOME, UNPACKED AND PUT his clothes in the laundry, and went to the kitchen. The toast he'd eaten at Holly's had just been an appetizer, so he poured himself a bowl of cereal and took it to the table to eat, then decided to check messages while he ate. The first message he saw was from his bank. It finally happened! The lottery money had been deposited into his new account this morning. That was weeks earlier than he'd expected, but he wasn't going to complain.

The first thing he did was sit down and make a phone call to the financial advisor his lawyer had set him up with. After a few minutes on the phone, he knew exactly what to do and when to do it.

But now that that had happened, he also accepted someone in the bank would leak the name, and he wanted to get to the precinct and tell them first. He already had his official resignation written and printed out, so he was taking that with him. He strapped on his gun, clipped his badge to his belt, and settled the black hat on his head as he headed for the garage.

After forty minutes and bypassing two wrecks on the Loop, he was pulling into the parking lot. He got the bulletproof vest out of the trunk and took everything inside with him.

Samuels's replacement turned out to be Lieutenant Greg Rance, an early riser who was already in the office.

Detectives were straggling in two and three at a time when Gunner walked in. Cliff was already at his desk, and Frankie Adams waved at him from across the room.

Gunner pointed at his hair with a questioning look.

"Passionate purple!" she shouted.

He gave her a thumbs-up, and their interchange got everyone else's attention. At that point, they began gathering around him, teasing him about being able to duck, and glad to see him back.

Cliff got up smiling. "Man, am I ever glad to see you. We all heard about Dixon. I guess the heat is off on you now."

"Hard to say. Samuels thinks it is. I had a text from him, but that was before his heart attack. That must have scared the shit out of all of you."

Cliff nodded. "Frankie and I started CPR and then switched out with two more and kept at it until the ambulance arrived. I don't want to have to do that again."

"He's doing good," Gunner said. "I went to see him yesterday. He was in there on his own. FYI… If you were with him at the hospital when they brought him in, he doesn't remember that. He thinks he's been there on his own. He said his daughter was due in yesterday afternoon, so I guess he's not alone now."

The detectives who'd gathered all stared at each other with a mixture of surprise and guilt. "We did go! At least ten or twelve of us… Everyone who wasn't out on a case. Thanks for letting us know. We'll check in on him today."

At that point, Tom Rowdy walked in carrying a Starbucks coffee and a half-eaten Danish.

"Kingston! As I live and breathe! Good to see you still ticking," Rowdy said.

Before Gunner could comment, he heard footsteps coming up behind him and turned around. Seeing this man's face was the last omen Gunner needed to know he was doing the right thing. He disliked the man intensely, and that man felt the same.

"Lieutenant Rance. You must be the boss's sub," Gunner drawled.

Rance glared. They'd gone through the police academy together and had struck sparks off each other from the start.

"Kingston. We're busy here. State your business."

Before he could answer, there was a shuffling at the door. As everyone turned to look, a half-dozen men in black suits walked in, paused to look over the room, then headed straight for Tom Rowdy.

Gunner saw them and stepped back. *Ah shit. His name was on that list.*

"Thomas Lee Rowdy?"

Rowdy nodded. "Yes, that's me."

The man flashed his badge. "Special Agent Ed Hanley. We have a warrant for your arrest. Charges include passing privileged information to Burgess Dixon in return for numerous monetary payments. Said information resulted in giving up the location of one of our safe houses, and the deaths of four FBI agents and the death of a material witness in the Burgess Dixon trial. You are also being charged with abetting in the hit and run of Dan Helford, also known as Yankee Dan, and abetting in the bounty that was issued for Gunner Kingston."

Rowdy had turned every shade of red before he turned an ashy pale.

"I didn't… Uh… You have to be mistaken; I would never…"

"Burgess Dixon's suicide letter was, in fact, a list with the names and contact info of all of his informants, and your name is on it. We have time, place, and details of the offshore bank where you're stashing the payouts you have received. They coincide with the crimes we have mentioned, and all of the solid evidence we need to prove it."

Greg Rance was in shock, as were the other detectives. The only one of them who didn't seem surprised was Gunner. As the Feds were taking Rowdy away, Greg Rance turned on Gunner.

"You knew? Was it you who gave him up?"

Gunner blinked. "Gave him up? What the fuck's wrong with you? Burgess Dixon gave him up—gave up all his informants. If I'd known, I would have already beaten the shit out of him for trying to get me killed. However, I did suspect there was a dirty cop in this department, as everyone here can attest. I said it often enough. The first one I suspected was my partner, Cliff, for acting so damn weird after we brought Yankee Dan in to get his statement. But I didn't say a damn thing. Not even when the old man was killed in a hit and run. Then I began wondering how Lieutenant Samuels had the knowledge to tell me that it was safe for me to come back to Dallas because the hit had been called off. But I didn't call him out, either. I never saw this coming until I talked to Samuels yesterday, and he mentioned it was Rowdy who told him the hit was off and I would be safe to come back. There was no way to know that unless that someone had gotten the info straight from Dixon."

Rance's face flushed with anger. "But—"

"But nothing," Gunner said. "Yesterday, I also learned that one of the special agents who died in that safe house was Tom Rowdy's brother-in-law. Even then, I could not wrap my head around a man low enough to sell out his sister's husband for a wad of dough."

"It's pretty convenient to just happen to be here when they come to get him," Rance said.

Gunner took a paper from his inside pocket. "I didn't come to see a rat dragged out of hiding. I came here to submit my resignation. Witnessing this was icing on the cake. Getting to watch the bastard who nearly got me killed get what was coming to him is the cherry on top." He slapped his resignation on the desk, took off his weapon and holster, dropped the bulletproof vest at his feet, and unclipped his badge. "Being targeted and hunted like a dog because some worthless piece of shit liked money more than God puts a whole new spin on a man's viewpoint of who he wants to work with. And you, standing there like the asshole you are, wanting to tar me with some kind of guilt just because you don't like me, says absolutely everything about your lack of honor and morals. I'm outta here. And just FYI...to all of you. If Andy Samuels does return to work, it might be in your best interests to make peace with him about the visitations."

Rance's face was purple with unspent rage, but he could not deny a word of it.

Before Gunner could leave, Cliff grabbed his arm.

"I'm sorry. I'm sorry I was such an ass. I'm sorry I lost your trust."

Gunner shrugged. "It's over."

"But where are you going? If you're not a cop, what are you going to do?" Cliff asked.

"I'm going to get my lady and live happily ever after, and I don't have to do a damn thing I don't want to do for the rest of my life, because I'm the one who won the Mega Millions lottery, and the payoff money just landed in my bank this morning. Before any of you ask, the answer is no."

He walked out, leaving the detectives shocked about the money and staring at Greg Rance in disbelief.

"What the hell, Boss? Defending the thin blue line is one thing, but you sure missed the point. A detective from our department just got hauled off by the FBI, charging him with abetting in six murders, and the attempted murder of one of our own, and you're ragging on Gunner? Why? Because the hit man missed? That's cold," Frankie Adams said and walked away.

Rance gathered up all of Gunner's gear and went into the office.

Cliff followed him in. "Sir."

"What the hell do you want?" Rance muttered.

"Just wanted you to know that I'll be making sure Kingston's official resignation does not get buried. We don't care what you thought about him, but he was my partner. He saved my life twice. And if you do anything to demean his name in his personal file, I will make sure you don't get away with it."

"I could ruin you for this insubordination," Rance said.

Cliff held up his phone. "But you won't, because I just recorded this conversation." He looked down at his phone as he began sending a text. "And I sent it to the captain's phone."

Rance's eyes widened. "But I had no intention of doing any such thing."

Cliff shrugged. "Well, now he knows anyway," he said and walked out, then threw out a question to the crowd. "What's the payout on seven hundred and eighty million dollars?"

"I'd guess something over four hundred and fifty million," someone said.

"Damn," Cliff said. "Just damn."

Gunner exited the building and didn't look back. Without the weight of responsibility that came with a badge and gun, he felt like he was floating.

He drove out of the parking lot and on the street leading to an on-ramp to the Loop and headed to Holly's work. He'd had flowers delivered there, but he'd never been there. That was about to change.

Holly walked into work with a smile on her face, got a doughnut and a cup of coffee from the breakroom, and took them to her desk. The yellow roses were still perky, but she added some water to the vase just in case, then picked up her work from where she'd stopped last night.

One hour passed, and then another, and then she pushed away from her desk, picked up a file, and carried it to Gene Morris's desk.

"The deed to the Powers property is officially cleared and up-to-date. You can finalize the sale."

Gene nodded. "Fantastic. Good work, Holly."

"Thanks," she said and took a quick break to wash up, then came back and sat down to check her to-do list to see what came next. She was shuffling through her notes when she heard footsteps in the hall outside their office.

The door opened.

Everybody looked up from their desks, including Holly; then she saw the look on his face. He was smiling. She stood up.

Without saying a word, Gunner went straight to her, took her in his arms, and laid a kiss on her lips that had every woman swooning.

When they came up for air, Holly grabbed his arms. "It's over, isn't it? Oh my God, Gunner. Tell me it's over!"

"I'm over it, that's for sure. Resigned, and turned in my gun and badge. The Feds came while I was there and arrested the informant in front of all of us." Then he turned around to face the room. "I have a house to sell. I want Holly Dillon to list it, and then I'm gonna steal your girl."

Holly looked straight at her boss. "Then that's where I'll be for a while. I have contracts in my briefcase, and I'm going to take the Nikon for the photos."

Gene nodded. He was all for another listing, while facing

the fact that he was going to lose a valuable employee. Nobody was as good as Holly with clearing deeds.

A few moments later, they were gone.

Leigh put her head on her desk. "Why can't that happen to me?" she groaned.

Josie leaned back in her chair. "OMG… What just happened?"

Lisa was dabbing her eyes with a tissue. "That's the most romantic thing I've ever witnessed. Straight out of *An Officer and a Gentleman*."

Leigh raised her head from the desk. "Never heard of it."

"Probably because it came out before you were born. Treat yourself some night. It's bound to be on some streaming service," Lisa muttered, then turned back to her computer, trying to remember what she'd been doing.

Holly buckled her seat belt and leaned back in the seat as Gunner gunned it out of the parking lot, heading for the nearest on-ramp to the Loop, then shooting out into traffic like he'd been launched.

"This is the first time we've been in a car together," she said.

Gunner arched an eyebrow. "But we have been in bed together."

Holly was still trying to catch her breath from their entry into traffic.

"True, and I can say with all honesty that I am forever grateful you are not this fast in bed."

He burst out laughing.

"What?" she said.

He shrugged. "You are going to be so freaking good for me. My whole life has been lived behind dark glasses."

"Oh, honey..." Holly's voice was suddenly shaky. "My heart is so sad for the little boy you were, and how damaged your faith in people became because of what happened."

"I have the best family. The best support group. I'm just missing the genetic component to adapting."

Holly shook her head. "It's not that. Don't ever think it's a fault of your own for what happened. It hit you the hardest because you were also the youngest. Children almost always form their first bond with their mother. The first nine months of becoming us happens inside our mothers' bellies. Even after a child is born, tiny pieces of the child's DNA stay with her. My mom told me something years ago that has stayed with me. The bond between mother and child is eternal, even if that mother fails to nurture. When your mother did what she did, she took that tiny piece of you with her but left nothing tangible of herself within you except a feeling of abandonment."

The hair crawled on the back of Gunner's neck. It all made sense. Emotions can be so complicated, but answers could be so simple.

"Damn, girl. You just nailed me to the wall with that. There's no denying everything you said."

"All you have to do is let people love you again. I'm the beginning, but it's going to get better... I promise. You don't have to keep running anymore."

Gunner was suddenly blinking back tears, and he didn't cry.

"Heard, with thanks. I love you, Holly Dillon." Then he noticed he was coming up on his exit. He shifted lanes and took the next off-ramp in one smooth move. "It's not far now, and you're gonna get the biggest hug when I get you out of this car."

"Something more to look forward to," she said. "And I can't wait to see your house."

"It's Spanish in design. Adobe walls, arches, and colorful

handmade tiles. Asher's house is similar, and neither of us knew we'd chosen similar styles until I went there when he and Nora were about to get married. My house is a three-bedroom, two and a half baths, with an office, a chef's kitchen, and a great fireplace. Oh...and a big, covered patio and a funky escape hatch from the back of my garage."

"The escape hatch is intriguing, and you just described my dream home," she said.

"Then we will recreate it in Crossroads, with everything you want in it," he said.

"I still can't believe this is all happening... Getting to move home. Making a forever life with you and filling a house with the sounds of children's laughter."

"We will be invincible when we work together," Gunner said. "It's going to be a hassle to move, but we'll get it done."

"I rent. Moving will be simple for me. What are we going to do with two sets of furniture?" she asked.

"Sell or donate, and buy new stuff? Anything we want."

Holly's eyes widened, and so did the smile on her face. "We are on such an adventure."

"Yes, we are, darlin'. It feels a little like a dream, doesn't it? Like a quest, but without any more dragons in wait."

As he neared his house, he tapped the remote. The garage was open when he went up the driveway and rolled inside. That's when Holly saw the Rubicon parked in the other bay, and a single exit door in that bay at the back of the garage.

"Oh wow... If that's an exit through your backyard, I can't wait to see."

"The remote to that exit also opens the back gate that leads into the alley. It's how I got out of town while the hit men were still hunting me. Nobody saw me leave this house, and I don't drive it around Dallas, so it was an unknown to anyone hunting me by car tag."

"Car tag? Those hit men were looking for you by the number on your tag?"

"So says the dude I sent flying into the concrete barrier."

She paled. "You must have been so afraid."

"Honestly, my first reaction was surprise, and then anger. It got scary later, not knowing the faces of my enemies. But that's over, and that back exit helped me get away unseen."

She shook her head. "A man with an escape hatch. Amazing."

As soon as they exited the car, Gunner hugged her, then kissed the top of her head.

"Okay, Miss Dillon. That's the hug I promised. Now put on your Realtor shoes and let's get down to business. I am in your hands."

Holly was a pro at her job.

She began with the exterior photos front and back and then moved to the interior. As she worked, it became apparent that Gunner was more of a neat freak than she would have believed. It made taking photos much easier.

He stayed out of her way, watching her setting up a shot by moving a pillow, tilting a lamp shade a certain way, and making sure all of the lights were on in every room. It was eye-opening, witnessing how adept she was at her job.

"Lighting is everything when selling a house. The curtains always need to be pulled back. The shades up, lamps and overhead lights on. Bright is uplifting. If people want to live in a cave-like atmosphere later, they can close shades to suit them," she said. When she got to his bedroom, her eyes widened at the sight of his bed. "That might be the biggest bed I've ever seen."

He grinned. "I have a foot and leg problem."

She turned, mirroring instant sympathy. "Why? What's wrong?"

"My legs are too long, and my feet hang over the edges. The bed and mattress were special orders."

She laughed. "You are always teasing. I should have known."

"I don't remember teasing you," he said.

"Remember that big barbeque they had at the high school to raise money for new equipment for the baseball team?"

"Vaguely," he said.

"You were serving in the food line. I was standing beside my mom. Extended my plate to the food you were serving, and I asked you what it was."

His eyebrows arched. "Are you talking about the calf fries?"

"You told me they were meat patties. Little pieces of beef."

He was smiling now. "I did not lie to you."

She rolled her eyes. "That was the worst joke anyone has ever played on me. I gagged for a week every time I thought about it."

Now he was laughing. He swooped her up in his arms and swung her feet off the floor. "I'm sorry, darlin'. I'm sorry." And then kissed the frown off her face.

By the time the kiss was over, she was breathless. "Truce. Let me finish up here with the pictures, and then we'll go over the contract."

"You've already taken all the pictures you need in the kitchen, right?"

She nodded.

"Then I'm going to make us some sandwiches. Not sure what's in the fridge, but I'm hungry."

"I'm not picky. As long as it's not calf fries, I'm good to go."

He was laughing as he left the room.

Two hours later, the photos and contract were all finished. The ham and cheese sandwiches had been eaten, and the kitchen was in order once more.

"It's a pity you have to go back to work. We could have tried out that bed."

"There's always tomorrow," Holly said and blew him a kiss from across the room. "I'm going to wash up before we leave."

"Then how about I take you back in the Jeep, and you can see how the back exit works, too?"

"Yes! That would be awesome," Holly said.

Gunner went to get the other set of keys.

Holly came back carrying her briefcase and the camera case.

Gunner was peeling off the wrapper of a Hershey's Kiss when she reached the counter.

"Dessert," he said. "Open wide," then he popped the little chocolate candy in her mouth. "Off we go, darlin'. I'm right behind you. I need to set the alarm as we go."

The chocolate was still melting on her tongue as he loaded her briefcase and camera bag in the back seat while she got inside and buckled up.

He tapped the remote as soon as he was behind the wheel, leaving Holly witness to both the garage door and the back gate at the fence opening in unison.

"This is genius, Gunner. Are you responsible for this?" she asked.

"No, it was here when I bought it, but it's also part of what sold me on the house."

He started the engine and drove straight out and through the gate. He pressed the remote again as he was clearing the gate, and Holly turned to watch both doors going shut.

"Oh, I can't wait to start showing this house," she said.

"And I can't wait to get the both of us back to Crossroads."

"I still keep pinching myself, that this is really happening. I guess we will be back in our parents' houses while our house is being built?"

"Not the ideal situation, but we'll figure it out as we go. Remember, we have all the time and the money we need to make it happen," he said.

She leaned back into the seat as they exited the alley and onto a street. This time when he launched them onto the Loop, she was prepared. Sitting in a seat beside Gunner Kingston as he drove was a little like sitting in the passenger seat of a plane taking off.

"Do you ever get speeding tickets?" she asked.

He laughed and pointed at the traffic they were in. "You drive in this traffic every day. Do you ever see anyone getting pulled over for speeding?"

She grinned. "Now that you mention it..."

"Right. The only cops and cars stopped on the Loop are working wrecks, or part of one. You're safe with me. Trying to catch a killer running a roadblock is way worse. I will never be sorry I stepped out of that job when I did. You and me... We're good. Not sure what your Daddy is going to think about this turn of events, having this all happen so fast."

"A... I'm way past the age of consent. B... I make my own decisions about my life. He wasn't crazy about me leaving Crossroads, but he got over it. He's going to be so happy that I'm back in his world, he will be beside himself."

"Good enough," Gunner said.

A short while later, he pulled up into the parking lot at her work.

"You don't have to get out," she said.

"Oh, but I do. It's bad manners not to walk your girl safely back inside."

"Okay then, but if Gene starts turning the porch light on and off, that means no more kissing in his presence. I thought he was going to faint where he sat."

Gunner's eyes narrowed. "That was just a male reaction to seeing another man intruding in his territory. He is the only guy in the room, right?"

She laughed. "I never thought of it that way."

"I'll get your things for you. He's already seen the light. He'll be fine. You'll see."

And Gunner was right. Gene was the first to get up to welcome them back. "All went well, I assume."

Gunner nodded. "Holly knows her business. It was a real lesson in organization just watching her work. I think the only thing she didn't photograph was me."

"Oh, I have a couple. You just weren't looking," she said.

He shook his head. "I should have known. Be safe going home later, darlin'. We'll talk tonight, okay?"

"Definitely okay," Holly said.

He brushed a quick kiss across her lips, then tipped his hat to the women. "Ladies… Mr. Morris… Pleasure to do business with you," he said, and then he was gone.

Leigh sighed. "I hate you, Holly Dillon."

Holly wiggled her eyebrows. "Jealousy is so high school, girl."

"How did you guys meet?" Josie asked.

"We didn't meet. We grew up in the same little town in West Texas, but with a five-year difference in age. When I was twelve, I was the bat girl for the boys' high school baseball team. I had such a crush, and he was so sweet about it, tolerating a little girl's fantasy."

"Does he have a brother?" Leigh asked.

"He has two. They're just as hunky as he is, and both married with children," Holly said.

Leigh sighed. "Drat."

Holly laughed. "Seriously, Leigh? You're married."

"Details, details," Leigh said and got up to refill her coffee.

Holly was excited to be doing something besides digging through old deeds at courthouses as she sat down at her desk. The first thing she did was call their appraiser and an inspector and give them the address of Gunner's house.

She told them both the same thing. "This one is kind of a rush. If you can move this appraisal up your agenda, it would be appreciated. The owner is moving back to West Texas to be closer to the elders in his family." They responded in kind with moving it to the top of their lists.

After that was settled, she stretched the tense muscles in her shoulders, finger-combed the curls out of her face, then reached for the camera, pulled the SIM card, and began uploading the photos into her system.

Now that the FBI had taken over the evidence from the suicide scene, they were running two connected cases. Rounding up the people on Dixon's informant list was part of their ongoing connection to the murders of their agents and witness, and re-examining the facts of Burgess Dixon's death played into it.

It was protocol to verify what they'd been given, and they were in the process of running their own set of labs for the collected evidence. Everything panned out except the video from the security system.

Colin Decker, the tech guru who was viewing the security footage, soon noticed something funky about the last visible images and decided to run it through a data recovery program.

It took him the better part of two days of cleanup, but by

the time he was finished, what was revealed blew the suicide theory out of the water.

The hair was standing up on the back of his neck as he picked up the phone and buzzed his boss.

"This is Lavinsky. What's up?"

"Sir, this is Decker. You need to see this. In the lab. Now."

"On the way," Lavinsky said, took the stairs down a floor to their tech lab, and went straight to where Decker was working. "What's up?"

"This is the security footage from the Dixon property. You have to see this," he said and got up. "Sit in my chair, sir. You need a front-row seat for this." He hit Start.

Lavinsky had seen it all before but sat through the entire footage again of all five of the security cameras on the property, waiting for some big reveal. When it got to the last few frames, where Dixon got out of the limo and went inside, and the chauffeur parked the limo and drove away, he frowned. "What am I supposed to be seeing?"

"Keep watching," Decker said and pointed.

"What the hell?" he said. "This wasn't on the original video."

"Sir. This *is* the original video. Give it a few minutes. You're going to see the chauffeur coming back to the estate on foot and climbing over the fence. There, right there."

"Well, damn," Lavinsky muttered, his eyes narrowing as the footage switched to another camera view showing the interior of the house, and there in plain sight was Beau Whistler going up the stairs and then into Dixon's office with a gun.

"Can you turn up the audio?" Lavinsky asked.

Decker nodded and reached over Lavinsky's shoulder.

At that point, there was nothing to do other than witness the ensuing murder and Whistler's exit.

"I did not see that coming," Lavinsky said. "Good work,

Decker. Good work. Make a copy, then bring both to me ASAP. I'll be in my office."

"Yes, sir," Decker said.

Lavinsky was already making mental notes of what he needed to do. They needed an arrest warrant. They had an address for Beau Whistler, but after seeing this, chances were that the man was already in the wind.

Within an hour, they had the warrant and sent a team to the address, only to discover that Whistler was gone—moved with no forwarding address. The hunt was on.

After a quick trip through Whole Foods and then home, Gunner put up the groceries, started a load of laundry, then sat down at his laptop and began searching for hydrogeologists in West Texas. He needed someone to find him a water source near the place where he wanted to build his house, and after a brief search, he found a couple within a reasonable distance of Crossroads and sent both of them a message. He was getting up to start a load of laundry when his cell phone rang.

It was Asher, and as soon as Gunner picked up, Asher started talking.

"I'm driving, so I don't have much time to talk. You know Burgess Dixon is dead, right?"

"Yeah, suicide," Gunner said.

"No. His bodyguard did it. They have security footage. The Feds recovered what had been erased, and he's in the wind. They're combing the streets of Dallas and found his truck in a used car lot. He sold it for cash. They don't know where he is or what he's driving. I was told they're going through security footage of every bus station and airport in the Dallas/Fort Worth area. Nobody knows what prompted him to off his boss, but he's considered armed and dangerous."

"That's the same man I put on the floor and handcuffed to a piece of furniture when I went to have it out with Dixon," Gunner said.

"Damn it," Asher muttered. "Just pay attention to your surroundings until they find and arrest him, okay?"

"Yes, and thanks for the heads-up," Gunner said.

"Are you okay, otherwise?" Asher asked.

"I turned in my resignation and told the guys in the department about the lottery. I am in the beginning stages of selling my house and moving back to Crossroads, and I'm bringing Holly with me."

"So, you two are a thing now?" Asher asked.

"Yes, we are officially a thing."

"What does she think about leaving Dallas?" Asher asked.

"The same thing that I think… That we both want to be close to home because of our dads. That week I spent with Dad and Pearl was the best time I've had in years. He's not getting any younger, and I want to be there for him, like he was there for us. The lottery win gave me so much more than just money. I have the freedom to go home again."

Asher could hear the longing in his brother's voice. "Then I am happy for you, and Dad will be ecstatic. Just stay aware and stay safe."

"I will. Love to little Jake and Nora for me, and decide how you want me to send you the money I promised: transfer into a bank account, or just write you a check. And tell Dylan I need the same info from him, too."

"Yeah, I will talk to Nora tonight. We will never be able to thank you enough."

"I don't need thanks. It isn't charity. It's just a gift from one brother to another. Talk to you later," Gunner said and hung up.

But now he had a whole new concern. Surely a man on the run for murder would not be hanging around to get revenge for being coldcocked, but he was definitely going to take Asher's advice and pay attention.

Chapter 15

Beau Whistler did not know the Feds had cleaned the security footage, and it wouldn't have occurred to him to wonder because he didn't know that was possible.

He was not trying to hide anywhere. He was preparing to move on and sleeping in a different motel every night because he had his own set of enemies who might be interested in taking him out.

He'd sold his old truck because he knew it wouldn't make it to Mexico, took the cash from that sale and a little more from his stash, and bought a Harley off a guy who'd won the bike in a poker game.

But there was one thing still eating at him. That cop who'd decked him in front of Dixon. That incident was what had driven the wedge between him and the boss. If that had never happened, then Dixon wouldn't have been looking for someone to replace him. Dixon paid for his decision, but in Whistler's mind, the cop still owed him.

By the time Holly headed home, she was ready to get out of her work clothes and put her feet up. She had leftovers in the fridge from her dinner with Gunner last night. The only downside was eating them alone. But when she drove into her neighborhood, the idea of a quiet night was looking iffy.

Residents at the far end of the complex were having a

party. She could see a faint pillar of smoke and guessed meat was cooking on a grill. A good half-dozen extra cars were lining the streets, and it appeared more guests were arriving.

"Please lord, don't let this be an all-nighter," she muttered as she drove into her garage. To her relief, the noise from down the street faded once she went inside and began her normal unwinding routine.

Upstairs to strip, shower, and get comfy.

Downstairs to graze through the contents of her fridge.

She shivered, wondering what life with Gunner Kingston would be like. For certain, it was going to be a wild ride.

After she ate, she called home. She wanted to hear her dad's voice. She would know by the sound of it if he was doing okay.

The phone rang a couple of times before Garrett answered.

"Hello, ladybug, it's good to hear your voice. Is everything okay?" he said.

Relief rolled through her. He'd called her *ladybug,* a name from her childhood. He was doing okay.

"Everything is very okay. How's Granny and Travis?"

"They're good. We all have our moments, but we're getting there, honey. What's going on in your world?"

"Work, and Gunner Kingston," she said.

"So, this is getting serious?" he asked.

"Yes, and you better be happy for us. He's moving back to Crossroads and building a house on the Kingston property. I'm coming home, too. We're making plans for life together. He'll be staying at their home, and I'm going to need a place to hang out until the house gets built. Any chance of my old room still being available?"

Delight was evident in Garrett's voice. "This is wonderful news, Holly. Your room will always be here if you need it. I'm happy for both of you… So happy, and your mom would be over the moon."

"I know, and thank you, Dad. I miss talking to her so much," Holly said.

"We all do, sugar. We all do."

"Tell Travis and Granny I said hello. I love you. Be safe," she said.

"I sure will. Take care. Love you, too," Garrett said and disconnected.

Holly put her phone down with a sigh. She had a bed for the duration of the construction, and she had Gunner. Life was good.

She turned on the TV for company and stretched out on the sofa to watch a show. Lulled by the voices, she fell asleep and was awakened a short while later when her phone rang.

She sat up and reached for her phone.

"Hello."

"Hey, baby… You sound sleepy. Did I wake you?"

"I was watching TV and dozed off. Glad you called. I talked to Dad tonight. All is well. I told him about us, and moving back to build a house. I have officially been welcomed back to my old room for the time being, and he is happy for us."

"Good to have that blessing, but I will officially talk to him, as well, when we get back. Did you get any flak from your boss after I left the office?"

"No, but my girlfriends gave me a little grief. They think you're hot. One of them asked if you had any brothers. I had to break the bad news that you had two and they were married with children." Then she heard him laugh, and that soft, husky voice in her ear made her ache. "I don't know what your favorite color is, or favorite songs, but I know you love me, and everything else will unfold in its own time."

"Blue like your eyes. My favorite color is blue. I like most music genres, but because of Dad and the bar, I grew up on country music. I live for the way your breath catches when we make love, and how you move when you walk. I love the weight of your breasts in my hands, and the curve of your hips. Even the way your hair curls around my fingers, holding me fast. In my eyes, you are so beautiful. That's what you need to know about me."

Holly swallowed past the lump in her throat. Every word he'd uttered was a caress. "I'm somewhat speechless. My God, Gunner. You make love with your words like you make love with me."

"Love does that to a man," he said. "Sleep well, darlin'. You are my heart."

"Love you," she said.

The call ended. She stood, set the security alarm, and made her way upstairs. She was certain she'd never fall asleep after that call, but she did, and dreamed of baseball and a tall, black-haired boy who ran like the wind.

By morning, Special Agent Lavinsky had made the decision to go public with the manhunt for Beau Whistler. Every local news station was running with the story that Burgess Dixon had not committed suicide but in fact was murdered by his own bodyguard, Beau Whistler. Whistler's face was all over every TV station. If spotted, there was a hotline number to call, but with a warning: do not approach; he was armed and dangerous.

Gunner caught the story as he was making breakfast. He paused to watch a clip of the special agent in charge of the case at a news conference being asked by a reporter in the audience how this tied into the informant list Dixon had left behind.

"This is an ongoing case, and we will not be commenting on it at this time," Lavinsky said and took another question.

Gunner pulled the last piece of bacon out of the skillet, then cracked a couple of eggs into the hot grease, turned down the flame on the burner, and put a lid on the skillet. He was putting bread in the toaster when his phone rang. He smiled. It was Holly.

"Good morning, Hollyberry. How's my best girl?"

She smiled. "Hollyberry is just fine. I'm on the way to work, but I called to ask if you saw the story about Dixon's suicide being a murder and the ongoing manhunt for the killer?"

"Yes, I did."

"He looks scary," she said.

"That's because he is scary. I suspect Dixon is only the latest in a long line of Whistler's murder and mayhem."

"Ewww, I hope they catch him soon."

"So do I, darlin'. What's on your agenda today?"

"I will be verifying that the deed to your place is up-to-date and waiting on my appraiser and an inspector to call me back. They have both promised to get to your house ASAP."

"I need to be here for that, right?"

"It would be a good idea, if you can," she said.

"Just give me a day and time," Gunner said. "Love you. Miss you. If you're up for a pajama party tonight, I would promise late-night pizza."

"Why late night?" she asked.

"I was sorta hoping we'd be trying out my bed first. You know... The big one...that I sleep in alone."

She laughed. "You are such a charmer. I will bring pajamas for eating pizza, but I will not be wearing pajamas in your bed."

He sighed. "This is going to be one long-ass day waiting for you to get here. I might go visit my lieutenant again. The one in the hospital. I want to tell him myself that I resigned and see how he's doing."

"Pay attention," Holly said. "Remember you knocked that Whistler man out once. He might be a man who holds a grudge."

"Noted," Gunner said. "Love you, honey. See you this evening."

"Love you, and I'll call when I'm headed your way."

His toast popped up. He put it and his eggs onto the plate with his bacon and carried it all to the table, then poured himself a cup of coffee and turned the volume back up on the TV.

Whistler was out of the shower and getting dressed when he heard his name being mentioned on the TV, and then he heard the rest of the bulletin and cursed beneath his breath.

"How the hell…?"

But then he stopped. It didn't matter how, but his ass was grass if he didn't get out of Dallas. They would be looking for his truck, and he was patting himself on the back that he'd already sold it. They wouldn't be looking for him on a Harley, and his helmet had a face guard.

He finished dressing, shoved everything into his pack, tossed the room key on the bed, and headed out the door. So much for that stack of pancakes and sausage he'd been planning to eat.

He mounted his bike and took off out of the parking lot, leaving rubber on the pavement as he went. One stop to fuel up, and he was gone.

Chapter 16

Gunner was getting ready to leave for a last visit to Lieutenant Samuels. He picked up the car keys, then remembered the manhunt for Beau Whistler and went back to his closet to get his personal handgun and took it with him to the car.

Asher told him to be aware.

Holly told him to pay attention.

He believed in heeding good advice. Whistler had to be desperate, and desperate men were dangerous men.

As Gunner was backing out of the garage, he noticed his gas gauge was low and headed for the Gas and Dash where he'd bought that winning lottery ticket, because it was on the same route he would take to get to the hospital.

The day was clear, which meant by noon it would be hot enough to melt a good mood. He was thinking about Samuels. The heart attack was probably going to be the push Samuels needed to retire.

A motorcycle came up behind him on the street and then passed him so fast it made his heart skip. Just for a second, he was remembering the dude on the purple Yamaha.

A block and a half later, Gunner pulled into the Gas and Dash and noticed that the rider who just passed him had stopped there, too. He pulled in at the other side of the fuel pump and got out.

He was reaching for his credit card when he glanced up and saw the rider staring at him. Recognition was instant. It was the eyes and that scar that cut his left eyebrow in half. Even with the face guard down on the helmet, he knew it was Whistler.

And Whistler knew he'd been made. Having a shootout in public was the fastest way to get caught, and since he'd already paid and replaced the gas nozzle, he decided to make a run for it. He swung his leg over the Harley and leaned forward, releasing the kickstand as he turned the key. The engine fired, and he gunned it. He was already shooting out of the parking lot when he saw a shadow on the pavement coming at him from behind.

Before he could react, he was hit in the back with such force that he lost his breath and then his balance. The bike was already tilting, and then he was on the pavement in an armlock, flat on his belly and trying to get enough air to breathe.

Even through his helmet, Whistler heard the man on his back shouting, "Call 911."

Whistler was struggling and kicking and pounding air trying to knock the man off his back, but he couldn't reach him to do any harm, and in that moment, he knew it was over.

Son of a bitch. How did Kingston move that fast? "I'm going to kill you!" Whistler shouted.

"No. You're not. You're going to prison for the rest of your life," Gunner said.

Whistler shifted tactics. "I can't breathe."

"You just shouted and threatened to kill me. Sounds like you're breathing just fine," Gunner said.

But hearing the sirens of the approaching patrol cars made Whistler fight harder and Gunner hold tighter.

They came from every direction. Patrol cars from the Dallas PD were the first to arrive. The Harley was on its side and still running. One officer quickly shut it off as another recognized Gunner.

"Who's your bosom buddy?" he asked as he reached for his handcuffs and put Whistler in restraints.

"The guy the Feds are looking for. Beau Whistler. Somebody needs to call them."

A couple of officers sat Whistler up and removed his helmet.

"In living color," the officer said. "Good catch, Kingston, but how the hell did you know it was him behind that face guard?"

"We've met before," Gunner said and then realized his arm was burning and looked down. His shirt sleeve was torn, and the skin from his elbow down was raw and bleeding from sliding across the concrete. He was bleeding from a long cut on his shoulder, and his jaw was starting to throb.

Whistler had fared better, mostly because the helmet he was wearing took the brunt of his fall when Gunner tackled him, but he was moving from shock to rage at being caught twice by the same man. If the security footage had been restored, then what they had was irrefutable. No lawyer was going to save him. No deals were to be made with the Feds because everybody connected to the safe house murders was dead except him and Tom Rowdy. And they already had Rowdy in custody.

"It's your fault, Kingston. This is all your fault," Whistler said.

"Shut it, Whistler. Your boss is the one who ordered the hit on me. He wouldn't admit it, but we both knew it."

But Whistler wouldn't give up. "You took me down. You shamed me in front of him. Because of you, I was no longer of use to him, which meant I was going to get axed. I did what I did to save myself."

"Then it's a good thing he's not alive to witness this, because he would really be through with you," Gunner said.

"Bastard," Whistler muttered.

"Asshole," Gunner drawled.

At that point, they pulled Whistler to his feet, put him in the back of a patrol car, and then drove away with one patrol car leading the way and four following, leaving an officer and a patrol car with Gunner.

"We called an ambulance for you, Kingston. Sit tight. I'm waiting with you until they arrive."

Gunner nodded. "Much appreciated."

Blood was still dripping down his arm and onto his boot and his jeans, and he was feeling a little dizzy, so he leaned against the back of the officer's car.

"Hey, Kingston, did you really run him down and tackle him from behind as he was rolling?"

"Too many people around to take a shot," Gunner said.

"But—"

Gunner shrugged. "I run fast."

"I guess we'll get to see the takedown on social media," the officer said.

It was at that moment that Gunner realized the size of the crowd around them, all with their phones aimed straight at him.

"Great," he muttered and pulled out his phone and called Holly. He needed to tell her before social media did it for him.

It rang twice before she picked up. He was about to ruin her day.

"Good morning," Holly said.

"Hey, darlin', just calling to let you know that Beau Whistler is in custody."

"Oh, Gunner! That's wonderful. Now we know you're finally safe."

"Well, almost," he said. "It took a bit of a tussle to take him down. I have a little cut on my arm, but there's an ambulance rolling up on the scene right now. As soon as they clean it up, I'm going home."

"*You* caught him?"

He winced. Her voice was clearly at the level of squeak.

"Yes. It was the darndest thing. We both stopped at the same place to get gas. What are the odds of that? I promise I'm okay except for a little road rash."

"You got into a fight with him at the gas station?"

"Ummm, sort of. More like I ran him down," Gunner said.

"Like you did with the guy who tried to shoot you?"

"No, I was on foot. More like a tackle. I took him down while the bike was rolling. We both went over the bike onto the pavement. It was epic. I think. It felt epic, and now not so much." The ambulance was coming up the street with lights flashing and the siren screaming. "The ambulance is here. I will be going home after they're through with me."

"And I will be sitting in your driveway waiting," she muttered and hung up in his ear.

Gunner sighed. "Have mercy."

Holly's hands were shaking as she turned off her computer and reached for her purse.

"Gunner just caught the guy from the manhunt. An ambulance is on scene, and he's bleeding. He swears he's going home afterward. I will be sitting in his driveway when he arrives to take him to the ER."

Her coworkers were horrified.

"Oh my God! Holly! What happened?" Gene asked.

She rolled her eyes. "I don't know, but from what he said, there were probably enough witnesses to splatter him and the incident all over social media."

The women immediately began searching social media sites on their phones as Holly went out the door.

"If you find any video of it, I want to see," Gene said.

The first EMT on the scene was wearing a shirt with the name Brewster stitched onto the pocket.

Brewster immediately removed Gunner's shirt and began assessing the bleeding injuries as his partner was examining his ribs and jaw.

Gunner's arm was burning like hell. It felt like he'd rolled in a nest of fire ants, and it was good he was sitting down.

"You need stitches. We'll get you bandaged up enough to slow down the bleeding, but you need to go to the ER. Stitches for sure, antibiotics, and X-rays," Brewster said.

Gunner frowned. "I didn't fall on my head or face. I got clocked by his helmet. It's fine. Just slosh some disinfectant on my arm and wrap it up so I don't bleed all over my car. I've had worse sliding into home plate."

Brewster grinned. "Noted, but still not letting you go until I'm satisfied."

The patrolman still on-site with Gunner saw a black SUV with tinted windows turn off the street and pull up behind the ambulance. When he saw the two men who got out, he knew the Feds had arrived.

"Hey, Gunner, you have company," he said.

Gunner glanced up. FBI. He could spot them anywhere. They were all wearing sunglasses, although the sunny day called for them, but they all had a tendency to walk like Tommy Lee Jones about to start a fight.

"Gunner Kingston?"

"Yes."

The man obviously in charge flashed his ID. "Special Agent Lavinsky. Heard you caught our man. Much appreciated. We're still working the case of the safe house murders."

"Ah...and I'm the guy who worked the case of your missing witness who was found dead in a warehouse."

Lavinsky blinked. "I don't think I knew that."

"So, Tom Rowdy isn't talking?" Gunner said. "I worked in the same homicide department. The information he kept leaking to Burgess Dixon also got a homeless man who went by the name Yankee Dan killed, and resulted in a fifty-thousand-dollar bounty on my head. You will be interested to know that Whistler just confessed in front of me and a dozen cops as to why he killed Dixon."

"I would be interested in knowing what he said," Lavinsky said.

"It was the day I sort of invaded Dixon's office. I had to remove the bodyguard to get in. Dropped him with one good karate chop and went in to express my displeasure to Dixon about the hit. Because I took Whistler out like that, Whistler believed Dixon was losing faith in him and guessed he'd be the next one to fall. He went all proactive and struck the first blow, which was fatal. Then he told me it was all my fault for making him look bad in his boss's eyes."

Lavinsky smiled. "Something as simple as 'losing face,'" he said, then pointed to Gunner's arm. "Are you going to be okay?"

"Yes."

"Thank you," Lavinsky said. "Maybe we'll see each other around."

"Nope. I turned in my resignation a few days ago."

Lavinsky frowned. "Shame. The PD is losing a good cop."

"They lose good cops every time one dies in the line of

duty. I'm going home to West Texas to be close to my dad. He's not going to be here forever."

"What is your dad's name?" Lavinsky asked.

"Jacob Kingston. My mother was Brenda Kingston, an accomplice in an armored car robbery over thirty years ago. Unknown to all, including the leader of the gang, she buried the stolen loot in the basement of our home, then swallowed a bottle of sleeping pills because she knew the FBI was coming. She died in their car on her way to jail. Thirty years later, that unclaimed money nearly got Dad killed. Maybe you remember. My brothers and I solved the crime, found the money, and your people flew to Crossroads in a chopper to pick it up."

Lavinsky reeled like he'd just been slapped. "You're that family? Damn. We're still holding our heads in shame for that one. I'd like to shake your hand...if you have one that doesn't hurt and isn't bleeding."

"The left one's good," he said, and the two men shook hands.

"You give your father my best," Lavinsky said. "Tell him I said he raised some really fine men."

Gunner said nothing as they drove away, then looked back at what Brewster was doing. "Are you about through here?"

"The driveway of a gas station is filthy. All of that detritus is in the wounds on your arm. Get yourself to the ER for a tetanus shot and let them finish this up. The cut isn't going to stop bleeding until you get stitches. They will give you meds and stuff for pain. If you don't feel like it, we can transport you there ourselves."

"My girl will take me," Gunner said, and in that moment, he felt a rush of emotion for the fact that he could claim that.

"Okay then, but you're a bloody mess, so if she doesn't

pass out at the sight of you, you've got a good one," Brewster said.

"Holly is not a fainter. She may give me hell for winding up in the middle of this again, and she will take me to the ER whether I want to go or not." Then he walked over to the gas pump where he'd left his car, pulled out his credit card to pay for gas, and began refueling.

Chapter 17

As Gunner was replacing the hose at the fuel pump, he was also concluding that driving himself home might not have been his best decision. He was beginning to get stiff, and everything was burning, but he was alive and still upright. It was enough, and it was over—finally over.

He eased in behind the steering wheel, wincing when he reached out to start the car, then drove back into traffic. No speeding for him today. About thirty minutes later he pulled into his driveway and saw Holly waiting in her car. She did not look happy.

He rolled slowly into the garage and eased himself out. When he turned around, Holly was already coming toward him.

"Jesus wept, Gunner Kingston. How are you still walking?"

"I swear it looks worse than it is. I have a cut on my arm, and I lost a lot of skin there when I took him down on the pavement. His damn helmet whacked my jaw. I probably have bruises, but it's all superficial. I'd hug you but…"

"Did you go to the ER?" she asked.

"No, but I—"

She glared. "Well, you're going, and don't argue with me. You look like the last rooster standing in a cockfight. Get a clean shirt and pants. They're going to cut all of this off of you when we get there, so you'll need something to wear home."

He was hurting like hell, but she'd just made him smile.

"Holly."

"What?"

"I sure do love you," Gunner said.

"I know. Inside now, please."

It hurt to laugh, but he did it anyway. He'd just gotten his first dose of how Holly dealt with crises. She was definitely a keeper.

As soon as they got the change of clothes, they left the house. She scooted the passenger seat back as far as it would go, buckled him in, and drove him to the ER in her SUV, then walked him straight in and up to the front desk.

The receptionist looked up, then shock followed as recognition dawned. "Detective Kingston! What happened?"

"Just Gunner Kingston now," he said. "I had a run-in with a perp. EMTs on scene patched me up to stop the bleeding, but it hasn't stopped, and they recommended I see a doctor."

A woman in the waiting room glanced up, then did a double take. "It's him! The man that caught that killer on the loose!"

Gunner gave the receptionist a pleading look. "This is only going to get worse."

The receptionist nodded. "Follow me," he said and led them through the double doors and up to the ER nurse's desk. "Is there a doctor who wouldn't mind taking Mr. Kingston now? It seems he's become something of a hero, and it's going to cause a stir in the waiting room. I've got to get back to the front desk, but they'll get you fixed up in no time, Mr. Kingston."

The nurse glanced at the schedule to see where the ER doctors were at the moment. "What kind of a hero are we talking about here?" she said, half joking.

Holly didn't like the way those words came out of the nurse's mouth and answered for him.

"He got hurt taking down the killer the FBI was looking for. He was a bloody mess when he got home, and he's hurting. A lot. But he's not going to say it, so I'm saying it for him."

The nurse gave Holly a look. "And you are?"

"She's mine," Gunner said.

Holly burst into tears.

He reached out with his good arm and pulled her close. "It's been a hard day. Is there somewhere we could sit until a room is available?"

The nurse's whole demeanor just changed, as she waved at one of the aides. "Shelly, take him to Room 8. If the linens haven't been changed yet, do it before you leave."

"Yes, ma'am," Shelly said. "This way, please."

A few minutes later Gunner was stretched out on the bed, and Holly was sitting in a chair beside him.

"This sure puts a kink in our pajama party," Gunner said.

Holly rolled her eyes, then managed a wry smile. "Yes, it does, but I do take rain checks. And don't fuss at me. When you hurt, I cry. That's how it's always going to be."

The words were stuck in the back of his throat. He held out his good hand, and she took it, holding on as if she was never going to let him go.

And while they were waiting for the doctor, Gunner's phone began to ring. He quickly handed it to Holly. "It's Asher. Would you do the honors and answer it, then put it on Speaker?"

She nodded. "Hey, Asher, this is Holly."

"Hey, Holly. My brother is all over social media. Is he okay?"

"More or less," she said. "Just a sec and I'll put the phone on Speaker." As soon as she had it switched, she laid it on the bed near his head.

"Hey, Ash, I'm just a little bruised. My right arm caught

the worst of the impact when we hit the pavement. I'm missing a little skin and have a cut that needs stitches," Gunner said.

"Oh, we saw the video. And the blood dripping down your arm afterward, and the cops hauling Whistler off to jail."

"Well, I'm sorry about the shock value. Nothing's broken. Everything will heal. It's just gonna hurt for a while, but this nightmare is finally over," Gunner said.

"I will not rest until you get your ass out of Dallas," Asher said. "Dad saw the video. Someone at the bar showed it to him. He's crowing like the only rooster in the pen about his son, the hero, and Dylan's only comment isn't for polite company."

When Gunner heard the rooster reference, he winked at Holly. "Holly drove me to the ER. Trust me when I say, I am in good hands. She's already squashed a nurse who made light of the situation."

"Good for her. Hey, Holly, thanks for being there for him, and welcome to the family."

Holly was beaming. "Happy to be here. Oh… The doctor's coming."

"Right! If the doctor decides his brain is falling out, let me know," Asher said and hung up.

"My brain is fine," Gunner muttered, and then the doctor walked in.

"I'm Dr. Stanley. This is my nurse, Rita. I know what brought you here, and I saw the video of you take a flying leap into the air and T-bone a man on a Harley. So, we need to remove your shirt and jeans. You don't have to move. Rita is going to cut them off for you."

Gunner eyed Rita. "Slowly, if you please."

She stifled a giggle. "You aren't my first victim, and yes, I will cut slow."

"Many thanks," Gunner said.

When the shirt came off, the doctor frowned at Gunner's chest and midriff. Severe bruising was already evident.

"If you don't have cracked ribs, I'll be surprised. They're bringing a portable X-ray machine."

Holly had moved out of the way as they were removing Gunner's clothing. First the shirt, then the jeans. That's when she saw the bruises already making themselves known. There was a big one on his right thigh, and another one near his right knee. All on the side he fell on. It was terrible to see him in so much pain, but she would not look away. *Have mercy, Lord. How is he still upright and walking?*

The portable X-ray arrived. The technician took photos as directed—of his chest and his jaw—then left to get them ready for the doctor.

Once they removed the field dressings from his arm, they began cleaning up the raw places and flushing the cut of any possible debris.

When they finally numbed the area where they were going to put stitches, she breathed a sigh of relief.

For Gunner, numbing was a godsend. He gave Holly a wink to let her know he was okay and then closed his eyes as the doctor took the first stitch.

When the homicide detectives in the downtown division of the Dallas PD found out Beau Whistler was in custody and that Gunner Kingston had taken him down, they were torn between pride that he'd been one of them and guilt for how he'd been treated when he'd turned in his resignation.

When Greg Rance saw the video, his first thought was that the man was crazy, and the second thought, that he was absolutely fearless. They'd lost a good man because of an informant, and he'd been a royal jerk. It was a hard pill to swallow.

Cliff Beale was proud on Gunner's behalf and didn't mind telling anyone who would listen that Kingston had once been his partner.

Frankie Adams was sitting quietly at her desk, watching the video over and over like some action-adventure movie. It was hard to imagine this wasn't fake. That there hadn't been any stunt men taking over to create this reality. The way Gunner held Whistler down—without a weapon to protect himself—without handcuffs to subdue him. Bleeding like a stuck pig without flinching. It was so damn heroic she wanted to cry. She didn't know what made men like that, but she wished one of them was hers.

Andy Samuels's daughter had taken her father home yesterday, and today he was in his favorite recliner, dozing off and on, just happy to still be alive. He could hear his daughter humming as she moved throughout the house.

A short while later, he turned on the TV, switched the channel to local news, and got the shock of his life. Not only was the manhunt over, but Gunner had been the one to catch him and take him down. As he was listening to the commentator and watching the video, he realized they had not once referred to Kingston as a detective, and he wondered if the lottery money had come in and Gunner opted out of law enforcement. If this was so, Andy didn't blame him. The stress of the job had been his downfall.

"Good job, Kingston. Godspeed."

Travis Dillon was the first one at the ranch to see the video and went to look for his dad. They'd been branding all day, and he found him taking a break with some of the hands.

"Dad! Y'all have to see this!" he said, then pulled up the video.

The hands gathered around Garrett, looking over his shoulder as Travis handed him the phone.

"That's Gunner. Catching the guy from the FBI manhunt."

They watched in awe, laughing and pointing at specific moments, and then watched it a half-dozen times more.

Garrett was grinning. "I guess my last concern for my daughter has just been answered. Having him for a son-in-law is going to ease my last fears for her safety. I would not want to make that man angry."

"He was bleeding quite a bit," Travis said.

"Yes, but he was still walking and talking, and he'll heal. Damn. That Whistler guy was big, too," Garrett said.

"I know…linebacker big," Travis said. "But Gunner sure can run. He looked like Superman taking flight when he took that man off a moving motorcycle. I sure hope he's okay."

"Call Holly. She'll know. She's likely with him."

"Yeah, I will. I'm gonna go show Granny," he said and went running back to the house.

Asher and Dylan Kingston were impressed with their little brother's prowess, while their wives were in tears that he was hurt. Man and woman. Yin and yang. Different feelings for the same event, but all from love.

While back in Dallas, Gunner was home and resting in bed and Holly was at his house, answering call after call from his phone. Most of them were from television stations or reporters from newspapers wanting an interview, and the answer from Gunner was no to all of it. Finally, he told Holly to let it all go to voicemail. He'd already talked to his family, and everybody else could wait.

The last time she went in to check on him, he had turned off the TV and was staring at the ceiling, lost in thought.

"Gunner? Sweetheart? Is there anything you need?"

He turned his head and patted the bed beside him. "Just you. Only you. Lie down with me."

She kicked off her shoes and crawled onto the left side of the bed nearest his uninjured arm and rolled over on her side to face him. "Travis called. The family sends their love and prayers for getting better, and Travis now thinks you've hung the moon."

Gunner had finally seen the video and was somewhat shocked that he'd done all of that without thinking. Part of it was the cop he was, not wanting a bad guy to get away, and the other part was all Kingston.

A half smile broke the somberness of his face. "He's a really good kid."

"Lieutenant Samuels called. He's out of the hospital and very proud of you. He knows that you resigned. Said to tell you it was a good decision and wishes you well."

Gunner sighed. "Well, damn. That's where I was heading when I stopped to get gas. I intended to tell him in person that I'd resigned. I guess he was already at home. It's just as well."

"Are you going to miss the people you worked with?"

He thought a few moments. "I don't think so. Without Samuels as lieutenant, it would have been hell to work under Greg Rance. Nobody needs that kind of grief every day when you're trying to solve murders. Cliff Beale was my partner up until the bounty thing happened and Samuels put me on a leave of absence until all that was resolved. Cliff and I worked well together, but his personal life, which he often brought with him to work, was a mess. He gambled. And his home life was screwed because of it."

"Oh wow…and you won all that money. If you'd stayed…"

"He would have hounded me for money…either to bet with, or to pay off debts."

He started to yawn, then winced and reached for his jaw. "That hurt."

"You need an ice pack."

"You are probably right. I didn't think of that when I laid down. I keep those frozen in the freezer at the bottom of the fridge," he said.

"I'll get one for you," she said.

"I could use another pain pill, too, if it's time," he added.

She blew him a kiss. "Be right back."

He listened to her footsteps flying down the hall and closed his eyes.

She was running.

Gunner fell asleep with an ice pack wrapped in a kitchen towel leaning against his jaw.

Holly pulled the covers up over his chest, taking care not to bump anything that hurt, and blew him a kiss as she left.

It was past noon, and he had already taken his second pain pill without eating. One more dose and she knew from experience that if he didn't put food in his stomach, he was going to get sick. A quick look through his refrigerator was useless. There was nothing there that he could comfortably chew.

She scanned several menus before getting to something

she thought would work and placed two orders for meatloaf, mashed potatoes, and gravy dinners with one side, and four orders of two different kinds of soup for other meals, then sent texts to the girls at the office and to Gene, her boss.

> I will work virtually tomorrow, but from Gunner's house. He's in a lot of pain. Sorry for bolting like I did. He was a bloody mess. Twelve stitches to close the cut on his shoulder, a really bad case of road rash on his arm below the elbow where he hit the pavement with the perp, a huge bruise on the side of his jaw from the biker's helmet, and bruises all over. But nothing is broken, and he will heal.
>
> Still waiting on the appraiser to get to Gunner's property. I have the photos for Zillow and Redfin ready to go. As soon as we get the appraisal and the inspection done, we can set a price. That's all for now.
>
> Holly

She was still sitting in the quiet of the room when her cell phone rang. It was Travis.

"Hey, little brother."

"I wanted to check on Gunner, but Dad said I should call you because he might not feel like talking," Travis said.

"He's going to be fine. He's hurting a lot now, but at the moment, he's asleep. I'm going to work virtually for a while and will be spending the next few nights here until he is able to get around on his own better."

"You will tell him we called and asked about him, okay?" Travis said.

"Oh, I will, honey. Everything okay there? Is Granny settling in?"

"All is well, and it's like Granny never left. She's doing the books. And Dad has a roping event coming up. Granny is all fired up about keeping times and announcing the competitors…like Mom used to do."

"Good. You know that was Granny's job before Mom and Dad were married, so she is an old hand at all of this, which is exactly what Dad needs. She's someone who can pick up the slack without having to be taught what to do."

"I guess I forgot about that," Travis said. "Dad said you are moving back to Crossroads with Gunner."

"I am…but we're going to have to build a house first, which means he's staying with his dad, and I'm staying at the ranch until the house is built."

"That's so cool, and so is Gunner. We've watched that video a thousand times. Dang, Holly. It's like looking at something out of a movie."

She chuckled. "I'm paraphrasing, but Gunner said flying through the air was epic. Coming down, not so much."

Travis laughed. "He's already become Crossroads' new hero."

"I can only imagine. Are you getting a little excited now about college?"

"Yeah. I found out that a guy I know from Tulia is also going there. We might room together."

"That's wonderful, honey. It will all work out. Life always does, whether we're ready for it or not. Listen, I just hear a car pulling up. It's probably DoorDash. Gotta go. Talk to you soon."

"Okay, bye. Love you," Travis said.

"Love you, too," Holly said and hung up just as the doorbell rang. By the time she got there, the driver was backing out of the drive, and the food was on the doorstep. "Awesome," she said and took it back inside.

She heard Gunner stirring and went to check on him. He was up and pulling on a pair of sweatpants with some effort.

"I'm so sorry, honey. Did the doorbell wake you? It was DoorDash."

"I was awake, just not moving. But the longer I stay still, the stiffer I'm getting. I need to move around a little," he said.

"Do you feel like eating anything?" she asked.

"If I don't have to do much chewing, yes."

"You need to eat something. Taking pain pills on an empty stomach isn't a good idea," she said. "I ordered meatloaf and mashed potatoes and gravy for you, or soups if you prefer."

"Meatloaf and mashed potatoes sound perfect," he said, and it was. It took a while to get it eaten, but most of it was gone by the time he quit. He got a fresh ice pack for his jaw and brushed a kiss across Holly's lips. "I've been sick a dozen times and still working on the job, had a broken nose, been shot once, and beaten up twice on the job before help arrived. All that time, I came home to this house alone and healed in spite of myself. You have no idea what this means to me."

"You were shot?"

He showed her a small scar on the side of his waist. "Flesh wound. Nothing serious, but it hurt a while."

"I will spend the rest of our lives together, loving all of the empty, lonely places within you. Just know that; now get yourself in bed."

Before he'd taken two steps, the doorbell rang.

"Are you expecting anyone?" she asked.

"No." He started to go to the door when Holly stopped him.

"You sit. If it's some reporter, I'll deal with them. You go to the door like that, and your picture will be front-page news."

He looked down at himself, wearing nothing but a pair

of sweatpants, purple bruises everywhere, and his arm bandaged in two places.

"Point taken," he said and sat in his recliner.

Holly looked through the peephole in the door. "Two people. A blond guy with sunglasses and a woman with purple hair."

Cliff and Frankie. Gunner sighed. "Let them in."

Holly opened the door. "I'm gonna need to see some IDs."

They looked startled and then laughed when they realized she was teasing. Cliff yelled out. "Damn it, Gunner. Call her off. It's just us."

Holly laughed. "Sorry. Couldn't resist," she said, then stood aside for them to enter.

But the moment they saw him, their smiles disappeared.

"Jesus," Cliff said.

Frankie's eyes welled.

"I'm sitting up and talking, not lying in a casket. Get your asses in here and sit down," Gunner said.

They sat.

"Everyone, this is Holly Dillon…soon to be Kingston. Once the best bat girl on my high school baseball team, and now a hotshot Realtor here in Dallas. Holly, this is Cliff Beale, my homicide partner. And Frankie Adams, the only female detective in Homicide with enough patience to put up with us."

"I've heard nothing but good things about both of you," Holly said.

Frankie rolled her eyes. "She must really love you if she's willing to lie for you, too."

Gunner started to laugh, then caught himself. "No jokes. My jaw is barely hanging on my face."

The huge purple bruise on the right side of his face was evident.

"Well, you look like hell," Cliff said.

"Good observation. I feel like hell, too, but Holly is taking really good care of me."

"Clearly," Frankie said. "When we didn't know the password, I wasn't sure she'd let me in."

Holly grinned. "I always wanted to say that, and it's a pleasure to meet you. Can I get you anything to drink? We have coffee already made."

"No, but thanks," Cliff said.

"I'm good," Frankie added, then poked Cliff on the shoulder.

He nodded, then took a deep breath in an effort to calm down. "Everybody in the department is proud of you, Gunner, but they… We…are also ashamed of the raw deal you got. Greg Rance is an ass. He caught hell from all of us after you left. I confronted him in his office afterward, and I might have recorded the conversation we had. And I might have sent it to Captain Edwards. Nobody contacted me personally, but as of yesterday, we have a new lieutenant."

"And I came just so you could razz me about the new hair color," Frankie said.

Cliff frowned. "She's lying. She's the one who said you needed to hear that from us. And she made me come because I didn't have the guts to face you on my own. You have been my rock. My advisor. My best friend. And I acted like an ass because of the mess I'd made of myself. I've been going to Gambler's Anonymous for a while now. I wanted you to know that. And you also need to know that after that video went viral, I claimed bragging rights to having been your partner. I'm really sorry."

Gunner smiled. "You're still a doofus, and thanks for that, Cliff. It means a lot. And thank you, Frankie, for coming with him."

"You're welcome," Frankie added.

Gunner saw the tears in her eyes. "I should probably confess that some days, your bullshit was the best thing that happened in that department. Thanks for making this happen, and I appreciate you both."

Frankie shrugged. "I can't help being superb."

In that moment, Holly saw the adoration she had for Gunner. Frankie was in love with him, and Holly couldn't blame her. He was a hard man to ignore, but an even harder man to love. She didn't know why he had, but she was glad he'd trusted her enough to let her into his life.

Cliff slapped his knees and stood. "Okay… Confession time is over, and I can tell by the way you're not blinking that you hurt like hell. We're wishing you and Holly happy ever after and a safe journey home."

When they left, Gunner felt the cord between them breaking. He no longer belonged in their world.

Holly closed the door behind them, then held out her hand and helped him up.

"Bed now."

He didn't argue, and when he stretched out and finally got comfortable, Holly pulled up his covers and then lay beside him and closed her eyes.

Gunner reached for her hand. "Love you, baby."

She threaded their fingers together. It was the only way she could hold him without hurting him. "Love you more. Close your eyes and sleep away the pain."

Around midnight, she brought him a cup of soup in bed. He sat up long enough to drink it, then made his way to the bathroom and back. Holly was waiting for him with a pain pill and a glass of water.

He moved in slow, measured steps to accommodate the aches, took the pill, and chased it with water.

"Did you set the security alarm?" he asked.

"Yes, I did. Just like you showed me. And I have your extra house key on my key chain. Do you want something else to eat? Ice cream?"

He shook his head. "I'm good. What time do you need to be up tomorrow to get to work from here?"

"I'm working virtually from here, but the office doesn't open until 8:00 a.m., so I'll get up about six. If you hear my alarm go off, ignore it. Tomorrow, you do what you need to do at your own pace. There will be food already made in the fridge, and we will heat and eat."

He frowned. "What? Have you been cooking for me?"

"You had nothing to cook. I ordered in. Don't fuss. You can't use your right arm. In the morning, do not get in the shower. You can't get that road rash wet. Sometime during the day when you feel like it, I'll help you get in your Jacuzzi. It will probably make all those achy muscles feel better, but I'll need to wrap your arm at least up to the elbow before the bath to keep it from getting wet."

He chuckled. "I shall obey, Dr. Dillon."

"It's your own fault for thinking you could fly," she said.

He laughed, then winced. "Have mercy, are they sure my jaw is just bruised?"

"Yes, they're sure. I saw the X-rays. And your ribs aren't even cracked, which means you could be a bit of a superman after all."

He cupped the side of her cheek. "Will you come to bed with me? I'm out of circulation in the sex department, but I love the sound of your breathing when you're asleep."

"Do I snore?" she asked.

"Not even a little."

"That's not what Travis says about me. He says he can hear me snoring from his room down the hall."

Gunner just shook his head. "He's been lying to you all along. He probably lies in bed laughing to himself about the trick he's played on you all these years."

She rolled her eyes. "Are all boys like this?"

"Pretty much. We have a really weird sense of humor, and one of the biggest kicks in my family was embarrassing your siblings."

"Lord... Well, so be it. Feel free to check the security anyway, so you can rest easy. I'll be here when you get back."

And she was, wearing nothing but a smile and waiting for him to get settled before she went to bed.

Gunner groaned. "Lord... You are beautiful."

She shook her head. "And you are so hurt. Lie down, sweetheart. This can wait."

He eased himself into bed. She adjusted his covers and then circled the bed and got in beside him. When she turned the light out, she heard him sigh.

"We're taking this bed to Crossroads," she said and rolled over on her side.

He patted her bare butt. "Yes, we are. Night, darlin'."

"I'm sleeping with a hero," she muttered.

"Shut it, girl. I don't want to laugh again tonight."

She smiled and closed her eyes. The last thing she remembered was the touch of his hand against her hip.

Holly wasn't in bed when Gunner woke up, but he remembered she was working from here and was probably in his office with the door closed.

Then he thought of Frankie Adams. She would either

still be at home or on her way to work, and he wanted to talk to her about her sister's beauty school debt.

He made a quick trip to the bathroom, eyed the black whiskers beginning to show on his face, and thought, *Tough shit. So, I look like a pirate for a while. No way am I dragging a razor down the side of that face.*

He put on his sweatpants again, picked up his phone, and walked into the kitchen. Holly had left his bottle of pain pills on the counter along with a note.

Whatever you're thinking, don't do it.
Your job today is taking your meds in a timely fashion.

He grinned. Her sense of humor was a delight. He took the pain pill, poured himself a cup of coffee, then sat down and pulled up Frankie's number.

It rang several times, and when she answered, she was breathless.

"Hello."

"Frankie, it's me, Gunner."

"I know… Caller ID," she said.

He grinned. "Okay. Duly noted. I have a question to ask you."

"Ask," she said.

"There's something I really want to do, but I don't want to insult you by the offer."

"Okay. If I promise not to be insulted, what is this thing you really want to do?"

"It's strictly between me and you. Nobody else in the department has to know."

"Jesus, Kingston, just spit it out!" Frankie said.

"Family means everything to me, and I admire the devotion and time you give to yours. Then I went and won all that money out of sheer luck, and I wondered how you'd feel if I paid for the rest of your sister's beauty school, with extra to help you take care of your mom. Like building that ramp off your porch for her wheelchair, and whatever else you needed to get your sister on her own path."

He heard a gasp, and then nothing.

"Frankie… If this was an intrusion into your private life, then—"

"I'm not insulted. I'm crying, damn it."

"So, you'll accept my offer?" he asked.

"Yes, with more gratitude than you will ever know," she said.

He sighed. "Awesome. You'll probably have to notify the new lieutenant about a chunk of money suddenly showing up in your account. You can tell him it came from me, for your sister's beauty school and handicap aids for your mom, and some minor repairs in your home. Something like that. And you can make a joke about how I always teased you about your colored hair to make the point. But I'd advise not mentioning it to any of the other detectives. People don't deal well with jealousy."

"Chunk of money? What are we talking about? There's less than two thousand dollars left of her schooling."

"I was thinking fifty thousand. It was the bounty for my life, and I want to give a real bounty to you. You spend it everywhere else you need, okay?" She was silent again, and he could hear her sobbing. "Don't cry."

"You have no idea what a difference this is going to make in my life. My father walked out on us when I was thirteen. My sister was four. Mom worked herself sick at two jobs to help me get through the police academy. My brother is a clone of my father. He has a dozen priors and at the moment is in jail somewhere in Mississippi, I think. Not for sure. Nobody has ever given us anything…until today. I am honored, and overjoyed, and grateful beyond words."

"Then it's a deal. You can either come by my house and pick up the check, or I'll have my bank transfer it to your account, but I'd have to have the bank tracking number and your account number for that."

"If we don't pick up a case I can't get away from, I could come by this evening."

"Holly is here, working virtually, but I'll have it written and in a sealed envelope, in case I'm asleep. Okay?"

"Yes, yes, and Gunner, thank you. So much," Frankie said.

"It's my honor to be able to do this," he said. "Have a good day."

"Oh. Well, shit Sherlock! It's already peaked. Whatever happens next will never top this."

Gunner was grinning as he hung up. Frankie Adams was one of a kind. Tough as an old boot, with a heart of gold.

He got up, immediately wrote the check with a good degree of pain, and slipped it into an envelope, then left it on the table by the door. He didn't know how Frankie was feeling, but he felt like he was walking on air. Doing something awesome for someone else was a true emotional high.

Chapter 18

Gunner got emails later in the day from both Asher and Dylan with bank information for the money transfers to them, and Asher had gone to the trouble to get their dad's information as well.

Gunner called his bank and asked for the president. Transferring amounts of that kind of money meant going straight to the big dog. But when he identified himself and asked for the president, his secretary launched into a full-blown fangirl moment regarding his takedown of Beau Whistler.

Gunner let her get it said, then asked again for her boss.

"Yes, of course. One moment."

Gunner waited; he heard a click and then Rimmer's voice.

"Mr. Kingston! Allow me to congratulate you on ending that FBI manhunt in a most remarkable way! Now, how can I help you?"

Gunner began to explain what he needed. "So, can we do this without me coming in? I look like I wrestled a bear and have the stitches and bruises to show for it. I'm also too sore to drive."

"Bless your heart," Mr. Rimmer said. "We can definitely do this for your father and your two brothers. It's most generous of you, too."

"They're family," Gunner said. "I have the tracking numbers and account numbers for their banks. Two are in Austin. One in Crossroads, Texas."

"Are you comfortable reading them to me over the phone?" Rimmer asked.

"Yes, sir. Tell me when you're ready."

Gunner read out each brother's given name, then the info for the bank, and then the same for his dad.

"Let me read these back to you," Rimmer said and read aloud what he'd written down.

"Yes, sir. They're all correct. How long will it take for the money to go through?"

"Oh, not long at all. You can check your account this afternoon and the transfers will show. And of course, check in with your family to let them know it was sent, so they can watch for it, too."

"Thank you," Gunner said. "Oh…and I'll also be writing a personal check for fifty thousand to a coworker who needs some help. That's all for now."

"Of course. A pleasure doing business with you," Rimmer said.

Gunner disconnected, pleased with his morning's work, and went to see what food Holly left for him. He found scrambled eggs in a bowl in the fridge, and already baked biscuits on a covered plate beside the microwave.

"Thank you, sweet lady," he said, then nuked the eggs, gave the biscuits a few seconds in the microwave, and sat down to eat.

By the time he finished, he knew he'd been up too long. He peeked in on her at work, blew her a kiss, and went back to bed, hoping that Beau Whistler was equally miserable facing the consequences of his actions.

Special Agent Lavinsky and his partner were in the interrogation room with Beauregard Whistler, taping their interview. A court-ordered attorney was sitting beside Whistler on the opposite side of the table.

Whistler was cuffed to the table, and his ankles were shackled. He and his lawyer had already seen the video of Dixon's last breath. As far as he was concerned, it would have made a hell of a snuff film, and he didn't know why they were so bent out of shape. They wanted Dixon put away. He'd just done it for them.

"What was your job within Dixon's organization?" Lavinsky asked.

"I wasn't mopping floors and cleaning toilets, if that's what you're asking," Whistler said.

"Did Dixon give you orders to get rid of people?" Lavinsky asked.

"You're not very smart for a fed. What the hell makes you think I'd answer that? I'm already going down for this."

"No problem," Lavinsky said. "We're about to interview an informant who claims to have info he'll trade for. We find that amusing, that an informant wants to make a deal with the FBI when he's already nailed for selling information to Dixon that got other people killed. Keep your seat. We're not through with you," he said.

Whistler frowned. He hadn't counted on that. Damn snitch. He hated them.

When Lewinsky and his partner walked into the interrogation down the hall, Tom Rowdy was already sweating. His lawyer whispered something in his ear, and Rowdy settled.

Lavinsky sat down with the full intention of breaking this man and his secrets wide open. No cop ever wants to go to prison, and that's where Rowdy was headed, but he was guessing the man was going to try to make them a deal.

They sat down and turned on the tape, went through the process of introducing the people in the room, and then began the questioning.

"Thomas Rowdy, you already know the charges you are facing…abetting in the murders of four of my special agents, one of whom was your brother-in-law; one attempted murder on a homicide detective in your own department; and selling confidential information to a crime lord."

Rowdy was fidgeting. "I had no idea that would be the end result. It was never my intent to get anyone hurt."

"What did you expect a man like Burgess Dixon was going to do with the information, then?" Lavinsky asked. "We know you don't do the dirty work. You're just one of the toads of the world who sells their soul for money. So, who wiped out the safe house? You remember the safe house. You gave up the location for money, and made your sister a widow and left your two nephews without a father."

Rowdy stifled a moan and gave his lawyer a frantic look. "My wife left me. My sister disowned me," he said.

"What did you expect? You destroyed their lives," Lavinsky said.

"I can't go to jail," Rowdy said. "I'll be dead in a month."

Lavinsky nodded. "Likely so…just like all those people you gave up to Dixon. It's called karma."

"I know who pulled the trigger on all of it. Even Garza and Letourneau."

Lavinsky frowned. "Who are Garza and Letourneau?"

"Two of Dixon's men who were supposed to bury Freddie Welsh's body where even God couldn't find it, and instead, they got high and dumped the body in some warehouse. Dixon sent his man to deal with them. If I give you his name, what's it worth to me?" Rowdy asked.

"You gave up Kingston, your own coworker, and a manhunt

and bounty on his head ensued. Fortunately for Kingston, he survived it."

"I want to make a deal," Rowdy said.

"I've already caught all the people involved," Lavinsky said. "You don't have squat to sell me."

"You don't have Beau Whistler. He's the trigger man for everything. I'll give you everything I know about him if you'll put me in an out-of-state prison."

"Actually, I do have Beau Whistler. We had an ongoing manhunt for him, and Gunner Kingston caught him for us. He's in the room next door, claiming guilt only on the death of Dixon."

"If I testify against him, would that get me out of a Texas penitentiary?"

"I'd have to talk to my people."

"I'll do it. I swear to God, I'll do it," Rowdy said.

Lavinsky frowned. "I don't know how far your testimony would go, considering the depth of your guilt in all of it. Who's going to trust you? They'll assume you're lying for a lighter sentence."

"Then I'm dead," Rowdy said.

"That's something you've caused, and your welfare in prison is out of my control," Lavinsky said. "I have four dead agents, four widows, and an accumulation of nine children between them now without their fathers. They're my concern."

Rowdy's lawyer whispered in his ear again.

Rowdy leaned forward. "There's more connected to your case that you don't know about. Whistler did the hit and run on Dan Helford. Yankee Dan, the man who found Freddie Welsh's body. He didn't know anything, but Dixon didn't like loose ends. It's also why he put the hit out on Gunner Kingston. He was the man who took Yankee Dan's statement." Rowdy dropped his head and started crying. "I'll testify."

"Even without a deal?" Lavinsky asked.

He nodded. "Even without a deal."

"Why?" Lavinsky asked.

"If I do the right thing, maybe God will forgive me. I know I'm going to jail and will likely not survive it. But I do not want to go to hell. I'll testify against Whistler."

Lavinsky nodded. "Interrogation ends at 4:44 p.m." Then he and his partner got up and walked out and back up the hall to Whistler.

They walked in and took a seat and started the tape again. Introduced themselves again, noted the time, and then began with more questions.

"Mr. Whistler, charges are being added to your existing one. You are also being charged with the murders of four FBI agents, a federal witness, the murders of Garza and Letourneau, the hit-and-run murder of Dan Helford, also known as Yankee Dan, and collaboration in the attempted murder of Gunner Kingston."

Whistler felt the blood run out of his face. *Son of a bitch. Rowdy gave me up because he knew I couldn't get to him.*

"So, you gave Rowdy a deal to lie about me? How far do you think that will go with a jury?"

"Oh, he isn't getting a deal. We don't make deals with killers, or the people who abet them. He has no illusions about his future. He just doesn't want to go to hell when he dies."

Whistler blinked. He never saw that coming. "I got nothing more to say. We're done here."

"Yes, yes you are. You are so done here, and so are we. We'll see you in court."

They walked out, and for the first time in his life, Whistler didn't have a Plan B.

Gunner woke just after 5:00 p.m., glanced at the time, and then groaned. "I'm turning into Rip van Winkle."

He rolled out of bed and headed to the bathroom mirror. The bruise on his jaw was so purple it was almost black, but it didn't feel as stiff as it had been. The ice packs were helping.

He combed his fingers through his hair, picked up the ice pack on his pillow, and took it to the kitchen to refreeze it. He was kind of hungry, but there was a note from Holly on the counter telling him she'd gone home to pack some clothes and would bring dinner to his house, so he opted for a cold pop and a couple of cookies and headed to the living room with his snack.

He thought about checking his email as he ate but decided to leave it until later and kicked back to watch TV. He was in the act of swallowing the last of his pop when the doorbell rang.

Frankie Adams was on his doorstep, and her money was on the table right beside the door.

"Catch any bad guys today?" he asked as he handed her the envelope.

"No, but they pulled a body out of the fountain in Fair Park. The victim has a hole in his head from an old-fashioned Colt revolver. Everybody seems more excited about the weapon than why the guy was killed. Like always, they'll calm down and figure it out."

He handed her the envelope.

She clasped it to her chest, her eyes welling again. "Thank you."

"I'm glad I could help. If you hustle, you can get it in the bank before they close."

She nodded. "My plan, exactly. Take care of you, Kingston."

He waited until she backed out of his drive before he

shut the door. *Mission accomplished.* He turned off the TV and went to the kitchen, took a pain pill, and went back to the bedroom to make the rest of his calls from his bed.

Both Asher and Dylan had responded to tell him the money had come through. He knew his dad was busy at the Tumbleweed and never checked his phone when he was working, and that he rarely checked his bank account. He'd have to call him tonight and remind him.

As he was scrolling through the messages, he noticed a reply from Lane Bowman, one of the hydrogeologists he'd reached out to, and quickly read it, then called the number. After a brief discussion, the date was set.

"My father, Jacob Kingston, will be your contact. The location is a bit south of his home and business. He will give you directions. I made a tower of rocks on the location where I want to build, and I need you to find the nearest water source. If I have to relocate the build site, then I will," Gunner said.

"Duly noted," Bowman said. "I'll be there tomorrow."

"I'll let my dad know, and thank you," Gunner said.

As soon as that call ended, Gunner called Jacob.

The phone rang a few times, and then his father's voice was in his ear.

"Hey, son! How are you feeling?"

"Like I got stomped by a herd of longhorns, but I'm healing. I called to ask you a favor."

"Ask away," Jacob said.

"I've hired a hydrogeologist by the name of Lane Bowman to locate the nearest water source to where I want to build. He's coming to Crossroads tomorrow, and I gave him your name as the contact. All you need to do is point him in the right direction. I told him there's small tower of rocks that I made to mark the place where I want to build."

"I can do that," Jacob said. "I am so happy you're coming

home, son. It will be wonderful to have you and Holly here again."

"I can't wait to be home. She's going to stay with Garrett, and I'll be bunking with you and Pearl again until the house is built, so we're looking at a few months here. I hope you're ready for that."

"This will always be your home, and your room is always there," Jacob said.

"One other thing, Dad. I had the money transfers made this morning. Asher and Dylan have already received theirs. First chance you get, check your bank account to see if your transfer came through and then let me know."

"That's awesome, Gunner! I will do that later when I get a chance. Thank you again for such a generous gift. We're going to remodel the kitchen here at the house."

"I can't wait to see it," Gunner said.

"You take it slow and take time to heal before you pull another stunt like that. I have been bragging about you a little, and you probably will need to know ahead of time that Pearl found the video online and got some kid to run the feed into her TV at the Rose. She lets it play over and over nonstop. Everybody in town has seen it countless times. She tells all the strangers who stop at the Rose that the hero who ended an FBI manhunt with that stunt is her stepson."

"I guess I'm never going to live that down," Gunner said.

"There's no shame in being a hero, son. Accept it with grace. It doesn't come to many men," Jacob said. "I need to get back to the bar. I'll let you know about the bank account. Take care."

"You, too, Dad," Gunner said and disconnected, then leaned back, thinking, *Life just kept happening of its own accord. All he had to do was hold on.*

Holly's boss had been out of the office all day showing houses, so she sent him an email.

> The appraiser for Gunner's house will be here at the residence tomorrow, and the inspector later in the day. Considering our client's current physical issues, I thought it would be best to be on hand to let him in and stay until all of this is finished. I will continue to work from the residence, so if anybody has questions, or needs me to do some research, just text me.
> Holly

She left Gunner a note, then made a quick trip home while Gunner was asleep to pack some clothes, gathered up the groceries in her refrigerator to use at his house before they ruined, then hurried home. She was anxious about his welfare and knew he was miserable, and that there was nothing she could do to heal him any faster.

One wreck and a car chase later, she exited off the Loop and took the route through the neighborhoods to get there. Pulling up to his house was a relief. She got out her key and suitcase and deactivated the security system as she entered. Two trips later, the food was inside, and so were her briefcase and laptop.

She turned the lock, then went down to check on him. He was asleep and lying on his left side holding his phone—a sign that his mobility was getting better.

She stepped out of her shoes, left them and her suitcase just inside his door, then went to put up the food. A short while later, she went back to check on him. He had rolled over onto his back.

"Hey, superman," Holly said and leaned over the bed to brush a kiss across his mouth.

"Hey, yourself, darlin'. Glad you're home."

“Our dinner won’t be here for another hour. Are you ready to try getting in the Jacuzzi? I think you would really benefit from the jets and the soak.”

“Heck yes.”

“Let me see your arm,” she said and began looking for blood spots on the bandages over the road rash area, but none of them looked fresh. “I can wrap your arm so the bandage there won’t get wet, but you can’t slide down into the water. You’re not to get that arm wet at all until we go back to get the bandages changed. Then they’ll reassess.”

He sat up on the side of the bed. “I was hurting enough in the ER that I didn’t pay much attention to what the doctor was saying about treatment afterward. Good thing you were listening.”

“That’s what I’m here for. I’ll start the water running, then go get some plastic wrap. Do you think you can get yourself in and out of the Jacuzzi okay? Your legs are so bruised, they must be stiff, but the soak in the tub should help the soreness.”

He nodded. “I can do it.”

She went into the bathroom to start water running, then went flying past his bed. “I’m going to get plastic wrap.”

“You don’t need to hurry,” he said, but she was already gone and back with a box of plastic wrap and a roll of Scotch tape before he knew it.

She tore off one long sheet and began wrapping it gently around his forearm beginning at the wrist, and she kept wrapping and adding sheet after sheet until she had the bandage covered from his wrist to his elbow and taped to hold.

“That should work on any unintentional splashes. You get in the tub to see where the water level is and I’ll either let it run some more or turn it off.”

“Best nurse ever,” Gunner said and followed her. He

stepped out of his sweatpants and into the tub, easing himself down, bracing his elbow on one side of the tub and his hand on the other until he was in. "This depth works. You can turn it off."

Holly nodded, turned off the faucets, handed him a washcloth and a bar of soap, and laid a bath towel on the lid of the commode.

"We're gonna need a bigger Jacuzzi when we build our house," he said.

"Why?"

"My legs are too long. There's nowhere for you to squeeze in. I'm gonna need one big enough for the both of us," he said.

She walked out laughing.

Gunner had never been so glad to be clean again. It was like washing away the last remnants of Whistler from his memory. He was out, dry, and dressed in clean sweatpants when he walked into the kitchen.

"Something smells good," he said.

"Our food arrived. Fried catfish and steak fries. I also heated up some baked beans I brought from my place. It's all done if you want supper now."

"Sounds good," he said, then pulled out a chair and sat down. "I'm really grateful you are here, and there's a bit of irony to it."

"How so?" Holly asked as she was making their plates.

"Remember how you used to chase all the fly balls, and dart about grabbing bats for all of us? I can still see that in you… Attacking projects with laser focus and picking up after me again like the bats that I threw. I had no idea back then how much you would come to mean to me now."

She paused, still holding his plate as her eyes lost focus. Gunner knew that she'd gone somewhere else in her mind.

"The hardest thing I've had to do is make peace with losing Mom. The best thing that came after was you. It was like the universe was trying to make up for what had been taken away by giving you back to me. There's nothing I wouldn't give up for you. Loving you is as necessary to me as breathing. The fact that you love me back is a gift I will never take for granted." She sighed, blinked, and finished making their plates and carried them to the table.

When she started to walk away, he reached for her wrist, stopping her, then tapped the side of his face. "Right here," he said.

She giggled, then leaned over and kissed him.

"And here," he said, tapping his lips.

She kissed him there, lingering enough to make him groan, then went back for their drinks and sat down with him. They talked as they ate, filling each other in on the progress of their day until they'd finished their food, and she'd cleared the table, but then they stayed, still planning for the day ahead.

"The hydrogeologist is going out to the house site sometime tomorrow. If he can't find a good water source there, then we'll have to choose another location, but I feel confident about it," Gunner said.

"Oh… You were asleep when I first got home, and then I forgot to tell you. The appraiser for this house will be here tomorrow around eleven. I will be here to let him in and for the duration of his inspection. The inspector is coming tomorrow afternoon. The day is going to be a hassle for you, but we'll be getting it over with at once. It's actually part of my job as a Realtor, and I left Gene a note letting him know I'm working virtually until you're much better. He was out of the office all day today showing houses, so it's not an issue. I can do all the research they need from my laptop as easily as the PC on my desk... If that's alright with you?" she added.

Gunner was listening, thinking of the days ahead when this was all behind them when he realized that the light coming through the stained-glass window behind her was bathing her in a multi-colored aura. A kind of heavenly halo. *She might not be an angel from heaven, but she's sure my angel.*

Then he realized she'd just asked him a question.

"Of course it's alright. It's all coming together, isn't it, Holly? Moving out of this house and building our new one. Going home to Crossroads."

She nodded. "I never thought about how much I would miss Crossroads until I was gone. Yes, I have a good job. But I never had a life outside of work. I didn't like the party life. I guess I was too much of a country girl to see the point in watching everyone else get drunk and make fools of themselves, so I quit accepting the invitations. I liked my own company better than what was offered to me here. Time passed. I got in such a rut that the only thing I had to look forward to was eating dinner in front of the TV and then going to bed. I always missed the noise a family makes, and you were the last person on earth I ever expected to see at Whole Foods. Even after I recognized you from that distance, I still couldn't believe it. Do you know what old song was playing in the background when I saw you?"

He shook his head. "I don't think I was even aware there was music."

"'Then Came You', an old Dionne Warwick song from before we were even born. One of my mom's favorite oldies. There's a line in the song... 'I never knew love before...and then came you.' It was like getting hit with a bolt of lightning. I couldn't move. I forgot to breathe. And then you started walking away, and I moved from shock to panic. I couldn't lose sight of you until I saw you as the man you had become, and you saw me."

"And the rest is history," Gunner said. "It took me about five minutes to get past thinking of you as the kid and realizing what a beautiful woman you'd grown up to be. Following up was the best impulse I ever had. Now, I cannot imagine life without you."

She sat for a few moments, watching the expressions changing on his face, before she spoke. "You have quite a gift, Gunner Kingston."

He arched an eyebrow. "If you mean running headfirst into situations without thinking of the dangers, I would agree."

She shrugged. "Well, there's that, too, but no. You make love with your eyes and your words before you ever touch my body. You give of yourself before you ever take from another."

It wasn't until her face blurred before him that he felt real tears in his eyes. Neither pain, anger, nor betrayal had ever made him cry, but love just did, and without warning.

Holly saw his tears, and then the flash of panic that followed, and calmly got up to refill their glasses. By the time she came back the tears were gone. But when she turned to walk away, he reached for her with his good arm and pulled her close.

His head was below her chin as she stood within his embrace. "It's hard to let down the walls you don't even know are there, isn't it, love?"

"I never asked you to marry me. I just asked you to love me. That was selfish as hell. Trusting a woman was always like a foreign language to me. I knew there was a need to be able to communicate, but I didn't know how to conjugate the verbs or which adjectives to use. Until the last time I went to Whole Foods. There I was, minding my own business in the cereal aisle when I heard this voice behind me and turned to see who was calling my name, and it was like watching my whole future roll out in front of me. A spurt of panic followed, wondering if you were unattached. Then another spurt of panic that you'd still see me as just a friend when I wanted you to see me as more. We'll pick out rings before we leave Dallas, but will you marry me, Holly Dillon?"

She was nodding through tears. "Yes, please, and thank you," she said. He pulled her into his lap and kissed her senseless.

That night she slept tucked up beside him with his hand against her back and dreamed of home, and the glorious sunrises and sunsets, and the sounds of coyotes yipping on the hunt, and the horses on her daddy's ranch, and her mother standing on the porch waving goodbye as she drove away, and she woke up crying.

Gunner woke at the sound and rolled over. "Holly, darlin', are you okay?"

"A good dream went bad," she said. "I'm good. I'm good."

Frustrated by the restriction of bandages on his right arm, he got up and circled the bed to sit beside her. "I'm sorry, baby…so sorry. You go wash away your tears and I'll go start the coffee. I can do that much without making a mess."

"Okay, I'll be right there as soon as I get dressed."

"You don't have to do that on my account," he said and then grinned.

She rolled her eyes. "You are incorrigible."

"So that means I can't go commando to make breakfast?"

"Like I said…incorrigible," she said, but she was laughing, and only later realized he'd said and done all that to erase the bad dream.

Chapter 19

By the time the appraiser was due, Gunner was semidressed in a pair of loose sweats and an athletic tank top and wearing flip-flops instead of shoes, and Holly was wearing sandals, light-blue slacks, and a white summer top.

"You look beautiful," Gunner said when he walked into the kitchen.

Holly looked up from the sandwiches she was making and smiled. "Thank you, honey. Gotta look professional for the appraiser, and look at you. Pants, a shirt, and shoes!"

"What are you doing?" he asked.

"Making some food so you can eat when you're hungry. George takes forever when he's doing an appraisal, but he's good and honest. He'll be in the attic, eyeing all of the HVAC, the security system, the system for exiting the property through the back gate, the windows, and the rooms. I'll be surprised if he finishes in two hours, and then we have Austin the inspector later. I've already made the bed and put out fresh towels in the bathroom and checked your extra rooms. They're photo-ready, but he'll be opening doors and drawers, too. Oh… Do you have your own weapon here in the house?"

Gunner nodded. "Yes, but it's a handgun in a lockbox, and he will have no need for me to open that box, because I'm taking it with me."

She smiled. "I was mostly asking for his well-being. George once opened a closet door during an appraisal, and a loaded shotgun that was leaning too near the door fell out and went off. Shot a huge hole in the wall beside him."

"Good lord," Gunner said. "Don't tell me. The guy who owned the house also had kids, right?"

She nodded. "Three. Don't worry about anything while he's here, okay? It's my responsibility to deal with him. Feel free to grab a sandwich and a cold drink and escape to the patio. Or, when he's finished at the back of the house, go to bed if you want to lie down and just close the door. I've got you."

He watched her spreading pimento cheese spread on both slices of bread, then adding thin slices of tomato on one slice and lettuce on the other before she put the pieces together. She cut it in half and wrapped it up, then put it on the platter with the other sandwich she'd already made and put it in the refrigerator.

"For whenever you want it," she said, then licked a bit of cheese spread off her thumb. "Just enough jalapeno to make it tasty. Maybe you'll be up to chewing steak again soon. Tomorrow is the day you go back to the doctor for them to check your progress. They said the risk of infection to your forearm is at its highest now, before it starts forming scabs."

"Yes, ma'am," Gunner said, and when she looked up, he grinned at her.

"Okay… I could be overcompensating, but you're the one who came home looking like you did."

"You mean, like that last rooster standing in a cockfight?" he asked.

She was trying not to smile. "You heard me," she said, and then the doorbell rang.

Gunner winked. "I'll just get myself a cold drink and journey to the back patio to dry my pin feathers, okay?"

"Lord," she muttered and took off to the front room while he snagged a pop and sandwich and went outside.

The day was hot, but the patio fan stirring air above him made it comfortable. He eased himself down in a lounge chair, opened the bottle of pop, and took a drink before he dug into the sandwich. The first bite was cool, crunchy, cheesy goodness. *Damn. She even makes cheese sandwiches taste good.* He finished the food and the drink and then leaned back and closed his eyes. He could hear muted voices that disappeared as they moved farther away from where he was at, and he dozed off.

He woke as they were coming outside, and got up from the chair.

"Oh shoot, Gunner. Sorry we woke you," Holly said.

"That's okay, honey. I'll just get out of your way," he said and started to go inside when the appraiser, who'd been watching the interchange, suddenly realized who he was.

He looked at Holly in shock. "Gunner? This is *the* Gunner Kingston, from the video?"

"Every black-and-blue piece of him," Gunner said, then winked at Holly as he went inside, closing the slider behind him. He could still hear George the appraiser talking. Clearly, meeting him had sidetracked his appraisal duties.

Holly finally refocused George on the task at hand. By the time he'd confirmed the square footage and the added features in the backyard, it was almost two o'clock. She walked him out the door, then started through the house, calling Gunner's name.

He stepped out into the hall. "Yes, darlin'?"

She laughed and walked into his arms. "The sight of you sure threw George off his game. I swear to God, he had the gall to ask if he could take a picture with you. Of course I told him no. That's all you need is to become a target for another nutcase."

The smile slid off Gunner's face. "You would have made a good cop's wife, and thank you for thinking of my welfare."

"I don't care what you do for a living, as long as I'm along for the ride," she said.

"You're already on that team," he said and then kissed her. "Have you eaten anything since breakfast?"

"A spoonful or two of pimento cheese while I was making sandwiches, but I can eat the other one now that he's gone," she said. "The inspector is due within the hour."

A short while later, the inspector arrived, along with storm clouds gathering on the horizon. It looked like rain.

They stayed out of his way while he rushed through his inspection, as anxious to get home before the storm hit as they were for him to be gone.

Finally, he was gone, and Holly and Gunner were in the living room eating biscuits and sausage gravy while keeping track of the intermittent weather updates. They could see the storm on radar, moving closer to the city, until the clouds finally blocked out the sunset and the wind began to rise.

At that point, Holly pulled her knees up beneath her chin and wrapped her arms around her legs. "I hate storms."

He slid closer to her and put his good arm around her shoulders. "I'm sorry, darlin'. I didn't know that, but we're safe. I have that Generac generator system for power losses, and you already know the walk-in closet in the first spare bedroom is also an F-5 storm shelter."

She nodded. "I know. George was impressed when I showed him. Those kinds of features up your appraisal value. I'm just a big baby about it."

"No. We all have cracks in our defenses. You already know mine. You are not in your condo. You are in a house that will keep you safe, and when we build our house, no matter what it looks like at ground level, there will be a decent basement beneath, just like the one we have at Dad's. He always said you can lose and replace things, but you can't replace people. That's why he had that one dug when he built the house onto the back of the Tumbleweed."

"I can't wait to go home," Holly said.

"If you want to give over selling this house to one of the other Realtors in your office, we can make it happen even sooner."

"Really?"

"We can put stuff in storage here, and sort through what we want to keep and what we want to bring to the new house after it's built. That way we'll be on-site from the beginning when the building begins," he said.

Lightning flashed, followed by a loud clap of thunder, but the tornado watch had not evolved into a warning.

"Lord," Holly said. "What do you usually do on nights like this?"

"Eat ice cream. It's my cure for just about everything that messes with my attitude," he said.

"I'm in," Holly said. "You sit and keep watching the weather. I'll get the ice cream."

"I require a minimum of four scoops," he said.

"Coming up," she said as she ran out of the room.

Pearl had already shut the Yellow Rose down for the night and was back at the house with Jacob. The bar up front was busy, but she knew Jacob would not close before midnight, and he needed to check in with Gunner about the man who'd come to find water. The stranger had some kind of fancy title, but in Pearl's world, he was just another man who witched for water. After she had Jacob's food on the table, she went to stand in for him while he ate and made his call, and the moment she showed up at the bar, everyone shouted out in unison, "Good evening, Miss Pearl."

She blew them a kiss and then whispered in Jacob's ear. "Your supper is ready, and don't forget to call Gunner before you come back. He's still in healing mode and might be going to bed earlier than usual."

"Thank you, sweetheart, for the food and the reminder," he said and then shouted out across the room. "Nobody gives Pearl a hard time."

"We're more afraid of her than we are of you," one of the men shouted, and then everyone laughed.

Pearl grabbed a bar rag and began cleaning off the empty tables as Jacob entered the house.

He washed up, then sat down at the table and called Gunner. He could eat while he talked. The phone rang a couple of times and then he heard his son's voice.

"Hey, Dad. We're having a really noisy thunderstorm right now. What's happening at home?"

"I just sat down to supper, so I might be chewing in your ear. Pearl's behind the bar, so I won't dally."

"I remember chewing," Gunner said.

Jacob frowned. "Is your jaw still giving you fits?"

"It's getting better. Did the hydrogeologist show up?" Gunner asked.

"He did. He stopped by when he was leaving and said to tell you it was good news, and he'd send you all the details via email."

"Fantastic!" Gunner said.

"Also, I'm confirming the money transfer came through. Nothing stays secret for long in Crossroads, but given our previous issue with being blamed for the armed car robbery, I would like permission to admit that it was a gift from you," Jacob said.

"Oh, dang it, Dad! I didn't even think about that. Yes, tell them it was a gift from me, and that I won the damn lottery, if you want. It will explain everything else I do when I get home."

"Thanks, son. Even though people finally knew the truth of that, it's still in the back of their minds, and I'm sorry."

"You have nothing to be sorry for," Gunner said. "Enjoy your supper. I know it has to be great because Pearl made it, and we'll be home before you know it."

"You have no idea how happy this makes me," Jacob said. "Take care of yourself and get well first."

"Yes, sir. It's my intention," Gunner said and then looked up as Holly returned with two bowls of ice cream. "We're still safe. It's noisy, but no funnels have formed. Enjoy your supper."

"I'll do that. Can't leave Pearl alone too long in the Weed. She'll have the men all using napkins and bringing their dirty glasses to the bar," Jacob said.

Gunner was still smiling when his dad disconnected, and moved a pillow so Holly could sit beside him.

Gunner took his first bite of ice cream. "Dad called. He said we have a good water source for the build, and the man will be sending me details via email."

"One more step accomplished," she said, but still chose the seat closest to him. Bruises and stitches aside, he would always be her safe place to fall.

Jacob ate his way through supper and finished it off with a bowl of banana pudding. Pearl never made a meal without dessert, which made him a happy man. When he finished, he rinsed the dishes and put them in the dishwasher, then went back into the bar.

"Thanks for standing in for me, and for that good food," Jacob said and kissed Pearl on the cheek.

She turned a sweet shade of pink and hustled out before the crowd got rowdy again.

The thunderstorms over Dallas passed with nothing more than minor wind damage, most of which consisted of trampolines blowing into neighbors' yards and dead or dying trees finally giving up the ghost.

Gunner woke up, heard Holly in the shower, and went to the guest bath to wash up. When he came back to the room, she was getting dressed for the day.

"Hey, honey, do you want me to wrap your arm again for the Jacuzzi?"

"I do, but I need my wake-up kiss first," he said.

"Your wake-up kisses make me wish for so much more," she said and then put her arms around his neck and leaned in for the onslaught of emotions she knew were coming.

And they did, like an avalanche.

The thudding heartbeat.

A growing ache without release until they stopped.

"Good morning, love. The storms are gone, and it's a new day," Gunner said.

Holly felt like a leaf, still floating in the wind, still trying to fall to earth.

"Yes, it is. I'm going to get the plastic wrap."

He went into the bathroom and started filling up the tub. The skin still pulled a little beneath the bandages, but he was sure ready to get them off. Maybe today was the day.

As soon as she had the arm wrapped up again, he got in the tub and turned on the jets.

"Take all the time you want," Holly said as she put out a fresh bath towel and handed him a washcloth. "I am going to verify the appointment time that was made with your doctor," she said and turned to walk out.

"Hey, Holly."

She paused and turned around. "Yes?"

"Thank you."

"I don't need thanks for taking care of the man I love." And then she was gone.

He emerged later with the whisker stubble gone, actual clothing, and slip-on loafers, minus the socks.

Holly was impressed. "Gunner, sweetheart! Look at you! I'm as proud of your progress as I was when Travis finally learned to tie his shoes."

Gunner laughed. "Darlin', your analogies are bumper stickers for life."

"Whatever," she said, but it made her happy when he laughed.

It was just after 10:00 a.m. when they left the house.

At Holly's insistence, he'd taken a pain pill. Not because he was in that much pain, but she was afraid when they started pulling off bandages, he would be.

When they arrived at the doctors' building, instead of parking in front, Holly circled the building and parked near a side entrance.

"Why are we parking here?" Gunner asked.

"Because we're not parading through the main lobby. People keep taking pictures of you and posting them on social media. All that's going to do is give someone who knew Whistler or that crooked detective the idea that they should finish the job," she said.

"Damn, girl. You think like a cop."

"Doctor Raines agreed with me. You're not sitting in the waiting room, either."

"You're calling the shots, darlin'," he said.

She nodded and sent a quick text. "Okay, out we go," she said and locked the doors behind them as they entered the building.

They were walking up a long hall when a nurse came around the corner and waved at them. "I'm your escort. Follow me."

They wound through one hallway after another, past a lab, past X-ray and digital imaging, and then through a door into the area where Doctor Raines's exam rooms were located.

"You're in Room 4," the nurse said. As soon as Gunner was sitting on the exam table, she took his blood pressure and temp. "We're going to need you to take off your shirt, sir."

"Right," Gunner said.

Holly got up without saying a word and helped him pull the T-shirt he was wearing over his head.

The nurse blinked. She'd seen the bandage on his arm and the bruise on his jaw but was not prepared for the rest of it, or the larger bandage on his shoulder. Wisely, she said nothing.

"Dr. Raines will be here shortly," she said and closed the door on her way out.

Holly sat back in her chair with his shirt on her lap and raised an eyebrow at the charts on the wall. "A hypochondriac would have a meltdown in here," she muttered.

Gunner nodded. "Very descriptive, but still better than reading autopsy reports. Trust me."

Holly leaned back against the wall for a more comfortable position. "We never went to the doctor unless we were really sick. With the closest doctor being in Amarillo, it wasn't convenient."

"Crossroads is lucky to have Urgent Care and two nurses on staff now, with a once-a-week doctor. It's not large enough to sustain an actual hospital."

"It doesn't really grow, does it?" Holly said.

"No, but that's due to lack of available jobs and housing. Finding a place to live there is almost impossible," he said.

Holly's eyes widened. "You could build an apartment building. Six up and six down, just to see if it would make a difference. If people took to the idea, you'd be in business."

"That is actually a really good idea. I've been thinking about the simpler ways I could make a difference there. I know nothing about leasing or renting homes, but I sure know someone who does. If we did that, it would have to be your business to run. Collecting rent, dealing with problems and repairs."

Her eyes lit up. "I could do that with my eyes closed," she said.

"Then that will be our first project," he said. "My wife, the real estate mogul."

"Considering the size of Crossroads, mogul might be stretching the point."

"Gotta start somewhere," Gunner said, and then the door opened and Doctor Raines walked in, followed by his nurse.

"Gunner Kingston, and who's the lovely lady you have with you?"

"Holly Dillon, my soon-to-be wife. Holly, this is Dr. Benjamin Raines. For my sins, I have been his patient ever since joining the force."

"A pleasure to meet you, and best wishes for the both of you." Then he took a look at Gunner and shook his head. "I knew when I saw that video that you would soon be gracing my clinic. And the word is, you did this one as a civilian. Did you really quit the force?"

"I did. Having a bounty put on my head and a dozen hit men after the money can ruin a whole lot of things," Gunner said.

"Good lord! The public knew nothing about that!"

Gunner nodded. "Yet another reason the bubble burst for me. It's hard to work in a department knowing there's a dirty cop somewhere in the bunch, and no one wanted to hear the words or consider the possibility. Bad look for the department, and all that."

"So, that guy on the Harley...?"

"Wanted by the FBI. His face was all over the news. I just happened to see him," Gunner said.

Raines frowned. He'd known Kingston long enough to recognize he was being redirected to a different subject, so he got down to business.

"I've read the ER report on these injuries. Let's get these bandages off so I can see where we're at."

With his nurse assisting, Raines began on the lower part of the arm. The bandaging was stuck in a couple of places, but he got it off without causing any scabbing to break loose and start bleeding.

"Is this painful?" Raines asked.

"Somewhat. Mostly. Is it at the point where I can get it wet?" Gunner asked.

Raines frowned. "You could let warm water run over it and gently wash it with soap on the palm of your hand, but not on a washcloth. Pat it dry, lightly apply Neosporin, then use nonstick gauze pads to cover it, and keep them in place with a wrap like an Ace bandage. We'll reapply a fresh bandage here for now. The rest will be up to you."

"I'll take that as progress," Gunner said.

"Let's take a look at the stitches," Raines said as he removed the large patch on Gunner's shoulder and checked that out. "These are healing properly. I don't see any undue inflammation. You can leave the bandage off here. It will heal faster without it, but you will still need to finish the prescription of antibiotics, and pain pills as needed. Of course, if you think it's become infected, don't waste time getting back to a doctor, wherever you are." Then he tapped lightly on the bruise on Gunner's jaw. "Did that hurt?"

Gunner nodded.

"Then don't do that," Raines said and grinned. "It's a heck of a bruise. Ice is the best medicine for that."

Gunner grinned. "You're still a wiseass."

"And you're still a badass," Raines said. "The real deal. I think we're done here." He glanced at Holly. "You've got your hands full with this one."

"I've known him for as long as I've been alive. I already knew he was pure gold."

Gunner winked. "Right now, she's *my* bodyguard, and I'm smart enough not to argue."

"Sit tight. My nurse will be back to rebandage the lower arm and bring the info I mentioned about wound care. There's one refill on those antibiotics. I suggest you refill it and finish it out. The stitches will heal faster than the injury on your lower arm."

They both left, leaving Holly to help him get dressed. When they were ready to leave, the same nurse who'd walked them in returned to walk them back to their exit. It was almost noon.

"I'm buying lunch," Gunner said as they got back in her car. "What's your pleasure? Food Truck? Fast food drive-in? Pick up an order to go? I know you have to work this afternoon, and I don't want you fussing around about trying to feed me," Gunner said.

"Anything pasta!" Holly said. "Like spaghetti with meatballs, and you can eat pasta without hurting your jaw. If you know a good Italian place close to home, you order it as I drive, and we'll pick it up on the way."

"Deal, and I'll let you know when we need to divert the route," he said as she headed for an on-ramp. Less than five minutes on the Loop and they witnessed a fender bender, and a mile further down, a fistfight happening on the shoulder of the road.

"Hell of a place to have a disagreement," Gunner said as they drove past.

Holly laughed. "You are the king of understatement."

He grinned, and as soon as they exited the Loop, he directed her to the Italian restaurant.

"It's already paid for," Gunner said as she parked.

"Okay, but I'll go in to get it. You stay."

"Woof," Gunner said and nodded his head.

She wasn't going to give him an inch. "Be a good boy. I'll see if they have pup cups."

He was still grinning when the entrance door closed behind her. *Lord, she is going to be so much fun to live with.*

That night, after Holly's workday had ended, they grilled wieners for hot dogs on the patio grill and ate supper by moonlight. It was a far cry from the storms of the night before and a peaceful way to spend an evening.

It had been so long since normal was even a part of Gunner's life that he was beginning to realize how much he'd given up for the job. He was having to relearn what it meant to relax.

Holly was snuggled up against him, with her head on his shoulder, when she suddenly sat up and turned to face him.

"Hey, Gunner, do you remember that wiener roast the coach had your senior year after baseball season was over?"

Gunner grinned. "Was that when you got the toasted marshmallow in your hair?"

She rolled her eyes. "Maybe. But I was referring to the

shiny gold crown the team gave me for being best bat girl of the year."

He smiled. "I remember. You were so dang cute."

"It was made out of cardboard, but someone had covered it with gold Christmas wrap and glued all kinds of glass 'jewels' on it. Mom took a picture of me with the team wearing the crown that night."

"Really? Wish I'd seen that," Gunner said.

"It's hanging on the wall in my old bedroom back home. I'm standing in front of you and Will Devlin. Each of you have a hand resting on my shoulders. I want to hang it in our house after we move in."

His teasing ended as he reached for her hand.

"Darlin', I would love it. That was our before, and now is our after. It needs to be there."

She leaned her head against his shoulder. Her childhood hero had become so much more to her than she could have imagined. That this was even happening still felt like a dream.

And so they stayed, lulled by the slight rocking of the glider in which they were sitting, with the night breeze stirring the air and muting the sounds out on the street. Interrupting the silence with their intermittent bursts of laughter that punctuated the moments between their kisses.

Later, as Gunner was getting into bed with her, he was wishing for so much more. "Holly, darlin', I want to make love to you so bad I ache."

Her hand was on his chest, feeling the steady thump of his heart. "I know… So do I, but while the epic leap you made knocking Whistler off the Harley solved the FBI's problem, it created another one for you. You're going to have to get better before you even think about stressing out the stitches on your shoulder or making your forearm start bleeding again."

Gunner sighed. "I know, I know. Last rooster standing, and all that."

Her silence lay between them until she leaned over and brushed a kiss across his lips. "I know you're frustrated, and tired of being frustrated, but I'm fine. However, if you promise to lie real still and close your eyes, I know how to rock *you* to sleep."

A muscle jerked at the side of his eye as he reached out and turned off the lamp. He was already hard, and she was nothing but a silhouette in the dark as he watched her sit up.

"Promise you won't move," she said.

"Promise," he said and closed his eyes.

He felt the bed give to her movements, then the weight of her straddling his hips as she eased herself down on his rock-hard erection. Tight. Warm. Soft as silk. Those were his last conscious thoughts as she began to move.

Her heart quickened when she heard a soft groan. Making love was the best feeling, and the most urgent feeling on earth—the only thing you never want to end, while chasing the climax you so desperately need to happen.

"Please say I'm not hurting you," she whispered, then heard a groan, followed by a softly muttered plea not to stop.

It was all the verification she needed. She went faster, took him deeper, over and over, closer to the climax building within them.

It came without warning, washing through them in waves, until the ripples had faded into a stupor of afterglow.

"Lord, woman…" He took a breath, and as she moved away, it was like losing a piece of himself. "That was so… You are… You gave…"

She put a finger over his lips. "Shh. It's just me loving you." She kissed him and slipped into the bathroom.

When she came back, he was asleep.

"Rock-a-bye, baby," she whispered, then pulled the covers up over both of them and fell asleep.

When she woke, her alarm was going off. She silenced it, then realized he was already in the shower. That meant he'd need her help replacing bandages. Today she was going back to her actual office to work, and Gunner would be on his own.

The rest of the week became a whirlwind of decisions. Gunner found an architect to draw up blueprints for the house and took himself back to the doctor to get the stitches out in his arm, and another checkup on his forearm.

When he walked into the waiting room wearing sunglasses and a long-sleeved shirt, nobody paid attention. He was becoming old news, which was a blessing. Time had a way of doing that.

Once he was back in an exam room, it was back off with the shirt, and then waiting. When Dr. Raines walked in and saw the sunglasses lying on his shirt, he smiled.

"Incognito. Perfect." Then he moved to the stitches. "These have healed great, so yes, they're coming out."

He and his nurse proceeded to remove the stitches in his arm, then moved down to his forearm and unwrapped all of the bandages.

"All of the raw places are healing beautifully. A few scabby places, and a whole lot of new pink skin, but that can still be re-injured easily, so proceed with caution. Don't stop the antibiotic ointment until all of the wounds have closed, and you will still need to keep the new skin soft. Maybe use Holly's moisturizer, or some of your own. I'd say another week or two and you should be good to go," Raines said.

"That's good news all the way around," Gunner said.

As soon as they finished rewrapping his forearm, he went back to his car and sent Holly a text.

> Stitches out. Forearm healing. Mustang on the move.
> If you need anything for tonight, now's the time to let me know.
> Love you,
> Roadrunner

Holly was walking out of the office on her way to the Tarrant County Courthouse when she got the text. She got into her car and started it up to cool off, then read it and smiled. All good news, but now she was back to concern for him. Gunner Kingston was off the "be careful" list, which also meant back to normal. His normal was usually someone else's nightmare, but she wouldn't want to change a thing about him. She responded to his message.

> Fabulous news. We're set for food, but if you're getting short of nonstick bandages or Neosporin, you might want to make a stop at your pharmacy before you go home. I'm on the way to the Tarrant County Courthouse. See you this evening.
> Love you more,
> Holly

Gunner had one special stop in mind. He was headed to a jewelry store in the Galleria. He'd borrowed one of her favorite rings for size and was coming home with their rings. If he hadn't pulled that motorcycle stunt, this would have already been done.

The Galleria was in its usual orderly chaos. Moving through the foot traffic inside the mall was almost as hectic as driving on the Loop, but he knew where he was going, and he knew what he wanted.

He got a few double takes but ignored them and kept walking until he got to Zales Jewelry. He began looking in display cases until he found engagement rings and ring sets and started looking for the ones with an oval cut. He'd noticed how pretty that shape looked on Holly's finger, and she clearly favored the style.

When a salesclerk approached, he handed him Holly's ring for size, then they began shopping what was on hand.

"I want an oval-cut diamond. White gold, at least a carat, and with a matching band."

The clerk nodded and pulled what they had in her size.

Gunner wasn't a man for waffling. He saw what he wanted and pointed. "That set. May I see that one, please?" He picked up the engagement ring and held it to the light, imagining the light in her eyes when she saw it and how it would look on her hand. He had no memory of ever seeing a ring on his mother's hand, but she must have had one at some time.

On the day of their wedding, he was going to be the man who put it on her finger. "These are perfect, and I need a wedding band for myself."

A short while later, he left the store with his purchases, stopped at one kiosk on his way out of the mall and bought flowers, then at another kiosk to buy a dozen macarons, and headed home.

Holly came home to see flowers on the dining table and three flavors of macarons beneath the glass dome of Gunner's cake stand. The table was set, and she could smell something savory in the warming oven.

Gunner was standing beside the island, smiling. She dumped her briefcase and purse and threw her arms around his neck.

"Honey! This is so beautiful! What's going on?" she asked.

"You've been taking such good care of me, I wanted to do something special for you," he said, then cupped her face.

She shivered. The way he looked at her said it all, and then he kissed her and took the ring out of his shirt pocket. At that point, she lost focus of everything around her but this man and the sound of his voice.

"I love you, Holly Dillon...with every breath in my body. I asked you before without rings. I'm asking you again with my heart in your hands. Will you marry me?"

"Yes, a thousand times, yes," she said, then watched him slip the ring on her finger. The overhead lights caught in the facets, sparkling like starlight on her hand. "It's beautiful, Gunner, and it's a perfect fit." She kissed him again and then threw back her head and laughed from the sheer joy of it.

He was grinning. "Not bad for the last standing rooster at the cockfight?"

She rolled her eyes. "You are never going to let me forget that, are you?"

"Honey... In the middle of a very painful, serious event, you made me laugh. It was the best moment of that day, so hell no, I'm not going to forget it," he said.

A timer went off behind them.

"Dinner is about to be served," he said.

"What are we having?" she asked.

"Chicken."

"Hopefully not that raggedy rooster," she said.

Gunner was still laughing as he went to get the casserole out of the oven.

"I'm taking it out. You don't want to add a burn to your arm, too," she said.

"Oops, good call," he said. "It's actually chicken pot pie from the Whole Foods deli, but they're good. I'll get the salad. It came out of a bag from the same place, and your favorite macarons for dessert."

They worked together as if they'd been doing it for years and then sat down together. Holly looked at the ring on her finger again and thought of the years to come, and then Gunner bowed his head.

"I am a blessed man. Amen, thank you Lord, and pass the pepper."

She giggled, pushed the shaker within reach, and took her first bite. "Ummm, Chef Kingston, you outdid yourself. This is so good."

It was the wee hours of the morning when Holly woke to a whisper in her ear.

"I can't sleep. I need you. Let me love you."

So, she did.

Chapter 20

Within three weeks, a local well driller out of Amarillo had drilled the water well for their home, and a pump installer had set the pump and provided the well house to cover it. A contractor and his crew were waiting to break ground the next week.

Gunner's house was under contract, and the belongings they planned to keep were in a Dallas storage facility. The rest had been donated to Habitat for Humanity Resale.

Gunner had driven the Rubicon back to Crossroads yesterday with most of his clothes, left it at his dad's, and flew back to Dallas the same day.

It was also Holly's last day at work, and her coworkers gave her a personal wedding shower at the office while Gene was out showing a house. The gifts were all sexy bits of lingerie. Holly accepted them with the proper gasps and blushes, without mentioning they both slept in the nude, and drove to the room she and Gunner had reserved at a hotel near the airport where he would be landing.

A couple of hours later, she heard sounds outside her room, and then a click. Gunner walked in the room with an overnight bag.

"You're back!" Holly said and rolled off the bed to meet him. "Did everything go okay?"

"Yes. The Jeep is parked at Dad's. My clothes are unloaded in my room, and my Mustang is now in the parking lot of this hotel, gassed up and ready. We're heading to the land of no Uber options, no DoorDash, and no freaking traffic jams," he said and gave her a quick kiss. "What about you?"

"The girls at the office gave me a personal wedding shower."

"What's a personal wedding shower?" he asked.

She pointed to the display of stuff straight out of Victoria's Secret. "Don't ever expect me to wear any of that stuff," she added.

"Good. I like you better nekkid," he drawled. "I'm starving. Let's go down to the restaurant, okay?"

"Whither thou goest," she said and went to get her shoes.

While they were in the restaurant, Gunner got a text. "Hey, honey, it's from Detective Frankie Adams. Remember her?"

"Yes! Read it. It might be important," she said.

Gunner opened the text. There was a picture and the words THANK YOU FROM THE ADAMS FAMILY. It was a picture of their home with a new roof, a shiny new handicap ramp, and a fresh paint job on the exterior of the house. In the photo, Frankie and her sister were standing on the porch with their mother in her wheelchair between them. They were all giving him a thumbs-up.

"Look at this, darlin'," he said and handed Holly his phone.

"That's a great photo. Is that her family with her? What are they thanking you for?"

He shrugged. "I always knew Detective Adams was struggling financially. About four years ago, she moved back to her childhood home to care for her handicapped mother, as well as footing the bill for her younger sister's beauty school. The day she and Cliff came to the house, I got to thinking how much I had, and how much she needed help, so I called her that night and said I wanted to offer a little financial assistance, but I didn't want to insult her. She was shocked. Then she cried, but she wasn't insulted. She accepted it with gratitude and came by the next day to pick up the check. I think that was the day you went home to pack some clothes."

Holly was in awe. "Just when I think you can't get any better, I find out something like this."

He shrugged. "I gave her the same amount of money that Burgess Dixon was offering to the first hit man who killed me. For me, it erased the ugliness of that. Now, when I think of that amount, I think of Frankie and her family doing okay. That's a new roof and paint job on the exterior. The handicap ramp she needed for her mother wasn't there before, and her hair is blue, which means she's still the model for her sister's lessons."

Holly was in tears. She could only imagine what that must have meant to the whole family. "I just love you," she said.

He grinned. "Thanks, I love you, too."

"Give me a sec to powder my nose, and I'll be ready to go," Holly said.

While she was gone, Gunner replied to Frankie's message.

> Freakin' awesome! Have a blessed life! Your hair is blue!

They woke up at daybreak. Gunner lifted a curly lock of hair away from the corner of Holly's eye and then kissed her on the nose.

"Up and at 'em, sleepyhead! This is the day we get the hell out of Dallas."

After that, it was a whirlwind of action. Packing up their overnight bags, eating a quick breakfast, and checking out of the hotel. It was just after 7:00 a.m. when they went out to valet parking. Because they were traveling together, but in two separate cars, they began discussing the trip.

"Don't drive too fast and lose me," Holly said.

"As if," Gunner said. "If we get separated in Dallas traffic, it's no big deal. I'll be watching our Life360 apps. I'll know when you get on the 287 that takes us home. If I'm ahead of you, I'll wait for you to catch up. If you're ahead of me, just keep driving; I'll catch up with you. When you need to stop for any reason, flash your lights or pass me. Then we'll pull off together at the next exit."

"There comes my car," Holly said, pointing to the white Chevy SUV pulling up.

"And mine's right behind it," Gunner said. "Do you need to gas up?"

"No, I did it before I got to the hotel last night," she said.

"I'm good to go, too," Gunner said. "Be careful. Love you," he said.

"You're the roadrunner. You be careful, and love you more," she said.

They traded a hug and a kiss and then loaded up the bags, then drove away with Holly in the lead and Gunner tailing her up. Even if they got separated in traffic it wouldn't matter. They knew the way home.

The drive turned out to be a combination of good weather and bad traffic, impeding the ETA Gunner and Holly had planned. But about ten minutes from home, Gunner got a call from his dad. "Just checking in on your progress," Jacob said.

"We're about ten minutes from home. There were a couple of traffic delays. See you soon," Gunner said.

"Is Holly with you or—"

"She's right behind me, driving her car and loaded for bear. I know she's tired. We both are," Gunner said.

"Garrett and Travis are here. I think one of them plans to drive her the rest of the way home," Jacob said. "Make sure she knows it."

"Good news, and thanks. I'll see if they've already called to let her know," Gunner said, disconnected, then called Holly. "Hey, darlin', have you heard from your dad or Travis about meeting you at the Tumbleweed?"

She was laughing. "Travis just called me not a minute ago. I need a great big goodbye hug and kiss before we part company. There are going to be some lonesome nights for the both of us before that house is ready, but we'll have the rest of our lives after to snore in each other's ears."

"I do not snore," he said.

"Yeah, me either," Holly said, and then they burst out laughing.

"Hug coming up in a very few minutes," he said and disconnected.

Less than a quarter of a mile from Crossroads, they began seeing cars lined up on both sides of the highway and people standing beside them holding up big signs.

"What the hell?" Gunner muttered, then his phone rang. It was Holly.

"Gunner! What's happening?"

"I don't know. They're holding up signs, and now I can hear horns honking and… I'll be damned," he whispered. "They're for us, Holly. The signs are for us. Welcome home! Welcome home, Gunner and Holly! Prodigals return! I don't get it!" he said, and then they began slowing down and turning into the parking lot at the Tumbleweed. Gunner was blocked from driving around back by the number of cars, and Holly had to pull in behind him just to get off the highway.

They emerged from their cars as both of their fathers came out of the bar. Pearl was beside them waving the Texas State flag, and Holly's brother Travis was filming the whole thing with the camera on his phone.

Still confused by the unexpected welcome, they finally made their way to the top of the steps to where Jacob and Garrett were waiting.

At that moment, Pearl pulled out her bullhorn, gave it a blast, and the crowd went silent as Mayor Belker, who was also the owner of Belker's supermarket, stepped out of the crowd and joined them on the steps.

"Gunner Kingston, welcome home! Chuck Norris has nothing on you. We understand you did suffer some injuries from that flying leap to catch a bad man, but that whole incident was amazing. Now to the reason for this welcome. Over the years, we have seen many young people grow up here, only to leave for further education or military service, or just a longing to see more of the world. And that's how life usually goes. But never in the history of Crossroads have we had young people come back here to live, and we are elated that you have. We understand congratulations are in order for you and Holly, and that you are in the process of building your new home. Holly Dillon, welcome home! You are a beloved daughter of Crossroads, and I know you had a great job in real estate in a thriving company that you gave up to come back here to live. We all wanted you two to know how delighted we are. You two are the first prodigal children of Crossroads to return to the nest. Welcome home! Welcome home!"

The crowd echoed his words.

All Holly and Gunner could do was smile and wave.

It was Pearl who thought enough was enough and ushered them both inside the bar, which triggered those gathered to get back to their cars and go home. But the moment they got inside out of the noise, Gunner went straight to Holly's dad.

"Garrett, I'm not asking for permission to marry your daughter, but I am asking for your blessing. I worship the ground she walks on. I will never let her down or betray her and would give my life to keep her safe."

Garrett shook his head and gave Gunner a big hug. "You have my blessings a hundred times over. I don't know what you two are going to do with yourselves here, or how you plan to make a living, but I'm behind you both, all the way."

Holly heard the last of her father's words as she walked up and slid her arm around Gunner's waist.

Gunner looked down at her and frowned. "I thought you would have told your dad by now about the—"

Holly shook her head. "That's your story to tell, honey."

Garrett looked from one to the other, then back again. "Tell me what?"

"I'm the guy who won the Mega Millions lottery. Just shy of eight hundred million dollars," Gunner said.

Garrett's eyes widened. His mouth opened and then closed, and then opened again in pure shock. "My sweet lord!" he mumbled.

"You can't imagine how I felt when I found out. It was a random thing. I bought a ticket as I was paying for gas. I took a cash payout of a little over half of that. Holly didn't even know for weeks. I had some shit going on in Homicide I had to deal with, and it got in the way of a whole lot of plans. But that's finally solved, and the money gave us both the freedom to come home. I'd really appreciate it if you kept that to yourself, though. I don't intend to turn myself into everybody's banker. Holly can fill you in on stuff later."

Garrett nodded, still speechless, still trying to wrap his mind around the fact that Gunner Kingston was a multi-millionaire.

"Dad, which one of you is driving me home? Travis is ready to go."

Garrett made himself refocus. "I'm driving you in your car. Tell Travis to take the truck and we'll be right behind him." Then he looked back at Gunner. "Blessings abound," he said, shook his hand, and winked at his daughter before heading out the door.

Gunner wrapped his arms around her. "Lord, I am going to miss you. I know we'll see each other constantly, but it's not the same thing, is it?"

"No, it's not," she said. There were tears in her eyes.

"Damn it, you're gonna make me cry, too," Gunner muttered, then kissed her hard and fast. "Your dad's waiting. Expect a call from me every night. I will not be able to sleep until I hear your voice before I close my eyes."

"I love you. So much," she said.

"Love you more."

And then she was gone, and so were the people who'd gathered earlier. Gunner got in his car, circled the bar to get to the house, and unloaded the last of his things.

On the Monday after they came home, Gunner and Holly were together in his Jeep, driving to the building site of their new house.

"This is so exciting. Our first official act together, our own little groundbreaking ceremony," she said.

"Actually, making love with you for the first time was number one on my list, but we can put shoveling dirt as number two," Gunner said.

She gave him the side-eye and grinned. "Well, okay… Yes. That was epic."

He winked. "You're welcome."

They parked and waved at the driver sitting on a bulldozer, who was waiting for them to proceed. Then they retrieved a shovel from the back of the Jeep as they got out.

Gunner took Holly's hand as they walked up to the pile of rocks that he'd left weeks ago to mark the spot.

"You first," Holly said.

Gunner stabbed the shovel into the ground, then stepped onto the rim to drive it deeper and lifted away the first shovel of dirt.

"The ground is hard, but we're in West Texas. Life is hard here, too," Gunner said, then stabbed the shovel into the ground several times to soften it up for her and handed the shovel to her.

"Here you go, Hollyberry."

She gripped it firmly and shoved it into the softened dirt, shoveled up a decent scoop, and tossed it aside.

"Done and done," Gunner said. "There comes the contractor. I'm going to talk to him a bit before we leave. Go ahead and get in out of the heat, honey. I'll be right there."

Holly took the shovel and carried it back to the Jeep, glad to get in out of the sun, then sat watching as the three men began a discussion. All she got out of it was a lot of hand-waving and pointing and assumed they knew what they were doing. She knew everything there was to know about buying and selling real estate, but she knew very little about building a house from the ground up.

As they were talking, she glanced up and saw an eagle soaring high in the sky above. "Yes, we're about to invade your space," she said and then watched as it soared out of sight.

Moments later, Gunner was back behind the wheel, and they were driving away.

"They're going to start by building a pad for the house, and then grade a road from the project to the highway that will come out on the east side of the Tumbleweed. We'll get it blacktopped ASAP before delivery trucks and cement trucks start coming and going. They'll bring a backhoe to dig out a basement. After that, the contractor and his crew will start building forms to pour concrete in the basement and then marking where electrical and plumbing have to go at the house site before they begin building forms for the footing."

"Do you have to be on-site every day?" she asked.

"No. I know nothing about carpentry and would only be in the way. But I will be available by phone every day to answer questions. Dylan gave me a thumbs-up on my choice of contractors, so I know he's good at his job."

"Armadillo!" she said abruptly, pointing right in front of them.

Gunner braked to let the critter pass. "We're probably disturbing their territory," he said.

"I saw an eagle flying over while you were talking to the men," she said.

"Really? That's a good omen, I think. Are you going home now or…"

"I'm picking up some stuff at the supermarket before I go home. Granny wants to make a cobbler, and I'm getting some baking stuff for her."

He pulled up and parked beside her car. "Be careful going home, then."

"I'll text you," she said.

"You don't have to unless you want. We have that Life360 app. It tells me when you leave home and when you get home. And if you look at the app, you can see where I am, too."

"Oh, I keep forgetting to look at that," she said.

"I need to turn on the notification for you, and then you'll hear it. Let me have your phone a sec," he said and then pulled up the app, scrolled through the system, turned on the notification signal, and then closed the app. "Now you're good to go. Every time I leave home, you'll hear it beep to let you know. And when I get home it will beep at you again, and I did the same for your phone. You don't have to check in with me all the time. I will know where you are, and you can track where I am at any given time, as long as my phone is on me."

She beamed. "I love that! You're the best," she said, gave him a quick kiss, then got in her car.

He watched her driving away before he went back into the house, then into the bar. "Hey, Dad, we're through shoveling dirt. What can I help with?"

"If I haven't said it before, I'm saying it now. It's so good to have you home."

"It's good to be home, and I am at your service. What do you need?"

A month later, the bones of the house were now visible from the highway, and both Gunner and Holly were becoming accustomed to a slower way of life.

Gunner already knew Holly would be at the ranch all day today, helping out at the sale barn and the arena for one of Garrett Dillon's roping competitions. The traffic passing through Crossroads consisted mostly of big pickup trucks pulling loaded horse trailers, and he knew where they were going.

After helping Jacob get set up to open, he went down to the Yellow Rose to have a late breakfast and see Pearl. She was always gone before they got up, and he missed her.

He could see firsthand how much she meant to his dad and how she adored the ground Jacob Kingston walked on. He had moments of wondering what their lives might have been like if she'd been their mother, then let it go. What had been did not control what is, or what the future might bring. Being a cop had taught Gunner one really important thing—to live in the now.

He was sitting at a table, sipping coffee and listening to the chatter of a dozen different conversations surrounding him without focusing on any of it—just letting the drone of voices be backup music to the beginning of this day.

And then a phone rang at the table beside him. He glanced up, watching as Dale Curry, the bank president, took the call, then watched the color fading from Curry's face.

"Oh my God!" he yelled. "The bank is being robbed! I have to go—"

Gunner was on his feet in seconds. "No! You'll either get yourself killed or become another hostage. Call the sheriff!" he said and was out the door in seconds, then in the Mustang and flying out of the parking lot. His loaded handgun was in the console, and he was seeing the layout of the bank in his mind as he raced up the street.

The getaway car was obvious—parked directly in front of the bank and a driver behind the wheel. He didn't know how many were inside, but he was about to find out. He reached for his gun and got out, then before he took a step, he saw the driver open his door a bit and spit. *Probably has a lip full of chewing tobacco, and the driver's door is not locked.*

Gunner wasn't the only one racing toward the bank.

Sonny Bluejacket, the rancher who lived south of

Crossroads, was feeding horses when he had one of his visions. He could see the robbers entering the bank and the getaway driver out front. And then he saw Gunner Kingston arriving on the scene and knew it was going to get dicey before the sheriff had time to arrive. He dropped what he was doing, snagged a handful of bungee cords, ran into the house long enough to tell his wife, Maggie, what was happening, then grabbed his rifle and took off running toward his truck.

The getaway driver, Jackie Rankin, was completely focused on the front door of the bank when the door against which he was leaning suddenly opened. He reached for the steering wheel to catch himself from falling when someone grabbed him by the collar, yanked him backward, and shoved the barrel of a gun so hard into his ear he felt it pop. The voice of the man behind him was a shock.

"Don't move. I will shoot you where you sit. How many are inside the bank?"

Jackie's life suddenly flashed before his eyes. He was twenty-four years old. There was a man he couldn't see holding a gun in his ear, and he'd just swallowed his chew and peed his pants. He didn't feel obliged to be a hero.

"Two… There's two. Don't kill me, mister. Don't kill me!"

"Thanks for the info," Gunner said, then knocked him out cold with the gun butt, dragged him out of the car, and popped the trunk before tossing him inside, then pocketed the keys and headed for the bank.

He had two choices. Go inside and possibly cause a gunfight, or wait for them to come out, but as he reached the bank, the decision was made for him. He caught a glimpse of two men running for the exit and stepped to the side of the bank. No sooner had they come flying out the door than Gunner stepped out behind them.

"Freeze. Drop the guns! Hands in the air, or I'll shoot you where you stand! Your driver is indisposed, and I have the keys to your car."

They looked at each other and turned in unison, firing wildly.

Gunner hit the ground belly first and shot one in the knee and the other one in the shoulder. Seconds later, he had confiscated both weapons and the money bags and was standing over them with his gun, calling the sheriff's office. The one with the shoulder wound was cursing and moaning, and the one with the shattered knee was screaming like a woman giving birth.

Fred Wilson, the vice president of the bank, came out holding a handkerchief to his nose to slow the bleeding from the sucker punch he hadn't seen coming. Customers who'd been inside were coming out in hysterics, as well as the tellers who'd been on duty.

"Everybody okay in there?" Gunner asked.

"Yes! Oh my God, you caught them!" Wilson said.

"You all need to stay to give statements to Sheriff Reddick. Go back inside where it's cool and take a seat. Somebody make up an ice pack and put it on the back of Mr. Wilson's neck. It will slow the bleeding. You're safe now," Gunner said, and then he heard the roar of a big engine coming in from the south and saw a red pickup truck coming toward them on the fly.

The truck slid sideways before coming to a stop, and Sonny Bluejacket emerged in one leap. He had a rifle in one hand and a bunch of bungee cords in the other and came running toward Gunner.

"You're good. Damn good, Kingston. I saw it happening.

Got here as fast as I could," Sonny said. "Didn't have any handcuffs. Thought these might work."

Gunner relaxed. Backup had arrived. "Good to see your face, Sonny. If you don't mind, bungee up their ankles for me. Without the badge and the cuffs, I am no longer an official officer of the law. We're waiting on Sheriff Reddick's men to show."

"They're five minutes away," Sonny said and knelt down beside the one with the shoulder wound who was lying on his back moaning and cursing, and trussed his ankles up tight, then moved to the other one. "I'm going to wrap this above your knee to slow down the bleeding, and you need to stop screaming. If you were man enough to pull a gun on people and rob them, you are man enough to take the pain."

But when Sonny began wrapping the bungee cord around his leg, just above the place where he'd been shot, the thief let out a shriek and passed out, leaving Sonny to finish the job in peace.

They were standing together when cars from the sheriff's department came flying past the Tumbleweed and the Yellow Rose and took a skidding turn south up the street to the bank.

Moments later, an ambulance rolled up behind them. Sheriff Reddick got out, as did a half-dozen deputies, saw the scene, and waved in the EMTs.

Gunner handed over his weapon. "I had the drop on them when they came out of the bank. They weren't inclined to give up, and both started firing first. I think you will find enough cartridges around where they are lying to back that up, along with some bullet holes in the side of the bank behind me. The getaway driver is in the trunk of the car," Gunner said, then remembered the car keys he'd confiscated. "Oh…and here are the keys to said car. All of the witnesses to the robbery are in the bank. I sent them back to wait where it was cool. The only injury is Mr. Wilson's broken nose."

Reddick glanced at Sonny. "And how, pray tell my psychic friend, did you come to be involved in all this?"

"I was at the ranch when I saw it happening. Unfortunately, I got here too late to assist, but I did furnish the bungee cords," Sonny said.

Reddick shook his head. "Dang psychic and a one-man army. You two would make quite a team."

"No, thanks. Maggie and horses are my world. Am I good here?" Sonny asked.

"Give one of the deputies your contact information for the record, and say hello to Maggie for me," Reddick said and reached out to shake Gunner's hand. "It is good you came back to Crossroads. They need a man like you here. You'll get your weapon back soon. You know the drill. It just needs to be processed." Then he went inside the bank.

"Thanks for the backup, Sonny," Gunner said. "It's my good fortune you aren't at the Dillon Ranch today with some of your horses."

"Some of my horses are there with Chris Jackson, my foreman. Maggie isn't well. Morning sickness. We are having twins."

Gunner beamed. "Congratulations, man! That's wonderful."

"Maggie told Pearl this morning. Likely you will be hearing all about it tonight." And then he tipped his hat, ran back to the truck with his long hair flying, and drove away.

Gunner gave his contact info to a deputy. "I'll email a written statement to the sheriff's office by the end of the day," he added, then got in his car and drove back to the Rose.

Dale Curry saw him enter and stood up, pale and shaky as he awaited the verdict.

"Crisis averted. Three thieves in custody. Mr. Wilson

probably has a broken nose. Everyone else is okay, and the money is back in the bank."

"Thank the lord!" Dale said. "What did you do?"

"Stopped them. You can go back to the bank now. The sheriff is on-site," Gunner said and then looked at the table where he'd been sitting. "Did someone eat my breakfast?"

When Pearl heard his voice, she came flying out of the kitchen.

"Are you hurt again?"

Gunner grinned. "No, ma'am."

"Then sit. I put your food in the warmer," she said. By the time he sat, she was on her way out with his eggs and bacon and a basket of fresh biscuits hot from the oven. She put them down at his place and then hugged his neck. "I said a prayer," she whispered, then patted the top of his head like he was six and went back into the kitchen.

Gunner grinned at the customers watching their moment. "I'm not in too much trouble. She brought hot biscuits."

The customers laughed, and the temperament in the room went back to normal. As he was eating, it occurred to him that gossip might be spreading faster than the butter melting on his biscuit, and he sent Holly a text.

> There was an attempted robbery at the bank. The thieves were caught. No one got hurt. I'm fine. Hope you're having a good day.

He was just finishing his meal when he got a text back from Holly.

> Last-rooster-standing-at-the-cockfight fine, or really, truly fine?

He grinned, turned the phone around and took a selfie, then sent it to her.

> Might be some butter and jelly on my face, but no blood. I swear.

He got an LOL and a heart emoji. Between Pearl and Holly's reactions, it was like getting a blessing from the pope.

What he didn't know was that his knee-jerk reaction to danger, and the way he'd stepped up to the plate for a town without any law, had started people thinking—wondering—hoping—talking…that the Kingston who'd come home might be the answer to their prayers.

Reddick returned Gunner's weapon a few weeks later, and one month spilled into another and another.

Gunner and Holly took all the stolen moments they could find to be together, until finally, the house was only days from completion, and they'd taken early residence inside. The contractor was still waiting for the chandelier that went over the dining table, and there were two big area rugs to be delivered. It was none too soon.

It was the first of October. The days were already cold, and the ever-present wind sharper than ever. The furniture from their storage unit in Dallas arrived the day before. The furniture was in place. The massive bed was in the primary bedroom, but they were digging through boxes, looking for linens and towels, and unpacking flatware and dishes, and pots and pans, and stocking the kitchen and the refrigerator and new freezer with food.

It was like playing house, furnishing rooms with the

things they'd kept and adding the new pieces they'd picked out.

The wedding was still pending, and the big bed still had not been made. They couldn't find the oversize sheets that fit it.

"I remember packing them. I remember loading up the U-Haul and unloading that box at the storage unit. They have to be here somewhere," he muttered, then realized Holly was no longer in the room and went to look for her, but she was nowhere in the house.

"Holly! Where are you?" he shouted.

Then he heard her shouting from the garage. "Gunner! In here! I'm in here!" He walked in just in time to see her climbing up a stack of boxes that had been lined up against a wall, and he ran. "Holly! Stop! You're gonna fall and break your pretty neck."

"I found the box with your linens. It says *linens* on the side, and that's your writing. It got mixed up with the boxes from my stuff. Is there anything breakable in this box, or is it all linens?"

"It's all linens, but lord, girl. You don't want to hurt yourself over a pair of sheets," he said and then stood back as she gave it a shove off the stack, then walked the floor beside her as she made her way down.

As soon as she was standing on the lowest box, he swooped her off and into his arms. "Don't ever fuss at me again for putting myself in danger," he muttered.

She wrapped her arms around his neck. "Don't be mad. This is important. We have to sleep in that bed together on our wedding night...with the sheets on and the covers ready to be pulled up against the cold. I dream about it in my sleep."

He sighed. "Heard. But I'm carrying the box in the house, and I will pull every one of these boxes down to single level before we leave this garage, so sit and wait."

"Heard," she echoed and plopped down on the box she'd knocked down.

A few minutes later, they were on their way inside and going down the hall to the primary. Together, they unpacked the sheets, and together, they made up the bed.

"Are you satisfied now?" Gunner asked.

"Maybe we should take a test drive," she said.

His eyes narrowed. "Test drive?"

She nodded.

"How far do you want to go?" he asked.

She put her hand in the middle of his chest, feeling the heart pounding beneath her hand. "As far as the ride will take us."

He pulled the sweater she was wearing over her head and stripped her down to the skin. "How fast do you want me to drive?"

She closed her eyes, already locked into the blood rush. "You're the roadrunner. Fast is the only gear you have. Just start the engine and gun it."

He took her at her word.

It was the fastest ride she'd ever taken, and the farthest away she'd been. But it was the fall back into his arms she would never forget—or the words he had whispered in her ear.

Chapter 21

LESS THAN A WEEK LATER, THE HOUSE WAS FINISHED. Holly had the photo from her childhood hanging in a hallway—the one that had been taken with the baseball team. She intended to hang one from their wedding right beside it.

The contractor was gone. All signs of building scraps removed. There would never be grass in the yard, but the wildlife in the area had become familiar enough with their presence now that they heard coyotes in the night and birdsong in the days.

The Spanish hacienda, with the adobe walls, the red terracotta roof, the arched windows and doorways, and the decorative ironwork, had become the cherry on top of the town of Crossroads. The blacktop road leading from the house to the highway was clearly visible, as was the NO TRESPASSING sign at the foot of the hill.

During the same time, Jacob had enlarged and updated the kitchen in their little home, and Pearl ruled it like the queen she was, polishing appliances after each use as if they were jewels. And to further please the love of his life, he announced a new closing time of 10:00 p.m. and warned the customers to get used to it, because life was passing way too fast. When they all began to moan, he silenced them with a truth they could not deny.

"One day, you will regret the time you spent here with me when you could have been home with your wife and family. People die. Children grow up and move away. Ten o'clock is closing time."

In the end, they lifted their drinks in a toast to Jacob and took the change in stride.

Pearl was happy. Jacob was happy, and when Pearl's bedtime came, she no longer went to bed alone.

The night before their wedding, Holly Dillon went home and slept in her childhood bedroom. Going back to the ranch for this night only had been symbolic—her last night as a single woman.

The next morning when she woke, her first thought was pure joy.

Today is the day I become Gunner's wife.

Their wedding was happening at the little church where she and Gunner were baptized as children—where the services for her grandpa Dillon and her mother's funerals had been held, where both their parents had been married.

The space within the walls of that small church still held the echoes of years and years of joy, grief, baptisms, and salvation, and it was only fitting that they added their own moments of joy to the energy within.

She and her granny Dillon had gone to Amarillo months ago and picked out the dress her granny would wear, but Holly had known from the start what she wanted. It had taken a heart-to-heart talk with her daddy to get the okay, and she could still remember the look on his face when she asked.

"Dad, when Gunner and I get married, would it hurt your heart too much if I wore the dress Mama wore to your wedding?"

Garrett's eyes welled, but he was smiling. "Baby girl, I can't think of anything better. Do you know where it is?"

She nodded. "After I turned thirteen, she let me try it on once a year. I needed to see how much growing I still had to do before it fit, but I told her every time that it was what I wanted to wear when I got married. She would laugh and tell me if I ever changed my mind, it would be okay. I didn't change my mind, and I know it still fits. I'll take it to Amarillo to have it cleaned and then bring it back here."

Garrett hugged her. "Sounds like a plan."

And she followed it through.

But that was then, and this was now, and their morning routines were all out of whack. By the time they got to the church, her grandmother, Trudy, was large and in charge, checking to see if the flowers had arrived and that Holly had "something old, something new, and a penny in her shoe," and then announcing it was all systems go. Holly's dress was something old, her engagement ring something new, and there was a penny in her shoe.

But taking the dress out of the garment bag was an emotional trigger. Her mom should have been the one pulling it over her head, zipping up the back, and fastening the little hook and eye above the zipper. The urge to cry was quelled by knowing that the man who held her heart would be waiting for her at the altar. But it was her granny doing the honors, and she was grateful she was there.

"There now!" Trudy said. "Just look at you," she said and turned Holly toward the full-length mirror. "You look so much like your mama. Such a beauty she was, just like you. Now, turn around. I need to get this veil pinned to your hair, and then my work here will be done. I'll be in the foyer with the rest of the wedding party. Your daddy is waiting, and Pastor Reeding is ready if you are."

"I'm ready, Granny," Holly said and took the bridal bouquet Trudy handed her.

"You are a beautiful bride. Be happy, love. Be so very happy."

Holly nodded. "With Gunner in my life, there's no other way to be."

Trudy blew her a kiss, and when she opened the door to leave, Garrett was waiting in the hall.

"Brace yourself," Trudy whispered to her son, as she hurried off to find Travis.

Garrett wasn't sure what that meant until he walked into the room, and in the space of a heartbeat, he saw what his mother meant. He only saw Helen as she'd been before, and then he blinked, and she was gone. He was frantically gathering his emotions before he transferred them to Holly and made both of them cry.

"Holly, sweetheart! You are absolutely stunning," he said. "Are you ready?"

She nodded, slipped her hand in the crook of his arm, and then they were walking up the hall, past the rooms where Sunday School was held, past the nursery where the youngest Kingstons could be heard giggling and playing, then into the foyer of the church where the other members of her wedding party were gathered. Without close friends here in Crossroads anymore, she had prevailed upon her new sisters-in-law to be her bridesmaids, and they had happily agreed.

As the moments passed, she felt her mother's absence now, more than ever before.

Mom... This isn't fair. This shouldn't be happening without you.

As if sensing her struggles, Garrett whispered in her ear. "Chin up. Look for Gunner. After that, it will all be easy."

She nodded. Her dad was right. Gunner was her North Star. With him, she would never be lost. She lifted her chin, her heart pounding, waiting for the moment when she would see his face.

Spending the night without Holly had been long and restless. It didn't feel right without her curled up in his arms, but Gunner woke to this day with a sense of relief.

Today was their wedding day, and he was at their new house alone, biding time until he needed to leave. He'd chosen his own clothes—a black Western-style suit and black alligator boots. A white-as-snow shirt, and a black string tie at the collar. He knew better than to worry about his hair because the wind was going to blow it six ways to Sunday before he got to the church. He'd deal with it there, later.

His brothers and their families had arrived yesterday and were all packed in at Jacob and Pearl's, and for once, the little house was noisier than the bar. Pearl was already excited about the expectation of Maggie and Sonny's twins, and Asher and Dylan's two boys were already calling her Grammy. It had taken her and Jacob half of their lives to get to this place, but he had finally given her the family she'd always wanted, and Gunner and Holly were about to add to it.

It was almost time, but not yet, so Gunner walked the halls of the house alone, admiring the Spanish influence in the colorful handmade tiles in the bathrooms and kitchen, and the adobe red floor tiles throughout the house. He stopped at the sliding doors in the dining room to look out from beneath the sheltered verandah at the eastern view. The place where daybreak happened, and each new day began. He was at peace within the solitude and silence of their new house, but Holly's boundless exuberance was missing.

The reverence of the day and the magnitude of the promises they were going to make was uppermost in his mind. The most important words he would ever say to her were in the vows. To cherish. To protect. To love her forever. In sickness and in health, in death and beyond. Those were his promises to her.

He kept watching the clock, wishing time would hurry up just this once. He wanted his ring on her finger and his mouth on her lips.

He'd kissed her countless times before, but never as his wife.

Then finally it was time. He got in the Mustang, backed out of the garage, and drove to the church, then went in through the back entrance. He walked in on his dad and brothers, who were waiting with the pastor.

"There you are! Good morning, Gunner," the pastor said. "I'll go check with the ladies and see how close we are to being ready," he said and left the room.

"See, I told you he'd be here when he was ready," Jacob said. "Still our loner." And then he gave him a big hug and a pat on the back.

"He won't be a loner anymore," Dylan added. "Proud of you, Gunner. You and Holly were made for each other."

Asher hugged him. "I am proud to be your brother."

"I know this was quite a trip to make with your families, but I sure appreciate that you made it happen," Gunner said.

"Oh… We had to see this in person, just to make sure we weren't dreaming," Dylan said. "Besides, who else would be your groomsmen?"

"All of you, Dad included, got me through a hell of a mess back in Dallas. I don't know how this would have turned out without your help."

"That's what dads and big brothers are for," Asher said. "Do you have the rings?"

Gunner took the little box out of his pocket and handed it to Asher, who immediately gave it to his dad.

"Take a breath. You've got this," Dylan said.

"I'm more at peace with myself than I have ever been," Gunner said. "This isn't nerves. It's anticipation. She broke down every wall I had between me and the world with nothing but sass and love."

Asher nodded. "I can see that, but I have a question. What does she mean when she sometimes refers you as 'that rooster'?"

Gunner grinned. "Oh, that's the day I knew I had to spend the rest of my life with her or die trying. It was right after my superman moment when I took Beau Whistler off the Harley. I was dripping blood from the cut on my shoulder, and the missing skin on my forearm and my clothes were slick with blood. It hurt to breathe enough that I thought I made have broken a rib or two. The bruise on my jaw was already turning purple, and I knew the right side of my body was going to be the same color. The EMT patched me up enough that I drove myself home. She was sitting in the driveway, waiting. I got out of the car, still dripping blood. She walked to the end of her car and then stopped. I expected shrieks of horror, or tears. Instead, I see this fierce glint in her eyes, and I'm watching her jaw set to keep from crying, when she lit into me. She told me to get in her car, and that she was taking me to the ER, and that I looked like the last rooster standing in a cockfight and not to argue."

They burst out laughing. "You're right. She's a keeper," Asher said.

"And she followed through," Gunner said. "Packed an overnight bag and spent the next few days helping me, feeding me, everything...until I could finally do it for myself. She was doing all that and working online at her job without a hint of a complaint, and today I'm going to marry her."

There was a knock at the door, and then the pastor walked in. "Everyone's ready. Follow me," he said and led the way into the nave.

Pastor Reeding took his place at the pulpit.

Gunner was standing below and to the right. Everybody else was in the foyer and out of his sight.

He knew Little Jake and CJ were in the church nursery with a lady from the church, and he knew every smiling face in the congregation.

There were no flower girls. No ring bearer.

They were all waiting for the bride.

When the organist struck the first chord, it was Jacob's signal. As the music began, he escorted Pearl to the pew and seated her before moving into place beside his son.

Travis and Trudy Dillon appeared next. Escorted by her grandson, Trudy walked down the aisle to take her place as matron of honor, then Travis took a seat in the pew beside Pearl.

Asher and Nora followed, each taking their place as bridesmaid and groomsman.

Dylan and Angie completed the procession and were standing in place when the music suddenly stopped.

The room went silent, waiting.

And then another chord was struck.

Garrett and Holly appeared in the doorway as the organist began playing the *Wedding March*. The congregation stood, watching father and daughter as they began walking down the aisle.

Holly's floor-length dress with an overlay of lace and

pearls had three-quarter sleeves, a sweetheart neckline with a flat unadorned bodice ending in a point just below the waist, and a full gathered skirt, and the auburn curls in her hair pillowed the sheer perfection of her veil.

The moment they walked into view, Jacob stifled a quick gasp.

Asher moved a step closer to his dad and whispered, "Are you okay?"

Jacob's voice was shaky. "I was best man at Garrett and Helen's wedding. Holly is wearing her mother's wedding dress."

Gunner hadn't taken his eyes off of her since they appeared in the doorway, but when he heard what his father said, his view of her blurred. She'd told him once that when he hurt, she cried. Now he knew what she meant.

The room was silent—like the world was holding its breath. And then they were at the altar, and Pastor Reeding was asking....

"Who gives this woman to this man?"

Garrett's voice rang out—steady and true. "I do. I give my daughter to this good man."

After that, everything faded but the sound of Holly's voice pledging her vows and his own words echoing in his head. The feel of her hand in his as he slipped the wedding ring on her finger, and the steady grasp of her hand as she did the same for him.

Then hearing the words, "I now pronounce you husband and wife. You may kiss the bride."

"I thought you'd never get to this part," Gunner said, unaware that he'd said it out loud until Holly laughed, and when she did, the congregation and the pastor laughed with her.

Gunner dipped his head just enough to reach the target, felt the soft yield of her lips against his mouth, and left them all in no doubt that Gunner Kingston had just kissed his bride.

Then they turned and walked down the aisle and across the hall to the dining room where the cake was to be cut, and mints and nuts in small cups were to be dispersed, and flowers frozen in ice floated in pink punch.

Everything became a whirlwind of laughter and joy.

When it was time to throw the bouquet, it fell into the hands of one of the new nurses working in their Urgent Care facility.

The party was still in full swing when they all realized Gunner and Holly were gone. It was getting late, and getting colder, and the smallest Kingstons had run out of patience.

The party was over for everyone but the bride and groom.

The thick adobe walls resisted the wind's intent. The central heat kept the temperature steady, and the gas logs in their fireplace were an added feature to the ambiance of their first night as husband and wife.

Although they'd been in and out of the house and slept here countless times, he carried her across the threshold.

"My wife," he said as he set her down.

Mischief was dancing in her eyes. "My husband. I thought we'd never get to this part."

He grinned. "I didn't know I'd said that out loud until it was too late. I also didn't know that my dad was best man at your parents' wedding."

"I did, but I've seen pictures," she said.

Gunner brushed a kiss across her lips. "He said you are wearing your mother's wedding dress. Is this true?"

She nodded. "I didn't want to say anything ahead of

time, because I needed you to see me in it, not the ghost of my mother. I asked Dad if it would bother him, and of course he said it would be great, but at the church, when he first saw me in it, I saw his face. It was hard for him." She laid her head against Gunner's chest. "I was all shaky at the church, and he knew it. Then he told me to just look for your face, and after that, nothing else would matter. He was right. Will you help me take off the dress? I want to change and hang it up."

"It would be my honor," he said.

Hours later, the only lights on the hill above Crossroads came from the security lights on the property. There was a faint glow through the curtains coming from the interior.

The newlyweds were wrapped close in each other's arms, sated from lovemaking and nestled down beneath the covers as the cold Texas wind blew its way south.

The next day, Gunner sent an email to his lawyer, Wes Bradley, with notes to change the beneficiaries in his will. Everything went to Holly, then any ensuing children if she preceded them in death.

It was the last *T* to cross and *I* to dot.

It was the new year, but winter was still holding on with icy fingers as Maggie Bluejacket gave birth to identical twin boys with a shock of black hair, wearing remnants of their father's face. She took to being a mother as easily as she took a brush and paint to create the masterpieces that were her art.

Every day that Sonny looked upon their faces, he could

see his vision from long ago coming to life. They would grow tall and strong like him, because he'd seen it. They would shadow her every step as babies and grow into men who would become her shadows as she walked through her life of fame. Pearl was the only grandmother Maggie could give her sons, just as Pearl had become the only mother Maggie could trust, but Sonny Bluejacket had a whole tribe of people who would ground them into the culture of their people.

It was a new beginning for them, just as Holly and Gunner were branching out into their new life.

Jacob was building a wing onto their house for his growing family, and Gunner was building that apartment building for Holly that she'd talked about before. The whole town was excited. It would mean an opportunity to keep Crossroads alive. With new people came growth, and the residents of Crossroads were watching the building going up one board at a time.

Gunner's whole purpose was putting delight in Holly's eyes.

Six up and six down, just like she suggested. Entrances at each end of the building, and one main entrance in the front. Covered parking circled the building, and all entrances to the apartments were from the interior hallways. Not like a motel, but a real apartment building.

Even though Jacob told the banker Gunner had given him the money, he'd hesitated on Gunner's behalf not to mention the lottery, which meant very few people knew, and every day Gunner lived within that anonymity was one more day of bliss.

But secrets never stay hidden.

And one cold day in March, the bubble popped.

Holly had driven out to the Dillon Ranch to have lunch, and Gunner was headed to the Yellow Rose to pick up food for him and his dad. He was wearing the old bomber-style leather jacket from his years in Homicide and opted out of a hat because of the wind. An armadillo was digging at the ground beneath a large boulder as he drove down the hill toward the highway.

"Someone else is digging for dinner," he said and kept driving, then turned left on the highway, passing the bar and a gas station to get to the Rose.

The parking lot was filling up, but he'd called in their order. All he had to do was pick it up. He parked near the highway, making it easier to drive away, and then entered the café.

The immediate absence of wind was a relief. A couple was headed to the door, so he stopped to open the door for them, then closed it behind them.

But before he could walk across the room to the pickup station at the register, he heard someone call out his name.

"Look who's here! It's Gunner Kingston. Hey, Gunner! How you likin' your castle on the hill?"

Gunner turned, gazing out across the room full of customers who, sensing an oncoming conflict, had now stopped their own meals and conversations. His expression was unreadable, and he had yet to respond.

"What? Don't you recognize your old friends anymore? It's me, Dave Randall."

"I don't remember calling you *friend*," Gunner said and kept walking toward the front register.

Randall shoved his chair back and stood up, as if itching for a fight.

"We see you slinging money around for that big house.

Your daddy's fancying up his place. You're building your wife an apartment building to run. How you doin' all that, boy? Maybe you dug up some more money Brenda Kingston buried and forgot to mention it to the Feds."

He was immediately bombarded with angry comments from locals, calling him a drunk and telling him to sit down and that he was making an ass of himself.

But when Pearl came flying out of the kitchen with her shotgun, everybody sitting behind Randall got up and moved to the other side of the room.

"It's okay, Pearl. No need to shoot his ass and mess up the dining room. I've got this," Gunner said, and then he made an announcement to the whole room. "Not that it's ever been anybody's damn business, but I have money. I have a whole hell of a lot of it now, because one morning on my way to work, I stopped at a Gas and Dash in Dallas to refuel. I also went inside and bought a candy bar and a bottle of pop, and on a whim, a lottery ticket."

Now the whole room was silent, and Dave Randall's belly was rolling, and he was wishing he hadn't ordered cheese on his fries, and Gunner was still talking.

"I went to work, then went home, went to bed, and went to work the next day just like every day, cleaning up the messes people make with their lives. And when I went to bed that second night, I was lying there watching TV when they began calling out the lottery numbers for that Mega Millions jackpot. And, because I'd bought that random ticket, I got it out of my wallet and glanced at it. To my eternal shock, every damn number they called was on the ticket I had in my hands. That night, I won just shy of eight hundred million dollars, and I was afraid to go to sleep. The next day I picked up my lawyer, and we went to the Dallas Claims Center of the Texas Lottery Commission to verify my winning number and agreed to a cash payout of a little over half. So, no, you sorry bastard, I did not dig up anybody's stolen money. The apartment in Crossroads will help this town grow. That's for all of us. Not for me. And I gave my dad money because I wanted to. The addition that Jacob Kingston is building onto his house is because he likes to have his freakin' family home for the holidays, and there isn't room enough anymore. You are a son of a bitch for even mentioning his name in such a derogatory way. And if I ever hear you denigrate my father's name by mentioning him and Brenda Kingston in the same breath, I will beat your ass clean into the dirt. And just for the record to everybody listening, I am not your next available ATM. You need to borrow money, Dale Curry and Fred Wilson are the men you go to. Not me or my wife. Understood?" Then he went to the register to pick up his to-go order, handed a waitress the money to pay for it, and hugged Pearl.

"Thank you for the food, Mama Pearl. Love you, but put up the gun."

She took his kiss on her cheek, glared at the whole room as he walked out, and then shouted. "Sit. Finish your food. Dave Randall will be leaving now."

Dave wasn't finished with his food, but he did not have enough guts left to even open his mouth, let alone argue or chew. He threw some money on the table and walked out with his head down.

By nightfall, everyone in Crossroads and beyond knew about Gunner's windfall, but they also knew him well enough to know he meant what he said.

The Tumbleweed was nearly empty at noon. By the time Gunner got back to the bar, Pearl had already called Jacob and told him what happened. When they sat down at a table usually reserved for domino games and began to eat, Jacob started the conversation.

"I sure like having you around. Between you and Pearl, I might start feeling like I was somebody," he said. "And for the record, Pearl called, I guess the second you walked out the door. Dave Randall is an ass. He lives in Tulia now, but I'd bet money you won't see him around Crossroads anymore. Pearl sent him packing."

Gunner dipped a french fry in his dad's ketchup, then grinned. "She pulled out the shotgun on him."

Jacob shook his head. "You'd think by now, all the locals would know better." And then he smiled. "But she sure is a dandy, isn't she?"

Gunner laughed. "She's that, and then some."

"Where's Holly at today?" Jacob asked.

"She went to the ranch to have lunch with Trudy. I suspect she'll hear all about the lottery revelation before she makes it home. Gossip has a way of traveling, but her family already knew. I told Garrett the day we came home."

Jacob nodded and pointed to the pickle on the side of Gunner's plate. "You plan on eatin' that?"

"Help yourself," Gunner said and sat listening to his dad's bar stories as he ate, like they were the fairy tales he told Gunner when he was little. All the years Jacob had put into making sure his smallest son still knew he was loved had not been in vain.

Gunner was right when he said Holly would find out, because she had. They'd talked about this a dozen times in the past few months, and now it had happened, she couldn't help thinking it was like peeling off a scab. Maybe it was time. She didn't know how she was going to be received now, but she'd soon find out, because she was going to Belker's for groceries before she went home. A short while later she pulled into the parking lot.

After a quick check in her purse to make sure she had her list, she went inside, grabbed a shopping cart and headed for the produce aisle, began gathering up what she needed there, then moved to the bread aisle. She was debating about sourdough or a loaf of plain bread when someone tapped her on the shoulder. It was the little nurse who'd caught her bridal bouquet.

"Hey, Holly, I don't know if you remember me. I'm Wendy Jennings."

Holly grinned. "The bridal bouquet! You caught it! Did it work?" she asked.

Wendy giggled. "Prospects abound, but nothing yet. I was wondering when you were going to start taking applications for the new apartments because I want to apply. I'm living out in the country with an aunt and uncle, and the drive back and forth is hard on my budget."

"Oh… I totally understand. I think we're less than a month from completion, and you're the first one who's asked, so your name will be at the top of the list. We'll have an open house, but if the apartment and the price suit you, you have first pick. Up or down. They're all two bedrooms, one bath. All appliances furnished. Utilities are on the renters."

"Oh my God… Thank you," Wendy said and handed her a card with her contact info. "I need to hurry. Aunt Pam is waiting for me and these groceries."

Holly dropped the card in her purse and finished shopping. But her chance meeting with Wendy had been witnessed by other shoppers, and they were elated to know there would be an open house. Everyone wanted to see the latest addition to their little town, and nobody seemed inclined to exhibit jealousy to the man who'd foiled a bank robbery, or his wife, who'd just lost her mother in such a tragic way.

Gunner was still at the bar with his dad when he glanced at the time, then checked the travel app to see if Holly was still at the ranch. When he realized she was already back in town and at the supermarket, he knew it was time to head home.

"Hey, Dad, I'm going home. Holly is at the supermarket, and I'm the bag boy at our house."

Jacob grinned. "You're learning your place early, boy. Good for you."

Gunner was smiling as he drove away. He already knew his place. Right by her side. He beat her to the house, but not by much. He backed up into the garage and was getting out when he saw her SUV coming up the road, so he waited.

Holly started smiling the moment she saw him. She pulled into the garage, parked, and killed the engine as he opened the door to help her out. Moments later she was in his arms.

"I missed you. I had lunch with Dad. Did you and Trudy have a good visit?"

She cupped his face and kissed him just enough to let him know she missed him, too. "We had the best time. I helped her make pie crusts to put in the freezer. She said Travis comes home from college about once a month, shops for his groceries in her pantry, and takes as many desserts as he can back to college with him. Dad thinks Travis is likely selling them for big bucks."

Gunner laughed. "A budding entrepreneur. That's priceless. I'll get the grocery bags, you get the door, okay?"

"With thanks," she said and closed the garage door as she

opened the one into the house, then waited for him to pass through.

"It feels so good to be home. The wind is exhausting just to listen to, and our house really buffers that sound."

Gunner was emptying the bags, and she was putting up the purchases when she paused and turned around.

"I heard enough about Dave Randall's asinine behavior to know Pearl pulled the shotgun off the wall," she said.

Gunner shrugged. "We knew the lottery thing would eventually come out, but I never thought about it happening like that."

She pulled a barstool up to the island and sat. "Tell me."

"He was drunk and itching for a fight. Everything he said was a challenge, trying to make me respond. And then he suggested that all this money being spent came from me digging up more stolen money that Brenda Kingston buried, and that since we built the house, and the apartment building, and Dad is adding on to his place, that the Kingstons might have held some back for their own purposes."

Holly groaned. "Oh my God. I didn't hear all that. Gunner… Sweetheart, I'm so sorry."

"So is Randall, now. Between realizing what a jerk he was, and Pearl coming out with the shotgun, he was wishing he'd never opened his mouth. I also made it clear that if there's any money being borrowed in Crossroads, I am not an ATM, and it will be happening at the bank, then I got Dad's lunch and left."

She frowned. "What can I do to take away your mad face?"

The corner of his mouth turned up just a little. "Do you have to ask?"

She slid off the barstool and started toward their bedroom, but Gunner caught up, swept her off her feet, and carried her the rest of the way.

They were still making love on that bed when the sun began to set. They fell asleep in each other's arms and woke up a couple of hours later to a house in total darkness.

"Did we finish putting up the groceries?" Holly asked.

"Hell if I know, darlin', but we can put some clothes on and find out."

"I'm kinda hungry, too," Holly said.

He turned on a lamp by their bed. "First one to the kitchen is first one to the kitchen," he said.

Holly burst out laughing and rolled out of bed.

Chapter 22

A FEW WEEKS LATER, THE DESIGNER HAD FINISHED SETting up all twelve apartments, and the contractor turned over the keys of the building to Gunner, who immediately handed them to Holly.

"We did it!" she said.

He shook his head. "You did it. And FYI... The deed to the property is in your name."

"I won't mess up," she said. "I know how this business works."

"I know you do. I've seen you in action," he said. "Give me the tour."

So, she did, talking about rental prices as they went.

"This is all free and clear of debt, and our intent was not to make a big profit, but rather furnish the opportunity for housing, and enough for taxes, insurance, repairs, and upkeep. I know the median monthly income around here, and this has to rent accordingly. Seven hundred a month for eight hundred and fifty square feet, we furnish all of the appliances, and they pay utilities."

"It's a go for me," he said.

"Open house is Saturday, and if it suits her, I already have my first renter. Wendy Jennings, the young nurse who caught the bouquet at our wedding," she said.

"That's amazing," Gunner said. "And you know how that goes. The first one is the seed that starts the garden growing. I predict you'll have it fully rented within months. Will they have restrictions to agree with?"

She nodded. "The usual. No drugs. No pets. Consideration toward your neighbors next door. Rent will come out with automatic withdrawal like the rest of the world. If they don't have a job and a bank account, then they need a motel, not an apartment."

By Saturday, the town was buzzing about the open house at Hollyberry Apartments.

Wendy Jennings was waiting for the doors to open and was the first one through the door. Gunner volunteered to handle security and was a silent presence as people walked inside. Holly was on the ground floor leading tours, and Trudy Dillon was on the top floor doing the same.

The moment Wendy learned the rent was within her budget, she chose the downstairs apartment at the south end of the building, facing east. She picked up an application and went home to fill it out. There was no required deposit, which was huge. Now she had to wait and see if her application was accepted. By the time the event was over, five other people had asked for applications.

It was a huge success.

Holly Kingston was in business.

Gunner was proud of her but was beginning to feel at loose ends. He was going to have to come up with some other projects just to stay busy.

There were business owners in Crossroads who had another plan in mind for Gunner. The problem was going to be convincing him. Most of them were doubtful, considering he had no need to work, but others disagreed.

They had everything figured out, and what they could contribute to the project to make it happen. There was nothing left to do but confront him, but finding the opportune time wasn't as simple as it seemed. They all wanted to be present when they asked him, and their own jobs and free time were out of sync with the plan.

Every day, Gunner went to the Tumbleweed to help his dad get ready to open, while Holly was in her office checking out credit scores and references for potential renters.

It was nearing noon. The last customer in the bar had gone home only a few minutes earlier, and Gunner was getting ready to get his dad's lunch when he heard a dog bark. Stray dogs in Crossroads weren't a thing. Dogs were either in someone's backyard or were little house dogs that got carried everywhere.

He turned around toward the front entrance and saw a big yellow dog at the door and a little boy covered in blood standing beside him.

"Dad! What the hell?" he said and bolted toward the door with Jacob at his heels.

The moment he stepped out on the porch, he could see the child was in shock. He touched the dog to make sure he'd let him close, and when the dog accepted his presence, he knelt in front of the boy.

"Hey, buddy, is this your dog?"

He nodded. "Buster."

"What's your name?" he asked.

"Sam."

"Sam, there's a lot of blood on you. Where are you hurt?" Gunner asked.

"Mommy's hurt. Her's a'bleedin'," Sam said.

"A wreck. It must be close by," Jacob said. "I'll take the boy and call Reddick."

Gunner picked up the little boy. "Hey, Sam, this is my daddy. His name is Jacob. I'm going to look for your mommy. Can you show me where to go look?"

The little boy pointed east, which explained why they'd stopped here. The bar was the first building at the edge of town.

"Tell Reddick," Gunner said and handed him to Jacob. "I'm about to see if Buster has any bloodhound in him."

Jacob went back inside with the child as Gunner walked off the porch.

He knew within reason that the wreck had to be close, or another driver would have surely seen them walking. He looked down. The dog was right beside him, looking up.

"Okay, Buster. Where is Sam's mommy? Show me! Show me!"

The dog took off running due east with Gunner right beside him, and it didn't take long to find what he went looking for. About a hundred yards down from where he was running, he saw a big white truck in a ditch on the wrong side of the road, lying driver's side down.

Buster kicked into high gear and took off running and was waiting beside the truck when Gunner caught up. He could see a woman behind the wheel, bloody and motionless.

"Good boy, Buster. Good boy," he said and patted the dog on the head, then stepped into the ditch and looked down into the open window on the passenger side—the one the boy and the dog had obviously crawled out of. He made a quick call to the sheriff's office to give the location, then leaned back into the open window. He couldn't reach her without crawling in, and without knowing what injuries she had, moving her could be fatal. "Lady! Lady! Can you hear me? Help is coming. Sam is safe. Buster is safe. Can you hear me?"

She hadn't moved, but blood was still running. That had to mean her heart was still pumping. Didn't it? It had to.

Don't be dead. Don't be dead. Please, God, don't take Sam's mommy, too.

Holly was in the kitchen, expecting Gunner to be home at any minute when her phone rang. One frantic phone call from Jacob, and she was driving down the road to the bar. She parked and got out running.

The little boy was sitting on the bar without a shirt, and Jacob was wiping the blood off his little face and arms with bar towels.

Before she could ask a question, Jacob's phone rang. "Holly, it's Gunner. Get that for me."

She answered. "Gunner, I'm here with Jacob. I'm going to put this on Speaker for him."

"Dad, can Sam hear us?" Gunner asked.

"Yes," Jacob said.

"Okay… Sam, this is Gunner. Buster took me straight to your mommy. The police are coming to help, and there is an ambulance coming with doctors. She's not by herself. Buster is here. I'm here. Okay?"

Sam nodded, then collapsed against Jacob's shoulder.

"He heard you, Gunner."

"And…here comes the cavalry," Gunner said. "Cops, ambulance, and all." He hung up.

Holly ran down the hall and into the house, grabbed the blanket from the foot of Gunner's old bed, and ran back into the bar.

Sam was somewhat clean, but he was shivering uncontrollably.

"Shock," Jacob said and picked up the bloody towels.

"I've got him," Holly said. "Hey, Sam, my name is Holly. Let's get you wrapped up so you can get warm, okay?" She wrapped the blanket around him, then carried him down the hall and into the family living room and sat down in the rocker-recliner, cradling him against her as she started rocking. "You're safe, Sammy, you're safe," she kept saying.

When she felt him relaxing, she looked down.

Emotionally and physically exhausted, between shock and self-preservation, he had fallen asleep.

Worried about a concussion, she combed her fingers through his hair, carefully feeling for bumps or indentations, but it seemed fine. It was just a little boy's head, slightly sweaty with dust and grass in his hair.

The rescue truck from the Silverton Fire Department arrived with a Texas Highway patrol car and, right behind them, a tow truck and two cars from the sheriff's department.

They put Buster in the back seat of a patrol car to make sure he didn't run away, then used the tow truck to pull the truck upright and out of the ditch before they could get to the driver. She was still breathing, but getting her immobilized enough to make it safe to move her took time they didn't have.

Gunner stayed back, watching the emergency workers moving in tandem, knowing what they needed to do to get their victim stabilized and ready to move. Then finally, as they were loading her up, one of the deputies from the sheriff's office came looking for him.

"Hey, Gunner, is that boy who was in the wreck still with your dad?"

"Yes, at the Tumbleweed."

"Give Jacob a call and tell him that the ambulance driver is going to stop at the Weed and pick up the boy. He's a wreck victim, too, and needs to be examined."

"On it," Gunner said and made the call. When Jacob picked up, Gunner started talking. "Dad… They have Sam's mother ready to go. They're going to pick up the boy on their way. Get Sam and be ready to meet them."

"Consider it done," Jacob said. He ran into their house and saw Holly holding the sleeping child in her arms.

"I wrapped him in the blanket at the foot of Gunner's bed," she said.

"It's fine. Leave him in it. It's old, and he needs it. The ambulance is coming to pick him up. I have to take him out to meet them."

Holly handed him over and followed their exit, watching as Jacob hastily carried the sleeping child beyond the parked cars to the highway beyond.

The scream of ambulance sirens announced their arrival as they came to a stop.

The back doors flew open.

Jacob handed off the child, and then they were gone.

Holly arms felt strangely empty. *Mother instinct, I guess.* Then she looked toward the east. Gunner was down there—somewhere in the midst of chaos. *Where he belongs.*

The only member of the wreck who was still in limbo was Buster. For the moment, he was in custody of the sheriff's office, and the sheriff began making calls.

Sam's grandparents were on the way to the hospital when

they got the call and sent a friend to meet the patrol car to retrieve the beloved pet.

Gunner finally left the scene as the truck was being towed away.

He began walking back on the shoulder of the highway when he saw a white SUV driving toward him.

It was Holly.

When she stopped, he got in without saying a word. She made a U-turn on the highway and headed back home.

"Are you okay?" she asked.

He nodded. "Hell of a run. Thank you for coming to look for me."

"I'm not about to lose you, and I knew where to look. That phone app. Remember?"

"The little boy... Sam... Is he okay?" he asked.

"Yes. Jacob cleaned him up, but he couldn't stop shaking. I wrapped him in the old blanket that was on the foot of your bed and rocked him to sleep. Your dad said it was okay. The ambulance stopped and took him with them."

He looked at her then, thinking one day she would rock their babies to sleep. "It's definitely okay." A few minutes later, she let him out to get his car, and then they both drove home.

By nightfall, Gunner's episode with the little boy and the dog, and being led to the wreck in time to save the mother's life, had just added to his story.

As for the men with the plan for Gunner's future, it solidified their purpose even more.

The next day, Gunner was at the bar, helping Jacob get ready to open when they saw a car drive up and watched a man and a dog walking up the steps.

"I don't know who the man is, but that's Buster," Gunner said.

Jacob headed to the door with Gunner beside him and unlocked it.

"You're a tad bit early, but come on it," Jacob said.

"I'm Sam Barnes. Are you the Kingstons? The people who saved my wife, Jenny, and son, Sam, yesterday?"

"That's us," Gunner said. "This is my father, Jacob Kingston. He took over Sam's welfare after Buster took me straight to your Jenny. Would you care to come in?"

"No, but thanks. I'm on the way home with Buster before I go back to the hospital. We've both had a long night. I wanted you to know that Jenny is alive, thanks to you. And little Sam has been talking about the giant men who saved him and his mama. I had to come meet you in person."

Gunner pointed at Buster, then gave the yellow dog a gentle rub on the head. "Your son and this dog saved your wife. Dad and I simply assisted in the rescue."

"You have a most remarkable son," Jacob said. "I have three rather remarkable sons of my own, and I know one when I see one. Thank you for letting us know. My wife and I said a prayer for them last night. She will be overjoyed to hear this."

Sam Barnes nodded. "Thank you again...for all you did."

They shook hands, then Sam and Buster were gone.

Jacob gave Gunner a pat on the back. "That's a really good way to start a day, isn't it, son?"

"Yes, it is, Dad. A really good way."

Two days later, Gunner was in the office with Holly when he got a phone call. He saw Caller ID and then showed Holly.

She arched an eyebrow. “Don’t look at me. I’m not overdrawn.”

He grinned and stepped out into the hall to answer. “Hello, this is Gunner.”

“Gunner! This is Dale Curry. I apologize for the late notice, but our business owners’ association is meeting at the church in about an hour, and we would appreciate your feedback regarding the current project we’re working on. It has to do with Crossroads. We have chicken salad sandwiches and coffee to ply you with, and we would really appreciate your input before we proceed.”

“Yes, sure, I can do that,” Gunner said.

“Wonderful! We’ll see you there.”

The odd query and then the abrupt end to the conversation made Gunner suspicious. He went back into the office.

“I received an invitation to lunch,” he said.

She glanced up. “With Curry? That’s nice…I guess. What’s going on?”

“See! Your Spidey sense is the same as mine. It was a strange call. Apparently, the entire business owners’ association is having a monthly meeting. Like in an hour. And they want my input on some city improvement project. I have been offered chicken salad sandwiches.”

She laughed. “Go! But be ready for chopped grapes.”

“Chopped grapes? What the hell, Holly?”

She was still smiling. “They won’t kill you. Just chew and swallow like a big boy. I’ll make you something yummy for supper.”

“Lord,” he muttered and walked off to change clothes and wipe the dust off his boots.

Gunner went straight to the church.

Dale was waiting for him in the vestibule and walked him down to the dining hall, still talking when they entered the room about chicken salad sandwiches and hand pies, and a choice between coffee or iced tea.

Every member of the business community was there, men and women alike—all of them milling about filling their plates and looking at him with an air of expectation.

His "on alert" shield went up.

"Help yourself, Gunner. Milly at the refreshment table will bring your drink and dessert. Just tell her what you want."

Following orders, Gunner put a sandwich and a bag of chips on a paper plate, chose an apple hand pie and sweet iced tea, and took the last vacant chair, which happened to be between Mayor Belker and Dale. They all seemed to be talking among themselves in a normal manner, but Gunner knew all eyes were on him, and he was even more suspicious of why he'd been invited.

When a decent amount of time had passed that had given everyone a chance to finish their meal, Dale Curry stood and raised a hand to get their attention.

"Everyone…a little silence please." He smiled and glanced down at Gunner. "You have to be wondering why you're here, and what we want, but I'll tell you right now, it's not money."

Everyone laughed, including Gunner. "That's good, because I don't have any cash on me. The church doesn't take credit cards, and I was afraid someone was going to suggest I wash dishes. Also, I was a detective too long not to know something was up, so spit it out. What, exactly, do you want to ask?"

"We need law in this town. We want to know if you'd consider being the first officer of the law in Crossroads, Texas. Our first chief of police. God knows you have the résumé for it. We have a donated location for a small police office. We have people willing to build a jail at the back of it. We will advertise for deputies and dispatchers. We're not sure how much we can pay them just yet, but we're all willing to pitch in. We all know why you came back…you and Holly…for your families. You are both already making a difference in this town. There are seven new residents since the apartment building opened, and one of the renters is planning to open a small business in town. We need law, but we don't want just anyone. We want you."

Gunner sat there, letting the request sink in, and at the same time, realizing that this was what had been missing. He had all he could ever want at his fingertips except purpose.

He stood. "I am honored. Beyond words. But I need to talk to my wife and my dad first."

"Oh, Jacob knows. He's one of us…a business owner. He said he's just happy you moved home. What you decide to do after you got here was totally up to you and fine with him," Dale said.

Gunner resisted the urge to roll his eyes. "I don't suppose you took it upon yourselves to also ask my wife?"

"No, lord no. You go home and talk it out, and whatever you decide to do, we will accept and understand."

Gunner nodded. "I'll be in touch, one way or another. Thank you for asking, and thanks for the lunch."

He walked out to silence, but the chatter that rose behind him as he headed for the door was obvious. They didn't want to give up without a fight, and Holly was going to be the one with the decision. He was giving her the last word. He drove home in silence, then went into the house and down the hall to her office.

She'd heard his footsteps and was smiling as he entered. "Sit and talk to me. What did they feed you, and what on earth did they want?"

"As you predicted, chicken salad sandwiches with

chopped-up grapes in it. It's not something I care to revisit. Salt and vinegar chips and an apple hand pie. And they asked me if I would take the job as the first law officer in Crossroads. If I would be their police chief."

Holly eyes widened. "Oh, my lord! Oh, Gunner! What did you say?"

"That I first had to talk to my wife."

She walked into his waiting arms. "My dearest rooster… You will never need my permission to follow your heart. If you want it, then do it. I've already glued you back together enough times to know the drill. I believe you told me once I'd make a good cop's wife, and I have known from the get-go that is what you are. You're one of those people who will always run into the fire. I love you. Follow your heart and make us proud."

The last knot in his gut was just unwound. "Lord, woman, how I love you," he said and held her without talking, without moving—until his phone rang.

"And still they persist." He picked it up to answer, then glanced at the number. It was his dad, and he knew why he was calling. "Hey, Dad."

"You can't haul beer kegs around for the rest of your life. No pressure, but what's the verdict?" Jacob said.

"Just call me Chief," Gunner said. "And since you're all in cahoots, you have my permission to tell them. Assure them that I will, of course, donate to the project, but my job is pro bono. This police chief does not receive paychecks."

Jacob let out a whoop and disconnected.

Gunner sighed. "In about two minutes or less, this phone is going to start ringing. If you want peace, darlin', you'll need to keep your door shut for a while."

"Heard," she said. His phone was already ringing when she went to shut the door. He'd called it.

Epilogue

Six months later, the American flag and the Texas State flag were flying from the flagpoles outside of the new police station with three jail cells in the back, waiting for baptism.

There were two dispatchers ready to go to work and three uniformed deputies standing at attention as Mayor Belker swore in Gunner Kingston as the town's first chief of police.

Asher had flown in on his private helicopter to witness the event and brought Dylan with him. Both Jacob and Pearl and Garrett and Trudy Dillon were on hand as the proud parents. Sheriff Reddick was on-site, along with the people of the town, to witness the auspicious event.

As his wife, Holly was standing beside Gunner, and when it came time to pin on the badge, the mayor handed it to her.

"Mrs. Kingston, will you do the honors?" he asked.

Holly took the badge, stepped directly in front of him, and pinned the badge to the shirt pocket of his uniform. She caught a glint in Gunner's eyes, but he never broke rank, keeping his head up and eyes forward as she stepped back in place.

Then the mayor turned to face the crowd. "Ladies and gentlemen, Chief Gunner Kingston is in the house."

The crowd roared and cheered.

The families gathered around them as Gunner and Holly waved.

The day was still and perfect. No wind, no clouds, just West Texas holding its breath for whatever came next.

The gun and holster around the police chief's waist, and the weight of the badge pulling against his shirt, were visual notices of his public identity.

Gunner Kingston would always be a cop to the world, but in the life that mattered most, he was just the man who belonged to Holly.

About the Author

New York Times and *USA Today* bestselling author Sharon Sala has 157+ books in print, published in eight different genres—romance, young adult, Western, general fiction, mystery, women's fiction, children's books, and nonfiction. First published in 1991, her industry awards include the Janet Dailey Award, five-time Career Achievement winner, five-time winner of the National Readers' Choice Award, five-time winner of the Colorado Romance Writers' Award of Excellence, the Heart of Excellence Award, the Booksellers Best Award, the Nora Roberts Lifetime Achievement Award, the Will Rogers Gold Medallion, and the Centennial Award in recognition of her 100th published novel. She lives in Oklahoma, the state where she was born.

Website: sharonsalaauthor.com
Facebook: sharonsala
Instagram: @sharonkaysala_